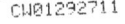

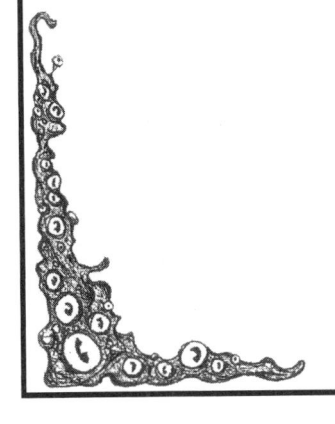

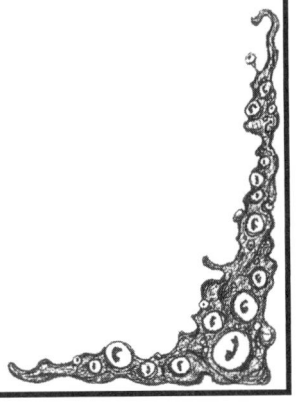

The Terror and other stories

Vol. 3 of the Best Weird Tales of Arthur Machen

Call of Cthulhu® Fiction

The Book of Eibon
The Disciples of Cthulhu 2
Singers of Strange Songs
Song of Cthulhu
Clark Ashton Smith's The Tsathoggua Cycle (forthcoming)
R. W. Chambers' The Yellow Sign (his complete weird fiction)
Robert E. Howard's Nameless Cults (his Mythos fiction)
Arthur Machen's The Three Impostors and Other Stories
Arthur Machen's The White People and Other Stories
Joseph S. Pulver's Nightmare's Disciple (original novel)

Miskatonic University® Archives

The Book of Dzyan

Miskatonic University Library Association

Caligo Accedendum Tournament
Cthulhu Invictus
End Time
First Book of Things
Machine Tractor Station Kharkov-37
Mysteries of Morocco
Parapsychologist's Handbook
Raising Up

The Terror
and Other Stories

The Best Weird Tales of Arthur Machen,
Volume 3

EDITED AND INTRODUCED BY S. T. JOSHI

*Chaosium thanks Andy and Michelle Dawson
for their help in producing this book.*

**A Chaosium Book
April 2005**

The Terror and Other Stories is published by Chaosium, Inc.

This book is ©2005 as a whole by Chaosium, Inc.

Introduction ©2005 by S. T. Joshi; all rights reserved.

The Terror and Other Stories is an original omnibus publication by Chaosium Inc. The tales included in this volume derive chiefly from Machen's late collections, *The Cosy Room and Other Stories* (London: Rich & Cowan, 1936) and *The Children of the Pool and Other Stories* (London: Hutchinson, 1936). The following stories appeared in *The Cosy Room* (original publication in magazines or anthologies given in parentheses): "The Lost Club" (*Whirlwind*, December 20, 1890); "Munitions of War" (in *The Ghost Book*, ed. Cynthia Asquith [London: Hutchinson, 1926]); "The Islington Mystery" (in *The Black Cap*, ed. Cynthia Asquith [London: Hutchinson, 1927]); "The Cosy Room" (in *Shudders*, ed. Cynthia Asquith [London: Hutchinson, 1931]); "Opening the Door" (in *When Churchyards Yawn*, ed. Cynthia Asquith [London: Hutchinson, 1931]). The following stories appeared in *The Children of the Pool* (all stories are original to that volume): "The Children of the Pool"; "The Bright Boy"; "Out of the Picture"; "Change." *The Terror* was first published (as "The Great Terror") in the London *Evening News* (October 16–31, 1916) and in book form by Duckworth (London), 1917. "Johnny Double" appeared in *The Treasure Cave*, ed. Cynthia Asquith (London: Jarrolds, 1928). "The Dover Road" appeared in *Missing from Their Homes* (London: Hutchinson, 1936). "Ritual" appeared in *Path and Pavement*, ed. John Rowland (London: Eric Grant, 1937).

An early essay on weird fiction, "The Literature of Occultism" (*Literature*, January 17, 1899), has been appended.

Cover art © 2005 by Harry Fassl. Cover and interior layout by Charlie Krank. Editorial by Lynn Willis. Additional copy editing by S. T. Joshi.

Similarities between characters in this book and persons living or dead are strictly coincidental.

The reproduction of material from within this book for the purposes of personal or corporate profit, by photographic, digital, or other means of storage and retrieval is prohibited.

Our web site is updated frequently; see **www.chaosium.com**.

This book is printed on 100% acid-free paper.

FIRST EDITION

10 9 8 7 6 5 4 3 2 1

Chaosium Publication 6036. Published in April 2005.

ISBN 1-56882-175-1   Printed in Canada

Contents

Introduction S. T. Joshi vii

The Terror (unabridged) 1

The Lost Club 110

Munitions of War 118

The Islington Mystery 122

Johnny Double 137

The Cosy Room 145

Opening the Door 153

The Children of the Pool 169

The Bright Boy 193

Out of the Picture 229

Change 259

The Dover Road 274

Ritual 310

Appendix: The Literature of
Occultism 316

Introduction

Arthur Machen (1863–1947) occupied a peculiar, even bizarre position in the English literary scene of the 1920s. In 1923 a first edition of his novel, *The Hill of Dreams* (1907), was fetching the fabulous price of £1500, or $7500, far more than most people earned in an entire year. And yet, Machen himself was struggling along as a journalist for a variety of British magazines and newspapers, making ends meet only by writing with unrelenting regularity for such papers as the *London Graphic*, *John O'London's Weekly*, the *Lyons Mail*, and the *Observer*; toward the end of the decade he had lapsed into such poverty that an extraordinary effort was made by British writers—T. S. Eliot among them—to garner a Civil List pension for an effort that succeeded in 1931. Thereafter Machen had an annual income of £100 from the British government, and this allowed him to live in comfort at his home in Old Amersham, Buckinghamshire, for the remaining sixteen years of his life.

Scarcely a year in the 1920s passed without some significant publication of Machen's work, but in the great majority of instances these presented stories, novels, or essays that he had written years or decades before. His major original works of the period were his three sensitive autobiographies, *Far Off Things* (1922), *Things Near and Far* (1923), and *The London Adventure* (1924), which alternately paint a bittersweet portrait of the poverty he endured when he left his native Wales in the early 1880s to work as a Grub Street hack during the day while spending the evenings writing those imperishable works of fantasy and terror—"The Great God Pan" (1890), "The White People" (1904), "A Fragment of Life" (1904), and preeminently *The Hill of Dreams* (written in 1897)—that have earned him a small but choice readership. Alfred A. Knopf began issuing a multivolume edition of his major works in the United States in 1923, and those volumes, with their familiar yellow covers, are still highly sought-after items for the book collector.

One wonders whether Machen gained a sense of being posthumous in his own time. He was being hailed for works he had written as a young man in the 1890s, and little of his new work found either critical esteem or popular favor; matters were certainly not helped when H. L. Mencken, then America's leading literary and cultural critic, delivered a towering condemnation of the Knopf volumes in his review column in the *Smart Set* for August 1923:

> For months past all the more passionate and bankrupt literary journals, both in London itself and in the colonies, have been full of encomiums upon him—some hymning his pellucid and insinuating style, others celebrating his adept evocations of the occult and horrible, yet others denouncing the human race bitterly for letting him slave away for years as a sub-editor, *i.e.*, a copy-reader, in Fleet Street. He becomes the Leo Ornstein, the Picasso of literature, the Gertrude Stein of prose. To admit that one finds him dull is as grave an offense as to let it be known, in Greenwich Village, that one believes in monogamy and belongs to the Elks. Literary Chicago is with him to a man—that is, all save the minority of literati who actually sell their literature. . . . Nevertheless, I have to confess shamelessly that this Machen entertains me only indifferently—that he seems to me, indeed, to be very positively a third-rater, both when he tries to charm with his rhetoric and when he tries to alarm with his cabbalism—that his is, in the main, a quite hollow and obvious fellow.

Machen was, however, himself only indifferently sensitive to the weird and fantastic: although appreciating Lord Dunsany's work with almost idolatrous fervour, and finding some merit in Algernon Blackwood's work, his review of Machen makes it evident that he did not even grasp the basic plot of such works as "A Fragment of Life" and "The White People," so his nose-thumbing need not be taken too seriously.

Machen's days as a fiction writer, indeed, seemed largely over. His last burst had occurred during World War I, when he gained notoriety with "The Bowmen" (1915), a poignant tale of mediaeval British soldiers coming to the aid of beleaguered British forces in France. A variant of that idea is found in the delicate story "Munitions of War" (written in 1915 but not published until 1926), contained in this volume. But Machen's chief war tale is of course *The Terror*, a short novel that has inspired a host of imitations of its basic plot—animals turning against human beings—ranging from Philip Macdonald's brief tale "Our Feathered Friends" to Daphne du Maurier's much better-known (but sadly mediocre) novelette, "The Birds."

The Terror reveals several features characteristic of Machen's later fiction. The first, perhaps, is frank autobiography. The first-person narrative voice not only seems to be Machen himself, but he plays upon his own role as a journalist and reporter—something we will find again in the later tale "Out of the Picture." Indeed, it is not insignificant that *The Terror* was first published as a serialisation in the London *Evening News* (October 16–31, 1916), under the title "The Great Terror." Is Machen attempting to pass off the narrative as a "true" story? To be sure, there is no deliberate intent to deceive; but the circumstantiality of his account, and its generally reportorial tone, make one wonder whether Machen is hoping to convey a deeper truth—the truth that the brief, fitful, and ultimately temporary "revolution" of the animals against humanity's reign over the earth is a signal that human morals are collapsing as a result of the hideous and unprecedented warfare that had broken out two years earlier.

The other feature that distinguishes *The Terror* is its mystery or even detective element. On the basis of several stories included here, one could easily imagine Machen writing an accomplished detective novel; but of course he would never have done so, for the notion of resolving all loose ends, and thereby emphasising the rational intellect's understanding of the world, was anathema to Machen, the religious mystic. For him, something of mystery must remain as a bulwark against the relentless march of science, which Machen felt was tearing away all the wonder and beauty of existence. And yet, in its way *The*

Terror is nothing more than a logical working out of all possibilities, so that, by a process of elimination, a single explanation—even if it is supernatural—remains as the only viable solution to the case.

Several other tales in this volume do indeed involve nothing supernatural—"The Islington Mystery" (1927), a murder tale pure and simple; "The Cosy Room" (1928), a *conte cruel* about the guilty conscience that plagues a murderer; "The Children of the Pool" (1936), a story that suggests the supernatural but proves to be one of psychological horror. And yet, Machen's witchery of words makes these works something more than mere crime stories; his vision, which always looks over the horizon of the known to the impenetrable mysteries beyond, infuses these works with a kind of *quasi-supernaturalism* that brings them close to the weird.

Machen actually wrote relatively few actual works of fiction in the 1920s, aside from a random set of stories for various anthologies edited by Cynthia Asquith; even *The Secret Glory*, a fine but non-supernatural novel, was written in 1907. In the 1930s he resumed somewhat greater productivity in fiction-writing, and published two late collections, *The Cosy Room* and *The Children of the Pool*, in 1936. The former volume contains stories written over a wide period, but the latter is an original collection of previously unpublished tales. They are, however, a sadly uneven mix, and some stories—such as "N," "The Exalted Omega," and "The Tree of Life"—are so poor that they have not been included here. But Machen could on occasion still wield the magic that makes his earlier works so shuddersomely memorable. In particular, "Out of the Picture" and "Change" seem to be among the final installments of what might be called his "Little People Mythos"—a loose series of tales, ranging from "The White People" to "The Red Hand" to "The Shining Pyramid," that probe the notion of a stunted race of primitive half-human creatures dwelling on the underside of civilisation. It is possible that "The Bright Boy" also belongs to this cycle.

Still other late works probe the notion of the *Doppelgänger* or double, sometimes (as perhaps in "Johnny Double") in the form of an astral body. "The Dover

Road" (1936), one of Machen's last works of fiction, is a brilliant and chilling exercise on this theme, and shows that his literary vitality, at the age of sixty-seven, was undiminished. And yet, Machen generated only one more work of fiction—"Ritual," published the next year, and testifying to his lifelong fascination with the eternal mystery of London.

One late work that is noticeably absent here is *The Green Round* (1933), a short novel later reprinted by Arkham House. But this insubstantial account of a man who goes to a quiet resort in Wales, only to be plagued by a strange, stunted being whom others can see but he cannot, is a disappointment in more ways than one. It is, really, a novella or even a short story stretched out to novel length, and its thinness of inspiration, verbosity, and failure to come to a satisfying conclusion must condemn it as a false start. Machen himself dismissed *The Terror* as a "shilling shocker," but that short novel stands leagues higher than the only other novel-length work of the supernatural that emerged from his pen.

In a career that spanned more than six decades, Arthur Machen produced some of the most evocative weird fiction in all literary history. Written with impeccably mellifluous prose, infused with a powerful mystical vision, and imbued with a wonder and terror that their author felt with every fibre of his being, his novels and tales will survive when works of far greater technical accomplishment fall by the wayside. Flawed as some of them are by certain crotchets—especially a furious hostility to science and secularism—that disfigure Machen's own philosophy, they are nonetheless as effective as they are because they echo the sincere beliefs of their author, whose eternal quest to preserve the mystery of the universe in an age of materialism is one to which we can all respond.

— S. T. Joshi

The Terror

I. The Coming of the Terror

After two years we are turning once more to the morning's news with a sense of appetite and glad expectation. There were thrills at the beginning of the war; the thrill of horror and of a doom that seemed at once incredible and certain; this was when Namur fell and the German host swelled like a flood over the French fields, and drew very near to the walls of Paris. Then we felt the thrill of exultation when the good news came that the awful tide had been turned back, that Paris and the world were safe; for awhile at all events.

Then for days we hoped for more news as good as this or better. Has von Muck been surrounded? Not to-day, but perhaps he will be surrounded to-morrow. But the days became weeks, the weeks drew out to months; the battle in the west seemed frozen. Now and again things were done that seemed hopeful, with promise of events still better. But Neuve Chapelle and Loos dwindled into disappointments as their tale was told fully; the lines in the west remained, for all practical purposes of victory, immobile. Nothing seemed to happen, there was nothing to read save the record of operations that were clearly trifling and insignificant. People speculated as to the reason of this inaction; the hopeful said that Joffre had a plan, that he was "nibbling," others declared that we were short of munitions, others again that the new levies were not yet ripe for battle. So the months went by, and almost two years of war had been completed before the motionless English line began to stir and quiver as if it awoke from a long sleep, and began to roll onward, overwhelming the enemy.

The secret of the long inaction of the British armies has been well kept. On the one hand it was rigorously protected by the censorship, which severe, and sometimes severe to the point of absurdity—"the captains and the . . . depart," for instance became in this particular matter ferocious. As soon as the real significance of that which was happening, of beginning to happen, was perceived by the authorities, an underlined circular was issued to the newspaper proprietors of Great Britain and Ireland. It warned each proprietor that he might impart the contents of this circular to one other person only, such person being the responsible editor of his paper, who was to keep the communication secret under the severest penalties. The circular forbade any mention of certain events that had taken place, that might take place; it forbade any kind of allusion to these events or any hint of their existence, or of the possibility of their existence, not only in the press, but in any form whatever. The subject was not to be alluded to in conversation, it was not to be hinted at, however obscurely, in letters; the very existence of the circular, its subject apart, was to be a dead secret.

These measures were successful. A wealthy newspaper proprietor of the north, warmed a little at the end of the Throwsters' Feast (which was held as usual, it will be remembered), ventured to say to the man next to him: "How awful it would be, wouldn't it, if. . . ." His words were repeated, as proof, one regrets to say, that it was time for "old Arnold" to "pull himself together"; and he was fined a thousand pounds. Then, there was the case of an obscure weekly paper published in the county town of an agricultural district in Wales. The Meiros *Observer* (we will call it) was issued from a stationer's back premises, and filled its four pages with accounts of local flower shows, fancy fairs at vicarages, reports of parish councils, and rare bathing fatalities. It also issued a visitors' list, which has been known to contain six names.

This enlightened organ printed a paragraph, which nobody noticed, which was very like paragraphs that small country newspapers have long been in the habit of printing, which could hardly give so much as a hint to any one—to any one, that is, who was not fully instructed in the secret. As a matter of fact, this piece of intelligence got into the paper because the proprietor, who was also the editor, incautiously left the last processes of this particular issue to the staff, who was the Lord-High-Everything-Else of the establishment; and the staff put in a bit of gossip he had heard in the market to fill up two inches on the back page. But the result was that the Meiros *Observer* ceased to appear, owing to "untoward circumstances," as the proprietor said; and he would say no more. No more, that is, by way of explanation, but a great deal more by way of execration of "damned, prying busybodies."

Now a censorship that is sufficiently minute and utterly remorseless can do amazing things in the way of hiding . . . what it wants to hide. Before the war, one would have thought otherwise; one would have said that, censor or no censor, the fact of the murder at X or the fact of the bank robbery at Y would certainly become known; if not through the press, at all events through rumour and the passage of the news from mouth to mouth. And this would be true—of England three hundred years ago, and of savage tribelands of to-day. But we have grown of late to such a reverence for the printed word and such a reliance on it, that the old faculty of disseminating news by word of mouth has become atrophied. Forbid the press to mention the fact that Jones has been murdered, and it is marvellous how few people will hear of it, and of those who hear how few will credit the story that they have heard. You meet a man in the train who remarks that he has been told something about a murder in Southwark; there is all the difference in the world between the impression you receive from such a chance communication and that given by half a dozen lines of print with name, and street and date and all the facts of the case. People in trains repeat all sorts of tales, many of them false; newspapers do not print accounts of murders that have not been committed.

Then another consideration that has made for secrecy. I may have seemed to say that the old office of rumour no longer exists; I shall be reminded of the strange legend of the Russians and the mythology of the angels of Mons. But let me point out, in the first place, that both these absurdities depended on the papers for their wide dissemination. If there had been no newspapers or magazines Russians and angels would have made but a brief, vague appearance of the most shadowy kind—a few would have heard of them, fewer still would have believed in them, they would have been gossiped about for a bare week or two, and so they would have vanished away.

And, then, again, the very fact of these vain rumours and fantastic tales having been so widely believed for a time was fatal to the credit of any stray mutterings that may have got abroad. People had been taken in twice; they had seen how grave persons, men of credit, had preached and lectured about the shining forms that had saved the British army at Mons, or had testified to the trains, packed with grey-coated Muscovites, rushing through the land at dead of night: and now there was a hint of something more amazing than either of the discredited legends. But this time there was no word of confirmation to be found in daily paper, or weekly review, or parish magazine, and so the few that heard either laughed, or, being serious, went home and jotted down notes for essays on "Wartime Psychology: Collective Delusions."

I followed neither of these courses. For before the secret circular had been issued, my curiosity had somehow been aroused by certain paragraphs concerning a "Fatal Accident to Well-known Airman." The propeller of the aeroplane had been shattered, apparently by a collision with a flight of pigeons; the blades had been broken and the machine had fallen like lead to the earth. And soon after I had seen this account, I heard of some very odd circumstances relating to an explosion in a great munition factory in the Midlands. I thought I saw the possibility of a connection between two very different events.

It has been pointed out to me by friends who have been good enough to read this record, that certain phrases I have used may give the impression that I ascribe all the delays of the war on the western front to the extraordinary circumstances which occasioned the issue of the secret circular. Of course this is not the case, there were many reasons for the immobility of our lines from October 1914 to July 1916. These causes have been evident enough and have been openly discussed and deplored. But behind them was something of infinitely greater moment. We lacked men, but men were pouring into the new army; we were short of shells, but when the shortage was proclaimed the nation set itself to mend this matter with all its energy. We could undertake to supply the defects of our army both in men and munitions—*if* the new and incredible danger could be overcome. It has been overcome; rather, perhaps, it has ceased to exist; and the secret may now be told.

I have said my attention was attracted by an account of the death of a well-known airman. I have not the habit of preserving cuttings, I am sorry to say, so that I cannot be precise as to the date of this event. To the best of my belief it was either towards the end of May or the beginning of June 1915. The newspaper paragraph announcing the death of Flight-Lieutenant

Western-Reynolds was brief enough; accidents, and fatal accidents, to the men who are storming the air for us are, unfortunately, by no means so rare as to demand an elaborated notice. But the manner in which Western-Reynolds met his death struck me as extraordinary, inasmuch as it revealed a new danger in the element that we have lately conquered. He was brought down, as I said, by a flight of birds; of pigeons, as appeared by what was found on the bloodstained and shattered blades of the propeller. An eyewitness of the accident, a fellow officer, described how Western-Reynolds set out from the aerodrome on a fine afternoon, there being hardly any wind. He was going to France; he had made the journey to and fro half a dozen times or more, and felt perfectly secure and at ease.

"'Wester' rose to a great height at once, and we could scarcely see the machine. I was turning to go when one of the fellows called out: 'I say! What's this?' He pointed up, and we saw what looked like a black cloud coming from the south at a tremendous rate. I saw at once it wasn't a cloud; it came with a swirl and a rush quite different from any cloud I've ever seen. But for a second I couldn't make out exactly what it was. It altered its shape and turned into a great crescent, and wheeled and veered about as if it was looking for something. The man who had called out had got his glasses, and was staring for all he was worth. Then he shouted that it was a tremendous flight of birds, 'thousands of them.' They went on wheeling and beating about high up in the air, and we were watching them, thinking it was interesting, but not supposing that they would make any difference to Wester, who was just about out of sight. His machine was just a speck. Then the two arms of the crescent drew in as quick as lightning, and these thousands of birds shot in a solid mass right up there across the sky, and flew away somewhere about nor'-nor'-by-west. Then

Henley, the man with the glasses, called out: 'He's down!' and started running, and I went after him. We got a car and as we were going along Henley told me that he'd seen the machine drop dead, as if it came out of that cloud of birds. He thought then that they must have mucked up the propeller somehow. That turned out to be the case. We found the propeller blades all broken and covered with blood and pigeon feathers, and carcasses of the birds had got wedged in between the blades, and were sticking to them."

This was the story that the young airman told one evening in a small company. He did not speak "in confidence," so I have no hesitation in reproducing what he said. Naturally, I did not take a verbatim note of his conversation, but I have something of a knack of remembering talk that interests me, and I think my reproduction is very near to the tale that I heard. And let it be noted that the flying man told his story without any sense or indication of a sense that the incredible, or all but the incredible, had happened. So far as he knew, he said, it was the first accident of the kind. Airmen in France had been bothered once or twice by birds—he thought they were eagles—flying viciously at them, but poor old Wester had been the first man to come up against a flight of some thousands of pigeons.

"And perhaps I shall be the next," he added, "but why look for trouble? Anyhow, I'm going to see *Toodle-oo* to-morrow afternoon."

Well, I heard the story, as one hears all the varied marvels and terrors of the air; as one heard some years ago of "air pockets," strange gulfs or voids in the atmosphere into which airmen fell with great peril; or as one heard of the experience of the airman who flew over the Cumberland Mountains in the burning summer of 1911, and as he swam far above the heights was suddenly and vehemently blown upwards, the hot air from the rocks striking his plane as if it had been a blast from a furnace chimney. We have just begun to navigate a strange region; we must expect to encounter strange adventures, strange perils. And here a new chapter in the chronicles of these perils and adventures had been opened by the death of Western-Reynolds; and no doubt invention and contrivance would presently hit on some way of countering the new danger.

It was, I think, about a week or ten days after the airman's death that my business called me to a northern town, the name of which, perhaps, had better remain unknown. My mission was to inquire into certain charges of extravagance which had been laid against the working people, that is, the munition workers of this especial town. It was said that the men who used to earn £2 10s. a week were now getting from seven to eight pounds, that "bits of girls" were being paid two pounds instead of seven or eight shillings, and that, in consequence, there was an orgy of foolish extravagance. The girls, I was told, were eating chocolates at four, five, and six shillings a pound, the women were ordering thirty-pound pianos which they couldn't play, and the men bought gold chains at ten and twenty guineas apiece.

I dived into the town in question and found, as usual, that there was a mixture of truth and exaggeration in the stories that I had heard. Gramophones, for example: they cannot be called in strictness necessaries, but they were undoubtedly finding a ready sale, even in the more expensive brands. And I thought that there were a great many very spick-and-span perambulators to be seen on the pavement; smart perambulators, painted in tender shades of colour and expensively fitted.

"And how can you be surprised if people will have a bit of a fling?" a worker said to me. "We're seeing money for the first time in our lives, and it's bright.

And we work hard for it, and we risk our lives to get it. You've heard of explosion yonder?"

He mentioned certain works on the outskirts of the town. Of course, neither the name of the works nor of the town had been printed; there had been a brief notice of "Explosion at Munition Works in the Northern District: Many Fatalities." The working man told me about it, and added some dreadful details.

"They wouldn't let their folks see bodies; screwed them up in coffins as they found them in shop. The gas had done it."

"Turned their faces black, you mean?"

"Nay. They were all as if they had been bitten to pieces."

This was a strange gas.

I asked the man in the northern town all sorts of questions about the extraordinary explosion of which he had spoken to me. But he had very little more to say. As I have noted already, secrets that may not be printed are often deeply kept; last summer there were very few people outside high official circles who knew anything about the "tanks," of which we have all been talking lately, though these strange instruments of war were being exercised and tested in a park not far from London. So the man who told me of the explosion in the munition factory was most likely genuine in his profession that he knew nothing more of the disaster. I found out that he was a smelter employed at a furnace on the other side of the town to the ruined factory; he didn't know even what they had been making there; some very dangerous high explosive, he supposed. His information was really nothing more than a bit of gruesome gossip, which he had heard probably at third or fourth or fifth hand. The horrible detail of faces "as if they had been bitten to pieces" had made its violent impression on him, that was all.

I gave him up and took a tram to the district of the disaster; a sort of industrial suburb, five miles from the centre of the town. When I asked for the factory, I was told that it was no good my going to it as there was nobody there. But I found it; a raw and hideous shed with a walled yard about it, and a shut gate. I looked for signs of destruction, but there was nothing. The roof was quite undamaged; and again it struck me that this had been a strange accident. There had been an explosion of sufficient violence to kill work-people in the building, but the building itself showed no wounds or scars.

A man came out of the gate and locked it behind him. I began to ask him some sort of question, or rather, I began to "open" for a question with "A terrible business here, they tell me," or some such phrase of convention. I got no farther. The man asked me if I saw a policeman walking down the street. I said I did, and I was given the choice of getting about my business forthwith or of being instantly given in charge as a spy. "Th'ast better be gone and quick about it," was, I think, his final advice, and I took it.

Well, I had come literally up against a brick wall. Thinking the problem over, I could only suppose that the smelter or his informant had twisted the phrases of the story. The smelter had said the dead men's faces were "bitten to pieces"; this might be an unconscious perversion of "eaten away." That phrase might describe well enough the effect of strong acids, and, for all I knew of the processes of munition-making, such acids might be used and might explode with horrible results in some perilous stage of their admixture.

It was a day or two later that the accident to the airman, Western-Reynolds, came into my mind. For one of those instants which are far shorter than any measure of time there flashed out the possibility of a link between the two disasters. But here was a wild impossibility, and I drove it away. And yet I think that the thought, mad as it seemed, never left me; it was the secret light that at last guided me through a sombre grove of enigmas.

It was about this time, so far as the date can be fixed, that a whole district, one might say a whole county, was visited by a series of extraordinary and terrible calamities, which were the more terrible inasmuch as they continued for some time to be inscrutable mysteries. It is, indeed, doubtful whether these awful events do not still remain mysteries to many of those concerned; for before the inhabitants of this part of the country had time to join one link of evidence to another the circular was issued, and thenceforth no one knew how to distinguish undoubted fact from wild and extravagant surmise.

The district in question is in the far west of Wales; I shall call it, for convenience, Meirion. In it there is one seaside town of some repute with holiday-makers for five or six weeks in the summer, and dotted about the county there are three or four small old towns that seem drooping in a slow decay, sleepy and grey with age and forgetfulness. They remind me of what I have read of towns in the west of Ireland. Grass grows between the uneven stones of the pavements, the signs above the shop windows decline, half the letters of these signs are missing, here and there a house has been pulled down, or has been allowed to slide into ruin, and wild greenery springs up through the fallen stones, and there is silence in all the streets. And it is to be noted, these are not places that were once magnificent. The Celts have never had the art of building, and so far as I can see, such towns as Towy and Merthyr Tegveth and Meiros must have been always much as they are now, clusters of poorish, meanly built houses, ill kept and down at heel.

And these few towns are thinly scattered over a wild country where north is divided from south by a wilder mountain range. One of these places is sixteen miles from any station; the others are doubtfully and deviously connected by single-line railways served by rare trains that pause and stagger and hesitate on their slow journey up mountain passes, or stop for half an hour or more at lonely sheds called stations, situated in the midst of desolate marshes. A few years ago I travelled with an Irishman on one of these queer lines, and he looked to right and saw the bog with its yellow and blue grasses and stagnant pools, and he looked to left and saw a ragged hill-side, set with grey stone walls. "I can hardly believe," he said, "that I'm not still in the wilds of Ireland."

Here, then, one sees a wild and divided and scattered region, a land of outland hills and secret and hidden valleys. I know white farms on this coast which must be separate by two hours of hard, rough walking from any other habitation, which are invisible from any other house. And inland, again, the farms are often ringed about by thick groves of ash, planted by men of old days to shelter their roof-trees from rude winds of the mountain and stormy winds of the sea; so that these places, too, are hidden away, to be surmised only by the wood smoke that rises from the green surrounding leaves. A Londoner must see them to believe in them; and even then he can scarcely credit their utter isolation.

Such, then, in the main is Meirion, and on this land in the early summer of last year terror descended—a terror without shape, such as no man there had ever known.

It began with the tale of a little child who wandered out into the lanes to pick flowers one sunny afternoon, and never came back to the cottage on the hill.

II. Death in the Village

The child who was lost came from a lonely cottage that stands on the slope of a steep hill-side called the Allt, or the height. The land about it is wild and ragged; here the growth of gorse and bracken, here a marshy hollow of reeds and rushes, marking the course of the stream from some hidden well, here thickets of dense and tangled undergrowth, the outposts of the wood. Down through this broken and uneven ground a path leads to the lane at the bottom of the valley; then the land rises again and swells up to the cliffs over the sea, about a quarter of a mile away. The little girl, Gertrude Morgan, asked her mother if she might go down to the lane and pick the purple flowers—these were orchids—that grew there, and her mother gave her leave, telling her she must be sure to be back by tea time, as there was apple tart for tea.

She never came back. It was supposed that she must have crossed the road and gone to the cliff's edge, possibly in order to pick the sea pinks that were then in full blossom. She must have slipped, they said, and fallen into the sea, two hundred feet below. And, it may be said at once, that there was no doubt some truth in this conjecture, though it stopped very far short of the whole truth. The child's body must have been carried out by the tide, for it was never found.

The conjecture of a false step or of a fatal slide on the slippery turf that slopes down to the rocks was accepted as being the only explanation possible. People thought the accident a strange one because, as a rule, country children living by the cliffs and the sea become wary at an early age, and Gertrude Morgan was almost ten years old. Still, as the neighbours said, "That's how it must have happened, and it's a great pity, to be sure." But this would not do when in a week's time a strong young labourer failed to come to his cottage after the day's work. His body was found on the rocks six or seven miles from the cliffs where the child was supposed to have fallen; he was going home by a path that he had used every night of his life for eight or nine years, that he used of dark nights in perfect security, knowing every inch of it. The police asked if he drank, but he was a teetotaller; if he were subject to fits, but he wasn't. And he was not murdered for his wealth, since agricultural labourers are not wealthy. It was only possible again to talk of slippery turf and a false step; but people began to be frightened. Then a woman was found with her neck broken at the bottom of a disused quarry near Llanfihangel, in the middle of the county. The "false step" theory was eliminated here, for the quarry was guarded with a natural hedge of gorse bushes. One would have to struggle and fight through sharp thorns to destruction in such a place as this; and indeed the gorse bushes were broken as if some one had rushed furiously through them, just above the place where the woman's body was found. And this was strange: there was a dead sheep lying beside her in the pit, as if the woman and the sheep together had been chased over the brim of the quarry. But chased by whom, or by what? And then there was a new form of terror.

This was in the region of the marshes under the mountain. A man and his son, a lad of fourteen or fifteen, set out early one morning to work and never reached the farm where they were bound. Their way skirted the marsh, but it was broad, firm and well metalled, and it had been raised about two feet above the bog. But when search was made in the evening of the same day Phillips and his son were found dead in the marsh, covered with black slime and pondweed. And they lay some ten yards from the path, which, it would seem, they must have left deliberately. It was useless, of course, to look for tracks in the black ooze, for if one threw a big stone into it a few seconds removed all marks of the disturbance. The men who found the two bodies beat about the verges and purlieus of the marsh in hope of finding some trace of the murderers; they went to and fro over the rising ground where the black cattle were grazing, they searched the alder thickets by the brook; but they discovered nothing.

Most horrible of all these horrors, perhaps, was the affair of the Highway, a lonely and unfrequented by-road that winds for many miles on high and lonely land. Here, a mile from any other dwelling, stands a cottage on the edge of a dark wood. It was inhabited by a labourer named Williams, his wife, and their three children. One hot summer's evening, a man who had been doing a day's gardening at a rectory three or four miles away, passed the cottage, and stopped for a few minutes to chat with Williams, the labourer, who was pottering about his garden, while the children were playing on the path by the door. The two talked of their neighbors and of the potatoes till Mrs. Williams appeared at the doorway and said supper was ready, and Williams turned to go into the house. This was about eight o'clock, and in the ordinary course the family would have their supper and be in bed by nine, or by half past nine at latest. At ten o'clock that night the local doctor was driving home along the Highway. His horse shied violently and then stopped dead just opposite the gate to the cottage. The doctor got down, frightened at what he saw; and there on the roadway lay Williams, his wife, and the three children, stone dead, all of them. Their skulls were battered in as if by some heavy iron instrument; their faces were beaten into a pulp.

III. THE DOCTOR'S THEORY

It is not easy to make any picture of the horror that lay dark on the hearts of the people of Meirion. It was no longer possible to believe or to pretend to believe that these men and women and children had met their deaths through strange accidents. The little girl and the young labourer might have slipped and fallen over the cliffs, but the woman who lay dead with the dead sheep at the bottom of the quarry, the two men who had been lured into the ooze of the marsh, the family who were found murdered on the Highway before their own cottage door; in these cases there could be no room for the supposition of accident. It seemed as if it were impossible to frame any conjecture or outline of a conjecture that would account for these hideous and, as it seemed, utterly purposeless crimes. For a time people said that there must be a madman at large, a sort of country variant of Jack the Ripper, some horrible pervert who was possessed by the passion of death, who prowled darkling about that lonely land, hiding in woods and in wild places, always watching and seeking for the victims of his desire.

Indeed, Dr. Lewis, who found poor Williams, his wife, and children miserably slaughtered on the Highway, was convinced at first that the presence of a concealed madman in the countryside offered the only possible solution to the difficulty.

"I felt sure," he said to me afterwards, "that the Williamses had been killed by a homicidal maniac. It was the nature of the poor creatures' injuries that convinced me that this was the case. Some years ago—thirty-seven or thirty-eight years ago as a matter of fact—I had something to do with a case which on the face of it had a strong likeness to the Highway murder. At that time I had a practice at Usk, in Monmouthshire. A whole family living in a cottage by the roadside were murdered one evening; it was called, I think, the Llangibby murder; the cottage was near the village of that name. The murderer was caught in Newport; he was a Spanish sailor, named Garcia, and it appeared that he had killed father, mother, and the three children for the sake of the brass works of an old Dutch clock, which were found on him when he was arrested.

"Garcia had been serving a month's imprisonment in Usk gaol for some small theft, and on his release he set out to walk to Newport, nine or ten miles away; no doubt to get another ship. He passed the cottage and saw the man working in his garden. Garcia stabbed him with his sailor's knife. The wife rushed out; he stabbed her. Then he went into the cottage and stabbed the three children, tried to set the place on fire, and made off with the clock-works. That looked like the deed of a madman, but Garcia wasn't mad—they hanged him, I may say—he was merely a man of a very low type, a degenerate who hadn't the slightest value for human life. I am not sure, but I think he came from one of the Spanish islands, where the people are said to be degenerates, very likely from too much interbreeding.

"But my point is that Garcia stabbed to kill and did kill, with one blow in each case. There was no senseless hacking and slashing. Now those poor people on the Highway had their heads smashed to pieces by what must have been a storm of blows. Any one of them would have been fatal, but the murderer must have gone on raining blows with his iron hammer on people who were already stone dead. And *that* sort of thing is the work of a madman, and nothing but a madman. That's how I argued the matter out to myself just after the event.

"I was utterly wrong, monstrously wrong. But who could have suspected the truth?"

Thus Dr. Lewis, and I quote him, or the substance of him, as representative of most of the educated opinion of the district at the beginnings of the terror. People seized on this theory largely because it offered at least the comfort of an explanation, and any explanation, even the poorest, is better than an intolerable and terrible mystery. Besides, Dr. Lewis's theory was plausible; it explained the lack of purpose that seemed to characterize the murders. And yet—there were difficulties even from the first. It was hardly possible that a strange madman should be able to keep hidden in a countryside where any stranger is instantly noted and noticed; sooner or later he would be seen as he prowled along the lanes or across the wild places. Indeed, a drunken, cheerful, and altogether harmless tramp was arrested by a farmer and his man in the fact and act of sleeping off beer under a hedge; but the vagrant was able to prove complete and undoubted alibis, and was soon allowed to go on his wandering way.

Then another theory, or rather a variant of Dr. Lewis's theory, was started. This was to the effect that the person responsible for the outrages was, indeed, a madman; but a madman only at intervals. It was one of the members of the Porth Club, a certain Mr. Remnant, who was supposed to have originated this more subtle explanation. Mr. Remnant was a middle-aged man, who, having nothing particular to do, read a great many books by way of conquering the hours. He talked to the club—doctors, retired colonels, parsons, lawyers—about "personality," quoted various psychological text-books in support of his contention that personality was sometimes fluid and unstable, went back to *Dr. Jekyll and Mr. Hyde* as good evidence of this proposition, and laid stress on Dr. Jekyll's speculation that the human soul, so far from being one and indivisible, might possibly turn out to be a mere polity, a state in which dwelt many strange and incongruous citizens, whose characters were not merely unknown but altogether unsurmised by that form of consciousness which so rashly assumed that it was not only the president of the republic but also its sole citizen.

"The long and the short of it is," Mr. Remnant concluded, "that any one of us may be the murderer, though he hasn't the faintest notion of the fact. Take Llewelyn there."

Mr. Payne Llewelyn was an elderly lawyer, a rural Tulkinghorn. He was the hereditary solicitor to the Morgans of Pentwyn. This does not sound anything tremendous to the Saxons of London; but the style is far more than noble to the Celts of west Wales; it is immemorial; Teilo Sant was of the collaterals of the first known chief of the race. And Mr. Payne Llewelyn did his best to look like the legal adviser of this ancient house. He was weighty, he was cautious, he was sound, he was secure. I have compared him to Mr. Tulkinghorn of Lincoln's Inn Fields; but Mr. Llewelyn would most certainly never have dreamed of employing his leisure in peering into the cupboards where the family skeletons were hidden. Supposing such cupboards to have existed, Mr. Payne Llewelyn would have risked large out-of-pocket expenses to furnish them with double, triple, impregnable locks. He was a new man, an *advena*, certainly; for he was partly of the Conquest, being descended on one side from Sir Payne Turberville; but he meant to stand by the old stock.

"Take Llewelyn now," said Mr. Remnant. "Look here, Llewelyn, can you produce evidence to show where you were on the night those people were murdered on the Highway? I thought not."

Mr. Llewelyn, an elderly man, as I have said, hesitated before speaking.

"I thought not," Remnant went on. "Now I say that it is perfectly possible that Llewelyn may be dealing death throughout Meirion, although in his present personality he may not have the faintest suspicion that there is another Llewelyn within him, a Llewelyn who follows murder as a fine art."

Mr. Payne Llewelyn did not at all relish Mr. Remnant's suggestion that he might well be a secret murderer, ravening for blood, remorseless as a wild beast. He thought the phrase about his following murder as a fine art was both nonsensical and in the worst taste, and his opinion was not changed when Remnant pointed out that it was used by De Quincey in the title of one of his most famous essays.

"If you had allowed me to speak," he said with some coldness of manner, "I would have told you that on Tuesday last, the night on which those unfortunate people were murdered on the Highway I was staying at the Angel Hotel, Cardiff. I had business in Cardiff, and I was detained till Wednesday afternoon."

Having given this satisfactory alibi, Mr. Payne Llewelyn left the club, and did not go near it for the rest of the week.

Remnant explained to those who stayed in the smoking-room that, of course, he had merely used Mr. Llewelyn as a concrete example of his theory, which, he persisted, had the support of a considerable body of evidence.

"There are several cases of double personality on record," he declared. "And I say again that it is quite possible that these murders may have been committed by one of us in his secondary personality. Why, I may be the murderer in my Remnant B state, though Remnant A knows nothing whatever about it, and is perfectly convinced that he could not kill a fowl, much less a whole family. Isn't it so, Lewis?"

Dr. Lewis said it was so, in theory, but he thought not in fact.

"Most of the cases of double or multiple personality that have been investigated," he said, "have been in connection with the very dubious experiments of hypnotism, or the still more dubious experiments of spiritualism. All that sort of thing, in my opinion, is like tinkering with the works of a clock—amateur tinkering, I mean. You fumble about with the wheels and cogs and bits of mechanism that you don't really know anything about; and then you find your clock going backwards or striking 240 at tea time. And I believe it's just the same thing with these psychical research experiments; the secondary personality is very likely the result of the tinkering and fumbling with a very delicate apparatus that we know nothing about. Mind, I can't say that it's impossible for one of us to be the Highway murderer in his B state, as Remnant puts it. But I think it's extremely improbable. Probability is the guide of life, you know, Remnant," said Dr. Lewis, smiling at that gentleman, as if to say that he also had done a little reading in his day. "And it follows, therefore, that improbability is also the guide of life. When you get a very high degree of probability, that is, you are justified in taking it as a certainty; and on the other hand, if a supposition is highly improbable, you are justified in treating it as an impossible one. That is, in nine hundred and ninety-nine cases out of a thousand."

"How about the thousandth case?" said Remnant. "Supposing these extraordinary crimes constitute the thousandth case?"

The doctor smiled and shrugged his shoulders, being tired of the subject. But for some little time highly respectable members of Porth society would look suspiciously at one another wondering whether, after all, there mightn't be "something in it." However, both Mr. Remnant's somewhat crazy theory and Dr. Lewis's plausible theory became untenable when two more victims of an awful and mysterious death were offered up in sacrifice, for a man was found dead in the Llanfihangel quarry, where the woman had been discovered. And on the same day a girl of fifteen was found broken on the jagged rocks under cliffs near Porth. Now, it appeared that these two deaths must have occurred at about the same time, within an hour of one another, certainly; and the distance between the quarry and the cliffs by Black Rock is certainly twenty miles.

"A motor could do it," one man said.

But it was pointed out that there was no high road between the two places; indeed, it might be said that there was no road at all between them. There was a network of deep, narrow, and tortuous lanes that wandered into one another at all manner of queer angles for, say, seventeen miles; this in the middle, as it were, between Black Rock and the quarry at Llanfihangel. But to get to the high land of the cliffs one had to take a path that went through two miles of fields; and the quarry lay a mile away from the nearest by-road in the midst of gorse and bracken and broken land. And, finally, there was no track of motor-car or motor bicycle in the lanes which must have been followed to pass from one place to the other.

"What about an aeroplane, then?" said the man of the motorcar theory. Well, there was certainly an aerodrome not far from one of the two places of death; but somehow, nobody believed that the Flying Corps harboured a homicidal maniac. It seemed clear, therefore, that there must be more than one person concerned in the terror of Meirion. And Dr. Lewis himself abandoned his own theory.

"As I said to Remnant at the club," he remarked, "improbability is the guide of life. I can't believe that there are a pack of madmen or even two madmen at large in the country. I give it up."

And now a fresh circumstance or set of circumstances became manifest to confound judgement and to awaken new and wild surmises. For at about this time people realized that none of the dreadful events that were happening all about them was so much as mentioned in the press. I have already spoken of the fate of the Meiros *Observer*. This paper was suppressed by the authorities because it had inserted a brief paragraph about some person who had been "found dead under mysterious circumstances"; I think that paragraph referred to the first death of Llanfihangel quarry. Thenceforth, horror followed on horror, but no word was printed in any of the local journals. The curious went to the newspaper offices— there were two left in the county—but found nothing save a firm refusal to discuss the matter. And the Cardiff papers were drawn and found blank; and the London press was apparently ignorant of the fact that crimes that had no parallel were terrorizing a whole countryside. Everybody wondered what could have happened, what was happening; and then it was whispered that the coroner would allow no inquiry to be made as to these deaths of darkness.

"In consequence of instructions received from the Home Office," one coroner was understood to have said, "I have to tell the jury that their business will be to hear the medical evidence and to bring in a verdict immediately in accordance with that evidence. I shall disallow all questions."

One jury protested. The foreman refused to bring in any verdict at all.

"Very good," said the coroner. "Then I beg to inform you, Mr. foreman and gentlemen of the jury, that under the Defense of the Realm Act, I have power to supersede your functions, and to enter a verdict according to the evidence which has been laid before the court as if it had been the verdict of you all."

The foreman and jury collapsed and accepted what they could not avoid. But the rumours that got abroad of all this, added to the known fact that the terror was ignored in the press, no doubt by official command, increased the panic that was now arising, and gave it a new direction. Clearly, people reasoned, these government restrictions and prohibitions could only refer to the war, to some great danger in connection with the war. And that being so, it followed that the outrages which must be kept so secret were the work of the enemy; that is, of concealed German agents.

IV. THE SPREAD OF THE TERROR

It is time, I think, for me to make one point clear. I began this history with certain references to an extraordinary accident to an airman whose machine fell to the ground after collision with a huge flock of pigeons; and then to an explosion in a northern munition factory, an explosion, as I noted, of a very singular kind. Then I deserted the neighbourhood of London, and the northern district, and dwelt on a mysterious and terrible series of events which occurred in the summer of 1915 in a Welsh county, which I have named, for convenience, Meirion.

Well, let it be understood at once that all this detail that I have given about the occurrences in Meirion does not imply that the county in the far west was alone or especially afflicted by the terror that was over the land. They tell me that in the villages about Dartmoor the stout Devonshire hearts sank as men's hearts used to sink in the time of plague and pestilence. There was horror, too, about the Norfolk Broads, and far up by Perth no one would venture on the path that leads by Scone to the wooded heights above the Tay. And in the industrial districts: I met a man by chance one day in an odd London corner who spoke with horror of what a friend had told him.

"'Ask no questions, Ned,' he says to me, 'but I tell yow a' was in Bairnigan t'other day, and a' met a pal who'd seen three hundred coffins going out of a works not far from there.'"

And then the ship that hovered outside the mouth of the Thames with all sails set and beat to and fro in the wind, and never answered any hail, and showed no light! The forts shot at her and brought down one of the masts, but she went suddenly about with a change of wind under what sail still stood, and then veered down Channel, and drove ashore at last on the sandbanks and pinewoods of Arcachon, and not a man alive on her, but only rattling heaps of bones! That last voyage of the *Semiramis* would be something horribly worth telling; but I only heard it at a distance as a yarn, and only believed it because it squared with other things that I knew for certain.

This, then, is my point; I have written of the terror as it fell on Meirion, simply because I have had opportunities of getting close there to what really happened. Third or fourth or fifth hand in the other places; but round about Porth and Merthyr Tegveth I have spoken with people who have seen the tracks of the terror with their own eyes.

Well, I have said that the people of that far-western county realized, not only that death was abroad in their quiet lanes and on their peaceful hills, but that for some reason it was to be kept all secret. Newspapers might not print any news of it, the very juries summoned to investigate it were allowed to investigate nothing. And so they concluded that this veil of secrecy must somehow be connected with the war; and from this position it was not a long way to a further inference: that the murderers of innocent men and women and children were either Germans or agents of Germany. It would be just like the Huns, everybody agreed, to think out such a devilish scheme as this; and they always thought out their schemes beforehand. They hoped to seize Paris in a few weeks, but when they were beaten on the Marne they had their trenches on the Aisne ready to fall back on: it had all been prepared years before the war. And so, no doubt, they had devised this terrible plan against England in case they could not beat us in open fight: there were people ready, very likely, all over the country, who were prepared to murder and destroy everywhere as soon as they got the word. In this way the Germans intended to sow terror throughout England and fill our hearts with panic and dismay, hoping so to weaken their enemy at home that he would lose all heart over the war abroad. It was the Zeppelin notion, in another form; they were committing these horrible and mysterious outrages thinking that we should be frightened out of our wits.

It all seemed plausible enough; Germany had by this time perpetrated so many horrors and had so excelled in devilish ingenuities that no abomination seemed too abominable to be probable, or too ingeniously wicked to be beyond the tortuous malice of the Hun. But then came the questions as to who the agents of this terrible design were, as to where they lived, as to how they contrived to move unseen from field to field, from lane to lane. All sorts of fantastic attempts were made to answer these questions; but it was felt that they remained unanswered. Some suggested that the murderers landed from submarines, or flew from hiding places on the west coast of Ireland, coming and going by night; but there were seen to be flagrant impossibilities in both these suggestions. Everybody agreed that the evil work was no doubt the work of Germany; but nobody could begin to guess how it was done. Somebody at the club asked Remnant for his theory.

"My theory," said that ingenious person, "is that human progress is simply a long march from one inconceivable to another. Look at that airship of ours that came over Porth yesterday: ten years ago that would have been an inconceivable sight. Take the steam engine, take printing, take the theory of gravitation: they were all inconceivable till somebody thought of them. So it is, no doubt, with this infernal dodgery that we're talking about: the Huns have found it out, and we haven't; and there you are. We can't conceive how these poor people have been murdered, because the method's inconceivable to us."

The club listened with some awe to this high argument. After Remnant had gone, one member said:

"Wonderful man, that." "Yes," said Dr. Lewis. "He was asked whether he knew something. And his reply really amounted to 'No, I don't.' But I have never heard it better put."

It was, I suppose, at about this time when the people were puzzling their heads as to the secret methods used by the Germans or their agents to accomplish their crimes that a very singular circumstance became known to a few of the Porth people. It related to the murder of the Williams family on the Highway in front of their cottage door. I do not know that I have made it plain that the old Roman road called the Highway follows the course of a long, steep hill that goes steadily westward till it slants down and droops towards the sea. On either side of the road the ground falls away, here into deep shadowy woods, here to high pastures, now and again into a field of corn, but for the most part into the wild and broken land that is characteristic of Arfon. The fields are long and narrow, stretching up the steep hill-side; they fall into sudden dips and hollows, a well springs up in the midst of one and a grove of ash and thorn bends over it, shading it; and beneath it the ground is thick with reeds and rushes. And then may come on either side of such a field territories glistening with the deep growth of bracken, and rough with gorse and rugged with thickets of blackthorn, green lichen hanging strangely from the branches; such are the lands on either side of the Highway.

Now on the lower slopes of it, beneath the Williams's cottage, some three or four fields down the hill, there is a military camp. The place has been used as a camp for many years, and lately the site has been extended and huts have been erected. But a considerable number of the men were under canvas here in the summer of 1915.

On the night of the Highway murder this camp, as it appeared afterwards, was the scene of the extraordinary panic of the horses.

A good many men in the camp were asleep in their tents soon after 9.30, when the last post was sounded. They woke up in panic. There was a thundering sound on the steep hill-side above them, and down upon the tents came half a dozen horses, mad with fright, trampling the canvas, trampling the men, bruising dozens of them and killing two.

Everything was in wild confusion, men groaning and screaming in the darkness, struggling with the canvas and the twisted ropes, shouting out, some of them, raw lads enough, that the Germans had landed, others wiping the blood from their eyes, a few, roused suddenly from heavy sleep, hitting out at one another, officers coming up at the double roaring out orders to the sergeants, a party of soldiers who were just returning to camp from the village seized with fright at what they could scarcely see or distinguish, at the wildness of the shouting and cursing and groaning that they could not understand, bolting out of the camp again and racing for their lives back to the village: everything in the maddest confusion of wild disorder.

Some of the men had seen the horses galloping down the hill as if terror itself was driving them. They scattered off into the darkness, and somehow or another found their way back in the night to their pasture above the camp. They were grazing there peacefully in the morning, and the only sign of the panic of the night before was the mud they had scattered all over themselves as they pelted through a patch of wet ground. The farmer said they were as quiet a lot as any in Meirion; he could make nothing of it.

"Indeed," he said, "I believe they must have seen the devil himself to be in such a fright as that: save the people!"

Now all this was kept as quiet as might be at the time when it happened; it became known to the men of the Porth Club in the days when they were discussing the difficult question of the German outrages, as the murders were commonly called. And this wild stampede of the farm horses was held by some to be evidence of the extraordinary and unheard-of character of the dreadful agency that was at work. One of the members of the club had been told by an officer who was in the camp at the time of the panic that the horses that came charging down were in a perfect fury of fright, that he had never seen horses in such a state, and so there was endless speculation as to the nature of the sight or the sound that had driven half a dozen quiet beasts into raging madness.

Then, in the middle of this talk, two or three other incidents, quite as odd and incomprehensible, came to be known, borne on chance trickles of gossip that came into the towns from outland farms, or were carried by cottagers tramping into Porth on market-day with a fowl or two and eggs and garden stuff; scraps and fragments of talk gathered by servants from the country folk and repeated to their mistresses. And in such ways it came out that up at Plas Newydd there had been a terrible business over swarming the bees; they had turned as wild as wasps and much more savage. They had come about the people who were taking the swarms like a cloud. They settled on one man's face so that you could not see the flesh for the bees crawling all over it, and they had stung him so badly that the doctor did not know whether he would get over it, and they had chased a girl who had come out to see the swarming, and settled on her and stung her to death. Then they had gone off to a brake below the farm and got into a hollow tree there, and it was not safe to go near it, for they would come out at you by day or by night.

And much the same thing had happened, it seemed, at three or four farms and cottages where bees were kept. And there were stories, hardly so clear or so credible, of sheep-dogs, mild and trusted beasts, turning as savage as wolves and injuring the farm boys in a horrible manner—in one case it was said with fatal results. It was certainly true that old Mrs. Owen's favourite Brahma-Dorking cock had gone mad; she came into Porth one Saturday morning with her face and her neck all bound up and plastered. She had gone out to her bit of a field to feed the poultry the night before, and the bird had flown at her and attacked her most savagely, inflicting some very nasty wounds before she could beat it off.

"There was a stake handy, lucky for me," she said, "and I did beat him and beat him till the life was out of him. But what is come to the world, whatever?"

Now Remnant, the man of theories, was also a man of extreme leisure. It was understood that he had succeeded to ample means when he was quite a young man, and after tasting the savours of the law, as it were, for half a dozen terms at the board of the Middle Temple, he had decided that it would be senseless to bother himself with passing examinations for a profession which he had not the faintest intention of practising. So he turned a deaf ear to the call of "Manger" ringing through the Temple Courts, and set himself out to potter amiably through the world. He had pottered all over Europe, he had looked at Africa, and had even put his head in at the door of the East, on a trip which included the Greek isles and Constantinople. Now, getting into the middle fifties, he had settled at Porth for the sake, as he said, of the Gulf Stream and the fuchsia hedges, and pottered over his books and his theories and the local gossip. He was no more brutal than the general public, which revels in the details of mysterious crime; but it must be said that the terror, black though it was, was a boon to him. He peered and investigated and poked about with the relish of a man to whose life a new zest has been added. He listened attentively to the strange tales of bees and dogs and poultry that came into Porth with the country baskets of butter, rabbits, and green peas; and he evolved at last a most extraordinary theory.

Full of this discovery, as he thought it, he went one night to see Dr. Lewis and take his view of the matter.

"I want to talk to you," said Remnant to the doctor, "about what I have called, provisionally, the Z Ray."

V. The Incident of the Unknown Tree

Dr. Lewis, smiling indulgently, and quite prepared for some monstrous piece of theorizing, led Remnant into the room that overlooked the terraced garden and the sea.

The doctor's house, though it was only a ten minutes' walk from the center of the town, seemed remote from all other habitations. The drive to it from the road came through a deep grove of trees and a dense shrubbery, trees were about the house on either side, mingling with neighbouring groves, and below, the garden fell down, terrace by green terrace, to wild growth, a twisted path amongst red rocks, and at last to the yellow sand of a little cove. The room to which the doctor took Remnant looked over these terraces and across the water to the dim boundaries of the bay. It had French windows that were thrown wide open, and the two men sat in the soft light of the lamp—this was before the days of severe lighting regulations in the far west—and enjoyed the sweet odours and the sweet vision of the summer evening. Then Remnant began:

"I suppose, Lewis, you've heard these extraordinary stories of bees and dogs and things that have been going about lately?"

"Certainly I have heard them. I was called in at Plas Newydd, and treated Thomas Trevor, who's only just out of danger, by the way. I certified for the poor child, Mary Trevor. She was dying when I got to the place. There was no doubt she was stung to death by bees, and I believe there were other very similar cases at Llantarnam and Morwen; none fatal, I think. What about them?"

"Well: then there are the stories of good-tempered old sheepdogs turning wicked and 'savaging' children?"

"Quite so. I haven't seen any of these cases professionally; but I believe the stories are accurate enough."

"And the old woman assaulted by her own poultry?"

"That's perfectly true. Her daughter put some stuff of their own concoction on her face and neck, and then she came to me. The wounds seemed going all right, so I told her to continue the treatment, whatever it might be."

"Very good," said Mr. Remnant. He spoke now with an italic impressiveness. *"Don't you see the link between all this and the horrible things that have been happening about here for the last month?"*

Lewis stared at Remnant in amazement. He lifted his red eyebrows and lowered them in a kind of scowl. His speech showed traces of his native accent.

"Great burning!" he exclaimed. "What on earth are you getting at now? It is madness. Do you mean to tell me that you think there is some connection between a swarm or two of bees that have turned nasty, a cross dog, and a wicked old barn-door cock and these poor people that have been pitched over the cliffs and hammered to death on the road? There's no sense in it, you know."

"I am strongly inclined to believe that there is a great deal of sense in it," replied Remnant with extreme calmness. "Look here, Lewis, I saw you grinning the other day at the club when I was telling the fellows that in my opinion all these outrages had been committed, certainly by the Germans, but by some method of which we have no conception. But what I meant to say when I talked about inconceivables was just this: that the Williamses and the rest of them have been killed in some way that's not in theory at all, not in our theory, at all events, some way we've not contemplated, not thought of for an instant. Do you see my point?"

"Well, in a sort of way. You mean there's an absolute originality in the method? I suppose that is so. But what next?"

Remnant seemed to hesitate, partly from a sense of the portentous nature of what he was about to say, partly from a sort of half unwillingness to part with so profound a secret.

"Well," he said, "you will allow that we have two sets of phenomena of a very extraordinary kind occurring at the same time. Don't you think that it's only reasonable to connect the two sets with one another."

"So the philosopher of Tenterden steeple and the Goodwin Sands thought, certainly," said Lewis. "But what is the connection? Those poor folks on the Highway weren't stung by bees or worried by a dog. And horses don't throw people over cliffs or stifle them in marshes."

"No; I never meant to suggest anything so absurd. It is evident to me that in all these cases of animals turning suddenly savage the cause has been terror, panic, fear. The horses that went charging into the camp were mad with fright, we know. And I say that in the other instances we have been discussing the cause was the same. The creatures were exposed to an infection of fear, and a frightened beast or bird or insect uses its weapons, whatever they may be. If, for example, there had been anybody with those horses when they took their panic they would have lashed out at him with their heels."

"Yes, I dare say that that is so. Well."

"Well; my belief is that the Germans have made an extraordinary discovery. I have called it the Z ray. You know that the ether is merely an hypothesis; we have to suppose that it's there to account for the passage of the Marconi current from one place to another. Now, suppose that there is a psychic ether as well as a material ether, suppose that it is possible to direct irresistible impulses across this medium, suppose that these impulses are towards murder or suicide; then I think that you have an explanation of the terrible series of events that have been happening in Meirion for the last few weeks. And it is quite clear to my mind that the horses and the other creatures have been exposed to this Z ray, and that it has produced on them the effect of terror, with ferocity as the result of terror. Now what do you say to that? Telepathy, you know, is well established; so is hypnotic suggestion. You have only to look in the *Encyclopedia Britannica* to see that, and suggestion is so strong in some cases as to be an irresistible imperative. Now don't you feel that putting telepathy and suggestion together, as it were, you have more than the elements of what I call the Z ray? I feel myself that I have more to go on in making my hypothesis than the inventor of the steam-engine had in making his hypothesis when he saw the lid of the kettle bobbing up and down. What do you say?"

Dr. Lewis made no answer. He was watching the growth of a new, unknown tree in his garden.

The doctor made no answer to Remnant's question. For one thing, Remnant was profuse in his eloquence—he has been rigidly condensed in this history—and Lewis was tired of the sound of his voice. For another thing, he found the Z-ray theory almost too extravagant to be bearable, wild enough to tear patience to tatters. And then as the tedious argument continued Lewis became conscious that there was something strange about the night.

It was a dark summer night. The moon was old and faint, above the Dragon's Head across the bay, and the air was very still. It was so still that Lewis had noted that not a leaf stirred on the very tip of a high tree that stood out against the sky; and yet he knew that he was listening to some sound that he could not determine or define. It was not the wind in the leaves, it was not the gentle wash of the water of the sea against the rocks; that latter sound he could distinguish quite easily. But there was something else. It was scarcely a sound; it was as if the air itself trembled and fluttered, as the air trembles in a church when they open the great pedal pipes of the organ.

The doctor listened intently. It was not an illusion, the sound was not in his own head, as he had suspected for a moment; but for the life of him he could not make out whence it came or what it was. He gazed down into the night over the terraces of his garden, now sweet with the scent of the flowers of the night; tried to peer over the tree-tops across the sea towards the Dragon's Head. It struck him suddenly that this strange fluttering vibration of the air might be the noise of a distant aeroplane or airship; there was not the usual droning hum, but this sound might be caused by a new type of engine. A new type of engine? Possibly it was an enemy airship; their range, it had been said, was getting longer; and Lewis was just going to call Remnant's attention to the sound, to its possible cause, and to the possible danger that might be hovering over them, when he saw something that caught his breath and his heart with wild amazement and a touch of terror.

He had been staring upward into the sky, and, about to speak to Remnant, he had let his eyes drop for an instant. He looked down towards the trees in the garden, and saw with utter astonishment that one had changed its shape in the few hours that had passed since the setting of the sun. There was a thick grove of ilexes bordering the lowest terrace, and above them rose one tall pine, spreading its head of sparse, dark branches dark against the sky.

As Lewis glanced down over the terraces he saw that the tall pine tree was no longer there. In its place there rose above the ilexes what might have been a greater ilex; there was the blackness of a dense growth of foliage rising like a broad and far-spreading and rounded cloud over the lesser trees.

Here, then, was a sight wholly incredible, impossible. It is doubtful whether the process of the human mind in such a case has ever been analysed and registered; it is doubtful whether it ever can be registered. It is hardly fair to bring in the mathematician, since he deals with absolute truth (so far as mortality can conceive absolute truth); but how would a mathematician feel if he were suddenly confronted with a two-sided triangle? I suppose he would instantly become a raging madman; and Lewis, staring wide-eyed and wild-eyed at a dark and spreading tree which his own experience informed him was not there, felt for an instant that shock which should affront us all when we first realize the intolerable antinomy of Achilles and the tortoise. Common sense tells us that Achilles will flash past the tortoise almost with the speed of the lightning; the inflexible truth of mathematics assures us that till the earth boils and the heavens cease to endure, the tortoise must still be in advance; and thereupon we should, in common decency, go mad. We do not go mad, because, by special grace, we are certified that, in the final court of appeal, all science is a lie, even the highest science of all; and so we simply grin at Achilles and the tortoise, as we grin at Darwin, deride Huxley, and laugh at Herbert Spencer.

Dr. Lewis did not grin. He glared into the dimness of the night, at the great spreading tree that he knew could not be there. And as he gazed he saw that what at first appeared the dense blackness of foliage was fretted and starred with wonderful appearances of lights and colours.

Afterwards he said to me: "I remember thinking to myself: 'Look here, I am not delirious; my temperature is perfectly normal. I am not drunk; I only had a pint of Graves with my dinner, over three hours ago. I have not eaten any poisonous fungus; I have not taken *Anhelonium Lewinii* experimentally. So, now then! What is happening?'"

The night had gloomed over; clouds obscured the faint moon and the misty stars. Lewis rose, with some kind of warning and inhibiting gesture to Remnant, who he was conscious was gaping at him in astonishment. He walked to the open French window, and took a pace forward on to the path outside, and looked, very intently, at the dark shape of the tree, down below the sloping garden, above the washing of the waves. He shaded the light of the lamp behind him by holding his hands on each side of his eyes.

The mass of the tree—the tree that couldn't be there—stood out against the sky, but not so clearly, now that the clouds had rolled up. Its edges, the limits of its leafage, were not so distinct. Lewis thought that he could detect some sort of quivering movement in it; though the air was at a dead calm. It was a night on which one might hold up a lighted match and watch it burn without any wavering or inclination of the flame.

"You know," said Lewis, "how a bit of burnt paper will sometimes hang over the coals before it goes up the chimney, and little worms of fire will shoot through it. It was like that, if you should be standing some distance away. Just threads and hairs of yellow light I saw, and specks and sparks of fire, and then a twinkling of a ruby no bigger than a pin point, and a green wandering in the black, as if an emerald were crawling, and then little veins of deep blue. 'Woe is me!' I said to myself in Welsh, 'What is all this color and burning?'

"And, then, at that very moment there came a thundering rap at the door of the room inside, and there was my man telling me that I was wanted directly up at the Garth, as old Mr. Trevor Williams had been taken very bad. I knew his heart was not worth much, so I had to go off directly and leave Remnant to make what he could of it all."

VI. Mr. Remnant's Z Ray

Dr. Lewis was kept some time at the Garth. It was past twelve when he got back to his house. He went quickly to the room that overlooked the garden and the sea and threw open the French window and peered into the darkness. There, dim indeed against the dim sky but unmistakable, was the tall pine with its sparse branches, high above the dense growth of the ilex-trees. The strange boughs which had amazed him had vanished; there was no appearance now of colours or of fires.

He drew his chair up to the open window and sat there gazing and wondering far into the night, till brightness came upon the sea and sky, and the forms of the trees in the garden grew clear and evident. He went up to his bed at last filled with a great perplexity, still asking questions to which there was no answer.

The doctor did not say anything about the strange tree to Remnant. When they next met, Lewis said that he had thought there was a man hiding amongst the bushes—this in explanation of that warning gesture he had used, and of his going out into the garden and staring into the night. He concealed the truth because he dreaded the Remnant doctrine that would undoubtedly be produced; indeed, he hoped that he had heard the last of the theory of the Z ray. But Remnant firmly reopened this subject.

"We were interrupted just as I was putting my case to you," he said. "And to sum it all up, it amounts to this: that the Huns have made one of the great leaps of science. They are sending 'suggestions' (which amount to irresistible commands) over here, and the persons affected are seized with suicidal or homicidal mania. The people who were killed by falling over the cliffs or into the quarry probably committed suicide; and so with the man and boy who were found in the bog. As to the Highway case, you remember that Thomas Evans said that he stopped and talked to Williams on the night of the murder. In my opinion Evans was the murderer. He came under the influence of the ray, became a homicidal maniac in an instant, snatched Williams's spade from his hand and killed him and the others."

"The bodies were found by me on the road."

"It is possible that the first impact of the ray produces violent nervous excitement, which would manifest itself externally. Williams might have called to his wife to come and see what was the matter with Evans. The children would naturally follow their mother. It seems to me simple. And as for the animals—the horses, dogs, and so forth, they as I say, were no doubt panic-stricken by the ray, and hence driven to frenzy."

"Why should Evans have murdered Williams instead of Williams murdering Evans? Why should the impact of the ray affect one and not the other?"

"Why does one man react violently to a certain drug, while it makes no impression on another man? Why is A able to drink a bottle of whisky and remain sober, while B is turned into something very like a lunatic after he has drunk three glasses?"

"It is a question of idiosyncrasy," said the doctor.

"Is 'idiosyncrasy' Greek for 'I don't know'?" asked Remnant.

"Not at all," said Lewis, smiling blandly. "I mean that in some diatheses whisky—as you have mentioned whisky—appears not to be pathogenic, or at all events not immediately pathogenic. In other cases, as you very justly observed, there seems to be a very marked cachexia associated with the exhibition of the spirit in question, even in comparatively small doses."

Under this cloud of professional verbiage Lewis escaped from the club and from Remnant. He did not want to hear any more about that dreadful ray, because he felt sure that the ray was all nonsense. But asking himself why he felt this certitude in the matter, he had to confess that he didn't know. An aeroplane, he reflected, was all nonsense before it was made; and he remembered talking in the early nineties to a friend of his about the newly discovered X rays. The friend laughed incredulously, evidently didn't believe a word of it, till Lewis told him that there was an article on the subject in the current number of the *Saturday Review*; whereupon the unbeliever said, "Oh, is that so? Oh, really. I *see*," and was converted on the X ray faith on the spot. Lewis, remembering this talk, marvelled at the strange processes of the human mind, its illogical and yet all-compelling *ergos*, and wondered whether he himself was only waiting for an article on the Z ray in the *Saturday Review* to become a devout believer in the doctrine of Remnant.

But he wondered with far more fervour as to the extraordinary thing he had seen in his own garden with his own eyes. The tree that changed all its shape for an hour or two of the night, the growth of strange boughs, the apparition of secret fires among them, the sparkling of emerald and ruby lights: how could one fail to be afraid with great amazement at the thought of such a mystery?

Dr. Lewis's thoughts were distracted from the incredible adventure of the tree by the visit of his sister and her husband. Mr. and Mrs. Merritt lived in a well-known manufacturing town of the Midlands, which was now, of course, a center of munition work. On the day of their arrival at Porth, Mrs. Merritt, who was tired after the long, hot journey, went to bed early, and Merritt and Lewis went into the room by the garden for their talk and tobacco. They spoke of the year that had passed since their last meeting, of the weary dragging of the war, of friends that had perished in it, of the hopelessness of an early ending of all this misery. Lewis said nothing of the terror that was on the land. One does not greet a tired man who is come to a quiet, sunny place for relief from black smoke and work and worry with a tale of horror. Indeed, the doctor saw that his brother-in-law looked far from well. And he seemed "jumpy"; there was an occasional twitch of his mouth that Lewis did not like at all.

"Well," said the doctor, after an interval of silence and port wine, "I am glad to see you here again. Porth always suits you. I don't think you're looking quite up to your usual form. But three weeks of Meirion air will do wonders."

"Well, I hope it will," said the other. "I am not up to the mark. Things are not going well at Midlingham."

"Business is all right, isn't it?"

"Yes. Business is all right. But there are other things that are all wrong. We are living under a reign of terror. It comes to that."

"What on earth do you mean?"

"Well, I suppose I may tell you what I know. It's not much. I didn't dare write it. But do you know that at every one of the munition works in Midlingham and all about it there's a guard of soldiers with drawn bayonets and loaded rifles day and night? Men with bombs, too. And machine-guns at the big factories."

"German spies?"

"You don't want Lewis guns to fight spies with. Nor bombs. Nor a platoon of men. I woke up last night. It was the machine-gun at Benington's Army Motor Works. Firing like fury. And then bang! bang! bang! That was the hand bombs."

"But what against?"

"Nobody knows."

"Nobody knows what is happening," Merritt repeated, and he went on to describe the bewilderment and terror that hung like a cloud over the great industrial city in the Midlands, how the feeling of concealment, of some intolerable secret danger that must not be named, was worst of all.

"A young fellow I know," he said, "was on short leave the other day from the front, and he spent it with his people at Belmont—that's about four miles out of Midlingham, you know. 'Thank God,' he said to me, 'I am going back to-morrow. It's no good saying that the Wipers salient is nice, because it isn't. But it's a damned sight better than this. At the front you know what you're up against anyhow.' At Midlingham everybody has the feeling that we're up against something awful and we don't know what; it's that that makes people inclined to whisper. There's terror in the air."

Merritt made a sort of picture of the great town cowering in its fear of an unknown danger.

"People are afraid to go about alone at nights in the outskirts. They make up parties at the stations to go home together if it's anything like dark, or if there are any lonely bits on their way."

"But why? I don't understand. What are they afraid of?"

"Well, I told you about my being awakened up the other night with the machine-guns at the motor works rattling away, and the bombs exploding and making the most terrible noise. That sort of thing alarms one, you know. It's only natural."

"Indeed, it must be very terrifying. You mean, then, there is a general nervousness about, a vague sort of apprehension that makes people inclined to herd together?"

"There's that, and there's more. People have gone out that have never come back. There were a couple of men in the train to Holme, arguing about the quickest way to get to Northend, a sort of outlying part of Holme where they both lived. They argued all the way out of Midlingham, one saying that the high road was the quickest though it was the longest way. 'It's the quickest going because it's the cleanest going,' he said.

"The other chap fancied a short cut across the fields, by the canal. 'It's half the distance,' he kept on. 'Yes, if you don't lose your way,' said the other. Well, it appears they put an even half-crown on it, and each was to try his own way when they got out of the train. It was arranged that they were to meet at the Wagon in Northend. 'I shall be at the Wagon first,' said the man who believed in the short cut, and with that he climbed over the stile and made off across the fields. It wasn't late enough to be really dark, and a lot of them thought he might win the stakes. But he never turned up at the Wagon—or anywhere else for the matter of that."

"What happened to him?"

"He was found lying on his back in the middle of a field—some way from the path. He was dead. The doctors said he'd been suffocated. Nobody knows how. Then there have been other cases. We whisper about them at Midlingham, but we're afraid to speak out."

Lewis was ruminating all this profoundly. Terror in Meirion and terror far away in the heart of England; but at Midlingham, so far as he could gather from these stories of soldiers on guard, of crackling machine-guns, it was a case of an organized attack on the munitioning of the army. He felt that he did not know enough to warrant his deciding that the terror of Meirion and of Stratfordshire were one.

Then Merritt began again:

"There's a queer story going about, when the door's shut and the curtain's drawn, that is, as to a place right out in the country over the other side of Midlingham; on the opposite side to Dunwich. They've built one of the new factories out there, a great red-brick town of sheds they tell me it is, with a tremendous chimney. It's not been finished more than a month or six weeks. They plumped it down right in the middle of the fields, by the line, and they're building huts for the workers as fast as they can but up to the present the men are billeted all about, up and down the line.

"About two hundred yards from this place there's an old footpath, leading from the station and the main road up to a small hamlet on the hill-side. Part of the way this path goes by a pretty large wood, most of it thick undergrowth. I should think there must be twenty acres of wood, more or less. As it happens, I used this path once long ago; and I can tell you it's a black place of nights.

"A man had to go this way one night. He got along all right till he came to the wood. And then he said his heart dropped out of his body. It was awful to hear the noises in that wood. Thousands of men were in it, he swears that. It was full of rustling, and pattering of feet trying to go dainty, and the crack of dead boughs lying on the ground as someone trod on them, and swishing of the grass, and some sort of chattering speech going on, that sounded, so he said, as if the dead sat in their bones and talked! He ran for his life, anyhow; across fields, over hedges, through brooks. He must have run, by his tale, ten miles out of his way before he got home to his wife, and beat at the door, and broke in, and bolted it behind him."

"There is something rather alarming about any wood at night," said Dr. Lewis.

Merritt shrugged his shoulders.

"People say that the Germans have landed, and that they are hiding in underground places all over the country."

VII. The Case of the Hidden Germans

Lewis gasped for a moment, silent in contemplation of the magnificence of rumour. The Germans already landed, hiding underground, striking by night, secretly, terribly, at the power of England! Here was a conception which made the myth of the Russians a paltry fable; before which the legend of Mons was an ineffectual thing.

It was monstrous. And yet—

He looked steadily at Merritt; a square-headed, black-haired, solid sort of man. He had symptoms of nerves about him for the moment, certainly, but one could not wonder at that, whether the tales he told were true, or whether he merely believed them to be true. Lewis had known his brother-in-law for twenty years or more, and had always found him a sure man in his own small world. "But then," said the doctor to himself, "those men, if they once get out of the ring of that little world of theirs, they are lost. Those are the men that believed in Madame Blavatsky."

"Well," he said, "what do you think yourself? The Germans landed and hiding somewhere about the country: there's something extravagant in the notion, isn't there?"

"I don't know what to think. You can't get over the facts. There are the soldiers with their rifles and their guns at the works all over Stratfordshire, and those guns go off. I told you I'd heard them. Then who are the soldiers shooting at? That's what we ask ourselves at Midlingham."

"Quite so; I quite understand. It's an extraordinary state of things."

"It's more than extraordinary; it's an awful state of things. It's terror in the dark, and there's nothing worse than that. As that young fellow I was telling you about said, 'At the front you do know what you're up against.'"

"And people really believe that a number of Germans have somehow got over to England and have hid themselves underground?"

"People say they've got a new kind of poison gas. Some think that they dig underground places and make the gas there, and lead it by secret pipes into the shops; others say that they throw gas bombs into the factories. It must be worse than anything they've used in France, from what the authorities say."

"The authorities? Do *they* admit that there are Germans in hiding about Midlingham?"

"No. They call it 'explosions.' But we know it isn't explosions. We know in the Midlands what an explosion sounds like and looks like. And we know that the people killed in these 'explosions' are put into their coffins in the works. Their own relations are not allowed to see them."

"And so you believe in the German theory?"

"If I do, it's because one must believe in something. Some say they've seen the gas. I heard that a man living in Dunwich saw it one night like a black cloud with sparks of fire in it floating over the tops of the trees by Dunwich Common."

The light of an ineffable amazement came into Lewis's eyes. The night of Remnant's visit, the trembling vibration of the air, the dark tree that had grown in his garden since the setting of the sun, the strange leafage that was starred with burning, with emerald and ruby fires, and all vanished away when he returned from his visit to the Garth; and such a leafage had appeared as a burning cloud far in the heart of England: what intolerable mystery, what tremendous doom was signified in this? But one thing was clear and certain: that the terror of Meirion was also the terror of the Midlands.

Lewis made up his mind most firmly that if possible all this should be kept from his brother-in-law. Merritt had come to Porth as to a city of refuge from the horrors of Midlingham; if it could be managed he should be spared the knowledge that the cloud of terror had gone before him and hung black over the western land. Lewis passed the port and said in an even voice:

"Very strange, indeed; a black cloud with sparks of fire?"

"I can't answer for it, you know; it's only a rumour."

"Just so; and you think, or you're inclined to think, that this and all the rest you've told me is to be put down to the hidden Germans?"

"As I say; because one must think something."

"I quite see your point. No doubt, if it's true, it's the most awful blow that has ever been dealt at any nation in the whole history of man. The enemy established in our vitals! But is it possible, after all? How could it have been worked?"

Merritt told Lewis how it had been worked, or rather, how people said it had been worked. The idea, he said, was that this was a part, and a most important part, of the great German plot to destroy England and the British Empire.

The scheme had been prepared years ago, some thought soon after the Franco-Prussian War. Moltke had seen that the invasion of England (in the ordinary sense of the term "invasion") presented very great difficulties. The matter was constantly in discussion in the inner military and high political circles, and the general trend of opinion in these quarters was that at the best, the invasion of England would involve Germany in the gravest difficulties, and leave France in the position of the *tertius gaudens*. This was the state of affairs when a very high Prussian personage was approached by the Swedish professor, Huvelius.

Thus Merritt, and here I would say in parenthesis that this Huvelius was by all accounts an extraordinary man. Considered personally and apart from his writings he would appear to have been a most amiable individual. He was richer than the generality of Swedes, certainly far richer than the average university professor in Sweden. But his shabby, green frock-coat, and his battered, furry hat were notorious in the university town where he lived. No one laughed, because it was well known that Professor Huvelius spent every penny of his private means and a large portion of his official stipend on works of kindness and charity. He hid his head in a garret, some one said, in order that others might be able to swell on the first floor. It was told of him that he restricted himself to a diet of dry bread and coffee for a month in order that a poor woman of the streets, dying of consumption, might enjoy luxuries in hospital.

And this was the man who wrote the treatise *De Facinore Humano*; to prove the infinite corruption of the human race.

Oddly enough, Professor Huvelius wrote the most cynical book in the world—Hobbes preaches rosy sentimentalism in comparison—with the very highest motives. He held that a very large part of human misery, misadventure, and sorrow was due to the false convention that the heart of man was naturally and in the main well disposed and kindly, if not exactly righteous. "Murderers, thieves, assassins, violators, and all the host of the abominable," he says in one passage, "are created by the false pretense and foolish credence of human virtue. A lion in a cage is a fierce beast, indeed; but what will he be if we declare him to be a lamb and open the doors of his den? Who will be guilty of the deaths of the men, women and children whom he will surely devour, save those who unlocked the cage?" And he goes on to show that kings and the rulers of the peoples could decrease the sum of human misery to a vast extent by acting on the doctrine of human wickedness. "War," he declares, "which is one of the worst of evils, will always continue to exist. But a wise king will desire a brief war rather than a lengthy one, a short evil rather than a long evil. And this not from the benignity of his heart towards his enemies, for we have seen that the human heart is naturally malignant, but because he desires to conquer, and to conquer easily, without a great expenditure of men or of treasure, knowing that if he can accomplish this feat his people will love him and his crown will be secure. So he will wage brief victorious wars, and not only spare his own nation, but the nation of the enemy, since in a short war the loss is less on both sides than in a long war. And so from evil will come good."

And how, asks Huvelius, are such wars to be waged? The wise prince, he replies, will begin by assuming the enemy to be infinitely corruptible and infinitely stupid, since stupidity and corruption are the chief characteristics of man. So the prince will make himself friends in the very councils of his enemy, and also amongst the populace, bribing the wealthy by proffering to them the opportunity of still greater wealth, and winning the poor by swelling words. "For, contrary to the common opinion, it is the wealthy who are greedy of wealth; while the populace are to be gained by talking to them about liberty, their unknown god. And so much are they enchanted by the words liberty, freedom, and such like, that the wise can go to the poor, rob them of what little they have, dismiss them with a hearty kick, and win their hearts and their votes for ever, if only they will assure them that the treatment which they have received is called liberty."

Guided by these principles, says Huvelius, the wise prince will entrench himself in the country that he desires to conquer; "nay, with but little trouble, he may actually and literally throw his garrisons into the heart of the enemy country before war has begun."

This is a long and tiresome parenthesis; but it is necessary as explaining the long tale which Merritt told his brother-in-law, he having received it from some magnate of the Midlands, who had travelled in Germany. It is probable that the story was suggested in the first place by the passage from Huvelius which I have just quoted.

Merritt knew nothing of the real Huvelius, who was all but a saint; he thought of the Swedish professor as a monster of iniquity, "worse," as he said, "than Neech"—meaning, no doubt, Nietzsche.

So he told the story of how Huvelius had sold his plan to the Germans; a plan for filling England with German soldiers. Land was to be bought in certain suitable and well-considered places, Englishmen were to be bought as the apparent owners of such land, and secret excavations were to be made, till the country was literally undermined. A subterranean Germany, in fact, was to be dug under selected districts of England; there were to be great caverns, underground cities, well drained, well ventilated, supplied with water, and in these places vast stores both of food and of munitions were to be accumulated, year after year, till "the day" dawned. And then, warned in time, the secret garrison would leave shops, hotels, offices, villas, and vanish underground, ready to begin their work of bleeding England at the heart.

"That's what Henson told me," said Merritt at the end of his long story. "Henson, head of the Buckley Iron and Steel Syndicate. He has been a lot in Germany."

"Well," said Lewis, "of course, it may be so. If it is so, it is terrible beyond words."

Indeed, he found something horribly plausible in the story. It was an extraordinary plan, of course; an unheard-of scheme; but it did not seem impossible. It was the Trojan horse on a gigantic scale; indeed, he reflected, the story of the horse with the warriors concealed within it which was dragged into the heart of Troy by the deluded Trojans themselves might be taken as a prophetic parable of what had happened to England—if Henson's theory were well founded. And this theory certainly squared with what one had heard of German preparations in Belgium and in France: emplacements for guns ready for the invader, German manufactories which were really German forts on Belgian soil, the caverns by the Aisne made ready for the cannon; indeed, Lewis thought he remembered something about suspicious concrete tennis-courts on the heights commanding London. But a German army hidden under English ground! It was a thought to chill the stoutest heart.

And it seemed from that wonder of the burning tree, that the enemy mysteriously and terribly present at Midlingham, was present also in Meirion. Lewis, thinking of the country as he knew it, of its wild and desolate hillsides, its deep woods, its wastes and solitary places, could not but confess that no more fit region could be found for the deadly enterprise of secret men. Yet, he thought again, there was but little harm to be done in Meirion to the armies of England or to their munitionment. They were working for panic terror? Possibly that might be so; but the camp under the Highway? That should be their first object, and no harm had been done there.

Lewis did not know that since the panic of the horses men had died terribly in that camp; that it was now a fortified place, with a deep, broad trench, a thick tangle of savage barbed wire about it, and a machine-gun planted at each corner.

VIII. What Mr. Merritt Found

Mr. Merritt began to pick up his health and spirits a good deal. For the first morning or two of his stay at the doctor's he contented himself with a very comfortable deck chair close to the house, where he sat under the shade of an old mulberry-tree beside his wife and watched the bright sunshine on the green lawns, on the creamy crests of the waves, on the headlands of that glorious coast, purple even from afar with the imperial glow of the heather, on the white farmhouses gleaming in the sunlight, high over the sea, far from any turmoil, from any troubling of men.

The sun was hot, but the wind breathed all the while gently, incessantly, from the east, and Merritt, who had come to this quiet place, not only from dismay, but from the stifling and oily airs of the smoky Midland town, said that that east wind, pure and clear and like well-water from the rock, was new life to him. He ate a capital dinner at the end of his first day at Porth and took rosy views. As to what they had been talking about the night before, he said to Lewis, no doubt there must be trouble of some sort, and perhaps bad trouble; still, Kitchener would soon put it all right.

So things went on very well. Merritt began to stroll about the garden, which was full of the comfortable spaces, groves, and surprises that only country gardens know. To the right of one of the terraces he found an arbor or summer-house covered with white roses, and he was as pleased as if he had discovered the pole. He spent a whole day there, smoking and lounging and reading a rubbishy sensational story, and declared that the Devonshire roses had taken many years off his age. Then on the other side of the garden there was a filbert grove that he had never explored on any of his former visits; and again there was a find. Deep in the shadow of the filberts was a bubbling well, issuing from rocks, and all manner of green, dewy ferns growing about it and above it, and an angelica springing beside it. Merritt knelt on his knees, and hollowed his hand and drank the well-water. He said (over his port) that night that if all water were like the water of the filbert well the world would turn to teetotalism. It takes a townsman to relish the manifold and exquisite joys of the country.

It was not till he began to venture abroad that Merritt found that something was lacking of the old rich peace that used to dwell in Meirion. He had a favourite walk which he never neglected, year after year. This walk led along the cliffs towards Meiros, and then one could turn inland and return to Porth by deep winding lanes that went over the Allt. So

Merritt set out early one morning and got as far as a sentry-box at the foot of the path that led up to the cliff. There was a sentry pacing up and down in front of the box, and he called on Merritt to produce his pass, or to turn back to the main road. Merritt was a good deal put out, and asked the doctor about this strict guard. And the doctor was surprised.

"I didn't know they had put their bar up there," he said. "I suppose it's wise. We are certainly in the far west here; still, the Germans might slip round and raid us and do a lot of damage just because Meirion is the last place we should expect them to go for."

"But there are no fortifications, surely, on the cliff?"

"Oh, no; I never heard of anything of the kind there."

"Well, what's the point of forbidding the public to go on the cliff, then? I can quite understand putting a sentry on the top to keep a look-out for the enemy. What I don't understand is a sentry at the bottom who can't keep a look-out for anything, as he can't see the sea. And why warn the public off the cliffs? I couldn't facilitate a German landing by standing on Pengareg, even if I wanted to."

"It is curious," the doctor agreed. "Some military reasons, I suppose."

He let the matter drop, perhaps because the matter did not affect him. People who live in the country all the year round, country doctors certainly, are little given to desultory walking in search of the picturesque.

Lewis had no suspicion that sentries whose object was equally obscure were being dotted all over the country. There was a sentry, for example, by the quarry at Llanfihangel, where the dead woman and the dead sheep had been found some weeks before. The path by the quarry was used a good deal, and its closing would have inconvenienced the people of the neighbourhood very considerably. But the sentry had his box by the side of the track and had his orders to keep everybody strictly to the path, as if the quarry were a secret fort.

It was not known till a month or two ago that one of these sentries was himself a victim of the terror. The men on duty at this place were given certain very strict orders, which from the nature of the case, must have seemed to them unreasonable. For old soldiers, orders are orders; but here was a young bank clerk, scarcely in training for a couple of months, who had not begun to appreciate the necessity of hard, literal obedience to an order which seemed to him meaningless. He found himself on a remote and lonely hillside, he had not the faintest notion that his every movement was watched; and he disobeyed a certain instruction that had been given him. The post was found deserted by the relief; the sentry's dead body was found at the bottom of the quarry.

This by the way; but Mr. Merritt discovered again and again that things happened to hamper his walks and his wanderings. Two or three miles from Porth there is a great marsh made by the Afon River before it falls into the sea, and here Merritt had been accustomed to botanize mildly. He had learned pretty accurately the causeways of solid ground that lead through the sea of swamp and ooze and soft yielding soil, and he set out one hot afternoon determined to make a thorough exploration of the marsh, and this time to find that rare bog bean, that he felt sure, must grow somewhere in its wide extent.

He got into the by-road that skirts the marsh, and to the gate which he had always used for entrance.

There was the scene as he had known it always, the rich growth of reeds and flags and rushes, the mild black cattle grazing on the "islands" of firm turf, the scented procession of the meadowsweet, the royal glory of the loosestrife, flaming pennons, crimson and golden, of the giant dock.

But they were bringing out a dead man's body through the gate.

A labouring man was holding open the gate on the marsh. Merritt, horrified, spoke to him and asked who it was, and how it had happened.

"They do say he was a visitor at Porth. Somehow he has been drowned in the marsh, whatever."

"But it's perfectly safe. I've been all over it a dozen times."

"Well, indeed, we did always think so. If you did slip by accident, like, and fall into the water, it was not so deep; it was easy enough to climb out again. And this gentleman was quite young, to look at him, poor man; and he has come to Meirion for his pleasure and holiday and found his death in it."

"Did he do it on purpose? Is it suicide?"

"They say he had no reasons to do that."

Here the sergeant of police in charge of the party interposed, according to orders, which he himself did not understand.

"A terrible thing, sir, to be sure, and a sad pity; and I am sure this is not the sort of sight you have come to see down in Meirion this beautiful summer. So don't you think, sir, that it would be more pleasantlike, if you would leave us to this sad business of ours? I have heard many gentlemen staying in Porth say that there is nothing to beat the view from the hill over there, not in the whole of Wales."

Every one is polite in Meirion, but somehow Merritt understood that, in English, this speech meant "move on."

Merritt moved back to Porth—he was not in the humour for any idle, pleasurable strolling after so dreadful a meeting with death. He made some inquiries in the town about the dead man, but nothing seemed known of him. It was said that he had been on his honeymoon, that he had been staying at the Porth Castle Hotel; but the people of the hotel declared that they had never heard of such a person. Merritt got the local paper at the end of the week; there was not a word in it of any fatal accident in the marsh. He met the sergeant of police in the street. That officer touched his helmet with the utmost politeness and a "hope you are enjoying yourself, sir; indeed you do look a lot better already"; but as to the poor man who was found drowned or stifled in the marsh, he knew nothing.

The next day Merritt made up his mind to go to the marsh to see whether he could find anything to account for so strange a death. What he found was a man with an armlet standing by the gate. The armlet had the letters "C. W." on it, which are understood to mean "Coast Watcher." The watcher said he had strict instructions to keep everybody away from the marsh. Why? He didn't know, but some said that the river was changing its course since the new railway embankment was built, and the marsh had become dangerous to people who didn't know it thoroughly.

"Indeed, sir," he added, "it is part of my orders not to set foot on the other side of that gate myself, not for one scrag-end of a minute."

Merritt glanced over the gate incredulously. The marsh looked as it had always looked; there was plenty of sound, hard ground to walk on; he could see the track that he used to follow as firm as ever. He did not believe in the story of the changing course of the river, and Lewis said he had never heard of anything of the kind. But Merritt had put the question in the middle of general conversation; he had not led up to it from any discussion of the death in the marsh, and so the doctor was taken unawares. If he had known of the connection in Merritt's mind between the alleged changing of the Afon's course and the tragical event in the marsh, no doubt he would have confirmed the official explanation. He was, above all things, anxious to prevent his sister and her husband from finding out that the invisible hand of terror that ruled at Midlingham was ruling also in Meirion.

Lewis himself had little doubt that the man who was found dead in the marsh had been struck down by the secret agency, whatever it was, that had already accomplished so much of evil; but it was a chief part of the terror that no one knew for certain that this or that particular event was to be ascribed to it. People do occasionally fall over cliffs through their own carelessness, and as the case of Garcia, the Spanish sailor, showed, cottagers and their wives and children are now and then the victims of savage and purposeless violence. Lewis had never wandered about the marsh himself; but Remnant had pottered round it and about it, and declared that the man who met his death there—his name was never known, in Porth at all events—must either have committed suicide by deliberately lying prone in the ooze and stifling himself, or else must have been held down in it. There were no details available, so it was clear that the authorities had classified this death with the others; still, the man might have committed suicide, or he might have had a sudden seizure and fallen in the slimy water face downwards. And so on: it was possible to believe that case A *or* B *or* C was in the category of ordinary accidents or ordinary crimes. But it was not possible to believe that A *and* B *and* C were all in that category. And thus it was to the end, and thus it is now. We know that the terror reigned, and how it reigned, but there were many dreadful events ascribed to its rule about which there must always be room for doubt.

For example, there was the case of the *Mary Ann*, the rowing-boat which came to grief in so strange a manner, almost under Merritt's eyes. In my opinion he was quite wrong in associating the sorry fate of the boat and her occupants with a system of signalling by flash-lights which he detected, or thought that he detected, on the afternoon in which the *Mary Ann* was capsized. I believe his signalling theory to be all nonsense, in spite of the naturalized German governess who was lodging with her employers in the suspected house. But, on the other hand, there is no doubt in my own mind that the boat was overturned and those in it drowned by the work of the terror.

IX. The Light on the Water

Let it be noted carefully that so far Merritt had not the slightest suspicion that the terror of Midlingham was quick over Meirion. Lewis had watched and shepherded him carefully. He had let out no suspicion of what had happened in Meirion, and before taking his brother-in-law to the club he had passed round a hint among the members. He did not tell the truth about Midlingham—and here again is a point of interest, that as the terror deepened the general public co-operated voluntarily, and, one would say, almost subconsciously, with the authorities in concealing what they knew from one another—but he gave out a desirable portion of the truth: that his brother-in-law was "nervy," not by any means up to the mark, and that it was therefore desirable that he should be spared the knowledge of the intolerable and tragic mysteries which were being enacted all about them.

"He knows about that poor fellow who was found in the marsh," said Lewis, "and he has a kind of vague suspicion that there is something out of the common about the case; but no more than that."

"A clear case of suggested, or rather commanded suicide," said Remnant. "I regard it as a strong confirmation of my theory."

"Perhaps so," said the doctor, dreading lest he might have to hear about the Z ray all over again. "But please don't let anything out to him; I want him to get built up thoroughly before he goes back to Midlingham."

Then, on the other hand, Merritt was as still as death about the doings of the Midlands; he hated to think of them, much more to speak of them; and thus, as I say, he and the men at the Porth Club kept their secrets from one another; and thus, from the beginning to the end of the terror, the links were not drawn together. In many cases, no doubt, A and B met every day and talked familiarly, it may be confidentially, on other matters of all sorts, each having in his possession half of the truth, which he concealed from the other. So the two halves were never put together to make a whole.

Merritt, as the doctor guessed had a kind of uneasy feeling—it scarcely amounted to a suspicion—as to the business of the marsh; chiefly because he thought the official talk about the railway embankment and the course of the river rank nonsense. But finding that nothing more happened, he let the matter drop from his mind, and settled himself down to enjoy his holiday.

He found to his delight that there were no sentries or watchers to hinder him from the approach to Larnac Bay, a delicious cove, a place where the ashgrove and the green meadow and the glistening bracken sloped gently down to red rocks and firm yellow sands. Merritt remembered a rock that formed a comfortable seat, and here he established himself of a golden afternoon, and gazed at the blue of the sea and the crimson bastions and bays of the coast as it bent inward to Sarnau and swept out again southward to the odd-shaped promontory called the Dragon's Head. Merritt gazed on, amused by the antics of the porpoises who were tumbling and splashing and gambolling a little way out at sea, charmed by the pure and radiant air that was so different from the oily smoke that often stood for heaven at Midlingham, and charmed, too, by the white farmhouses dotted here and there on the heights of the curving coast.

Then he noticed a little row-boat at about two hundred yards from the shore. There were two or three people aboard, he could not quite make out how many, and they seemed to be doing something with a line; they were no doubt fishing, and Merritt (who disliked fish) wondered how people could spoil such an afternoon, such a sea, such pellucid and radiant air by trying to catch white, flabby, offensive, evil-smelling creatures that would be excessively nasty when cooked. He puzzled over this problem and turned away from it to the contemplation of the crimson headlands. And then he says that he noticed that signalling was going on. Flashing lights of intense brilliance, he declares, were coming from one of those farms on the heights of the coast; it was as if white fire was spouting from it. Merritt was certain, as the light appeared and disappeared, that some message was being sent, and he regretted that he knew nothing of heliography. Three short flashes, a long and very brilliant flash, then two short flashes. Merritt fumbled in his pocket for pencil and paper so that he might record these signals, and, bringing his eyes down to the sea level, he became aware, with amazement and horror, that the boat had disappeared. All that he could see was some vague, dark object far to westward, running out with the tide.

Now it is certain, unfortunately, that the *Mary Ann* was capsized and that two school-boys and the sailor in charge were drowned. The bones of the boat were found amongst the rocks far along the coast, and the three bodies were also washed ashore. The sailor could not swim at all, the boys only a little, and it needs an exceptionally fine swimmer to fight against the outward suck of the tide as it rushes past Pengareg Point.

But I have no belief whatever in Merritt's theory. He held (and still holds, for all I know), that the flashes of light which he saw coming from Penyrhaul, the farmhouse on the height, had some connection with the disaster to the *Mary Ann*. When it was ascertained that a family were spending their summer at the farm, and that the governess was a German, though a long-naturalized German, Merritt could not see that there was anything left to argue about, though there might be many details to discover. But, in my opinion, all this was a mere mare's nest; the flashes of brilliant light were caused, no doubt, by the sun lighting up one window of the farmhouse after the other.

Still, Merritt was convinced from the very first, even before the damning circumstance of the German governess was brought to light; and on the evening of the disaster, as Lewis and he sat together after dinner, he was endeavouring to put what he called the common sense of the matter to the doctor.

"If you hear a shot," said Merritt, "and you see a man fall, you know pretty well what killed him."

There was a flutter of wild wings in the room. A great moth beat to and fro and dashed itself madly against the ceiling, the walls, the glass bookcase. Then a sputtering sound, a momentary dimming of the lamp. The moth had succeeded in its mysterious quest.

"Can you tell me," said Lewis as if he were answering Merritt, "why moths rush into the flame?"

Lewis had put his question as to the strange habits of the common moth to Merritt with the deliberate intent of closing the debate on death by heliograph. The query was suggested, of course, by the incident of the moth in the lamp, and Lewis thought that he had said: "Oh, shut up!" in a somewhat elegant manner. And, in fact Merritt looked dignified, remained silent, and helped himself to port.

That was the end that the doctor had desired. He had no doubt in his own mind that the affair of the *Mary Ann* was but one more item in a long account of horrors that grew larger almost with every day; and he was in no humour to listen to wild and futile theories as to the manner in which the disaster had been accomplished. Here was a proof that the terror that was upon them was mighty not only on the land but on the waters; for Lewis could not see that the boat could have been attacked by any ordinary means of destruction. From Merritt's story, it must have been in shallow water. The shore of Larnac Bay shelves very gradually, and the Admiralty charts showed the depth of water two hundred yards out to be only two fathoms; this would be too shallow for a submarine. And it could not have been shelled, and it could not have been torpedoed; there was no explosion. The disaster might have been due to carelessness; boys, he considered, will play the fool anywhere, even in a boat; but he did not think so; the sailor would have stopped them. And, it may be mentioned, that the two boys were as a matter of fact extremely steady, sensible young fellows, not in the least likely to play foolish tricks of any kind.

Lewis was immersed in these reflections, having successfully silenced his brother-in-law; he was trying in vain to find some clue to the horrible enigma. The Midlingham theory of a concealed German force, hiding in places under the earth, was extravagant enough, and yet it seemed the only solution that approached plausibility; but then again even a subterranean German host would hardly account for this wreckage of a boat, floating on a calm sea. And then what of the tree with the burning in it that had appeared in the garden there a few weeks ago, and the cloud with a burning in it that had shown over the trees of the Midland village?

I think I have already written something of the probable emotions of the mathematician confronted suddenly with an undoubted two-sided triangle. I said, if I remember, that he would be forced, in decency, to go mad; and I believe that Lewis was very near to this point. He felt himself confronted with an intolerable problem that most instantly demanded solution, and yet, with the same breath, as it were, denied the possibility of there being any solution. People were being killed in an inscrutable manner by some inscrutable means, day after day, and one asked why and how; and there seemed no answer. In the Midlands, where every kind of munitionment was manufactured, the explanation of German agency was plausible; and even if the subterranean notion was to be rejected as savoring altogether too much of the fairy-tale, or rather of the sensational romance, yet it was possible that the backbone of the theory was true; the Germans might have planted their agents in some way or another in the midst of our factories. But here in Meirion, what serious effect could be produced by the casual and indiscriminate slaughter of a couple of school-boys in a boat, of a harmless holiday-maker in a marsh? The creation of an atmosphere of terror and dismay? It was possible, of course, but it hardly seemed tolerable, in spite of the enormities of Louvain and of the *Lusitania*.

Into these meditations, and into the still dignified silence of Merritt broke the rap on the door of Lewis's man, and those words which harass the ease of the country doctor when he tries to take any ease: "You're wanted in the surgery, if you please, sir." Lewis bustled out, and appeared no more that night.

The doctor had been summoned to a little hamlet on the outskirts of Porth, separated from it by half a mile or three quarters of road. One dignifies, indeed, this settlement without a name in calling it a hamlet;

it was a mere row of four cottages, built about a hundred years ago for the accommodation of the workers in a quarry long since disused. In one of these cottages the doctor found a father and mother weeping and crying out to "doctor *bach*, doctor *bach*," and two frightened children, and one little body, still and dead. It was the youngest of the three, little Johnnie, and he was dead.

The doctor found that the child had been asphyxiated. He felt the clothes; they were dry; it was not a case of drowning. He looked at the neck; there was no mark of strangling. He asked the father how it had happened, and father and mother, weeping most lamentably, declared they had no knowledge of how their child had been killed: "unless it was the People that had done it." The Celtic fairies are still malignant. Lewis asked what had happened that evening; where had the child been?

"Was he with his brother and sister? Don't they know anything about it?"

Reduced into some sort of order from its original piteous confusion, this is the story that the doctor gathered.

All three children had been well and happy through the day. They had walked in with the mother, Mrs. Roberts, to Porth on a marketing expedition in the afternoon; they had returned to the cottage, had had their tea, and afterwards played about on the road in front of the house. John Roberts had come home somewhat late from his work, and it was after dusk when the family sat down to supper. Supper over, the three children went out again to play with other children from the cottage next door, Mrs. Roberts telling them that they might have half an hour before going to bed.

The two mothers came to the cottage gates at the same moment and called out to their children to come along and be quick about it. The two small families had been playing on the strip of turf across the road, just by the stile into the fields. The children ran across the road; all of them except Johnnie Roberts. His brother Willie said that just as their mother called them he heard Johnnie cry out:

"Oh, what is that beautiful shiny thing over the stile?"

X. THE CHILD AND THE MOTH

The little Robertses ran across the road, up the path, and into the lighted room. Then they noticed that Johnnie had not followed them. Mrs. Roberts was doing something in the back kitchen, and Mr. Roberts had gone out to the shed to bring in some sticks for the next morning's fire. Mrs. Roberts heard the children run in and went on with her work. The children whispered to one another that Johnnie would "catch it" when their mother came out of the back room and found him missing; but they expected he would run in through the open door any minute. But six or seven, perhaps ten, minutes passed, and there was no Johnnie. Then the father and mother came into the kitchen together, and saw that their little boy was not there.

They thought it was some small piece of mischief—that the two other children had hidden the boy somewhere in the room in the big cupboard perhaps.

"What have you done with him then?" said Mrs. Roberts. "Come out, you little rascal, directly in a minute."

There was no little rascal to come out, and Margaret Roberts, the girl, said that Johnnie had not come across the road with them: he must be still playing all by himself by the hedge.

"What did you let him stay like that for?" said Mrs. Roberts. "Can't I trust you for two minutes together?

Indeed to goodness, you are all of you more trouble than you are worth." She went to the open door.

"Johnnie! Come in directly, or you will be sorry for it. Johnnie!"

The poor woman called at the door. She went out to the gate and called there:

"Come you, little Johnnie. Come you, *bachgen*, there's a good boy. I do see you hiding there."

She thought he must be hiding in the shadow of the hedge, and that he would come running and laughing—"He was always such a happy little fellow"—to her across the road. But no little merry figure danced out of the gloom of the still, dark night; it was all silence.

It was then, as the mother's heart began to chill, though she still called cheerfully to the missing child, that the elder boy told how Johnnie had said there was something beautiful by the stile: "And perhaps he did climb over, and he is running now about the meadow, and has lost his way."

The father got his lantern then, and the whole family went crying and calling about the meadow, promising cakes and sweets and a fine toy to poor Johnnie if he would come to them.

They found the little body, under the ash-grove in the middle of the field. He was quite still and dead, so still that a great moth had settled on his forehead, fluttering away when they lifted him up.

Dr. Lewis heard this story. There was nothing to be done; little to be said to these most unhappy people.

"Take care of the two that you have left to you," said the doctor as he went away. "Don't let them out of your sight if you can help it. It is dreadful times that we are living in."

It is curious to record that all through these dreadful times the simple little "season" went through its accustomed course at Porth. The war and its consequences had somewhat thinned the numbers of the summer visitors; still a very fair contingent of them occupied the hotels and boarding-houses and lodginghouses and bathed from the old-fashioned machines on one beach, or from the new-fashioned tents on the other, and sauntered in the sun, or lay stretched out in the shade under the trees that grow down almost to the water's edge. Porth never tolerated Ethiopians or shows of any kind on its sands, but the Rockets did very well during that summer in their garden entertainment, given in the castle grounds, and the fit-up companies that came to the Assembly Rooms are said to have paid their bills to a woman and to a man.

Porth depends very largely on its Midland and northern custom, custom of a prosperous, well-established sort. People who think Llandudno overcrowded and Colwyn Bay too raw and red and new come year after year to the placid old town in the south-west and delight in its peace; and as I say, they enjoyed themselves much as usual there in the summer of 1915. Now and then they became conscious, as Mr. Merritt became conscious, that they could not wander about quite in the old way; but they accepted sentries and coast watchers and people who politely pointed out the advantages of seeing the view from this point rather than from that as very necessary consequences of the dreadful war that was being waged; nay, as a Manchester man said, after having been turned back from his favourite walk to Castell Coch, it was gratifying to think that they were so well looked after.

"So far as I can see," he added, "there's nothing to prevent a submarine from standing out there by Ynys Sant and landing half a dozen men in a collapsible boat in any of these little coves. And pretty fools we should look, shouldn't we, with our throats cut on the sands; or carried back to Germany in the submarine?" He tipped the coast watcher half a crown.

"That's right, lad," he said, "you give us the tip."

Now here was a strange thing. The North-countryman had his thoughts on elusive submarines and German raiders; the watcher had simply received instructions to keep people off the Castell Coch fields, without reason assigned. And there can be no doubt that the authorities themselves, while they marked out the fields as in the "terror zone," gave their orders in the dark and were themselves profoundly in the dark as to the manner of the slaughter that had been done there; for if they had understood what had happened, they would have understood also that their restrictions were useless.

The Manchester man was warned off his walk about ten days after Johnnie Roberts's death. The watcher had been placed at his post because, the night before, a young farmer had been found by his wife lying in the grass close to the castle, with no scar on him, nor any mark of violence, but stone dead.

The wife of the dead man, Joseph Cradock, finding her husband lying motionless on the dewy turf, went white and stricken up the path to the village and got two men who bore the body to the farm. Lewis was sent for, and knew at once when he saw the dead man that he had perished in the way that the little Roberts boy had perished whatever that awful way might be. Cradock had been asphyxiated; and here again there was no mark of a grip on the throat. It might have been a piece of work by Burke and Hare, the doctor reflected; a pitch plaster might have been clapped over the man's mouth and nostrils and held there.

Then a thought struck him; his brother-in-law had talked of a new kind of poison gas that was said to be used against the munition workers in the Midlands: was it possible that the deaths of the man and the boy were due to some such instrument? He applied his tests but could find no trace of any gas having been employed. Carbonic acid gas? A man could not be killed with that in the open air; to be fatal that required a confined space, such a position as the bottom of a huge vat or of a well.

He did not know how Cradock had been killed; he confessed it to himself. He had been suffocated; that was all he could say. It seemed that the man had gone out at about half past nine to look after some beasts. The field in which they were was about five minutes' walk from the house. He told his wife he would be back in a quarter of an hour or twenty minutes. He did not return, and when he had gone for three quarters of an hour Mrs. Cradock went out to look for him. She went into the field where the beasts were, and everything seemed all right, but there was no trace of Cradock. She called out; there was no answer.

Now the meadow in which the cattle were pastured is high ground; a hedge divides it from the fields which fall gently down to the castle and the sea. Mrs. Cradock hardly seemed able to say why, having failed to find her husband among his beasts, she turned to the path which led to Castell Coch. She said at first that she had thought that one of the oxen might have broken through the hedge and strayed, and that Cradock had perhaps gone after it. And then, correcting herself, she said:

"There was that; and then there was something else that I could not make out at all. It seemed to me that the hedge did look different from usual. To be sure, things do look different at night, and there was a bit of sea mist about, but somehow it did look odd to me, and I said to myself: "Have I lost my way, then?'"

She declared that the shape of the trees in the hedge appeared to have changed, and besides, it had a look "as if it was lighted up, somehow," and so she went on towards the stile to see what all this could be, and when she came near everything was as usual. She looked over the stile and called and hoped to see her husband coming towards her or to hear his voice;

but there was no answer, and glancing down the path she saw, or thought she saw, some sort of brightness on the ground, "a dim sort of light like a bunch of glow-worms in a hedge-bank.

"And so I climbed over the stile and went down the path, and the light seemed to melt away; and there was my poor husband lying on his back, saying not a word to me when I spoke to him and touched him."

So for Lewis the terror blackened and became altogether intolerable, and others, he perceived, felt as he did. He did not know, he never asked whether the men at the club had heard of these deaths of the child and the young farmer; but no one spoke of them. Indeed, the change was evident; at the beginning of the terror men spoke of nothing else; now it had become all too awful for ingenious chatter or laboured and grotesque theories. And Lewis had received a letter from his brother-in-law at Midlingham; it contained the sentence, "I am afraid Fanny's health has not greatly benefited by her visit to Porth; there are still several symptoms I don't at all like." And this told him, in a phraseology that the doctor and Merritt had agreed upon, that the terror remained heavy in the Midland town.

It was soon after the death of Cradock that people began to tell strange tales of a sound that was to be heard of nights about the hills and valleys to the northward of Porth. A man who had missed the last train from Meiros and had been forced to tramp the ten miles between Meiros and Porth seems to have been the first to hear it. He said he had got to the top of the hill by Tredonoc, somewhere between half past ten and eleven, when he first noticed an odd noise that he could not make out at all; it was like a shout, a long, drawn-out, dismal wail coming from a great way off, faint with distance. He stopped to listen, thinking at first that it might be owls hooting in the woods; but it was different, he said, from that: it was a long cry, and then there was silence and then it began over again. He could make nothing of it, and feeling frightened, he did not quite know of what, he walked on briskly and was glad to see the lights of Porth station.

He told his wife of this dismal sound that night, and she told the neighbors, and most of them thought that it was "all fancy"—or drink, or the owls after all. But the night after, two or three people, who had been to some small merry-making in a cottage just off the Meiros road, heard the sound as they were going home, soon after ten. They, too, described it as a long, wailing cry, indescribably dismal in the stillness of the autumn night; "Like the ghost of a voice," said one; "As if it came up from the bottom of the earth," said another.

XI. At Treff Loyne Farm

Let it be remembered, again and again, that, all the while that the terror lasted, there was no common stock of information as to the dreadful things that were being done. The press had not said one word upon it, there was no criterion by which the mass of the people could separate fact from mere vague rumour, no test by which ordinary misadventure or disaster could be distinguished from the achievements of the secret and awful force that was at work.

And so with every event of the passing day. A harmless commercial traveller might show himself in the course of his business in the tumbledown main street of Meiros and find himself regarded with looks of fear and suspicion as a possible worker of murder, while it is likely enough that the true agents of the terror went quite unnoticed. And since the real nature of all this mystery of death was unknown, it followed easily that the signs and warnings and omens of it were all the more unknown. Here was horror, there was horror; but there was no link to join one horror with another; no common basis of knowledge from which the connection between this horror and that horror might be inferred.

So there was no one who suspected at all that this dismal and hollow sound that was now heard of nights in the region to the north of Porth, had any relation at all to the case of the little girl who went out one afternoon to pick purple flowers and never returned, or to the case of the man whose body was taken out of the peaty slime of the marsh, or to the case of Cradock, dead in his fields, with a strange glimmering of light about his body, as his wife reported. And it is a question as to how far the rumour of this melancholy, nocturnal summons got abroad at all. Lewis heard of it, as a country doctor hears of most things, driving up and down the lanes, but he heard of it without much interest, with no sense that it was in any sort of relation to the terror. Remnant had been given the story of the hollow and echoing voice of the darkness in a coloured and picturesque form; he employed a Tredonoc man to work in his garden once a week. The gardener had not heard the summons himself, but he knew a man who had done so.

"Thomas Jenkins, Pentoppin, he did put his head out late last night to see what the weather was like, as he was cutting a field of corn the next day, and he did tell me that when he was with the Methodists in Cardigan he did never hear no singing eloquence in the chapels that was like to it. He did declare it was like a wailing of Judgement Day."

Remnant considered the matter, and was inclined to think that the sound must be caused by a subterranean inlet of the sea; there might be, he supposed, an imperfect or half-opened or tortuous blowhole in the Tredonoc woods, and the noise of the tide, surging up below, might very well produce that effect of a hollow wailing, far away. But neither he nor any one else paid much attention to the matter; save the few who heard the call at dead of night, as it echoed awfully over the black hills.

The sound had been heard for three or perhaps four nights, when the people coming out of Tredonoc church after morning service on Sunday noticed that there was a big yellow sheep-dog in the churchyard. The dog, it appeared, had been waiting for the congregation; for it at once attached itself to them, at first to the whole body, and then to a group of half a dozen who took the turning to the right. Two of these presently went off over the fields to their respective houses, and four strolled on in the leisurely Sunday-morning manner of the country, and these the dog followed, keeping to heel all the time. The men were talking hay, corn, and markets and paid no attention to the animal, and so they strolled along the autumn lane till they came to a gate in the hedge, whence a roughly made farm road went through the fields, and dipped down into the woods and to Treff Loyne farm.

Then the dog became like a possessed creature. He barked furiously. He ran up to one of the men and looked up at him, "as if he were begging for his life," as the man said, and then rushed to the gate and stood by it, wagging his tail and barking at intervals. The men stared and laughed.

"Whose dog will that be?" said one of them.

"It will be Thomas Griffith's, Treff Loyne," said another.

"Well, then, why doesn't he go home? Go home then!" He went through the gesture of picking up a stone from the road and throwing it at the dog. "Go home, then! Over the gate with you."

But the dog never stirred. He barked and whined and ran up to the men and then back to the gate. At last he came to one of them, and crawled and abased himself on the ground and then took hold of the man's coat and tried to pull him in the direction of the gate. The farmer shook the dog off, and the four went on their way; and the dog stood in the road and watched them and then put up its head and uttered a long and dismal howl that was despair.

The four farmers thought nothing of it; sheep-dogs in the country are dogs to look after sheep, and their whims and fancies are not studied. But the yellow dog—he was a kind of degenerate collie—haunted the Tredonoc lanes from that day. He came to a cottage door one night and scratched at it, and when it was opened lay down, and then, barking, ran to the garden gate and waited, entreating, as it seemed, the cottager to follow him. They drove him away and again he gave that long howl of anguish. It was almost as bad, they said, as the noise that they had heard a few nights before. And then it occurred to somebody, so far as I can make out with no particular reference to the odd conduct of the Treff Loyne sheep-dog, that Thomas Griffith had not been seen for some time past. He had missed market-day at Porth, he had not been at Tredonoc church, where he was a pretty regular attendant on Sunday; and then, as heads were put together, it appeared that nobody had seen any of the Griffith family for days and days.

Now in a town, even in a small town, this process of putting heads together is a pretty quick business. In the country, especially in a countryside of wild lands and scattered and lonely farms and cottages, the affair takes time. Harvest was going on, everybody was busy in his own fields, and after the long day's hard work neither the farmer nor his men felt inclined to stroll about in search of news or gossip. A harvester at the day's end is ready for supper and sleep and for nothing else.

And so it was late in that week when it was discovered that Thomas Griffith and all his house had vanished from this world. I have often been reproached for my curiosity over questions which are apparently of slight importance, or of no importance at all. I love to inquire, for instance, into the question of the visibility of a lighted candle at a distance. Suppose, that is, a candle lighted on a still, dark night in the country; what is the greatest distance at which you can see that there is a light at all? And then as to the human voice; what is its carrying distance, under good conditions, as a mere sound, apart from any matter of making out words that may be uttered?

They are trivial questions, no doubt, but they have always interested me, and the latter point has its application to the strange business of Treff Loyne. That melancholy and hollow sound, that wailing summons that appalled the hearts of those who heard it was, indeed, a human voice, produced in a very exceptional manner; and it seems to have been heard at points varying from a mile and a half to two miles from the farm. I do not know whether this is anything extraordinary; I do not know whether the peculiar method of production was calculated to increase or to diminish the carrying power of the sound.

Again and again I have laid emphasis in this story of the terror on the strange isolation of many of the farms and cottages in Meirion. I have done so in the effort to convince the townsman of something that he has never known. To the Londoner a house a quarter of a mile from the outlying suburban lamp, with no other dwelling within two hundred yards, is a lonely house, a place to fit with ghosts and mysteries and terrors. How can he understand then, the true loneliness of the white farmhouses of Meirion, dotted here and there, for the most part not even on the little lanes and deep winding by-ways, but set in the very heart of the fields, or alone on huge bastioned headlands facing the sea, and whether on the high verge of the sea or on the hills or in the hollows of the inner country, hidden from the sight of men, far from the sound of any common call. There is Penyrhaul, for example, the farm from which the foolish Merritt thought he saw signals of light being made: from seaward it is of course, widely visible; but from landward, owing partly to the curving and indented configuration of the bay, I doubt whether any other habitation views it from a nearer distance than three miles.

And of all these hidden and remote places, I doubt if any is so deeply buried as Treff Loyne. I have little or no Welsh, I am sorry to say, but I suppose that the name is corrupted from Trellwyn, or Tref-y-Ilwyn, "the place in the grove," and, indeed, it lies in the very heart of dark, overhanging woods. A deep, narrow valley runs down from the high lands of the Allt, through these woods, through steep hill-sides of bracken and gorse, right down to the great marsh, whence Merritt saw the dead man being carried. The valley lies away from any road, even from that by-road, little better than a bridle-path, where the four farmers, returning from church were perplexed by the strange antics of the sheep-dog. One cannot say that the valley is overlooked, even from a distance, for so narrow is it that the ash-groves that rim it on either side seem to meet and shut it in. I, at all events, have never found any high place from which Treff Loyne is visible; though, looking down from the Allt, I have seen blue woodsmoke rising from its hidden chimneys.

Such was the place, then, to which one September afternoon a party went up to discover what had happened to Griffith and his family. There were half a dozen farmers, a couple of policemen, and four soldiers, carrying their arms; those last had been lent by the officer commanding at the camp. Lewis, too, was of the party; he had heard by chance that no one knew what had become of Griffith and his family; and he was anxious about a young fellow, a painter, of his acquaintance, who had been lodging at Treff Loyne all the summer.

They all met by the gate of Tredonoc churchyard, and tramped solemnly along the narrow lane; all of them, I think, with some vague discomfort of mind, with a certain shadowy fear, as of men who do not quite know what they may encounter. Lewis heard the corporal and the three soldiers arguing over their orders.

"The captain says to me," muttered the corporal, "'Don't hesitate to shoot if there's any trouble.' 'Shoot what, sir,' I says. 'The trouble,' says he, and that's all I could get out of him."

The men grumbled in reply; Lewis thought he heard some obscure reference to rat-poison, and wondered what they were talking about.

They came to the gate in the hedge, where the farm road led down to Treff Loyne. They followed this track, roughly made, with grass growing up between its loosely laid stones, down by the hedge from field to wood, till at last they came to the sudden walls of the valley, and the sheltering groves of the ash-trees. Here the way curved down the steep hill-side, and bent southward, and followed henceforward the hidden hollow of the valley, under the shadow of the trees.

Here was the farm enclosure; the outlying walls of the yard and the barns and sheds and outhouses. One of the farmers threw open the gate and walked into the yard, and forthwith began bellowing at the top of his voice:

"Thomas Griffith! Thomas Griffith! Where be you, Thomas Griffith?"

The rest followed him. The corporal snapped out an order over his shoulder, and there was a rattling metallic noise as the men fixed their bayonets and became in an instant dreadful dealers out of death, in place of harmless fellows with a feeling for beer.

"Thomas Griffith!" again bellowed the farmer.

There was no answer to this summons. But they found poor Griffith lying on his face at the edge of the pond in the middle of the yard. There was a ghastly wound in his side, as if a sharp stake had been driven into his body.

XII. The Letter of Wrath

It was a still September afternoon. No wind stirred in the hanging woods that were dark all about the ancient house of Treff Loyne; the only sound in the dim air was the lowing of the cattle; they had wandered, it seemed, from the fields and had come in by the gate of the farmyard and stood there melancholy, as if they mourned for their dead master. And the horses; four great, heavy, patient-looking beasts they were there too, and in the lower field the sheep were standing, as if they waited to be fed.

"You would think they all knew there was something wrong," one of the soldiers muttered to another. A pale sun showed for a moment and glittered on their bayonets. They were standing about the body of poor, dead Griffith, with a certain grimness growing on their faces and hardening there. Their corporal snapped something at them again; they were quite ready. Lewis knelt down by the dead man and looked closely at the great gaping wound in his side.

"He's been dead a long time," he said. "A week, two weeks, perhaps. He was killed by some sharp pointed weapon. How about the family? How many are there of them? I never attended them."

"There was Griffith, and his wife, and his son Thomas and Mary Griffith, his daughter. And I do think there was a gentleman lodging with them this summer."

That was from one of the farmers. They all looked at one another, this party of rescue, who knew nothing of the danger that had smitten this house of quiet people, nothing of the peril which had brought them to this pass of a farmyard with a dead man in it, and his beasts standing patiently about him, as if they waited for the farmer to rise up and give them their food. Then the party turned to the house. It was an old, sixteenth-century building, with the singular round, Flemish chimney that is characteristic of Meirion. The walls were snowy with whitewash, the windows were deeply set and stone-mullioned, and a solid, stone-tiled porch sheltered the doorway from any winds that might penetrate to the hollow of that hidden valley. The windows were shut tight. There was no sign of any life or movement about the place. The party of men looked at one another, and the churchwarden amongst the farmers, the sergeant of police, Lewis, and the corporal drew together.

"What is it to goodness, doctor?" said the churchwarden.

"I can tell you nothing at all—except that that poor man there has been pierced to the heart," said Lewis.

"Do you think they are inside and they will shoot us?" said another farmer. He had no notion of what he meant by "they," and no one of them knew better than he. They did not know what the danger was, or where it might strike them, or whether it was from without or from within. They stared at the murdered man, and gazed dismally at one another.

"Come!" said Lewis, "we must do something. We must get into the house and see what is wrong."

"Yes, but suppose they are at us while we are getting in," said the sergeant. "Where shall we be then, Doctor Lewis?"

The corporal put one of his men by the gate at the top of the farmyard, another at the gate by the bottom of the farmyard, and told them to challenge and shoot. The doctor and the rest opened the little gate of the front garden and went up to the porch and stood listening by the door. It was all dead silence. Lewis took an ash stick from one of the farmers and beat heavily three times on the old, black, oaken door studded with antique nails.

He struck three thundering blows, and then they all waited. There was no answer from within. He beat again, and still silence. He shouted to the people within, but there was no answer. They all turned and looked at one another, that party of quest and rescue who knew not what they sought, what enemy they were to encounter. There was an iron ring on the door. Lewis turned it but the door stood fast; it was evidently barred and bolted. The sergeant of police called out to open, but again there was no answer.

They consulted together. There was nothing for it but to blow the door open, and some one of them called in a loud voice to anybody that might be within to stand away from the door, or they would be killed. And at this very moment the yellow sheepdog came bounding up the yard from the woods and licked their hands and fawned on them and barked joyfully.

"Indeed now," said one of the farmers, "he did know that there was something amiss. A pity it was, Thomas Williams, that we did not follow him when he implored us last Sunday."

The corporal motioned the rest of the party back, and they stood looking fearfully about them at the entrance to the porch. The corporal disengaged his bayonet and shot into the keyhole, calling out once more before he fired. He shot and shot again; so heavy and firm was the ancient door, so stout its bolts and fastenings. At last he had to fire at the massive hinges, and then they all pushed together and the door lurched open and fell forward. The corporal raised his left hand and stepped back a few paces. He hailed his two men at the top and bottom of the farmyard. They were all right, they said. And so the party climbed and struggled over the fallen door into the passage, and into the kitchen of the farmhouse.

Young Griffith was lying dead before the hearth, before a dead fire of white wood ashes. They went on towards the parlour, and in the doorway of the room was the body of the artist, Secretan, as if he had fallen in trying to get to the kitchen. Upstairs the two women, Mrs. Griffith and her daughter, a girl of eighteen, were lying together on the bed in the big bedroom, clasped in each other's arms.

They went about the house, searched the pantries, the back kitchen and the cellars; there was no life in it.

"Look!" said Dr. Lewis, when they came back to the big kitchen, "look! It is as if they had been besieged. Do you see that piece of bacon, half gnawed through?"

Then they found these pieces of bacon, cut from the sides on the kitchen wall, here and there about the house. There was no bread in the place, no milk, no water.

"And," said one of the farmers, "they had the best water here in all Meirion. The well is down there in the wood; it is most famous water. The old people did use to call it Ffynnon Teilo; it was Saint Teilo's Well, they did say."

"They must have died of thirst," said Lewis. "They have been dead for days and days."

The group of men stood in the big kitchen and stared at one another, a dreadful perplexity in their eyes. The dead were all about them, within the house and without it; and it was in vain to ask why they had died thus. The old man had been killed with the piercing thrust of some sharp weapon; the rest had perished, it seemed probable, of thirst; but what possible enemy was this that besieged the farm and shut in its inhabitants? There was no answer.

The sergeant of police spoke of getting a cart and taking the bodies into Porth, and Dr. Lewis went into the parlour that Secretan had used as a sitting-room, intending to gather any possessions or effects of the dead artist that he might find there. Half a dozen portfolios were piled up in one corner, there were some books on a side table, a fishing-rod and basket behind the door—that seemed all. No doubt there would be clothes and such matters upstairs, and Lewis was about to rejoin the rest of the party in the kitchen, when he looked down at some scattered papers lying with the books on the side table. On one of the sheets he read to his astonishment the words: "Dr. James Lewis, Porth." This was written in a staggering trembling scrawl, and examining the other leaves he saw that they were covered with writing.

The table stood in a dark corner of the room, and Lewis gathered up the sheets of paper and took them to the window-ledge and began to read, amazed at certain phrases that had caught his eye. But the manuscript was in disorder; as if the dead man who had written it had not been equal to the task of gathering the leaves into their proper sequence; it was some time before the doctor had each page in its place. This was the statement that he read, with ever-growing wonder, while a couple of the farmers were harnessing one of the horses in the yard to a cart, and the others were bringing down the dead women.

> I do not think that I can last much longer. We shared out the last drops of water a long time ago. I do not know how many days ago. We fall asleep and dream and walk about the house in our dreams, and I am often not sure whether I am awake or still dreaming, and so the days and nights are confused in my mind. I awoke not long ago, at least I suppose I awoke and found I was lying in the passage. I had a confused feeling that I had had an awful dream which seemed horribly real, and I thought for a moment what a relief it was to know

that it wasn't true, whatever it might have been. I made up my mind to have a good long walk to freshen myself up, and then I looked round and found that I had been lying on the stones of the passage; and it all came back to me. There was no walk for me.

I have not seen Mrs. Griffith or her daughter for a long while. They said they were going upstairs to have a rest. I heard them moving about the room at first, now I can hear nothing. Young Griffith is lying in the kitchen, before the hearth. He was talking to himself about the harvest and the weather when I last went into the kitchen. He didn't seem to know I was there, as he went gabbling on in a low voice very fast, and then he began to call the dog, Tiger.

There seems no hope for any of us. We are in the dream of death. . . .

Here the manuscript became unintelligible for half a dozen lines. Secretan had written the words "dream of death" three or four times over. He had begun a fresh word and had scratched it out and then followed strange, unmeaning characters, the script, as Lewis thought, of a terrible language. And then the writing became clear, clearer than it was at the beginning of the manuscript, and the sentences flowed more easily, as if the cloud on Secretan's mind had lifted for a while. There was a fresh start, as it were, and the writer began again, in ordinary letter form:

Dear Lewis,

I hope you will excuse all this confusion and wandering. I intended to begin a proper letter to you, and now I find all that stuff that you have been reading—if this ever gets into your hands. I have not the energy even to tear it up. If you read it you will know to what a sad pass I had come when it was written. It looks like delirium or a bad dream, and even now, though my mind seems to have cleared up a good deal, I have to hold myself in tightly to be sure that the experiences of the last days in this awful place are true, real things, not a long nightmare from which I shall wake up presently and find myself in my rooms at Chelsea.

I have said of what I am writing, "if it ever gets into your hands," and I am not at all sure that it ever will. If what is happening here is happening everywhere else, then I suppose, the world is coming to an end. I cannot understand it, even now I can hardly believe it. I know that I dream such wild dreams and walk in such mad fancies that I have to look out and look about me to make sure that I am not still dreaming.

Do you remember that talk we had about two months ago when I dined with you? We got on, somehow or other, to space and time, and I think we agreed that as soon as one tried to reason about space and time one was landed in a maze of contradictions. You said something to the effect that it was very curious but this was just like a dream. "A man will sometimes wake himself from his crazy dream," you said, "by realizing that he is thinking nonsense." And we both wondered whether these contradictions that one can't avoid if one begins to think of time and space may not really be proofs that the whole of life is a dream, and the moon and the stars bits of nightmare. I have often thought over that lately. I kick at the walls as Dr. Johnson kicked at the stone, to make sure that the things about me are there. And then that other question gets into my mind—is the world really coming to an end, the world as we have always known it; and what on earth will this new world be like? I can't imagine it; it's a story like Noah's Ark and the Flood. People used to talk about the end of the world and fire, but no one ever thought of anything like this.

And then there's another thing that bothers me. Now and then I wonder whether we are not all mad together in this house. In spite of what I see and know, or, perhaps, I should say, because what I see and know is so impossible, I wonder whether we are not all suffering from a delusion. Perhaps we are our own gaolers, and we are really free to go out and live. Perhaps what we think we see is not there at all. I believe I have heard of whole families going mad together, and I may have come under the influence of the house, having lived in it for the last four months. I know there have been people who have been kept alive by their keepers forcing food down their throats, because they are quite sure that their throats are closed, so that they feel they are unable to swallow a morsel. I wonder now and then whether we are all like this in Treff Loyne; yet in my heart I feel sure that it is not so.

Still, I do not want to leave a madman's letter behind me, and so I will not tell you the full story of what I have seen, or believe I have seen. If I am a sane man you will be able to fill in the blanks for yourself from your own knowledge. If I am mad, burn the letter and say nothing about it. Or perhaps—and indeed, I am not quite sure—I may wake up and hear Mary Griffith calling to me in her cheerful sing-song that breakfast will be ready "directly, in a minute," and I shall enjoy it and walk over to Porth and tell you the queerest, most horrible dream that a man ever had, and ask what I had better take.

I think that it was on a Tuesday that we first noticed that there was something queer about, only at the time we didn't know that there was anything really queer in what we noticed. I had been out since nine o'clock in the morning trying to paint the marsh, and I found it a very tough job. I came home about five or six o'clock and found the family at Treff Loyne laughing at old Tiger, the sheepdog. He was making short runs from the farmyard to the door of the house, barking, with quick, short yelps. Mrs. Griffith and Miss Griffith were standing by the porch, and the dog would go to them, look in their faces, and then run up the farmyard to the gate, and then look back with that eager yelping bark, as if he were waiting for the women to follow him. Then, again and again, he ran up to them and tugged at their skirts as if he would pull them by main force away from the house.

Then the men came home from the fields and he repeated this performance. The dog was running all up and down the farmyard, in and out of the barn and sheds yelping, barking; and always with that eager run to the person he addressed, and running away directly, and looking back as if to see whether we were following him. When the house-door was shut and they all sat down to supper, he would give them no peace, till at last they turned him out of doors. And then he sat in the porch and scratched at the door with his claws, barking all the while. When the daughter brought in my meal, she said: "We can't think what is come to old Tiger, and indeed, he has always been a good dog, too."

The dog barked and yelped and whined and scratched at the door all through the evening. They let him in once, but he seemed to have become quite frantic. He ran up to one member of the family after another; his eyes were bloodshot and his mouth was foaming, and he tore at their clothes till they drove him out again into the darkness. Then he broke into a long, lamentable howl of anguish, and we heard no more of him.

XIII. THE LAST WORDS OF MR. SECRETAN

I slept ill that night. I awoke again and again from uneasy dreams, and I seemed in my sleep to hear strange calls and noises and a sound of murmurs and beatings on the door. There were deep, hollow voices, too, that echoed in my sleep, and when I woke I could hear the autumn wind, mournful, on the hills above us. I started up once with a dreadful scream in my ears; but then the house was all still, and I fell again into uneasy sleep.

It was soon after dawn when I finally roused myself. The people in the house were talking to each other in high voices, arguing about something that I did not understand.

"It is those damned gipsies, I tell you," said old Griffith.

"What would they do a thing like that for?" asked Mrs. Griffith. "If it was stealing now—"

"It is more likely that John Jenkins has done it out of spite," said the son. "He said that he would remember you when we did catch him poaching."

They seemed puzzled and angry, so far as I could make out, but not at all frightened. I got up and began to dress. I don't think I looked out of the window. The glass on my dressing-table is high and broad, and the window is small; one would have to poke one's head round the glass to see anything.

The voices were still arguing downstairs. I heard the old man say, "Well, here's for a beginning anyhow," and then the door slammed.

A minute later the old man shouted, I think, to his son. Then there was a great noise which I will not describe more particularly, and a dreadful screaming and crying inside the house and a sound of rushing feet. They all cried out at once to each other. I heard the daughter crying, "it is no good, mother, he is dead, indeed they have killed him," and Mrs. Griffith screaming to the girl to let her go. And then one of them rushed out of the kitchen and shot the great bolts of oak across the door, just as something beat against it with a thundering crash.

I ran downstairs. I found them all in wild confusion, in an agony of grief and horror and amazement. They were like people who had seen something so awful that they had gone mad.

I went to the window looking out on the farmyard. I won't tell you all that I saw. But I saw poor old Griffith lying by the pond, with blood pouring out of his side.

I wanted to go out to him and bring him in. But they told me that he must be stone dead, and such things also that it was quite plain that any one who went out of the house would not live more than a moment. We could not believe it, even as we gazed at the body of the dead man; but it was there. I used to wonder sometimes what one would feel like if one saw an apple drop from the tree and shoot up into the air and disappear. I think I know now how one would feel.

Even then we couldn't believe that it would last. We were not seriously afraid for ourselves. We spoke of getting out in an hour or two, before dinner anyhow. It couldn't last, because it was impossible. Indeed, at twelve o'clock young Griffith said he would go down to the well by the back way and draw another pail of water. I went to the door and stood by it. He had not gone a dozen yards before they were on him. He ran for his life, and we had all we could do to bar the door in time. And then I began to get frightened.

Still we could not believe in it. Somebody would come along shouting in an hour or two and it would all melt away and vanish. There could not be any real danger. There was plenty of bacon in the house, and half the weekly baking of loaves and some beer in the cellar and a pound or so of tea, and a whole pitcher of water that had been drawn from the well the night before. We could do all right for the day and in the morning it would have all gone away.

But day followed day and it was still there. I knew Treff Loyne was a lonely place—that was why I had gone there, to have a long rest from all the jangle and rattle and turmoil of London, that makes a man alive and kills him too. I went to Treff Loyne because it was buried in the narrow valley under the ash trees, far away from any track. There was not so much as a footpath that was near it; no one ever came that way. Young Griffith had told me that it was a mile and a half to the nearest house, and the thought of the silent peace and retirement of the farm used to be a delight to me.

And now this thought came back without delight, with terror. Griffith thought that a shout might be heard on a still night up away on the Allt, "if a man was listening for it," he added, doubtfully. My voice was clearer and stronger than his, and on the second night I said I would go up to my bedroom and call for help through the open window. I waited till it was all dark and still, and looked out through the window before opening it. And when I saw over the ridge of the long barn across the yard what looked like a tree, though I knew there was no tree there. It was a dark mass against the sky, with wide-spread boughs, a tree of thick, dense growth. I wondered what this could be, and I threw open the window, not only because I was going to call for help, but because I wanted to see more clearly what the dark growth over the barn really was.

I saw in the depth of the dark of it points of fire, and colours in light, all glowing and moving, and the air trembled. I stared out into the night, and the dark tree lifted over the roof of the barn and rose up in the air and floated towards me. I did not move till at the last moment when it was close to the house; and then I saw what it was and banged the window down only just in time. I had to fight, and I saw the tree that was like a burning cloud rise up in the night and sink again and settle over the barn.

I told them downstairs of this. They sat with white faces, and Mrs. Griffith said that ancient devils were let loose and had come out of the trees and out of the old hills because of the wickedness that was on the earth. She began to murmur something to herself, something that sounded to me like broken-down Latin.

I went up to my room again an hour later, but the dark tree swelled over the barn. Another day went by, and at dusk I looked out, but the eyes of fire were watching me. I dared not open the window.

And then I thought of another plan. There was the great old fireplace, with the round Flemish chimney going high above the house. If I stood beneath it and shouted I thought perhaps the sound might be carried better than if I called out of the window; for all I knew the round chimney might act as a sort of megaphone. Night after night, then, I stood in the hearth and called for help from nine o'clock to eleven. I thought of the lonely place, deep in the valley of the ash trees, of the lonely hills and lands about it. I thought of the little cottages far away and hoped that my voice might reach to those within them. I thought of the winding lane high on the Allt, and of the few men that came there of nights; but I hoped that my cry might come to one of them.

But we had drunk up the beer, and we would only let ourselves have water by little drops, and on the fourth night my throat was dry, and I began to feel strange and weak; I knew that all the voice I had in my lungs would hardly reach the length of the field by the farm.

It was then we began to dream of wells and fountains, and water coming very cold, in little drops, out of rocky places in the middle of a cool wood. We had given up all meals; now and then one would cut a lump from the sides of bacon on the kitchen wall and chew a bit of it, but the saltness was like fire.

There was a great shower of rain one night. The girl said we might open a window and hold out bowls and basins and catch the rain. I spoke of the cloud with burning eyes. She said, "we will go to the window in the dairy at the back, and one of us can get some water at all events." She stood up with her basin on the stone slab in the dairy and looked out and heard the plashing of the rain, falling very fast. And she unfastened the catch of the window and had just opened it gently with one hand, for about an inch, and had her basin in the other hand. "And then," said she, "there was something that began to tremble and shudder and shake as it did when we went to the Choral Festival at St. Teilo's, and the organ played, and there was the cloud and the burning close before me."

And then we began to dream, as I say. I woke up in my sitting-room one hot afternoon when the sun was shining, and I had been looking and searching in my dream all through the house, and I had gone down to the old cellar that wasn't used, the cellar with the pillars and the vaulted room, with an iron pike in my hand. Something said to me that there was water there, and in my dream I went to a heavy stone by the middle pillar and raised it up, and there beneath was a bubbling well of cold, clear water, and I had just hollowed my hand to drink it when I woke. I went into the kitchen and told young Griffith. I said I was sure there was water there. He shook his head, but he took up the great kitchen poker and we went down to the old cellar. I showed him the stone by the pillar, and he raised it up. But there was no well.

Do you know, I reminded myself of many people whom I have met in life? I would not be convinced. I was sure that, after all, there was a well there. They had a butcher's cleaver in the kitchen and I took it down to the old cellar and hacked at the ground with it. The others didn't interfere with me. We were getting past that. We hardly ever spoke to one another. Each one would be wandering about the house, upstairs and downstairs, each one of us, I suppose, bent on his own foolish plan and mad design, but we hardly ever spoke. Years ago, I was an actor for a bit, and I remember how it was on first nights; the actors treading softly up and down the wings, by their entrance, their lips moving and muttering over the words of their parts, but without a word for one another. So it was with us. I came upon young Griffith one evening evidently trying to make a subterranean passage under one of the walls of the house. I knew he was mad, as he knew I was mad when he saw me digging for a well in the cellar; but neither said anything to the other.

Now we are past all this. We are too weak. We dream when we are awake and when we dream we think we wake. Night and day come and go and we mistake one for another; I hear Griffith murmuring to himself about the stars when the sun is high at noonday, and at midnight I have found myself thinking that I walked in bright sunlit meadows beside cold, rushing streams that flowed from high rocks.

Then at the dawn figures in black robes, carrying lighted tapers in their hands pass slowly about and about; and I hear great rolling organ music that sounds as if some tremendous rite were to begin, and voices crying in an ancient song shrill from the depths of the earth.

Only a little while ago I heard a voice which sounded as if it were at my very ears, but rang and echoed and resounded as if it were rolling and reverberated from the vault of some cathedral, chanting in terrible modulations. I heard the words quite clearly.

Incipit liber ire Domini Dei nostri. (Here beginneth The Book of the Wrath of the Lord our God.)

And then the voice sang the word *Aleph*, prolonging it, it seemed through ages, and a light was extinguished as it began the chapter:

In that day, saith the Lord, there shall be a cloud over the land, and in the cloud a burning and a shape of fire, and out of the cloud shall issue forth my messengers; they shall run all together, they shall not turn aside; this shall be a day of exceeding bitterness, without salvation. And on every high hill, saith the Lord of Hosts, I will set my sentinels, and my armies shall encamp in the place of every valley; in the house that is amongst rushes I will execute judgment, and in vain shall they fly for refuge to the munitions of the rocks. In the groves of the woods, in the places where the leaves are as a tent above them, they shall find the sword of the slayer; and they that put their trust in walled cities shall be confounded. Woe unto the armed man, woe unto him that taketh pleasure in the strength of his artillery, for a little thing shall smite him, and by one that hath no might shall he be brought down into the dust. That which is low shall be set on high; I will make the lamb and the young sheep to be as the lion from the swellings of Jordan; they shall not spare, saith the Lord, and the doves shall be as eagles on the hill Engedi; none shall be found that may abide the onset of their battle.

Even now I can hear the voice rolling far away, as if it came from the altar of a great church and I stood at the door. There are lights very far away in the hollow of a vast darkness, and one by one they are put out. I hear a voice chanting again with that endless modulation that climbs and aspires to the stars, and shines there, and rushes down to the dark depths of the earth, again to ascend; the word is *Zain*.

Here the manuscript lapsed again, and finally into utter, lamentable confusion. There were scrawled lines wavering across the page on which Secretan seemed to have been trying to note the unearthly music that swelled in his dying ears. As the scrapes and scratches of ink showed, he had tried hard to begin a new sentence. The pen had dropped at last out of his hand upon the paper, leaving a blot and a smear upon it.

Lewis heard the tramp of feet along the passage; they were carrying out the dead to the cart.

XIV. The End of the Terror

Dr. Lewis maintained that we should never begin to understand the real significance of life until we began to study just those aspects of it which we now dismiss and overlook as utterly inexplicable, and therefore, unimportant.

We were discussing a few months ago the awful shadow of the terror which at length had passed away from the land. I had formed my opinion, partly from observation, partly from certain facts which had been communicated to me, and the passwords having been exchanged, I found that Lewis had come by very different ways to the same end.

"And yet," he said, "it is not a true end, or rather, it is like all the ends of human inquiry, it leads one to a great mystery. We must confess that what has happened might have happened at any time in the history of the world. It did not happen till a year ago as a matter of fact, and therefore we made up our minds that it never could happen; or, one would better say, it was outside the range even of imagination. But this is our way. Most people are quite sure that the Black Death—otherwise the plague—will never invade Europe again. They have made up their complacent minds that it was due to dirt and bad drainage. As a matter of fact the plague had nothing to do with dirt or with drains; and there is nothing to prevent its ravaging England tomorrow. But if you tell people so, they won't believe you. They won't believe in anything that isn't there at the particular moment when you are talking to them. As with the plague, so with the terror. We could not believe that such a thing could ever happen. Remnant said, truly enough, that whatever it was, it was outside theory, outside our theory. Flatland cannot believe in the cube or the sphere."

I agreed with all this. I added that sometimes the world was incapable of seeing, much less believing, that which was before its own eyes.

"Look," I said, "at any eighteenth-century print of a Gothic cathedral. You will find that the trained artistic eye even could not behold in any true sense the building that was before it. I have seen an old print of Peterborough Cathedral that looks as if the artist had drawn it from a clumsy model, constructed of bent wire and children's bricks.

"Exactly; because Gothic was outside the aesthetic theory (and therefore vision) of the time. You can't believe what you don't see: rather, you can't see what you don't believe. It was so during the time of the terror. All this bears out what Coleridge said as to the necessity of having the idea before the facts could be of any service to one. Of course, he was right; mere facts, without the correlating idea, are nothing and lead to no conclusion. We had plenty of facts, but we could make nothing of them. I went home at the tail of that dreadful procession from Treff Loyne in a state of mind very near to madness. I heard one of the soldiers saying to the other: 'There's no rat that'll spike a man to the heart, Bill!' I don't know why, but I felt that if I heard any more of such talk as that I should go crazy; it seemed to me that the anchors of reason were parting. I left the party and took the short cut across the fields into Porth. I looked up Davies in the High Street and arranged with him that he should take on any cases I might have that evening, and then I went home and gave my man his instructions to send people on. And then I shut myself up to think it all out—if I could.

"You must not suppose that my experiences of that afternoon had afforded me the slightest illumination. Indeed, if it had not been that I had seen poor old Griffith's body lying pierced in his own farmyard, I think I should have been inclined to accept one of Secretan's hints, and to believe that the whole family had fallen a victim to a collective delusion or hallucination, and had shut themselves up and died of thirst through sheer madness. I think there have been such cases. It's the insanity of inhibition, the belief that you can't do something which you are really perfectly capable of doing. But; I had seen the body of the murdered man and the wound that had killed him.

"Did the manuscript left by Secretan give me no hint? Well, it seemed to me to make confusion worse confounded. You have seen it; you know that in certain places it is evidently mere delirium, the wanderings of a dying mind. How was I to separate the facts from the phantasms—lacking the key to the whole enigma. Delirium is often a sort of cloud-castle, a sort of magnified and distorted shadow of actualities, but it is a very difficult thing, almost an impossible thing, to reconstruct the real house from the distortion of it, thrown on the clouds of the patient's brain. You see, Secretan in writing that extraordinary document almost insisted on the fact that he was not in his proper sense; that for days he had been part asleep, part awake, part delirious. How was one to judge his statement, to separate delirium from fact? In one thing he stood confirmed; you remember he speaks of calling for help up the old chimney of Treff Loyne; that did seem to fit in with the tales of a hollow, moaning cry that had been heard upon the Allt: so far one could take him as a recorder of actual experiences. And I looked in the old cellars of the farm and found a frantic sort of rabbit-hole dug by one of the pillars; again he was confirmed. But what was one to make of that story of the chanting voice, and the letters of the Hebrew alphabet, and the chapter out of some unknown minor prophet? When one has the key it is easy enough to sort out the facts, or the hints of facts from the delusions; but I hadn't the key on that September evening. I was forgetting the 'tree' with lights and fires in it; that, I think, impressed me more than anything with the feeling that Secretan's story was, in the main, a true story. I had seen a like appearance down there in my own garden; but what was it?

"Now, I was saying that, paradoxically, it is only by the inexplicable things that life can be explained. We are apt to say, you know, 'a very odd coincidence' and pass the matter by, as if there were no more to be said, or as if that were the end of it. Well, I believe that the only real path lies through the blind alleys."

"How do you mean?"

"Well, this is an instance of what I mean. I told you about Merritt, my brother-in-law, and the capsizing of that boat, the *Mary Ann*. He had seen, he said, signal lights flashing from one of the farms on the coast, and he was quite certain that the two things were intimately connected as cause and effect. I thought it all nonsense, and I was wondering how I was going to shut him up when a big moth flew into the room through that window, fluttered about, and succeeded in burning itself alive in the lamp.

That gave me my cue; I asked Merritt if he knew why moths made for lamps or something of the kind; I thought it would be a hint to him that I was sick of his flash-lights and his half-baked theories. So it was—he looked sulky and held his tongue.

"But a few minutes later I was called out by a man who had found his little boy dead in a field near his cottage about an hour before. The child was so still, they said, that a great moth had settled on his forehead and only fluttered away when they lifted up the body. It was absolutely illogical; but it was this odd 'coincidence' of the moth in my lamp and the moth on the dead boy's forehead that first set me on the track. I can't say that it guided me in any real sense; it was more like a great flare of red paint on a wall; it rang up my attention, if I may say so; it was a sort of shock like a bang on the big drum. No doubt Merritt was talking great nonsense that evening so far as his particular instance went; the flashes of light from the farm had nothing to do with the wreck of the boat. But his general principle was sound; when you hear a gun go off and see a man fall it is idle to talk of 'a mere coincidence.' I think a very interesting book might be written on this question: I would call it *A Grammar of Coincidence*.

"But as you will remember, from having read my notes on the matter, I was called in about ten days later to see a man named Cradock, who had been found in a field near his farm quite dead. This also was at night. His wife found him, and there were some very queer things in her story. She said that the hedge of the field looked as if it were changed; she began to be afraid that she had lost her way and got into the wrong field. Then she said the hedge was lighted up as if there were a lot of glow-worms in it, and when she peered over the stile there seemed to be some kind of glimmering upon the ground, and then the glimmering melted away, and she found her husband's body near where this light had been. Now this man Cradock had been suffocated just as the little boy Roberts had been suffocated, and as that man in the Midlands who took a short cut one night had been suffocated. Then I remembered that poor Johnnie Roberts had called out about 'something shiny' over the stile just before he played truant. Then, on my part, I had to contribute the very remarkable sight I witnessed here, as I looked down over the garden; the appearance as of a spreading tree where I knew there was no such tree, and then the shining and burning of lights and moving colours. Like the poor child and Mrs. Cradock, I had seen something shiny, just as some man in Stratfordshire had seen a dark cloud with points of fire in it floating over the trees. And Mrs. Cradock thought that the shape of the trees in the hedge had changed.

"My mind almost uttered the word that was wanted; but you see the difficulties. This set of circumstances could not, so far as I could see, have any relation with the other circumstances of the terror. How could I connect all this with the bombs and machine-guns of the Midlands, with the armed men who kept watch about the munition shops by day and night. Then there was the long list of people here who had fallen over the cliffs or into the quarry; there were the cases of the men stifled in the slime of the marshes; there was the affair of the family murdered in front of their cottage on the Highway; there was the capsized *Mary Ann.* I could not see any thread that could bring all these incidents together; they seemed to me to be hopelessly disconnected. I could not make out any relation between the agency that beat out the brains of the Williamses and the agency that overturned the boat. I don't know, but I think it's very likely if nothing more had happened that I should have put the whole thing down as an unaccountable series of crimes and accidents which chanced to occur in Meirion in the summer of 1915. Well, of course, that would have been an impossible standpoint in view of certain incidents in Merritt's story. Still, if one is confronted by the insoluble, one lets it go at last. If the mystery is inexplicable, one pretends that there isn't any mystery. That is the justification for what is called free thinking.

"Then came that extraordinary business of Treff Loyne. I couldn't put that on one side. I couldn't pretend that nothing strange or out of the way had happened. There was no getting over it or getting round it. I had seen with my eyes that there was a mystery, and a most horrible mystery. I have forgotten my logic, but one might say that Treff Loyne demonstrated the existence of a mystery in the figure of death.

"I took it all home, as I have told you, and sat down for the evening before it. It appalled me, not only by its horror, but here again by the discrepancy between its terms. Old Griffith, so far as I could judge, had been killed by the thrust of a pike or perhaps of a sharpened stake: how could one relate this to the burning tree that had floated over the ridge of the barn. It was as if I said to you: 'Here is a man drowned, and here is a man burned alive: show that each death was caused by the same agency!' And the moment that I left this particular case of Treff Loyne, and tried to get some light on it from other instances of the terror, I would think of the man in the Midlands who heard the feet of a thousand men rustling in the wood, and their voices as if dead men sat up in their bones and talked. And then I would say to myself: 'And how about that boat overturned in a calm sea?' There seemed no end to it, no hope of any solution.

"It was, I believe, a sudden leap of the mind that liberated me from the tangle. It was quite beyond logic. I went back to that evening when Merritt was boring me with his flash-lights, to the moth in the candle, and to the moth on the forehead of poor Johnnie Roberts. There was no sense in it; but I suddenly determined that the child and Joseph Cradock the farmer, and that unnamed Stratfordshire man, all found at night, all asphyxiated, had been choked by vast swarms of moths. I don't pretend even now that this is demonstrated, but I'm sure it's true.

"Now suppose you encounter a swarm of these creatures in the dark. Suppose the smaller ones fly up your nostrils. You will gasp for breath and open your mouth. Then, suppose some hundreds of them fly into your mouth, into your gullet, into your windpipe, what will happen to you? You will be dead in a very short time, choked; asphyxiated."

"But the moths would be dead too. They would be found in the bodies."

"The moths? Do you know that it is extremely difficult to kill a moth with cyanide of potassium? Take a frog, kill it, open its stomach. There you will find its dinner of moths and small beetles, and the 'dinner' will shake itself and walk off cheerily, to resume an entirely active existence. No; that is no difficulty.

"Well, now I came to this. I was shutting out all the other cases. I was confining myself to those that came under the one formula. I got to the assumption or conclusion, whichever you like, that certain people had been asphyxiated by the action of moths. I had accounted for that extraordinary appearance of burning or colored lights that I had witnessed myself, when I saw the growth of that strange tree in my garden. That was clearly the cloud with points of fire in it that the Stratfordshire man took for a new and terrible kind of poison gas, that was the shiny something that poor little Johnnie Roberts had seen over the stile, that was the glimmering light that had led Mrs. Cradock to her husband's dead body, that was the assemblage of terrible eyes that had watched over Treff Loyne by night. Once on the right track I understood all this, for coming into this room in the dark, I have been amazed by the wonderful burning and the strange fiery colours of the eyes of a single moth, as it crept up the pane of glass, outside. Imagine the effect of myriads of such eyes, of the movement of these lights and fires in a vast swarm of moths, each insect being in constant motion while it kept its place in the mass: I felt that all this was clear and certain.

"Then the next step. Of course, we know nothing really about moths; rather, we know nothing of moth reality. For all I know there may be hundreds of books which treat of moth and nothing but moth. But these are scientific books, and science only deals with surfaces; it has nothing to do with realities—it is impertinent if it attempts to do with realities. To take a very minor matter, we don't even know why the moth desires the flame. But we do know what the moth does not do; it does not gather itself into swarms with the object of destroying human life. But here, by the hypothesis, were cases in which the moth had done this very thing; the moth race had entered, it seemed, into a malignant conspiracy against the human race. It was quite impossible, no doubt—that is to say, it had never happened before— but I could see no escape from this conclusion.

"These insects, then, were definitely hostile to man; and then I stopped, for I could not see the next step, obvious though it seems to me now. I believe that the soldiers' scraps of talk on the way to Treff Loyne and back flung the next plank over the gulf. They had spoken of 'rat-poison,' of no rat being able to spike a man through the heart; and then, suddenly, I saw my way clear. If the moths were infected with hatred of men, and possessed the design and the power of combining against him, why not suppose this hatred, this design, this power shared by other non-human creatures?

"The secret of the terror might be condensed into a sentence: the animals had revolted against men.

"Now, the puzzle became easy enough; one had only to classify. Take the cases of the people who met their deaths by falling over cliffs or over the edge of quarries. We think of sheep as timid creatures, who always ran away. But suppose sheep that don't run away; and, after all, in reason why should they run away? Quarry or no quarry, cliff or no cliff; what would happen to you if a hundred sheep ran after you instead of running from you? There would be no help for it; they would have you down and beat you to death or stifle you. Then suppose man, woman, or child near a cliff's edge or a quarry-side, and a sudden rush of sheep. Clearly there is no help; there is nothing for it but to go over. There can be no doubt that that is what happened in all these cases.

"And again; you know the country and you know how a herd of cattle will sometimes pursue people through the fields in a solemn, stolid sort of way. They behave as if they wanted to close in on you. Townspeople sometimes get frightened and scream and run; you or I would take no notice, or at the utmost, wave our sticks at the herd, which will stop dead or lumber off. But suppose they don't lumber off. The mildest old cow, remember, is stronger than any man. What can one man or half a dozen men do against half a hundred of these beasts no longer restrained by that mysterious inhibition, which has made for ages the strong the humble slaves of the weak? But if you are botanizing in the marsh, like that poor fellow who was staying at Porth, and forty or fifty young cattle gradually close round you, and refuse to move when you shout and wave your stick, but get closer and closer instead, and get you into the slime. Again, where is your help? If you haven't got an automatic pistol, you must go down and stay down, while the beasts lie quietly on you for five minutes. It was a quicker death for poor Griffith of Treff Loyne—one of his own beasts gored him to death with one sharp thrust of its horn into his heart. And from that morning those within the house were closely besieged by their own cattle and horses and sheep; and when those unhappy people within opened a window to call for help or to catch a few drops of rain water to relieve their burning thirst, the cloud waned for them with its myriad eyes of fire. Can you wonder that Secretan's statement reads in places like mania? You perceive the horrible position of those people in Treff Loyne; not only did they see death advancing on them, but advancing with incredible steps, as if one were to die not only in nightmare but by nightmare. But no one in his wildest, most fiery dreams had ever imagined such a fate. I am not astonished that Secretan at one moment suspected the evidence of his own senses, at another surmised that the world's end had come."

"And how about the Williamses who were murdered on the Highway near here?"

"The horses were the murderers; the horses that afterwards stampeded the camp below. By some means which is still obscure to me they lured that family into the road and beat their brains out; their shod hoofs were the instruments of execution. And, as for the *Mary Ann*, the boat that was capsized, I have no doubt that it was overturned by a sudden rush of the porpoises that were gambolling about in the water of Larnac Bay. A porpoise is a heavy beast—half a dozen of them could easily upset a light rowing-boat. The munition works? Their enemy was rats. I believe that it has been calculated that in greater London the number of rats is about equal to the number of human beings, that is, there are about seven millions of them. The proportion would be about the same in all the great centres of population; and the rat, moreover, is, on occasion, migratory in its habits. You can understand now that story of the

Semiramis, beating about the mouth of the Thames, and at last cast away by Arcachon, her only crew dry heaps of bones. The rat is an expert boarder of ships. And so one can understand the tale told by the frightened man who took the path by the wood that led up from the new munition works. He thought he heard a thousand men treading softly through the wood and chattering to one another in some horrible tongue; what he did hear was the marshalling of an army of rats—their array before the battle.

"And conceive the terror of such an attack. Even one rat in a fury is said to be an ugly customer to meet; conceive then, the irruption of these terrible, swarming myriads, rushing upon the helpless, unprepared, astonished workers in the munition shops."

There can be no doubt, I think, that Dr. Lewis was entirely justified in these extraordinary conclusions. As I say, I had arrived at pretty much the same end, by different ways; but this rather as to the general situation, while Lewis had made his own particular study of those circumstances of the terror that were within his immediate purview, as a physician in large practice in the southern part of Meirion. Of some of the cases which he reviewed he had, no doubt, no immediate or first-hand knowledge; but he judged these instances by their similarity to the facts which had come under his personal notice. He spoke of the affairs of the quarry at Llanfihangel on the analogy of the people who were found dead at the bottom of the cliffs near Porth, and he was no doubt justified in doing so. He told me that, thinking the whole matter over, he was hardly more astonished by the terror in itself than by the strange way in which he had arrived at his conclusions.

"You know," he said, "those certain evidences of animal malevolence which we knew of, the bees that stung the child to death, the trusted sheep-dog's turning savage, and so forth. Well, I got no light whatever from all this; it suggested nothing to me—simply because I had not got that 'idea' which Coleridge rightly holds necessary in all inquiry; facts *qua* facts, as we said, mean nothing and, come to nothing. You do not believe, therefore you cannot see.

"And then, when the truth at last appeared it was through the whimsical 'coincidence,' as we call such signs, of the moth in my lamp and the moth on the dead child's forehead. This, I think, is very extraordinary."

"And there seems to have been one beast that remained faithful; the dog at Treff Loyne. That is strange."

"That remains a mystery."

It would not be wise, even now, to describe too closely the terrible scenes that were to be seen in the munition areas of the north and the Midlands during the black months of the terror. Out of the factories issued at black midnight the shrouded dead in their coffins, and their very kinsfolk did not know how they had come by their deaths. All the towns were full of houses of mourning, were full of dark and terrible rumours; incredible, as the incredible reality. There were things done and suffered that perhaps never will be brought to light, memories and secret traditions of these things will be whispered in families, delivered from father to son, growing wilder with the passage of the years, but never growing wilder than the truth.

It is enough to say that the cause of the Allies was for awhile in deadly peril. The men at the front called in their extremity for guns and shells. No one told them what was happening in the places where these munitions were made.

At first the position was nothing less than desperate; men in high places were almost ready to cry mercy to the enemy. But, after the first panic, measures were taken such as those described by Merritt in his account of the matter. The workers were armed with special weapons, guards were mounted, machine-guns were placed in position, bombs and liquid flame were ready against the obscene hordes of the enemy, and the "burning clouds" found a fire fiercer than their own. Many deaths occurred amongst the airmen; but they, too, were given special guns, arms that scattered shot broadcast, and so drove away the dark flights that threatened the airplanes.

And, then, in the winter of 1915–16, the terror ended suddenly as it had begun. Once more a sheep was a frightened beast that ran instinctively from a little child; the cattle were again solemn, stupid creatures, void of harm; the spirit and the convention of malignant design passed out of the hearts of all the animals. The chains that they had cast off for a while were thrown again about them.

And, finally, there comes the inevitable "why?" Why did the beasts who had been humbly and patiently subject to man, or affrighted by his presence, suddenly know their strength and learn how to league together, and declare bitter war against their ancient master?

It is a most difficult and obscure question. I give what explanation I have to give with very great diffidence, and an eminent disposition to be corrected, if a clearer light can be found.

Some friends of mine, for whose judgment I have very great respect, are inclined to think that there was a certain contagion of hate. They hold that the fury of the whole world at war, the great passion of death that seems driving all humanity to destruction, infected at last these lower creatures, and in place of their native instinct of submission, gave them rage and wrath and ravening.

This may be the explanation. I cannot say that it is not so, because I do not profess to understand the working of the universe. But I confess that the theory strikes me as fanciful. There may be a contagion of hate as there is a contagion of smallpox; I do not know, but I hardly believe it.

In my opinion, and it is only an opinion, the source of the great revolt of the beasts is to be sought in a much subtler region of inquiry. I believe that the subjects revolted because the king abdicated. Man has dominated the beasts throughout the ages, the spiritual has reigned over the rational through the peculiar quality and grace of spirituality that men possess, that makes a man to be that which he is. And when he maintained this power and grace, I think it is pretty clear that between him and the animals there was a certain treaty and alliance. There was supremacy on the one hand, and submission on the other; but at the same time there was between the two that cordiality which exists between lords and subjects in a well-organized state. I know a socialist who maintains that Chaucer's *Canterbury Tales* give a picture of true democracy. I do not know about that, but I see that knight and miller were able to get on quite pleasantly together, just because the knight knew that he was a knight and the miller knew that he was a miller. If the knight had had conscientious objections to his knightly grade, while the miller saw no reason why he should not be a knight, I am sure that their intercourse would have been difficult, unpleasant, and perhaps murderous.

So with man. I believe in the strength and truth of tradition. A learned man said to me a few weeks ago: "When I have to choose between the evidence of tradition and the evidence of a document, I always believe the evidence of tradition. Documents may be falsified, and often are falsified; tradition is never falsified." This is true; and, therefore, I think, one may put trust in the vast body of folk-lore which asserts that there was once a worthy and friendly alliance between man and the beasts. Our popular tale of Dick Whittington and his cat no doubt represents the adaptation of a very ancient legend to a comparatively modern personage, but we may go back into the ages and find the popular tradition asserting that not only are the animals the subjects, but also the friends of man.

All that was in virtue of that singular spiritual element in man which the rational animals do not possess. "Spiritual" does not mean "respectable," it does not even mean "moral," it does not mean "good" in the ordinary acceptation of the word. It signifies the royal prerogative of man, differentiating him from the beasts.

For long ages he has been putting off this royal robe, he has been wiping the balm of consecration from his own breast. He has declared, again and again, that he is not spiritual, but rational, that is, the equal of the beasts over whom he was once sovereign. He has vowed that he is not Orpheus but Caliban.

But the beasts also have within them something which corresponds to the spiritual quality in men—we are content to call it instinct. They perceived that the throne was vacant—not even friendship was possible between them and the self-deposed monarch. If he were not king he was a sham, an impostor, a thing to be destroyed.

Hence, I think, the terror. They have risen once—they may rise again. ✢

The Lost Club

One hot afternoon in August a gorgeous young gentleman, one would say the last of his race in London, set out from the Circus end, and proceeded to stroll along the lonely expanse of Piccadilly Deserta. True to the traditions of his race, faithful even in the wilderness, he had not bated one jot or tittle of his regulation equipage; a glorious red and yellow blossom in his wholly and exquisitely-cut frock coat proclaimed him a true son of the carnation; hat and boots and chin were all polished to the highest pitch; though there had not been rain for many weeks his trouser-ends were duly turned up, and the poise of the gold-headed cane was in itself a liberal education. But ah! the heavy changes since June, when the leaves glanced green in the sunlit air, and the club windows were filled, and the hansoms flashed in long processions through the streets, and girls smiled from every carriage. The young man sighed; he thought of the quiet little evening at the Phoenix, of encounters of the Row, of the drive to Hurlingham, and many pleasant dinners in joyous company. Then he glanced up and saw a bus, half empty, slowly lumbering along the middle of the street, and in front of the 'White Horse Cellars' a four-wheeler had stopped still (the driver was asleep on his seat), and in the 'Badminton' the blinds were down. He half expected to see the Briar Rose trailing gracefully over the Hotel Cosmopole; certainly the Beauty, if such a thing were left in Piccadilly, was fast asleep.

Absorbed in these mournful reflections the hapless Johnny strolled on without observing that an exact duplicate of himself was advancing on the same pavement from the opposite direction; save that the inevitable carnation was salmon colour, and the cane a silver-headed one, instruments of great magnifying power would have been required to discriminate between them. The two met; each raised his eyes simultaneously at the strange sight of a well-dressed man, and each adjured the same old-world deity.

"By Jove! old man, what the deuce are you doing here?"

The gentleman who had advanced from the direction of Hyde Park Corner was the first to answer.

"Well, to tell the truth, Austin, I am detained in town on—ah—legal business. But how is it you are not in Scotland?"

"Well, it's curious; but the fact is, I have legal business in town also."

"You don't say so? Great nuisance, ain't it? But these things must be seen to, or a fellow finds himself in no end of a mess, don't you know?"

"He does, by Jove! That's what I thought."

Mr. Austin relapsed into silence for a few moments.

"And where are you off to, Phillips?"

The conversation had passed with the utmost gravity on both sides; at the joint mention of legal business, it was true, a slight twinkle had passed across their eyes, but the ordinary observer would have said that the weight of ages rested on those unruffled brows.

"I really couldn't say. I thought of having a quiet dinner at Azario's. The Badminton is closed, you know, for repairs or somethin', and I can't stand the Junior Wilton. Come along with me, and let's dine together."

"By Jove! I think I will. I thought of calling on my solicitor, but I dare say he can wait."

"Ah! I should think he could. We'll have some of that Italian wine—stuff in salad-oil flasks—you know what I mean."

The pair solemnly wheeled around, and solemnly paced towards the Circus, meditating, doubtless, on many things. The dinner in the little restaurant pleased them with a grave pleasure, as did the Chianti, of which they drank a good deal too much; "quite a light wine, you know," said Phillipps, and Austin agreed with him, so they emptied a quart flask between them and finished up with a couple of glasses apiece of Green Chartreuse. As they came out into the quiet street smoking vast cigars, the two slaves to duty and 'legal business' felt a dreamy delight in all things, the streets seemed full of fantasy in the dim light of the lamps, and a single star shining in the clear sky above seemed to Austin exactly of the same colour as Green Chartreuse. Phillipps agreed with him. "You know, old fellow," he said, "there are times when a fellow feels all sorts of strange things—you know, the sort of things they put in magazines, don't you know, and novels. By Jove, Austin, old man, I feel as if I could write a novel myself."

The pair wandered aimlessly on, not quite knowing where they were going, turning from one street to another, and discoursing in a maudlin strain. A great cloud had been slowly moving up from the south, darkening the sky, and suddenly it began to rain, at first slowly with great heavy drops, and then faster and faster in a pitiless, hissing shower; the gutters flooded over, and the furious drops danced up from the stones. The two Johnnies walked on as fast they could, whistling and calling "Hansom!" in vain; they were really getting very wet.

"Where the dickens are we?" said Phillipps. "Confound it all, I don't know. We ought to be in Oxford Street."

They walked on a little farther, when suddenly, to their great joy, they found a dry archway, leading into a dark passage or courtyard. They took shelter silently, too thankful and too wet to say anything. Austin looked at his hat; it was a wreck; and Phillipps shook himself feebly, like a tired terrier.

"What a beastly nuisance this is," he muttered: "I only wish I could see a hansom."

Austin looked into the street; the rain was still falling in torrents; he looked up the passage, and noticed for the first time that it led to a great house, which towered grimly against the sky. It seemed all dark and gloomy, except that from some chink in a shutter a light shone out. He pointed it out to Phillipps, who stared vacantly about him, then exclaimed:

"Hang it! I know where we are now. At least, I don't exactly know, you know, but I once came by here with Wylliams, and he told me there was some club or somethin' down this passage; I don't recollect exactly what he said. Hullo! why there goes Wylliams. I say, Wylliams, tell us where we are!"

A gentleman had brushed past them in the darkness and was walking fast down the passage. He heard his name and turned round, looking rather annoyed.

"Well, Phillipps, what do you want? Good evening, Austin; you seem rather wet, both of you."

"I should think we were wet; got caught in the rain. Didn't you tell me once there was some club down here? I wish you'd take us in, if you're a member."

Mr. Wylliams looked steadfastly at the two forlorn young men for a moment, hesitated, and said:

"Well, gentlemen, you may come with me if you like. But I must impose a condition; that you both give me your word of honour never to mention the club, or anything that you see while you are in it, to any individual whatsoever."

"Certainly not," replied Austin; "of course we shouldn't dream of doing so, should we, Phillipps?"

"No, no; go ahead, Wylliams, we'll keep it dark enough."

The party moved slowly down the passage till they came to the house. It was a very large house and very old; it looked as though it might have been an embassy of the last century. Wylliams whistled, knocked twice at the door, and whistled again, and it was opened by a man in black.

"Friends of yours, Mr. Wylliams?"

Wylliams nodded and they passed on.

"Now mind," he whispered, as they paused at a door, "you are not to recognise anybody, and nobody will recognise you."

The two friends nodded, and the door was opened, and they entered a vast room, brilliantly lighted with electric lamps. Men were standing in knots, walking up and down, and smoking at little tables; it was just like any club smoking room. Conversation was going on, but in a low murmur, and every now and then someone would stop talking, and look anxiously at the door at the other end of the room, and then turn round again. It was evident that they were waiting for someone or somebody. Austin and Phillipps were sitting on a sofa, lost in amazement; nearly every face was familiar to them. The flower of the Row was in that strange club room; several young noblemen, a young fellow who had just come into an enormous fortune, an eminent actor, and a well-known canon. What could it mean? They were all supposed to be scattered far and wide over the habitable globe, and yet here they were. Suddenly there came a loud knock at the door; and every man started, and those who were sitting got up. A servant appeared.

"The President is awaiting you, gentlemen," he said, and vanished.

One by one the members filed out, and Wylliams and the two guests brought up the rear. They found themselves in a room still larger than the first, but almost quite dark. The President sat at a long table and before him burned two candles, which barely lit up his face. It was the famous Duke of Dartington, the largest landowner in England. As soon as the members had entered he said in a cold, hard voice, "Gentlemen, you know our rules; the book is prepared. Whoever opens it at the black page is at the disposal of the committee and myself. We had better begin." Someone began to read out the names in a low distinct voice, pausing after each name, and the member called came up to the table and opened at random the pages of a big folio volume that lay between the two candles. The gloomy light made it difficult to distinguish features, but Phillipps heard a groan beside him, and recognised an old friend. His face was working fearfully, the man was evidently in an agony of terror. One by one the members opened the book; as each man did so he passed out by another door. At last there was only one left; it was Phillipps's friend. There was foam upon his lips as he passed up the table, and his hand shook as he opened up the leaves. Wylliams had passed out after whispering to the President, and had returned to his friends' side. He could hardly hold them back as the unfortunate man groaned in agony and leant against the table; he had opened the book at the black page. "Kindly come with me, Mr. D'Aubigny," said the President, and they passed out together.

"We can go now," said Wylliams, "I think the rain has gone off. Remember your promise, gentlemen. You have been at a meeting of the Lost Club. You will never see that young man again. Good night."

"It isn't *murder*, is it?" gasped Austin.

"Oh no, not at all. Mr. D'Aubigny will, I hope, live for many years; he has disappeared, merely disappeared. Good night; there's a hansom that will do for you."

The two friends went to their homes in dead silence. They did not meet again for three weeks, and each thought the other looked ill and shaken. They walked drearily, with grave averted faces, down Piccadilly, each afraid to begin the recollection of the terrible club. Of a sudden Phillipps stopped as if he had been shot. "Look there, Austin," he muttered, "look at that." The posters of the evening papers were spread out beside the pavement, and on one of them Austin saw in large blue letters, 'Mysterious disappearance of a Gentleman.' Austin bought a copy and turned over the leaves with shaking fingers till he found the brief paragraph:

> Mr. St. John D'Aubigny, of Stoke D'Aubigny, in Sussex, has disappeared under mysterious circumstances. Mr. D'Aubigny was staying at Strathdoon, in Scotland, and came up to London, as is stated, on business, on August 16th. It has been ascertained that he arrived safely at King's Cross, and drove to Piccadilly Circus, where he got out. It is said that he was last seen at the corner of Glass House Street, leading from Regent Street into Soho. Since the above date the unfortunate gentleman, who was much liked in London society, has not been heard of. Mr. D'Aubigny was to have been married in September. The police are extremely reticent.

"Good God! Austin, this is dreadful. You remember the date. Poor fellow, poor fellow!"

"Phillipps, I think I shall go home, I feel sick."

D'Aubigny was never heard of again. But the strangest part of the story remains to be told. The two friends called upon Wylliams, and charged him with being a member of the Lost Club, and an accomplice in the fate of D'Aubigny. The placid Mr. Wylliams at first stared at the two pale, earnest faces, and finally roared with laughter.

"My dear fellows, what on earth are you talking about? I never heard such a cock-and-bull story in my life. As you say, Phillipps, I once pointed out to you a house said to be a club, as we were walking through Soho; but that was a low gambling club, frequented by

German waiters. I am afraid the fact is that Azario's Chianti was rather too strong for you. However, I will try to convince you of your mistake."

Wylliams forthwith summoned his man, who swore that he and his master were in Cairo during the whole of August, and offered to produce the hotel bills. Phillipps shook his head, and they went away. Their next step was to try and find the archway where they had taken shelter, and after a good deal of trouble they succeeded. They knocked at the door of the gloomy house, whistling as Wylliams had done. They were admitted by a respectable mechanic in a white apron, who was evidently astonished at the whistle; in fact he was inclined to suspect the influence of a 'drop too much.' The place was a billiard table factory, and had been so (as they learnt in the neighbourhood) for many years. The rooms must once have been large and magnificent, but most of them had been divided into three or four separate workshops by wooden partitions.

Phillipps sighed; he could do no more for his lost friend; but both he and Austin remained unconvinced. In justice to Mr. Wylliams, it must be stated that Lord Henry Harcourt assured Phillipps that he had seen Wylliams in Cairo about the middle of August; he thought, but could not be sure, on the 16th; and also, that the recent disappearances of some well known men about town are patient of explanations which would exclude the agency of the Lost Club. ✦

Munitions of War

There was a thick fog, acrid and abominable, all over London when I set out for the West. And at the heart of the fog, as it were, was the shudder of the hard frost that made one think of those winters in Dickens that had seemed to have become fabulous. It was a day on which to hear in dreams the iron ring of the horses' hoofs on the Great North Road, to meditate on the old inns with blazing fires, the coach going onward into the darkness, into a frozen world.

A few miles out of London the fog lifted. The horizon was still vague in a purple mist of cold, but the sun shone brilliantly from a pale clear sky of blue, and all the earth was a magic of whiteness: white fields stretched to that dim violet mist far away, white hedges divided them, and the trees were all snowy white with the winter blossom of the frost. The train had been delayed a little by the thick fog about London; now it was rushing at a tremendous speed through this strange white world.

My business with the famous town in the West was to attempt to make some picture of it as it faced the stress of war, to find out whether it prospered or not. From what I had seen in other large towns, I expected to find it all of a bustle on the Saturday, its shops busy, its streets thronged and massed with people. Therefore, it was with no small astonishment that I found the atmosphere of Westpool wholly different from anything I had observed at Sheffield or Birmingham. Hardly anybody seemed to leave the train at the big station, and the broad road into the town wore a shy, barred-up air; it reminded one somewhat of the streets by which the traveller passes into forgotten places, little villages that once were great cities. I remember how in the town of my birth,

Caerleon-on-Usk, the doctor's wife would leave the fire and run to the window if a step sounded in the main street outside; and strangely I was reminded of this as I walked from the Westpool station. Save for one thing: at intervals there were silent parties huddled together as if for help and comfort, and all making for the outskirts of the city.

There is a fair quarter of an hour's walk between Westpool station and the centre of the town. And here I would say that though Westpool is one of the biggest and busiest cities in England, it is also, in my judgment, one of the most beautiful. Not only on account of the ancient timbered houses that still overhang many of its narrower streets, not only because of its glorious churches and noble old traditions of splendour—I am known to be weak and partial where such things are concerned—but rather because of its site. For through the very heart of the great town a narrow, deep river runs, full of tall ships, bordered by bustling quays; and so you can often look over your garden walls and see a cluster of masts, and the shaking out of sails for a fair wind. And this bringing of deep-sea business into the middle of the dusty streets has always seemed to me an enchantment; there is something of Sindbad and Basra and Bagdad and the Nights in it. But this is not all the delight of Westpool; from the very quays of the river the town rushes up to great heights, with streets so steep that often they are flights of steps as in St. Peter Port, and ladder-like ascents. And as I came to Middle Quay in Westpool that winter day, the sun hovered over the violet mists, and the windows of the houses on the heights flamed and flashed red, vehement fires.

But the slightest astonishment with which I had noted the shuttered and dismal aspect of the station road now became bewilderment. Middle Quay is the heart of Westpool, and all its business. I had always seen it swarm like an anthill. There were scarcely half a dozen people there on Saturday afternoon; and they seemed to be hurrying away. The Vintry and the Little Vintry, those famous streets, were deserted. I saw in a moment that I had come on a fool's errand: in Westpool assuredly there was no hurry or rush of war-business, no swarm of eager shoppers for me to describe. I had an introduction to a well-known Westpool man. "Oh, no," he said, "we are very slack in Westpool. We are doing hardly anything. There's an aeroplane factory out at Oldham, and they're making high explosives by Portdown, but that doesn't affect us. Things are quiet, very quiet." I suggested that they might brighten up a little at night. "No," he said, "it really wouldn't be worth your while to stay on; you wouldn't find anything to write about, I assure you."

I was not satisfied. I went out and about the desolate streets of the great city; I made inquiries at random, and always heard the same story—"things were very slack." And I began to receive an extraordinary impression: that the few I met were frightened, and were making the best of their way, either out of the town, or to the safety of their own bolted doors and barred shutters. It was only the very special mention of a friendly commercial traveller of my acquaintance that got me a room for the night at the Pineapple on Middle Quay, overlooking the river. The landlord assented with difficulty, after praising the express to town. "It's a noisy place, this," he said, "if you're not used to it." I looked at him. It was as quiet as if we were in the heart of the forest or the desert. "You see," he said, "we don't do much in munitions, but there's a lot of night transport for the docks at Portdown. You know those climbing motors that they use in the Army, caterpillars or whatever they call them. We get a lot of them through Westpool; we get all sorts of heavy stuff, and I expect they'll wake you at night. I wouldn't go to the window, if I were you, if you do wake up. They don't like anybody peering about."

And I woke up in the dead of night. There was a thundering and a rumbling and a trembling of the earth such as I had never heard. And shouting too; and rolling oaths that sounded like judgment. I got up and drew the blind a little aside, in spite of the landlord's warning, and there was that desolate Middle Quay swarming with men, and the river full of great ships, faint and huge in the frosty mist, and sailing-ships too. Men were rolling casks by the hundred down to the ships. "Hurry up, you lazy lubbers, you damned sons of guns, damn ye!" bellowed a huge voice. "Shall the King's Majesty lack powder?" "No, by God, he shall not!" roared the answer. "I rolled it aboard for old King George, and young King George shall be none the worse for me."

"And who the devil are you to speak so bold?"

"Blast ye, bos'n; I fell at Trafalgar." ✢

The Islington Mystery

I.

The public taste in murders is often erratic, and sometimes, I think, fallible enough. Take, for example, that Crippen business. It happened seventeen years ago, and it is still freshly remembered and discussed with interest. Yet it was by no means a murder of the first rank. What was there in it? The outline is crude enough; simple, easy, and disgusting, as Dr. Johnson observed of another work of art. Crippen was cursed with a nagging wife of unpleasant habits; and he cherished a passion for his typist. Whereupon he poisoned Mrs. Crippen, cut her up and buried the pieces in the coal-cellar. This was well enough, though elementary; and if the foolish little man had been content to lie quietly and do nothing, he might have lived and died peaceably. But he must needs disappear from his house—the action of a fool—and cross the Atlantic with his typist absurdly and obviously disguised as a boy: sheer, bungling imbecility. Here surely, there is no single trace of the master's hand; and yet, as I say, the Crippen Murder is reckoned amongst the masterpieces. It is the same tale in all the arts: the low comedian was always sure of a laugh if he cared to tumble over a pin; and the weakest murderer is sure of a certain amount of respectful attention if he will take the trouble to dismember his subject. And then, with respect to Crippen: he was caught by means of the wireless device, then in its early stages. This, of course, was utterly irrelevant to the true issue; but the public wallows in irrelevance. A great art critic may praise a great picture, and make his criticism a masterpiece in itself. He will be unread; but let some asinine paragraphist say that the painter always sings "Tom Bowling" as he sets his palette, and dines on boiled fowl and apricot sauce three times a week—then the world will proclaim the artist great.

II.

The success of the second-rate is deplorable in itself; but it is more deplorably in that it very often obscures the genuine masterpiece. If the crowd runs after the false, it must neglect the true. The intolerable *Romola* is praised; the admirable *Cloister and the Hearth* is waived aside. So, while the very indifferent and clumsy performance of Crippen filled the papers, the extraordinary Battersea Murder was served with a scanty paragraph or two in obscure corners of the Press. Indeed, we were so shamefully starved of detail that I only retain a bare outline of this superb crime in my memory; but, roughly, the affair was shaped as follows: In the first floor of one of the smaller sets of flats in Battersea a young fellow (18–20) was talking to an actress, a "touring" actress of no particular fame, whose age, if I recollect, was drawing on from thirty to forty. A shot, a near shot, broke in suddenly on their talk. the young man dashed out of the flat, down the stairs, and there, in the entry of the flats, found his own father, shot dead. The father, it should be remarked, was a touring actor, and an old friend of the lady upstairs. But here comes the magistral element in this murder. Beside the dead man, or in the hand of the dead man, or in a pocket of the dead man's coat—I am not sure how it was—there was found a weapon made of heavy wire—a vile and most deadly contraption, fashioned with curious and malignant ingenuity. It was night-time, but the bright light of a moon ten days old was shining, and the young man said he saw someone running and leaping over walls.

But mark the point: the dead actor was hiding beneath his friend's flat hiding and lying in wait, with his villainous weapon to his hand. He was expecting an encounter with some enemy, on whom he was resolved to work at least deadly mischief, if not murder.

Who was that enemy? Whose bullet was it that was swifter than the dead man's savage and premeditated desire?

We shall probably never know. A murder that might have stood in the very first rank, that might have view with the affair of Madeleine smith—there were certain indications that made this seem possible—was suffered to fade into obscurity, while the foolish crowd surged about elementary Crippen and his bungling imbecilities. So there were once people who considered *Robert Elsmere* as a literary work of palmary significance.

III.

Naturally, and with some excuse, the war was responsible for a good deal of this sort of neglect. In those appalling years there was but one thing in men's heads; all else was blotted out. So little attention was paid to the affair of the woman's body, carefully wrapped in sacking, which was found in Regent's Square, by the Gray's Inn Road. A man was hanged without phrases, but there were one or two curious points in the case.

Then, again, there was the Wimbledon Murder, a singular business. A well-to-do family had just moved into a big house facing the Common, so recently that many of their goods and chattels were still in the packing-cases. The master of the house was murdered one night by a man who made off with his booty. It was a curious haul, consisting of a mackintosh worth, perhaps, a couple of pounds, and a watch which would have been dear at ten shillings. This murderer, too, was hanged without comment; and yet, on the face of it, his conduct seems in need of explanation. But the most singular case of all those that suffered from the preoccupations of the war was, there is no doubt, the Islington Mystery, as the Press called it. It was a striking headline, but the world was too busy to attend. The affair got abroad, so far as it did get abroad, about the time of the first employment of the tanks; and people were trying not to see through the war correspondents, not to perceive that the inky fandangoes and corroborees of these gentlemen hid a sense of failure and disappointment.

IV.

But as to the Islington Mystery—this is how it fell out. There is an odd street, not far from the region which was once called Spa Fields, not far from Pentonville or Islington Fields, where Grimaldi the clown was once accused of inciting the mob to chase an overdriven ox. It goes up a steep hill, and the rare adventurer who pierces now and then into this unknown quarter of London is amazed and bewildered at the very outset, since there are no steep hills in the London of his knowledge, and the contours of the scene remind him of the cheap lodging-house area at the back of hilly seaside resorts. But if the site is strange, the buildings on it are far stranger. They were no doubt set up at the high tide of Sir Walter Scott Gothic, which has left such queer memories behind it. The houses of Lloyd Street are in couples, and the architect, combining the two into one design, desired to create an illusion of a succession of churches, in the Perpendicular or Third Pointed manner, climbing up the hill. The detail is rich, there are finials to rejoice the heart, and gargoyles of fine fantasy, all carried out in the purest stucco. At the lowest house on the right-hand side lived Mr. Harold Boale and his wife, and a brass plate on the Gothic door said, "Taxidermist: Skeletons Articulated." As it chanced, this lowest house of Lloyd Street had a longer garden than its fellows, giving on a contractor's yard, and at the end of the garden Mr. Boale had set up the apparatus of his craft in an outhouse, away from the noses of his fellow-men.

So far as can be gathered, the stuffer and articulator was a harmless and inoffensive little fellow. His neighbours liked him, and he and the Boule cabinet-maker from next door, the Shell box-maker over the way, the seal-engraver and the armourer from Baker Square at the top of the hill, and the old mercantile marine skipper who lived round the corner in Marchmont Street, at the house with the ivory junk in the window, used to spend many a genial evening together in the parlour of the Quill in the days before everything was spoilt by the war.

They did not drink very much or talk very much, any of them; but they enjoyed their moderate cups and the snug comfort of the place, and stared solemnly at the old coaching prints that were upon the walls, and at the large glass painting depicting the landing of England's Injured Queen, which hung over the mantelpiece, between two Pink Dogs with gold collars. Mr. Boale passed as a very nice sort of man in this circle, and everybody was sorry for him. Mrs. Boale was a tartar and a scold. The men of the quarter kept out of her way; the women were afraid of her. She led poor Boale the devil's own life. Her voice, often enough, would be heard at the Quill door vomiting venom at her husband's address; and he, poor man, would tremble and go forth, lest some worse thing might happen. Mrs. Boale was a short dark woman. Her hair was coal-black, her face wore an expression of acid malignity, and she walked quickly but with a decided limp. She was full of energy and the pest of the neighbourhood, and more than a pest to her husband.

The war, with its scarcity and its severe closing-hours, made the meetings at the Quill rarer than before, and deprived them of a good deal of their old comfort. Still, the circle was not wholly broken up, and one evening Boale announced that his wife had gone to visit relations in Lancashire and would most likely be away for a considerable time.

"Well, there's nothing like a change of air, so they say," said the skipper, "though I've had more than enough of it myself."

The others said nothing, but congratulated in their hearts. One of them remarked afterwards that the only change that would do Mrs. Boale good was a change to Kingdom Come, and they all agreed. They were not aware that Mrs. Boale was enjoying the advantages of the recommended treatment.

V.

As I recollect, Mr. Boale's worries began with the appearance of Mrs. Boale's sister, Mary Aspinall, a woman almost as ill-tempered and malignant as Mrs. Boale herself. She had been for some years a nurse with a family in Capetown, and had come home with her mistress. In the first place, the woman had written two or three letters to her sister, and there had been no reply. This struck her as odd, for Mrs. Boale had been a very good correspondent, filling her letters with "nasty things" about her husband. So, on her first afternoon off after her return, Mary Aspinall called at the house in Lloyd Street to get the truth of the matter from her sister's own lips. She strongly suspected Boale of having suppressed her letters. "The dirty little tyke; I'll serve him," she said to herself. So came Miss Aspinall to Lloyd Street and brought out Boale from his workshop. And when he saw her his heart sank. He had read her letters. But the decision to return to England had been taken suddenly; Miss Aspinall had therefore said not a word about it. Boale had thought of his wife's sister as established at the other end of the world for the next ten, twenty years, perhaps; and he meant to go away and lose himself under a new name in a year or two. And so when he saw the woman his heart sank.

Mary Aspinall went straight to the point.

"Where's Elizabeth?" she asked. "Upstairs? I wonder she didn't come down when she heard the bell."

"No," said Boale. He comforted himself with the thought of the curious labyrinth he had drawn about his secret; he felt secure in the centre of it.

"No, she's not upstairs. She's not in the house."

"Oh, indeed. Not in the house. Gone to see some friends, I suppose. When do you expect her back?"

"The truth is, Mary, that I don't expect her back. She's left me—three months ago, it is."

"You mean to tell me that! Left you! Showed her sense, I think. Where has she gone?"

"Upon my word, Mary, I don't know. We had a bit of a to-do one evening, though I don't think I said much. But she said she'd had enough, and she packed a few things in a bag and off she went. I ran after her and called to her to come back, but she wouldn't so much as turn her head, and went off King's Cross way. And from that day to this I've never seen her, nor had a word from her. I've had to send all of her letters back to the post office."

Mary Aspinall stared hard at her brother-in-law and pondered. Beyond telling him that he had brought it on himself, there seemed nothing to say. So she dealt with Boale on those lines very thoroughly, and made an indignant exit from the parlour. He went back to stuff peacocks, for all I know. He was feeling comfortable again. There had been a very unpleasant sensation in the stomach for a few seconds—a very horrible fear at the moment that one of the outer walls of that labyrinth of his had been breached; but now all was well again.

And all might have been permanently well if Miss Aspinall had not happened to meet Mrs. Horridge in the main road, close to the bottom of Lloyd Street. Mrs. Horridge was the wife of the shell box-maker, and the two had met once or twice long ago at Mrs. Boale's tea-table. they recognized each other, and after a few unmeaning remarks Mrs. Horridge asked Miss Aspinall if she had seen her sister since her return to England.

"How could I see her when I don't know where she is?" asked Miss Aspinall with some ferocity.

"Dear me, you haven't seen Mr. Boale, then?"

"I've just come from him this minute."

"But he can't have lost the Lancashire address, surely?"

And so one thing led to another, and Mary Aspinall gathered quite clearly that Boale had told his friends that his wife was paying a long visit to relations in Lancashire. In the first place, the Aspinalls had no relations in Lancashire—they came from Suffolk—and secondly, Boale had informed her that Elizabeth had gone away in a rage, he knew not where. She did not pay him another visit then and there, as she had first intended. It was growing later, and she took her considerations back with her to Wimbledon, determined on thinking the matter out.

Next week she called again at Lloyd Street. She charged Boale with deliberate lying, placing frankly before him the two tales he had told. Again that horrid sinking sensation lay heavy upon Boale. But he had reserves.

"Indeed," he said, "I've told you no lies, Mary. It all happened just as I said before. But I did make up that tale about Lancashire for the people about here. I didn't like them to have my troubles to talk over, especially as Elizabeth is bound to come back some time, and I hope it will be soon."

Miss Aspinall stared at the little man in a doubtful, threatening fashion of a moment, and then hurried upstairs. She came down soon afterwards.

I've gone through Elizabeth's drawers," she said with defiance. "There's a good many things missing. I don't see those bits of lace she had from Granny, and the set of jet is gone, and so is the garnet necklace, and the coral brooch. I couldn't find the ivory fan, either."

I found all the drawers wide open after she'd gone," sighed Mr. Boale. "I supposed she'd taken the things away with her."

It must be confessed that Mr. Boale, taught, perhaps, by the nicety of his craft, had paid every attention to detail. He had realized that it would be vain to tell a tale of his wife going away and leaving her treasures behind her. And so the treasures had disappeared.

Really, the Aspinall vixen did not know what to say. She had to confess that Boale had explained the difficulty of his two stories quite plausibly. So she informed him that he was more like a worm than a man, and banged the hall door. Again Boale went back to his workshop with a warmth about his heart. His labyrinth was still secure, its secret safe. At first, when confronted again by the accusing Aspinall, he had thought of bolting the moment he got the woman out of the house; but that was unreasoning panic. He was in no danger. And he remembered, like the rest of us, the Crippen case. It was running away that brought Crippen to ruin; if he had sat tight he would have sat secure, and the secret of the cellar would never have been known. Though, as Mr. Boale reflected, anybody was welcome to search his cellar, to search here and there and anywhere on his premises, from the hall door in front to the workshop at the back. And he proceeded to give his calm, whole-souled attention to a fine raven that had been sent round in the morning.

Miss Aspinall took the extraordinary disappearance of her sister back with her to Wimbledon and thought it over. She thought it over again and again, and she could make nothing of it. She did not know that people are constantly disappearing for all sorts of reasons; that nobody hears anything about such cases unless some enterprising paper sees matter for a "stunt," and rouses all England to hunt for John Jones or Mrs. Carraway. To Miss Aspinall, the vanishing of Elizabeth Boale seemed a portent and a wonder, a unique and terrible event; and she puzzled her head over it, and still could find no exit from her labyrinth—a different structure from the labyrinth maintained by the serene Boale. The Aspinall had no suspicions of her brother-in-law; both his manner and his matter were straightforward, clear, and square. He was a worm, as she had informed him, but he was certainly telling the truth. But the woman was fond of her sister, and wanted to know where she had gone and what had happened to her; and so she put the matter into the hands of the police.

VI.

She furnished the best description that she could of the missing woman, but the officer in charge of the case pointed out that she had not seen her sister for many years, and that Mr. Boale was obviously the person to be consulted in the matter. So the taxidermist was once again drawn from his scientific labours. He was shown the information laid by Miss Aspinall and the description furnished by her. He told his simple story once more, mentioning the incident of his lying to his neighbours to avoid unpleasant gossip, and added several details to Miss

Aspinall's picture of his wife. He then furnished the constable with two photographs, pointed out the better likeness of the two, and saw his visitor off his premises with cheerful calm.

In due course, the "Missing" bill, garnished with a reproduction of the photograph selected by Mr. Boale, with minute descriptive details, including the "marked limp," was posted up at the police-stations all over the country, and glanced at casually by a few passers-by here and there. There was nothing sensational about the placard; and the statement, "Last seen going in the direction of King's Cross," was not a very promising clue for the amateur detective. No hint of the matter got into the Press; as I have pointed out, hardly one per cent of these cases of "missing" does get into the Press. And just then we were all occupied in reading the paeans of the war correspondents, who were proving that an advance of a mile and a half on a nine-mile front constituted a victory which threw Waterloo into the shade. There was no room for discussing the whereabouts of an obscure woman whom Islington knew no more.

It was sheer accident that brought about the catastrophe. James Curry, a medical student who had rooms in Percy Street, Tottenham Court Road, was prowling about his quarter one afternoon in an indefinite and idle manner, gazing at shop windows and mooning at street corners. He knew that he would never want a cash register, but he inspected the stock with the closest attention, and chose a fine specimen listed at £75. Again, he invested heavily in costly Oriental rugs, and furnished a town mansion in the Sheraton manner at very considerable expense. And so his tour of inspection brought him to the police-station; and there he proceeded to read the bills posted outside, including the bill related to Elizabeth Boale.

"Walks with a marked limp."

James Curry felt his breath go out of his body in a swift grasp. He put out a hand towards the railing to steady himself as he read that amazing sentence over again. And then he walked straight into the police-station.

The fact was that he had bought from Harold Boale, three weeks after the date on which Elizabeth Boale was last seen, a female skeleton. He had got it comparatively cheaply because of the malformation of one of the thigh-bones. And now it struck him that the late owner of that thigh-bone must have walked with a very marked limp.

VII.

M'Aulay made his reputation at the trial. He defended Harold Boale with magnificent audacity. I was in court—it was a considerable part of my business in those days to frequent the Old Bailey—and I shall never forget the opening phrases of his speech for the prisoner. He rose slowly, and let his glance go slowly round the court. His eyes rested at last with grave solemnity on the jury. At length he spoke, in a low, clear, deliberate voice, weighing, as it seemed, every word he uttered.

"Gentlemen," he began, "a very great man, and a very wise man, and a very good man once said that probability is the guide of life. I think you will agree with me that this is a weighty utterance. When we once leave the domain of pure mathematics, there is very little that is certain. Supposing we have money to invest: we weigh the pros and cons of this scheme and that, and decide at last on probable grounds. Or it may be our lot to have to make an appointment; we have to choose a man to fill a responsible position in which both honesty and sagacity are of the first consequence. Again probability must guide us to a decision. No one man can form a certain and infallible judgement of another. And so through all the affairs of life: we must be content with probability, and again and again with probability. Bishop Butler was right.

"But every rule has its exception. The rule which we have just laid down has its exception. That exception confronts you terribly, tremendously, at this very moment. You may think—I do not say that you do think—but you may think that Harold Boale, the prisoner at the bar, in all probability murdered his wife, Elizabeth Boale."

There was a long pause at this point. Then:

"*If* you think that, then it is your imperative duty to acquit the prisoner at the bar. The only verdict which you dare give is a verdict of 'Not Guilty.'"

Up to this moment, Counsel had maintained the low, deliberate utterance with which he had begun his speech, pausing now and again and seeming to consider within himself the precise value of every word that came to his lips. Suddenly his voice rang out, resonant, piercing. One word followed swiftly on another:

"This, remember, is not a court of probability. Bishop Butler's maxim does not apply here. Here there is no place for probability. This is a court of certainty. And unless you are certain that my client is guilty, unless you are as certain of his guilt as you are certain that two and two make four, then you must acquit him.

"Again, and yet again—this is a court of certainty. In the ordinary affairs of life, as we have seen, we are guided by probability. We sometimes make mistakes; in most cases these mistakes may be rectified. A disastrous investment may be counter balanced by a prosperous investment; a bad servant may be replaced by a good one. But in this place, where life and death may hang in the balances which are in your hands, there is no room for mistakes, since here mistakes are irreparable. You cannot bring a dead man back to life. You must not say, 'This man is probably a murderer, and therefore he is guilty.' Before you bring in such a verdict, you must be able to say, 'This man is certainly a murderer.' And *that* you cannot say, and I will tell you why."

M'Aulay then took the evidence piece by piece. Scientific witnesses had declared that the malformation of the thigh-bone in the skeleton exhibited would produce exactly the sort of limp which had characterized Elizabeth Boale. Counsel for the defence had worried the doctors, had made them admit that such a malformation was by no means unique. It was uncommon. Yes, but not very uncommon? Perhaps not. Finally, one doctor admitted that in the course of thirty years of hospital and private practice he had known of five such cases of malformation of the thigh-bone. M'Aulay gave an inaudible sigh of relief; he felt that he had got his verdict.

He made all this quite clear to the jury. He dwelt on the principle that no one can be condemned unless the *corpus delecti*, the body, or some identifiable portion of the body of the murdered person can be produced. He told them the story of the Campden Wonder; how the "murdered" man walked into his village two years after the three people had been hanged for murdering him. "Gentlemen," he said, "for all I know, and for all you know, Elizabeth Boale may walk into this court at any moment. I say boldly that we have no earthly right to assume that she is dead."

Of course Boale's defence was a very simple one. The skeleton which he sold to Mr. Curry had been gradually assembled by him in the course of the last three years. He pointed out that the two hands were not a very good match; and, indeed, this was a little detail that he had not overlooked.

The jury took half an hour to consider their verdict. Harold Boale was found "Not Guilty."

He was seen by an old friend a couple of years ago. He had emigrated to America, and was doing prosperously in his old craft in a big town of the Middle West. He had married a pleasant girl of Swedish extraction.

"You see," he explained, "the lawyers told me I should be safe in presuming poor Elizabeth's death."

He smiled amiably.

And finally, I beg to state that this account of mine is a grossly partial narrative. For all I know, assuming for a moment the severe standards of M'Aulay, Boale was an innocent man. It is possible that his story was a true one. Elizabeth Boale may, after all, be living; she may return after the fashion of the "murdered" man in the Campden Wonder. All the thoughts, devices, meditations that I have put into the heart and mind of Boale may be my own malignant inventions without a shadow of true substance behind them.

In theory, then, the Islington Mystery is an open question. Certainly; but in fact? ✢

Johnny Double

I.

The worst of it was that Johnny Marchant had nothing particular to complain of. He did not live in a slum in the most miserable part of London. He lived in a beautiful old house in the country. His father did not beat him when he came home drunk, because his father very rarely left his house and therefore he couldn't come home. And besides, his father never got drunk. His old grandmother never thought of shutting him up in dark cupboards. All the cupboards at Johnny's home were full of books and of curious and beautiful things, so there was no room for Johnny. Besides, his grandmother, who came on visits about twice a year, would never have dreamt of doing such a silly thing. In the first place she was as kind as kind could be; and then she was not the sort of woman to take a lot of rare china out of a cupboard for the sake of putting a little boy into it; in fact, as I say, Johnny Marchant had nothing whatever to complain of, and that's a pity. People are not interested in a child who isn't shut up in the dark, starved, or beaten. It is true that Johnny's mother had died when he was a year old. But he never remembered her, and his nurse Mary knew what a boy's feelings are, and generally had gooseberry jam for tea. Or if not, blackberry jelly in the blue Chinese pot with the yellow dragons.

II.

So, since we cannot pretend that Johnny Marchant had a rough time, we may as well make the best of the smooth things that he enjoyed. To begin with, the house that he lived in was old and odd and beautiful.

It was in a hollow looking over a quiet bay of a calm blue sea. About it were groves of dark ilex trees, green all the year round; and then there were huge old laurels of a brighter green that blossomed and bore a crimson-purple fruit. There was a lawn in front of the house with fuchsia hedges twenty feet high. On one side was the kitchen garden, where the peaches grew from pale green to yellow, and from yellow to pink, and from pink to crimson all through the spring and summer. On the other side were the dessert apples and pears in an orchard sloping to the south and the sea. Then from the first lawn steps went down to the second lawn, called Johnny Summerhouse Lawn, for here was a summer house that had tried to look like a Chinese temple, before the white roses had grown all over it. And then another flight of steps went down to Well Lawn, where a tall pine tree grew off a red rock, and all manner of green boughs shaded a bubbling well, with white sand always stirring at the bottom of it, as the water rose clear and cold out of the heart of the hill. And, after that, below again was the wild place where all the trees grew thick together and the ground was rich with ferns, and a steep path twisted in and out of the wildness down to the sea.

III.

As for the house; it was about a hundred and twenty years old. There was a ground floor and a first floor, and that was all, and then a thatched roof. The walls were painted white, and the veranda was painted green, and purple clematis covered it. And on the path, in front of the house, were six great green tubs, and in the six great green tubs there were six great green bushes of box, as old as the house. The man who had built it was a captain in the Navy, who had fought in all the fights against Napoleon and had sailed all over the world besides. He had made the builders paint the walls white, and had called his house Casabianca, or White House. But when the box trees in the tubs grew big and round, as they soon did, the country people called the place "The Bunches," and at last it was known as Casabianca Bunches, and Johnny never heard the last of it when he went to school and told his best friend where he lived. In fact he was called "Bunches" at Oxford; and for all I know his fellow-judges call him "Brother Bunches" to this day—except when they are all dressed in scarlet and white and wear great wigs.

IV.

So there were all sorts of nice things outside the house, and one could always get lost in the wild place. And when it rained, there were all sorts of nice things inside the house. There were Chinese monsters and junks and temples made of ivory and lacquer cabinets, rich red and gold and mother-of-pearl, and Japanese pictures in deep fine colours, with people making horrible faces in the front, and blue mountains and rivers and bridges in the distance, and Indian gods with too many arms, and elephants' heads, and serpents and everything a boy can want. As for books, there were plenty everywhere: Baxter's *Saints' Rest*, *The Arabian Nights*, Jeremy Taylor, *Roderick Random*, the Poetical Works of Akenside, the Waverley Novels, *Gil Blas*, *Gulliver's Travels*, all Dickens', Jortin's *Sermons*, and *Don Quixote*. In due time Johnny tried them all—very small bits of some of them, and, as his father said, gave himself a liberal education. And yet his father and his grandmother and his Aunt Letitia were sometimes "quite uneasy" about him. He was so very odd at times. The old doctor came over from Nantgaron and heard all about it, and looked at Johnny's tongue, and punched him in the proper places, and sent powders; and that was no good. Then

Johnny was taken to the doctor at Bristol, who said he must live on cream and mutton chops done pink; and that was no good. Then Johnny was taken to the doctor in London, and he said that raw carrots, finely sliced, with plenty of nuts, would make an immense change for the better; but that did no good. Though his doctor spoke of "irritability of the nervous system," "marked psychological cachexia," "idiosyncrasy," and "pathogenic" at considerable length.

V.

Johnny's trouble was a very odd one, and for some time his relations didn't think much about it. It began by his telling long stories about where he had been and what he had seen, all the most wonderful things that he hadn't seen and couldn't have seen. Mary, the nurse, heard most of these tales in the morning and at tea-time and at bed-time, and she only said, "Yes, dear"; "Of course, darling"; "I see, Master Johnny"; and "Well, I'm sure!" not heeding a word of it. So she heard how Johnny had been a long way off to a big town, ever so much bigger than Nantgaron, and there were houses and houses, and then a sort of country in the middle of the houses, full of trees and grass, and there all the wild beasts in the picture-books came alive, elephants and everything. And Mary cut more bread-and-butter, for this was at tea, and said, "Beautiful, I'm sure." Another time there was a story of a great place, full of lights, and seats rising one behind another; and then something dark went away, and there was a wood beyond, and people in queer dresses talking and singing. "That's the way," said Mary, "and here's your nightshirt, Master Johnny, nice and warm, as I've aired it myself by the kitchen fire." Then it was a tale about another country in the middle of the big town, not the country where the beasts in the picture-book came to life, but a different one, and big soldiers in scarlet and gold with bright swords in their hands riding through the country, and a band playing. And Mary went on cutting the bread-and-butter and helping the jam and brushing Johnny's hair, and not putting herself out a bit. Sometimes Johnny would tell his adventures to his father, who let him run on as he liked. Imaginative children, he said to himself, will always "make up" and "make believe," and it is absurd to punish them for lying. So he would listen almost as quietly as Mary; and one night Johnny told him a long and confused story of one of the bright places with rows of seats rising one above another and the dark place getting bright, and then all sorts of wonderful things happening: a man all white and misty, who talked in a deep voice and seemed to frighten everybody very much, and a king and queen sat on thrones, and a man in a black cloak, who seemed very miserable, talked to them, and at last they all killed each other, and so everybody was dead, and there was a great noise. Mr. Marchant went on reading his paper, and said, "I see," and "Very good, and what did they do then?" "Did you say a churchyard and a rather cross clergyman with a bald head? Dear me! About your bedtime, isn't it?" He thought nothing about it, and he didn't think anything about it when his cousin Anna—one of the "Dawson girls," aged fifty-five—wrote to him from London and said amongst many other things: "Do you think *Hamlet* quite a suitable play for Johnny? He is surely very young for all the horrors. I must say he seemed to be enjoying himself when I saw him two or three weeks ago at the Lyceum. Irving is certainly very fine. Was Johnny staying with the Gascoignes? I did not recognize the lady next to him." Mr. Marchant simply said, "Tut, tut, tut: Anna talking nonsense as usual," and paid no more attention to the matter. He had not listened to half Johnny's story of the misty man and the miserable man and the king and queen and the cross clergyman, and he had forgotten all about the rest. And, anyhow, he knew that Johnny had been at Casabianca Bunches all the summer, and Anna had always been a muddlehead.

VI.

Mr. Marchant only began to get seriously disturbed about the boy one hot day in August, when Johnny was about nine. There was some business to be done at Nantgaron, the market town, eight miles away, and Mr. Marchant drove over in the dog-cart. As he was lunching in the coffee-room of The Three Salmons, his friend, Captain Lloyd, came in and sat down at another table and began to munch bread and cheese and to drink beer out of a great silver tankard with a lid. At first he talked of the harvest, which, as he said, was the earliest for twenty years, and then he remarked:

"What have you done with Johnny? Turned him loose in the tuck shop?"

"Johnny?" said Mr. Marchant. "What d'you mean? I left him at home. Nothing to amuse him at Nantgaron."

"Nonsense, I saw him in the High Street ten minutes ago. He was staring at those steeplejacks mending the weathercock on the spire of St. Mary's."

"I left Johnny reading on the veranda at home an hour and a half ago, and I've only just come. He could hardly have walked the distance in the time. You must have mistaken some other body for him."

"Well, that's very strange. I was quite close to him. He was wearing a straw hat with a green ribbon and a pheasant's feather stuck in it."

Mr. Marchant looked very oddly at Captain Lloyd.

"Queer things boys will wear," was all he said, and that was not much to the point. But the fact was that he had noticed the pheasant's feather in the straw hat with the green ribbon on Johnny's head when he said good-bye to him on the veranda, and had told Johnny that that style of hat was very little worn in town just now. Clearly Johnny had managed to get a lift into Nantgaron, and the only thing to do was to ask him what he meant by it. And so when Mr. Marchant got home about tea-time, the first thing he did was to ask Mary, the nurse, whether Master Johnny had come back.

"He's not been away, sir. He's reading in the Rose Bower, and I'm just going to call him for his tea."

"Not been away, Mary? Do you mean he was in to dinner?"

"As usual, sir, at one o'clock. Roast chicken and raspberry tart. And I thought to myself how children can eat so well and the weather so hot."

Mr. Marchant looked hard at the nurse and then said:

"Oh, I see. Thank you, Mary. That's all right, then."

He didn't see at all. But he thought the matter over, and decided that it was quite possible that some other little boy might have a straw hat with a green ribbon and stick a pheasant's tail feather in it. Soon after tea Mr. Marchant was enjoying his hollyhocks and his pipe on the Summerhouse Lawn, and Johnny was helping, and putting in a word about the Templar in *Ivanhoe*. And then he said: "Daddy! weren't those men wonderful to-day, right upon on the very top of the church?"

And Mr. Marchant's pipe dropped out of his mouth.

VII.

It was no good to try to get Johnny to explain. He didn't seem to think that there was anything to explain. He said he wondered what his father was doing at Nantgaron, so he thought he would go and see; and that was all, and that was how all his relations got "quite uneasy," as they said. And the doctors' medicines and chopped carrots and nuts made no difference whatever. Till at last the parson said there was nothing for it but school, and the boy was "Packed off," first of all to a big preparatory school, and then to a bigger public school. Odd things happened once or twice at both places. He began to tell the other boys one of his queer stories and was promptly kicked and clouted as a young liar. Then he got into trouble for being about the town at midnight, and things looked extremely serious. But as he was able to prove that he was fast asleep in the dormitory at the time, his house-master only gave him lines on general principles. Johnny was cured, or so his father and the people at home thought.

VIII.

But many years afterwards, only three years ago as a matter of fact, and some time after Johnny had become Mr. Justice Marchant, it was appointed that he should try Henry Farmer, who was accused of the dreadful Hetton murder. When the court was opened, and the judge and the prisoner faced each other, a few people noticed that the two men in their different places "looked as if they had seen a ghost." The prisoner in the dock gasped and shuddered, and muttered something about "the man in scarlet," and the judge on the bench turned ghastly white, and his head almost fell on the desk before him. Mr. Justice Marchant said in a faint voice that he feared a somewhat severe indisposition would prevent him trying the case. The prisoner was put back: it was another judge who sentenced Farmer to death a few days later. Mr. Justice Marchant never told anyone that he had seen the man in the dock before—and with the red knife in his hand. ✤

The Cosy Room

I.

And he found to his astonishment that he came to the appointed place with a sense of profound relief. It was true that the window was somewhat high up in the wall, and that, in case of fire, it might be difficult, for many reasons, to get out that way; it was barred like the basement windows that one sees now and then in London houses, but as for the rest it was an extremely snug room. There was a gay flowering paper on the walls, a hanging bookshelf—his stomach sickened for an instant—a little table under the window with a board and draughtsmen on it, two or three good pictures, religious and ordinary, and the man who looked after him was arranging the tea-things on the table in the middle of the room. And there was a nice wicker chair by a bright fire. It was a thoroughly pleasant room; cosy you would call it. And, thank God, it was all over, anyhow.

II.

It had been a horrible time for the last three months, up to an hour ago. First of all there was the trouble; all over in a minute, that was, and couldn't be helped, though it was a pity and the girl wasn't worth it. But then there was the getting out of the town. He thought at first of just going about his ordinary business and knowing nothing about it; he didn't think that anybody had seen him following Joe down to the river. Why not loaf about as usual, and say nothing, and go into the Ringland Arms for a pint? It might be days before they found the body under the alders;

and there would be an inquest, and all that. Would it be the best plan just to stick it out, and hold his tongue if the police came asking him questions? But then, how could he account for himself and his doings that evening? He might say he went for a stroll in Bleadon Woods and home again without meeting anybody. There was nobody who could contradict him that he could think of.

And now, sitting in the snug room with the bright wallpaper, sitting in the cosy chair by the fire—all so different from the tales they told of such places—he wished he had stuck it out and faced it out, and let them come on and find out what they could. But, then, he had got frightened. Lots of men had heard him swearing it would be outing does for Joe if he didn't leave the girl alone. And he had shown his revolver to Dick Haddon, and "Lobster" Carey, and Finniman, and others, and then they would be fitting the bullet into the revolver, and it would be all up. He got into a panic and shook with terror, and knew he could never stay in Ledham, not another hour.

III.

Mrs. Evans, his landlady, was spending the evening with her married daughter at the other side of the town, and would not be back till eleven. He shaved off his stubbly black beard and moustache, and slunk out of the town in the dark and walked all through the night by a lonely by-road, and got to Darnley, twenty miles away, in the morning in time to catch the London excursion. There was a great crowd of people, and, so far as he could see, nobody that he knew, and the carriages packed full of Darnleyites and Lockwood weavers all in high spirits and taking no notice of him. They all got out at King's Cross, and he strolled about with the rest and looked round here and there as they did and had a glass of beer at a crowded bar. He didn't see how anybody was to find out where he had gone.

IV.

He got a back room in a quiet street off the Caledonian Road, and waited. There was something in the evening paper that night, something that you couldn't very well make out. By the next day Joe's body was found, and they got to Murder—the doctor said it couldn't be suicide. Then his own name came in, and he was missing and was asked to come forward. And then he read that he was supposed to have gone to London, and he went sick with fear. He went hot and he went cold. Something rose in his throat and choked him. His hands shook as he held the paper, his head whirled with terror. He was afraid to go home to his room, because he knew he could not stay still in it; he would be tramping up and down, like a wild beast, and the landlady would wonder. And he was afraid to be in the streets, for fear a policeman would come behind him and put a hand on his shoulder. There was a kind of small square round the corner and he sat down on one of the benches there and held up the paper before his face, with the children yelling and howling and playing all about him on the asphalt paths. They took no notice of him, and yet they were company of a sort; it was not like being all alone in that little, quiet room. But it soon got dark and the man came to shut the gates.

V.

And after that night; nights and days of horror and sick terrors that he never had known a man could suffer and live. He had brought enough money to keep him for a while, but every time he changed a note he shook with fear, wondering whether it could be traced.

What could he do? Where could he go? Could he get out of the country? But there were passports and papers of all sorts; that would never do. He read that the police held a clue to the Ledham Murder Mystery; and he trembled to his lodgings and locked himself in and moaned in his agony, and then found himself chattering words and phrases at random, without meaning or relevance; strings of gibbering words: "all right, all right, all right . . . yes, yes, yes, yes . . . there, there, there . . . well, well, well, well . . ." just because he must utter something, because he could not bear to sit still and silent, with that anguish tearing his heart, with that sick horror choking him, with that weight of terror pressing on his breast. And then, nothing happened; and a little, faint trembling hope fluttered in his breast for a while, and for a day or two he felt he might have a chance after all.

One night he was in such a happy state that he ventured round to the little public-house at the corner, and drank a bottle of Old Brown Ale with some enjoyment, and began to think of what life might be again, if by a miracle—he recognized even then that it would be a miracle—all this horror passed away, and he was once more just like other men, with nothing to be afraid of. He was relishing the Brown Ale, and quite plucking up a spirit, when a chance phrase from the bar caught him: "looking for him not far from here, so they say." He left the glass of beer half full, and went out wondering whether he had the courage to kill himself that night. As a matter of fact the men at the bar were talking about a recent and sensational cat burglar; but every such word was doom to this wretch. And ever and again, he would check himself in his horrors, in his mutterings and gibberings, and wonder with amazement that the heart of a man could suffer such bitter agony, such rending torment. It was as if he had found out and discovered, he along of all men living, a new world of which no man before had ever dreamed, in which no man could believe, if he were told the story of it. He had woken up in his past life from such nightmares, now and again, as most men suffer. They were terrible, so terrible that he remembered two or three of them that had oppressed him years before; but they were pure delight to what he now endured. Not endured, but writhed under as a worm twisting amidst red, burning coals.

He went out into the streets, some noisy, some dull and empty, and considered in his panic-stricken confusion which he should choose. They were looking for him in that part of London; there was deadly peril in every step. The streets where people went to and fro and laughed and chattered might be the safer; he could walk with the others and seem to be of them, and so be less likely to be noticed by those who were hunting on his track. But then, on the other hand, the great electric lamps made these streets almost as bright as day, and every feature of the passers-by was clearly seen. True, he was clean-shaven now, and the pictures of him in the papers showed a bearded man, and his own face in the glass still looked strange to him. Still, there were sharp eyes that could penetrate such disguises; and they might have brought down some man from Ledham who know him well, and knew the way he walked; and so he might be haled and held at any moment. He dared not walk under the clear blaze of the electric lamps. He would be safe in the dark, quiet by-ways.

He was turning aside, making for a very quiet street close by, when he hesitated. This street, indeed, was still enough after dark, and not over well lighted. It was a street of low, two-storied houses of grey brick that had grimed, with three or four families in each house. Tired men came home here after working hard all day, and people drew their blinds early and stirred very little abroad, and went early to bed; footsteps were rare in the this street and in other streets into which it led, and the lamps were few and dim compared with those in the big thoroughfares. And yet, the very fact that few people were about made such as were all the more noticeable and conspicuous. And the police went slowly on their beats in the dark streets as in the bright, and with few people to look at no doubt they looked all the more keenly at such as passed on the pavement. In his world, that dreadful world that he had discovered and dwelt in alone, the darkness was brighter than the daylight, and solitude more dangerous that a multitude of men. He dared not go into the light, he feared the shadows, and went trembling to his room and shuddered to himself his infernal rosary: "all right, all right, all right . . . splendid, splendid . . . that's the way, that's the way, that's the way, that's the way . . . yes, yes, yes . . . first rate, first rate . . . all right . . . one, one, one, one"—gabbled in a low mutter to keep himself from howling like a wild beast.

VI.

It was somewhat in the manner of a wild beast that he beat and tore against the cage of his fate. Now and again it struck him as incredible. He would not believe that it was so. It was something that he would wake from, as he had waked from those nightmares that he remembered, for things did not really happen so. He could not believe it, he would not believe it. Or, if it were so indeed, then all these horrors must be happening to some other man into whose torments he had mysteriously entered. Or he had got into a book, into a tale which one read and shuddered at, but did not for one moment credit; all make-believe, it must be, and presumably everything would be all right again. And then the truth came down on him like a heavy hammer, and beat him down, and held him down—on the burning coals of his anguish.

Now and then he tried to reason with himself. He forced himself to be sensible, as he put it; not to give way, to think of his chances. After all, it was three weeks since he had got into the excursion train at Darnley, and he was still a free man, and every day of freedom made his chances better. These things often die down. There were lots of cases in which the police never got the man they were after. He lit his pipe and began to think things over quietly. It might be a good plan to give his landlady notice, and leave at the end of the week, and make for somewhere in South London, and try to get a job of some sort: that would help to put them off his track. He got up and looked thoughtfully out of the window; and caught his breath. There, outside the little newspaper shop opposite, was the bill of the evening paper: New Clue in Ledham Murder Mystery.

VII.

The moment came at last. He never knew the exact means by which he was hunted down. As a matter of fact, a woman who knew him well happened to be standing outside Darnley station on the Excursion Day morning, and she had recognized him, in spite of his beardless chin. And then, at the other end, his landlady, on her way upstairs, had heard his mutterings and gabblings, though the voice was low. She was interested, and curious, and a little frightened, and wondered whether her lodger might be dangerous, and naturally she talked to her friends. So the story trickled down to the police, and the police asked about the date of the lodger's arrival. And there you were. And there was our nameless friend, drinking a good, hot cup of tea, and polishing off the bacon and eggs with rare appetite; in the cosy room with the cheerful paper; otherwise the Condemned Cell. ✛

Opening the Door

The newspaper reporter, from the nature of the case, has generally to deal with the commonplaces of life. He does his best to find something singular and arresting in the spectacle of the day's doings; but, in spite of himself, he is generally forced to confess that whatever there may be beneath the surface, the surface itself is dull enough.

I must allow, however, that during my ten years or so in Fleet Street, I came across some tracks that were not devoid of oddity. There was that business of Campo Tosto, for example. That never got into the papers. Campo Tosto, I must explain, was a Belgian, settled for many years in England, who had left all his property to the man who looked after him.

My news editor was struck by something odd in the brief story that appeared in the morning paper, and sent me down to make inquiries. I left the train at Reigate; and there I found that Mr. Campo Tosto had lived at a place called Burnt Green—which is a translation of his name into English—and that he shot at trespassers with a bow and arrows. I was driven to his house, and saw through a glass door some of the property which he had bequeathed to his servant: fifteenth-century triptychs, dim and rich and golden; carved statues of the saints; great spiked altar candlesticks; storied censers in tarnished silver; and much more of old church treasure. The legatee, whose name was Turk, would not let me enter; but, as a treat, he took my newspaper from my pocket and read it upside down with great accuracy and facility. I wrote this very queer story, but Fleet Street would not suffer it. I believe it struck them as too strange a thing for their sober columns.

And then there was the affair of the J.H.V.S. Syndicate, which deal with a Cabalistic cypher, and the phenomenon, called in the Old Testament, "the Glory of the Lord," and the discovery of certain objects buried under the site of the Temple at Jerusalem; that story was left half told, and I never heard the ending of it. And I never understood the affair of the hoard of coins that a storm disclosed on the Suffolk coast near Aldeburgh. From the talk of the longshoremen, who were on the look-out amongst the dunes, it appeared that a great wave came in and washed away a slice of the sand cliff just beneath them. They saw glittering objects as the sea washed back, and retrieved what they could. I viewed the treasure—it was a collection of coins; the earliest of the twelfth century, the latest, pennies, three or four of them, of Edward VII, and a bronze medal of Charles Spurgeon. There are, of course, explanations of the puzzle; but there are difficulties in the way of accepting any one of them. It is very clear, for example, that the hoard was not gathered by a collector of coins; neither the twentieth-century pennies nor the medal of the great Baptist preacher would appeal to a numismatologist.

But perhaps the queerest story to which my newspaper connections introduced me was the affair of the Reverend Secretan Jones, the "Canonbury Clergyman," as the headlines called him.

To begin with, it was a matter of sudden disappearance. I believe people of all sorts disappear by dozens in the course of every year, and nobody hears of them or their vanishings. Perhaps they turn up again, or perhaps they don't; anyhow, they never get so much as a line in the papers, and there is an end of it. Take, for example, that unknown man in the burning car, who cost the amorous commercial traveller his life. In a certain sense, we all heard of him; but he must have disappeared from somewhere in space, and nobody knew that he had gone from his world. So it is often; but now and then there is some circumstance that draws attention to the fact that A. or B. was in his place on Monday and missing from it on Tuesday and Wednesday; and then inquiries are made and usually the lost man is found, alive or dead, and the explanation is often simple enough.

But as to the case of Secretan Jones. This gentleman, a cleric as I have said, but seldom, it appeared, exercising his sacred office, lived retired in a misty, 1830–40 square in the recesses of Canonbury. He was understood to be engaged in some kind of scholarly research, was a well-known figure in the Reading Room of the British Museum, and looked anything between fifty and sixty. It seems probable that if he had been content with that achievement he might have disappeared as often as he pleased, and nobody would have troubled; but one night as he sat late over his books in the stillness of that retired quarter, a motor-lorry passed along a road not far from Tollit Square, breaking thence with a heavy rumble and causing a tremor of the ground that penetrated into Secretan Jones's study. A teacup and saucer on a side-table trembled slightly, and Secretan Jones's attention was taken from his authorities and note-books.

This was in February or March of 1907, and the motor industry was still in its early stages. If you preferred a horse-bus, there were plenty left in the streets. Motor coaches were non-existent, hansom cabs still jogged and jingled on their cheerful way; and there were very few heavy motor-vans in use. But to Secretan Jones, disturbed by the rattle of his cup and saucer, a vision of the future, highly coloured, was vouchsafed, and he began to write to the papers. He saw the London streets almost as we know them to-day; streets where a horse-vehicle would be almost a matter to show one's children for them to remember in their old age; streets in which a great procession of huge omnibuses carrying fifty, seventy, a hundred people was continually passing; streets in which vans and trailers loaded far beyond the capacity of any manageable team of horses would make the ground tremble without ceasing.

The retired scholar, with the happy activity which does sometimes, oddly enough, distinguish the fish out of water, went on and spared nothing. Newton saw the apple fall, and built up a mathematical universe; Jones heard the teacup rattle, and laid the universe of London in ruins. He pointed out that neither the roadways nor the houses beside them were constructed to withstand the weight and vibration of the coming traffic. He crumbled all the shops in Oxford Street and Piccadilly into dust; he cracked the dome of St. Paul's, brought down Westminster Abbey, reduced the Law courts to a fine powder. What was left was dealt with by fire, flood and pestilence. The prophetic Jones demonstrated that the roads must collapse, involving the various services beneath them. Here, the water-mains and the main drainage would flood the streets; there, huge volumes of gas would escape, and electric wires fuse; the earth would be rent with explosions, and the myriad streets of London would go up in a great flame of fire. Nobody really believed that it would happen, but it made good reading, and Secretan Jones gave interviews, started discussions, and enjoyed himself thoroughly. Thus he became the "Canonbury Clergyman." "Canonbury Clergyman says that Catastrophe is Inevitable"; "Doom of London pronounced by Canonbury Clergyman"; "Canonbury Clergyman's Forecast: London a Carnival of Flood, Fire and Earthquake"— that sort of thing.

And thus Secretan Jones, though his main interests were liturgical, was able to secure a few newspaper paragraphs when he disappeared—rather more than a year after his great campaign in the Press, which was not quite forgotten, but not very clearly remembered.

A few paragraphs, I said, and stowed away, most of them, in out-of-the-way corners of the papers. It seemed that Mrs. Sedger, the woman who shared with her husband the business of looking after Secretan Jones, brought in tea on a tray to his study at four o'clock as usual, and came, again as usual, to take it away at five. And, a good deal to her astonishment, the study was empty. She concluded that her master had gone out for a stroll, though he never went out for strolls between tea and dinner. He didn't come back for dinner; and Sedger, inspecting the hall, pointed out that the master's hats and coats and sticks and umbrellas were all on their pegs and in their places. The Sedgers conjectured this, that, and the other, waited a week, and then went to the police, and the story came out and perturbed a few learned friends and correspondents: Prebendary Lincoln, author of *The Roman Canon in the Third Century*; Dr. Brightwell, wise on the Rite of Malabar; and Stokes, the Mozarabic man. The rest of the populace did not take very much interest in the affair, and when, at the end of six weeks, there was a line or two stating that "the Rev. Secretan Jones, whose disappearance at the beginning of last month from his house in Tollit Square, Canonbury, caused some anxiety to his friends, returned yesterday," there was neither enthusiasm nor curiosity. The last line of the paragraph said that the incident was supposed to be the result of a misunderstanding; and nobody even asked what that statement meant.

And there would have been the end of it—if Sedger had not gossiped to the circle in the private bar of The King of Prussia. Some mysterious and unofficial person, in touch with this circle, insinuated himself into the presence of my news editor and told him Sedger's tale. Mrs. Sedger, a careful woman, had kept all the rooms tidy and well-dusted. On the Tuesday after she had opened the study door and saw, to her amazement and delight, her master sitting at his table with a great book open beside him and a pencil in his hand. She exclaimed:

"Oh, sir, I *am* glad to see you back again!"

"Back again?" said the clergyman. "What do you mean? I think I should like some more tea."

"I don't know in the least what it's all about," said the news editor, "but you might go and see Secretan Jones and have a chat with him. There may be a story in it." There was a story in it, but not for my paper, or any other paper.

I got into the house in Tollit Square on some unhandsome pretext connected with Secretan Jones's traffic scare of the year before. He looked at me in a dim, abstracted way at first—the "great book" of his servant's story, and other books, and many black quarto notebooks were about him—but my introduction of the proposed design for a "mammoth carrier" clarified him, and he began to talk eagerly, and as it seemed to me lucidly, of the grave menace of the new mechanical transport.

"But what's the use of talking?" he ended. "I tried to wake people up to the certain dangers ahead. I seemed to succeed for a few weeks; and then they forgot all about it. You would really say that the great majority are like dreamers, like sleepwalkers. Yes; like men walking in a dream; shutting out all the actualities, all the facts of life. They know that they are, in fact, walking on the edge of a precipice; and yet they are able to believe, it seems, that the precipice is a garden path; and they behave as if it were a garden path, as safe as that path you see down there, going to the door at the bottom of my garden."

The study was at the back of the house, and looked on the long garden, heavily overgrown with shrubs run wild, mingling with one another, some of them flowering richly, and altogether and happily obscuring and confounding the rigid grey walls that doubtless separated each garden from its neighbours. Above the tall shrubs, taller elms and planes and ash trees grew unlopped and handsomely neglected; and under this deep concealment of green boughs the path went down to a green door, just visible under a cloud of white roses.

"As safe as that path you see there," Secretan Jones repeated, and, looking at him, I thought his expression changed a little; very slightly, indeed, but to a certain questioning, one might say to a meditative doubt. He suggested to me a man engaged in an argument, who puts his case strongly, decisively; and then hesitates for the fraction of a second as a point occurs to him of which he had never thought before; a point as yet unweighed, unestimated; dimly present, but more as a shadow than a shape.

The newspaper reporter needs the gestures of the serpent as well as its wisdom. I forget how I glided from the safe topic of the traffic peril to the dubious territory which I had been sent to explore. At all events, my contortions were the most graceful that I could devise; but they were altogether vain. Secretan Jones's kind, lean, clean-shaven face took on an expression of distress. He looked at me as one in perplexity; he seemed to search his mind not for the answer that he should give me, but rather for some answer due to himself.

"I am extremely sorry that I cannot give you the information you want," he said, after a considerable pause. "But I really can't go any farther into the matter. In fact, it is quite out of the question to do so. You must tell your editor or sub-editor; which is it?—that the whole business is due to a misunderstanding, a misconception, which I am not at liberty to explain.

But I am really sorry that you have come all this way for nothing."

There was real apology and regret, not only in his words, but in his tones and in his aspect. I could not clutch my hat and get on my way with a short word in the character of a disappointed and somewhat disgusted emissary; so we fell on general talk, and it came out that we both came from the Welsh borderland, and had long ago walked over the same hills and drunk of the same wells. Indeed, I believe we proved cousinship, in the seventh degree or so, and tea came in, and before long Secretan Jones was deep in liturgical problems, of which I knew just enough to play the listener's part. Indeed, when I had told him that the *hwyl*, or chanted eloquence, of the Welsh Methodists was, in fact the Preface Tone of the Roman Missal, he overflowed with grateful interest, and made a note in one of his books, and said the point was most curious and important. It was a pleasant evening, and we strolled through the french windows into the green-shadowed, blossoming garden, and went on with our talk, till it was time—and high time—for me to go. I had taken up my hat as we left the study, and as we stood by the green door in the wall at the end of the garden, I suggested that I might use it.

"I am so sorry," said Secretan Jones, looking, I thought, a little worried, "but I am afraid it's jammed, or something of that kind. It has always been an awkward door, and I hardly ever use it."

So we went through the house, and on the doorstep he pressed me to come again, and was so cordial that I agreed to his suggestion of the Saturday sennight. And so at last I got an answer to the question with which my newspaper had originally entrusted me; but an answer by no means for newspaper use. The tale, or the experience, or the impression, or whatever it may be called, was delivered to me by very slow degrees, with hesitations, and in a manner of tentative suggestion that often reminded me of our first talk together. It was as if Jones were again and again questioning himself as to the matter of his utterances, as if he doubted whether they should not rather be treated as dreams, and dismissed as trifles without consequence.

He said once to me: "People do tell their dreams, I know; but isn't it usually felt that they are telling nothing? That's what I am afraid of."

I told him that I thought we might throw a great deal of light on very dark places if more dreams were told.

"But there," I said "is the difficulty. I doubt whether the dreams that I am thinking of *can* be told. There are dreams that are perfectly lucid from beginning to end, and also perfectly insignificant. There are others which are blurred by a failure of memory, perhaps only on one point: you dream of a dead man as if he were alive. Then there are dreams which are prophetic: there seems, on the whole, no doubt of that. Then you may have sheer clotted nonsense; I once chased Julius Caesar all over London to get his recipe for curried eggs. But, besides these, there is a certain dream of another order: utter lucidity up to the moment of waking, and then perceived to be beyond the power of words to express. It is neither sense nor nonsense; it has, perhaps, a notation of its own, but . . . well, you can't play Euclid on the violin."

Secretan Jones shook his head. "I am afraid my experiences are rather like that," he said. It was clear, indeed, that he found great difficulty in finding a verbal formula which should convey some hint of his adventures.

But that was later. To start with, things were fairly easy; but, characteristically enough, he began his story before I realised that the story was begun. I had been talking of the queer tricks a man's memory sometimes plays him. I was saying that a few days before, I was suddenly interrupted in some work I was doing. It was necessary that I should clear my desk in a hurry. I shuffled a lot of loose papers together and put them away, and awaited my caller with a fresh writing-pad before me. The man came. I attended to the business with which he was concerned, and went back to my former affair when he had gone. But I could not find the sheaf of papers. I thought I had put them in a drawer. They were not in the drawer; they were not in any drawer, or in the blotting book, or in any place where one might reasonably expect to find them. They were found next morning by the servant who dusted the room, stuffed hard down into the crevice between the seat and the back of an arm-chair, and carefully hidden under a cushion.

"And," I finished, "I hadn't the faintest recollection of doing it. My mind was blank on the matter."

"Yes," said Secretan Jones, "I suppose we all suffer from that sort of thing at times. About a year ago I had a very odd experience of the same kind. It troubled me a good deal at the time. It was soon after I had taken up that question of the new traffic and its probable—its certain—results. As you may have gathered, I have been absorbed for most of my life in my own special studies, which are remote enough from the activities and interests of the day. It hasn't been at all my way to write to the papers to say there are too many dogs in London, or to denounce street musicians. But I must say that the extraordinary dangers of using our present road system for a traffic for which it was not designed did impress themselves very deeply upon me; and I dare say I allowed myself to be over-interested and over-excited.

"There is a great deal to be said for the Apostolic maxim: 'Study to be quiet and to mind your own business.' I am afraid I got the whole on the brain, and neglected my own business, which at that particular time, if I remember, was the investigation of a very curious question—the validity or non-validity of the Consecration Formula of the *Grand Saint Graal: Car chou est li sanc di ma nouviele loy, li miends meismes.* Instead of attending to my proper work, I allowed myself to be drawn into the discussion I had started, and for a week or two I thought of very little else: even when I was looking up authorities at the British Museum, I couldn't get the rumble of the motor-van out of my head. So, you see, I allowed myself to get harried and worried and distracted, and I put down what followed to all the bother and excitement I was going through. The other day, when you had to leave your work in the middle and start on something else, I dare say you felt annoyed and put out, and shoved those papers of yours away without really thinking of what you were doing, and I suppose something of the same kind happened to me. Though it was still queerer, I think."

He paused, and seemed to meditate doubtfully, and then broke out with an apologetic laugh, and: "it really sounds quite crazy!" And then: "I forgot where I lived."

"Loss of memory, in fact, through overwork and nervous excitement?"

"Yes, but not quite in the usual way. I was quite clear about my name and my identity. And I knew my address perfectly well: Thirty-nine, Tollit Square, Canonbury."

"But you said you forgot where you lived."

"I know; but there's the difficulty of expression we were talking about the other day. I am looking for the notation, as you called it. But it was like this: I had been working all the morning in the Reading Room with the motor danger at the back of my mind, and as I left the Museum, feeling a sort of heaviness and confusion, I made up my mind to walk home. I thought the air might freshen me a little. I set out at a good pace. I knew every foot of the way, as I had often done the walk before, and I went ahead mechanically, with my mind wrapt up in a very important matter relating to my proper studies. As a matter of fact, I had found in a most unexpected quarter a statement that threw an entirely new light on the rite of the Celtic Church, and I felt that I might be on the verge of an important discovery. I was lost in a maze of conjectures, and when I looked up I found myself standing on the pavement by the Angel, Islington, totally unaware of where I was to go next.

"Yes, quite so: I knew the Angel when I saw it, and I knew I lived in Tollit Square; but the relation between the two had entirely vanished from my consciousness. For me, there were no longer any points of the compass; there was no such thing as direction, neither north nor south, nor left nor right, an extraordinary sensation, which I don't feel I have made plain to you at all. I was a good deal disturbed, and felt that I must move somewhere, so I set off—and found myself at King's Cross railway station. Then I did the only thing there was to be done: took a hansom and got home, feeling shaky enough."

I gathered that this was the first incident of significance in a series of odd experiences that befell this learned and amiable clergyman. His memory became thoroughly unreliable, or so he thought at first.

He began to miss important papers from his table in the study. A series of notes, on three sheets lettered A, G, and C, were placed by him on the table under a paperweight one night, just before he went up to bed. They were missing when he went into his study the next morning. He was certain that he had put them in that particular place, under the bulbous glass weight with the pink roses embedded in its depths: but they were not there. Then Mrs. Sedger knocked at the door and entered with the papers in her hand. She said she had found them between the bed and the mattress in the master's bedroom, and thought they might be wanted.

Secretan Jones could not make it out at all. He supposed he must have put the papers where they were found and then forgotten all about it, and he was uneasy, feeling afraid that he was on the brink of a nervous breakdown. Then there were difficulties about his books, as to which he was very precise, every book having its own place. One morning he wanted to consult the *Missale de Arbuthnott*, a big red quarto, which lived at the end of a bottom shelf near the window. It was not there. The unfortunate man went up to his bedroom, and felt the bed all over and looked under his shirts in the chest of drawers, and searched all the room in vain. However, determined to get what he wanted, he went to the Reading Room, verified his reference, and returned to Canonbury: and there was the red quarto in its place. Now here, it seemed certain, there was no room for loss of memory; and Secretan Jones began to suspect his servants of playing tricks with his possessions, and tried to find a reason for their imbecility or villainy—he did not know what to call it. But it would not do at all. Papers and books disappeared and reappeared, or now and then vanished without return. One afternoon, struggling, as he told me, against a growing sense of confusion and bewilderment, he had with considerable difficulty filled two quarto sheets of ruled paper with a number of extracts necessary to the subject he had in hand. When this was done, he felt his bewilderment thickening like a cloud about him: "It was, physically and mentally, as if the objects in the room because indistinct, were presented in a shimmering mist or darkness." He felt afraid, and rose, and went out into the garden. The two sheets of paper he had left on his table were lying on the path by the garden door.

I remember he stopped dead at this point. To tell the truth, I was thinking that all these instances were rather matter for the ear of a mental specialist than for my hearing. There was evidence enough of a bad nervous breakdown, and it seemed to me, of delusions. I wondered whether it was my duty to advise the man to go to the best doctor he knew, and without delay. Then Secretan Jones began again:

"I won't tell you any more of these absurdities. I known they are drivel, pantomime tricks and traps, children's conjuring; contemptible, all of it.

"But it made me afraid. I felt like a man walking in the dark, beset with uncertain sounds and faint echoes of his footsteps that seem to come from a vast depth, till he begins to fear that he is treading by the edge of some awful precipice. There was something unknown about me; and I was holding on hard to what I knew, and wondering whether I should be sustained.

"One afternoon I was in a very miserable and distracted state. I could not attend to my work. I went out into the garden, and walked up and down trying to calm myself. I opened the garden door and looked into the narrow passage which runs at the end of all the gardens on this side of the square. There was nobody there—except three children playing some game or other. They were queer, stunted little creatures, and I turned back into the garden and walked into the study. I had just sat down, and had turned to my work hoping to find relief in it, when Mrs. Sedger, my servant, came into the room and cried out, in an excited sort of way, that she was glad to see me back again.

"I made up some story. I don't know whether she believes it. I suppose she thinks I have been mixed up in something disreputable."

"And what had happened?"

"I haven't the remotest notion."

We sat looking at each other for some time.

"I suppose what happened was just this," I said at last. "Your nervous system had been in a very bad way for some time. It broke down utterly; you lost your memory, your sense of identity—everything. You may have spent the six weeks in addressing envelopes in the City Road."

He turned to one of the books on the table and opened it. Between the leaves there were the dimmed red and white petals of some flower that looked like an anemone.

"I picked this flower," he said, "as I was walking down the path that afternoon. It was the first of its kind to be in bloom—very early. It was still in my hand when I walked back into this room, six weeks later, as everybody declares. But it was quite fresh."

There was nothing to be said. I kept silent for five minutes, I suppose, before I asked him whether his mind was an utter blank as to the six weeks during which no known person had set eyes on him; whether he had no sort of recollection, however vague.

"At first, nothing at all. I could not believe that more than a few seconds came between my opening the garden door and shutting it. Then in a day or two there was a vague impression that I had been somewhere where everything was absolutely right. I can't say more than that. No fairyland joys, or bowers of bliss, or anything of that kind; no sense of anything strange or unaccustomed. But there was no care there at all. *Est enim magnum chaos.*"

But that means "For there is a great void," or "A great gulf."

We never spoke of the matter again. Two months later he told me that his nerves had been troubling him, and that he was going to spend a month or six weeks at a farm near Llanthony, in the Black Mountains, a few miles from his old home. In three weeks I got a letter addressed in Secretan Jones's hand. Inside was a slip of paper on which he had written the words:

Est enim magnum chaos.

The day on which the letter was posted he had gone out in wild autumn weather, late one afternoon, and had never come back. No trace of him has ever been found. ✢

The Children of the Pool

A couple of summers ago I was staying with old friends in my native county, on the Welsh border. It was in the heat and drought of a hot and dry year, and I came into those green, well-watered valleys with a sense of a great refreshment. Here was relief from the burning of London streets, from the close and airless nights, when all the myriad walls of brick and stone and concrete and the pavements that are endless give out into the heavy darkness the fires that all day long have been drawn from the sun. And from those roadways that have become like railways, with their changing lamps, and their yellow globes, and their bars and studs of steel; from the menace of instant death if your feet stray from the track: from all this what a rest to walk under the green leaf in quiet, and hear the stream trickling from the heart of the hill.

My friends were old friends, and they were urgent that I should go my own way. There was breakfast at nine, but it was equally serviceable and excellent at ten; and I could be in for something cold for lunch, if I liked; and if I didn't like I could stay away till dinner at half past seven; and then there was all the evening for talks about old times and about the changes, with comfortable drinks, and bed soothed by memories and tobacco, and by the brook that twisted under dark alders through the meadow below. And not a red bungalow to be seen for many a mile around! Sometimes, when the heat even in that green land was more than burning, and the wind from the mountains in the west ceased, I would stay all day under shade on the lawn, but more often I went afield and trod remembered ways, and tried to find new ones, in that happy and bewildered country. There, paths go wandering into undiscovered valleys, there from deep and narrow lanes with overshadowing hedges, still smaller tracks that I suppose are old bridle-paths, creep obscurely, obviously leading nowhere in particular.

It was on a day of cooler air that I went adventuring abroad on such an expedition. It was a "day of the veil." There were no clouds in the sky, but a high mist, grey and luminous, had been drawn all over it. At one moment, it would seem that the sun must shine through, and the blue appear; and then the trees in the wood would seem to blossom, and the meadows lightened; and then again the veil would be drawn. I struck off by the stony lane that led from the back of the house up over the hill; I had last gone that way many years ago, of a winter afternoon, when the ruts were frozen into hard ridges, and dark pines on high places rose above snow, and the sun was red and still above the mountain. I remembered that the way had given good sport, with twists to right and left, and unexpected descents, and then risings to places of thorn and bracken, till it darkened to the hushed stillness of a winter's night, and I turned homeward reluctant. Now I took another chance with all the summer day before me, and resolved to come to some end and conclusion of the matter.

I think I had gone beyond the point at which I had stopped and turned back as the frozen darkness and the bright stars came on me. I remembered the dip in the hedge, from which I saw the round tumulus on high at the end of the mountain wall; and there was the white farm on the hill-side, and the farmer was still calling to his dog, as he—or his father—had called before, his voice high and thin in the distance. After this point, I seemed to be in undiscovered country; the ash trees grew densely on either side of the way and met above it: I went on and on into the unknown in the manner of the only good guide-books, which are the tales of old knights.

The road went down, and climbed, and again descended, all through the deep of the wood. Then, on both sides, the trees ceased, though the hedges were so high that I could see nothing of the way of the land about me. And just at the wood's ending, there was one of those tracks or little paths of which I have spoken, going off from my lane on the right, and winding out of sight quickly under all its leafage of hazel and wild rose, maple and hornbeam, with a holly here and there, and honeysuckle golden, and dark briony shining and twining everywhere. I could not resist the invitation of a path so obscure and uncertain, and set out on its track of green and profuse grass, with the ground beneath still soft to the feet, even in the drought of that fiery summer. The way wound, as far as I could make out, on the slope of a hill, neither ascending nor descending, and after a mile or more of this rich walking, it suddenly ceased, and I found myself on a bare hill-side, on a rough track that went down to a grey house. It was now a farm by its looks and surroundings, but there were signs of old state about it: good sixteenth-century mullioned windows and a Jacobean porch projecting from the centre, with dim armorial bearings mouldering above the door.

It struck me that bread and cheese and cider would be grateful, and I beat upon the door with my stick, and brought a pleasant woman to open it.

"Do you think," I began, "you could be so good as. . . ."

And then came a shout from somewhere at the end of the stone passage; and a great voice called:

"Come in, then, come in, you old scoundrel, if your name is Meyrick, as I'm sure it is."

I was amazed. The pleasant woman grinned and said:

"It seems you are well known here, sir, already. But perhaps you had heard that Mr. Roberts was staying here."

My old acquaintance, James Roberts, came tumbling out from his den at the back. He was a man whom I had known a long time, but not very well. Our affairs in London moved on different lines, and so we did not often meet. But I was glad to see him in that unexpected place: he was a round man, always florid and growing redder in the face with his years. He was a countryman of mine, but I had hardly known him before we both went to town, since his home had been at the northern end of the county.

He shook me cordially by the hand, and looked as if he would like to smack me on the back—he was, a little, that kind of man—and repeated his "Come in, come in!" adding to the pleasant woman: "And bring you another plate, Mrs. Morgan, and all the rest of it. I hope you've not forgotten how to eat Caerphilly cheese, Meyrick. I can tell you, there is none better than Mrs. Morgan's making. And, Mrs. Morgan, another jug of cider, and *seidr dda*, mind you."

I never knew whether he had been brought up as a boy to speak Welsh. In London he had lost all but the faintest trace of accent, but down here in Gwent the tones of the country had richly returned to him; and he smacked as strongly of the land in his speech as the cheerful farmer's wife herself. I judged his accent was a part of his holiday.

He drew me into the little parlour with its old furniture and its pleasant old-fashioned ornaments and faintly flowering wallpaper, and set me in an elbow-chair at the round table, and gave me, as I told him, exactly what I had meant to ask for; bread and cheese and cider. All very good; Mrs. Morgan, it was clear, had the art of making a Caerphilly cheese that was succulent—a sort of white *bel paese*—far different from those dry and stony cheeses that often bring dishonour on the Caerphilly name. And afterwards there was gooseberry jam and cream. And the tobacco that the country uses: Shag-on-the-Back, from the Welsh Back, Bristol. And then there was gin.

This last we partook of out of doors, in an old stone summerhouse, in the garden at the side. A white rose had grown all over the summer-house, and shaded and glorified it. The water in the big jug had just been drawn from the well in the limestone rock—and I told Roberts gratefully that I felt a great deal better than when I had knocked at the farmhouse door. I told him where I was staying—he knew my host by name—and he, in turn, informed me that it was his first visit to Lanypwll, as the farm was called. A neighbour of his at Lee had recommended Mrs. Morgan's cooking very highly: and, as he said, you couldn't speak too well of her in that way or any other.

We sipped and smoked through the afternoon in that pleasant retreat under the white roses. I meditated gratefully on the fact that I should not dare to enjoy Shag-on-the-Back so freely in London: a potent tobacco, of full and ripe savour, but not for the hard streets.

"You say the farm is called Lanypwll," I interjected, "that means 'by the pool,' doesn't it? Where is the pool? I don't see it."

"Come you," said Roberts, "and I will show you."

He took me by a little gate through the garden hedge of laurels, thick and high, and round to the left of the house, the opposite side to that by which I had made my approach. And there we climbed a green rounded bastion of the old ages, and he pointed down to a narrow valley, shut in by steep wooded hills. There at the bottom was a level, half marshland and half black water lying in still pools, with green islands of iris and of all manner of rank and strange growths that love to have their roots in slime.

"There is your pool for you," said Roberts.

It was the most strange place, I thought, hidden away under the hills as if it were a secret. The steeps that went down to it were a tangle of undergrowth, of all manner of boughs mingled, with taller trees rising above the mass, and down at the edge of the marsh some of these had perished in the swampy water, and stood white and bare and ghastly, with leprous limbs.

"An ugly looking place," I said to Roberts.

"I quite agree with you. It is an ugly place enough. They tell me at the farm it's not safe to go near it, or you may get fever and I don't know what else. And, indeed, if you didn't go down carefully and watch your steps, you might easily find yourself up to the neck in that black muck there."

We turned back into the garden and to our summer-house, and soon after, it was time for me to make my way home.

"How long are you staying with Nichol?" Roberts asked me as we parted. I told him, and he insisted on my dining with him at the end of the week.

"I will 'send' you," he said. "I will take you by a short cut across the fields and see that you don't lose your way. Roast duck and green peas," he added alluringly, "and something good for the digestion afterwards."

It was a fine evening when I next journeyed to the farm, but indeed we got tired of saying "fine weather" throughout that wonderful summer. I found Roberts cheery and welcoming, but, I thought, hardly in such rosy spirits as on my former visit. We were having a cocktail of his composition in the summer-house, as the famous duck gained the last glow of brown perfection; and I noticed that his speech was not bubbling so freely from him as before. He fell silent once or twice and looked thoughtful. He told me he'd ventured down to the pool, the swampy place at the bottom. "And it looks no better when you see it close at hand. Black, oily stuff that isn't like water, with a scum upon it, and weeds like a lot of monsters. I never saw such queer, ugly plants. There's one rank-looking thing down there covered with dull crimson blossoms, all bloated out and speckled like a toad."

"You're no botanist," I remarked.

"No, not I. I know buttercups and daisies and not much more. Mrs. Morgan here was quite frightened when I told her where I'd been. She said she hoped I mightn't be sorry for it. But I feel as well as ever. I don't think there are many places left in the country now where you can get malaria."

We proceeded to the duck and the green peas and rejoiced in their perfection. There was some very old ale that Mr. Morgan had bought when an ancient tavern in the neighbourhood had been pulled down; its age and original excellence had combined to make a drink like a rare wine. The "something good for the digestion" turned out to be a mellow brandy that Roberts had brought with him from town. I told him that I had never known a better hour. He warmed up with the good meat and drink and was cheery enough; and yet I thought there was a reserve, something obscure at the back of his mind that was by no means cheerful.

We had a second glass of the mellow brandy, and Roberts, after a moment's indecision, spoke out. He dropped his holiday game of Welsh countryman completely.

"You wouldn't think, would you," he began, "that a man would come down to a place like this to be blackmailed at the end of the journey?"

"Good Lord!" I gasped in amazement, "I should think not indeed. What's happened?"

He looked very grave. I thought even that he looked frightened.

"Well, I'll tell you. A couple of nights ago, I went for a stroll after my dinner; a beautiful night, with the moon shining, and a nice, clean breeze. So I walked up over the hill, and then took the path that leads down through the wood to the brook. I'd got into the wood, fifty yards or so, when I heard my name called out: 'Roberts! James Roberts!' in a shrill, piercing voice, a young girl's voice, and I jumped pretty well out of my skin, I can tell you. I stopped dead and stared all about me. Of course I could see nothing at all—bright moonlight and black shadow and all those trees—anybody could hide. Then it came to me that it was some girl of the place having a game with her sweetheart: James Roberts is a common enough name; especially in this part of the country. So I was just going on, not bothering my head about the local love-affairs, when that scream came right in my ear: 'Roberts! Roberts! James Roberts!'—and then half a dozen words that I won't trouble you with; not yet, at any rate."

I have said that Roberts was by no means an intimate friend of mine. But I had always known him as a genial, cordial fellow, a thoroughly good-natured man; and I was sorry and shocked, too, to see him sitting there wretched and dismayed. He looked as if he had seen a ghost; he looked much worse than that. He looked as if he had seen terror.

But it was too early to press him closely. I said:
"What did you do then?"

"I turned about, and ran back through the wood, and tumbled over the stile. I got home here as quick as ever I could, and shut myself up in this room, dripping with fright and gasping for breath. I was almost crazy, I believe. I walked up and down. I sat down in the chair and got up again. I wondered whether I should wake up in my bed and find I'd been having a nightmare. I cried at last. I'll tell you the truth: I put my head in my hands, and the tears ran down my cheeks. I was quite broken."

"But, look here," I said, "isn't this making a great to-do about very little? I can quite see it must have been a nasty shock. But, how long did you say you had been staying here; ten days, was it?"

"A fortnight, to-morrow."

"Well; you know country ways as well as I do. You may be sure that everybody within three or four miles of Lanypwll knows about a gentleman from London, a Mr. James Roberts, staying at the farm. And there are always unpleasant young people to be found, wherever you go. I gather that this girl used very abusive language when she hailed you. She probably thought it was a good joke. You had taken that walk through the wood in the evening a couple of times before? No doubt, you had been noticed going that way, and the girl and her friend or friends planned to give you a shock. I wouldn't think any more of it, if I were you."

He almost cried out.

"Think any more of it! What will the world think of it?" There was an anguish of terror in his voice. I thought it was time to come to cues. I spoke up pretty briskly:

"Now, look here, Roberts, it's no good beating about the bush. Before we can do anything, we've got to have the whole tale, fair and square. What I've gathered is this: you go for a walk in a wood near here one evening, and a girl—you say it was a girl's voice—hails you by your name, and then screams out a lot of filthy language. Is there anything more in it than that?"

"There's a lot more than that. I was going to ask you not to let it go any further; but as far as I can see, there won't be any secret in it much longer. There's another end to the story, and it goes back a good many years—to the time when I first came to London as a young man. That's twenty-five years ago."

He stopped speaking. When he began again, I could feel that he spoke with unutterable repugnance. Every word was a horror to him.

"You know as well as I do, that there are all sorts of turnings in London that a young fellow can take; good, bad, and indifferent. There was a good deal of bad luck about it, I do believe, and I was too young to know or care much where I was going; but I got into a turning with the black pit at the end of it."

He beckoned me to lean forward across the table, and whispered for a minute or two in my ear. In my turn, I heard not without horror. I said nothing.

"*That* was what I heard shrieked out in the wood. What do you say?"

"You've done with all that long ago?"

"It was done with very soon after it was begun. It was no more than a bad dream. And then it all flashed back on me like deadly lightning. What do you say? What can I do?"

I told him that I had to admit that it was no good to try to put the business in the wood down to accident, the casual filthy language of a depraved village girl. As I said, it couldn't be a case of a bow drawn at a venture.

"There must be somebody behind it. Can you think of anybody?"

"There may be one or two left. I can't say. I haven't heard of any of them for years. I thought they had all gone; dead, or at the other side of the world."

"Yes; but people can get back from the other side of the world pretty quickly in these days. Yokohama is not much farther off than Yarmouth. But you haven't heard of any of these people lately?"

"As I said, not for years. But the secret's out."

"But, let's consider. Who is this girl? Where does she live? We must get at her, and try if we can't frighten the life out of her. And, in the first place, we'll find out the source of her information. Then we shall know where we are. I suppose you have discovered who she is?"

"I've not a notion of who she is or where she lives."

"I daresay you wouldn't care to ask the Morgans any questions. But to go back to the beginning: you spoke of blackmail. Did this damned girl ask you for money to shut her mouth?"

"No; I shouldn't have called it blackmail. She didn't say anything about money."

"Well; that sounds more hopeful. Let's see; tonight is Saturday. You took this unfortunate walk of yours a couple of nights ago; on Thursday night. And you haven't heard anything more since. I should keep away from that wood, and try to find out who the young lady is. That's the fast thing to be done, clearly."

I was trying to cheer him up a little; but he only stared at me with his horror-stricken eyes.

"It didn't finish with the wood," he groaned. "My bedroom is next door to this room where we are. When I had pulled myself together a bit that night, I had a stiff glass, about double my allowance, and went off to bed and to sleep. I woke up with a noise of tapping at the window, just by the head of the bed. Tap, tap, tap, it went. I thought it might be a bough beating on the glass. And then I heard that voice calling me: 'James Roberts: open, open!'

"I tell you, my flesh crawled on my bones. I would have cried out, but I couldn't make a sound. The moon had gone down, and there's a great old pear tree close to the window, and it was quite dark. I sat up in my bed, shaking for fear. It was dead still, and I began to think that the fright I had got in the wood had given me nightmare. Then the voice called again, and louder:

"'James Roberts! Open. Quick.'

"And I had to open. I leaned half out of bed, and got at the latch, and opened the window a little. I didn't dare to look out. But it was too dark to see anything in the shadow of the tree. And then she began to talk to me. She told me all about it from the beginning. She knew all the names. She knew where my business was in London, and where I lived, and who my friends were. She said that they should all know. And she said: 'And you yourself shall tell them, and you shall not be able to keep back a single word!'"

The wretched man fell back in his chair, shuddering and gasping for breath. He beat his hands up and down, with a gesture of hopeless fear and misery; and his lips grinned with dread.

I won't say that I began to see light. But I saw a hint of certain possibilities of light or—let us say—of a lessening of the darkness. I said a soothing word or two, and let him get a little more quiet. The telling of this extraordinary and very dreadful experience had set his nerves all dancing; and yet, having made a clean breast of it all, I could see that he felt some relief. His hands lay quiet on the table, and his lips ceased their horrible grimacing. He looked at me with a faint expectancy, I thought; as if he had begun to cherish a dim hope that I might have some sort of help for him. He could not see himself the possibility of rescue; still, one never knew what resources and freedoms the other man might bring.

That, at least, was what his poor, miserable face seemed to me to express; and I hoped I was right, and let him simmer a little, and gather to himself such twigs and straws of hope as he could. Then, I began again:

"This was on the Thursday night. And last night? Another visit?"

"The same as before. Almost word for word."

"And it was all true, what she said? The girl was not lying?"

"Every word of it was true. There were some things that I had forgotten myself; but when she spoke of them, I remembered at once. There was the number of a house in a certain street, for example. If you had asked me for that number a week ago I should have told you, quite honestly, that I knew nothing about it. But when I heard it, I knew it in the instant: I could see that number in the light of a street lamp. The sky was dark and cloudy, and a bitter wind was blowing, and driving the leaves on the pavement—that November night."

"When the fire was lit?"

"That night. When they appeared."

"And you haven't seen this girl? You couldn't describe her?"

"I was afraid to look; I told you. I waited when she stopped speaking. I sat there for half an hour or an hour. Then I lit my candle and shut the window-latch. It was three o'clock and growing light."

I was thinking it over. I noted that Roberts confessed that every word spoken by his visitant was true. She had sprung no surprises on him; there had been no suggestion of fresh details, names, or circumstances. That struck me as having a certain—possible—significance; and the knowledge of Roberts's present circumstances, his City address, and his home address, and the names of his friends: that was interesting, too.

There was a glimpse of a possible hypothesis. I could not be sure; but I told Roberts that I thought something might be done. To begin with, I said, I was going to keep him company for the night. Nichol would guess that I had shirked the walk home after nightfall; that would be quite all right. And in the morning he was to pay Mrs. Morgan for the two extra weeks he had arranged to stay, with something by way of compensation. "And it should be something handsome," I added with emotion, thinking of the duck and the old ale. "And then," I finished, "I shall pack you off to the other side of the island."

Of that old ale I made him drink a liberal dose by way of sleeping-draught. He hardly needed a hypnotic; the terror that he had endured and the stress of telling it had worn him out. I saw him fall into bed and fall asleep in a moment, and I curled up, comfortably enough, in a roomy arm-chair. There was no trouble in the night, and when I writhed myself awake, I saw Roberts sleeping peacefully. I let him alone, and wandered about the house and the shining morning garden, till I came upon Mrs. Morgan, busy in the kitchen.

I broke the trouble to her. I told her that I was afraid that the place was not agreeing at all with Mr. Roberts. "Indeed," I said, "he was taken so ill last night that I was afraid to leave him. His nerves seem to be in a very bad way."

"Indeed, then, I don't wonder at all," replied Mrs. Morgan, with a very grave face. But I wondered a good deal at this remark of hers, not having a notion as to what she meant.

I went on to explain what I had arranged for our patient, as I called him: east-coast breezes, and crowds of people, the noisier the better, and, indeed, that was the cure that I had in mind. I said that I was sure Mr. Roberts would do the proper thing.

"That will be all right, sir, I am sure: don't you trouble yourself about that. But the sooner you get him away after I have given you both your breakfasts, the better I shall be pleased. I am frightened to death for him, I can tell you."

And she went off to her work, murmuring something that sounded like "Plant y pwll, plant y pwll."

I gave Roberts no time for reflection. I woke him up, bustled him out of bed, hurried him through his breakfast, saw him pack his suitcase, make his farewells to the Morgans, and had him sitting in the shade on Nichol's lawn well before the family were back from church. I gave Nichol a vague outline of the circumstances—nervous breakdown and so forth—introduced them to one another, and left them talking about the Black Mountains, Roberts's land of origin.

The next day I saw him off at the station, on his way to Great Yarmouth, via London. I told him with an air of authority that he would have no more trouble, "from any quarter," I emphasized. And he was to write to me at my town address in a week's time.

"And, by the way," I said, just before the train slid along the platform, "here's a bit of Welsh for you. What does 'plant y pwll' mean? Something of the pool?"

"'Plant y pwll,'" he explained, "means 'children of the pool.'"

When my holiday was ended, and I had got back to town, I began my investigations into the case of James Roberts and his nocturnal visitant. When he began his story I was extremely distressed—I made no doubt as to the bare truth of it, and was shocked to think of a very kindly man threatened with overwhelming disgrace and disaster. There seemed nothing impossible in the tale stated at large, and in the first outline. It is not altogether unheard of for very decent men to have had a black patch in their lives, which they have done their best to live down and atone for and forget. Often enough, the explanation of such misadventure is not hard to seek. You have a young fellow, very decently but very simply brought up among simple country people, suddenly pitched into the labyrinth of London, into a maze in which there are many turnings, as the unfortunate Roberts put it, which lead to disaster, or to something blacker than disaster. The more experienced man, the man of keen instincts and perceptions, knows the aspect of these tempting passages and avoids them; some have the wit to turn back in time; a few are caught in the trap at the end. And in some cases, though there may be apparent escape, and peace and security for many years, the teeth of the snare are about the man's leg all the while, and close at last on highly reputable chairmen and churchwardens and pillars of all sorts of seemly institutions. And then gaol, or at best, hissing and extinction.

So, on the first face of it, I was by no means prepared to pooh-pooh Roberts's tale. But when he came to detail, and I had time to think it over, that entirely illogical faculty, which sometimes takes charge of our thoughts and judgments, told me that there was some huge flaw in all this, that somehow or other, things had not happened so. This mental process, I may say, is strictly indefinable and unjustifiable by any laws of thought that I have ever heard of. It won't do to take our stand with Bishop Butler, and declare with him that probability is the guide of life; deducing from this premise the conclusion that the improbable doesn't happen. Any man who cares to glance over his experience of the world and of things in general is aware that the most wildly improbable events are constantly happening. For example, I take up today's paper, sure that I shall find something to my purpose, and in a minute I come across the headline: "Damaging a Model Elephant." A father, evidently a man of substance, accuses his son of this strange offence. Last summer, the father told the court, his son constructed in their front garden a large model of an elephant, the material being bought by witness. The skeleton of the elephant was made of tubing, and it was covered with soil and fibre, and held together with wire netting. Flowers were planted on it, and it cost £3 5s.

A photograph of the elephant was produced in court, and the clerk remarked: "It is a fearsome-looking thing."

And then the catastrophe. The son got to know a married woman much older than himself, and his parents frowned, and there were quarrels. And so, one night, the young man came to his father's house, jumped over the garden wall and tried to push the elephant over. Failing, he proceeded to disembowel the elephant with a pair of wire clippers.

There! Nothing can be much more improbable than that tale, but it all happened so, as the *Daily Telegraph* assures me, and I believe every word of it. And I have no doubt that if I care to look I shall find something as improbable, or even more improbable, in the newspaper columns three or perhaps four times a week. What about the old man, unknown, unidentified, found in the Thames: in one pocket, a stone Buddha; in the other, a leather wallet, with the inscription: "The hen that sits on the china egg is best off"?

The improbable happens and is constantly happening; but, using that faculty which I am unable to define, I rejected Roberts's girl of the wood and the window. I did not suspect him for a moment of leg-pulling of an offensive and vicious kind. His misery and terror were too clearly manifest for that, and I was certain that he was suffering from a very serious and dreadful shock—and yet I didn't believe in the truth of the story he had told me. I felt convinced that there was no girl in the case; either in the wood or at the window. And when Roberts told me, with increased horror, that every word she spoke was true, that she had even reminded him of matters that he had himself forgotten, I was greatly encouraged in my growing surmise. For, it seemed to me at least probable that if the case had been such as he supposed it, there would have been new and damning circumstances in the story, utterly unknown to him and unsuspected by him. But, as it was, everything that he was told he accepted; as a man in a dream accepts without hesitation the wildest fantasies as matters and incidents of his daily experience. Decidedly, there was no girl there.

On the Sunday that he spent with me at the Wern, Nichol's place, I took advantage of his calmer condition—the night's rest had done him good—to get some facts and dates out of him, and when I returned to town, I put these to the test. It was not altogether an easy investigation since, on the surface, at least, the matters to be investigated were eminently trivial; the early days of a young man from the country up in London in a business house; and twenty-five years ago. Even really exciting murder trials and changes of ministries become blurred and uncertain in outline, if not forgotten, in twenty-five years, or in twelve years for that matter: and compared with such events, the affair of James Roberts seemed perilously like nothing at all.

However, I made the best use I could of the information that Roberts had given me; and I was fortified for the task by a letter I received from him. He told me that there had been no recurrence of the trouble (as he expressed it), that he felt quite well, and was enjoying himself immensely at Yarmouth. He said that the shows and entertainments on the sands were doing him "no end of good. There's a retired executioner who does his old business in a tent, with the drop and everything. And there's a bloke who calls himself Archbishop of London, who fasts in a glass case, with his mitre and all his togs on." Certainly, my patient was either recovered, or in a very fair way to recovery: I could set about my researches in a calm spirit of scientific curiosity, without the nervous tension of the surgeon called upon at short notice to perform a life-or-death operation.

As a matter of fact it was all more simple than I thought it would be. True, the results were nothing, or almost nothing, but that was exactly what I had expected and hoped. With the slight sketch of his early career in London, furnished me by Roberts, the horrors omitted by my request; with a name or two and a date or two, I got along very well. And what did it come to? Simply this: here was a lad—he was just seventeen—who had been brought up amongst lonely hills and educated at a small grammar school, furnished through a London uncle with a very small stool in a City office. By arrangement, settled after a long and elaborate correspondence, he was to board with some distant cousins, who lived in the Cricklewood-Kilburn-Brondesbury region, and with them he settled down, comfortably enough, as it seemed, though Cousin Ellen objected to his learning to smoke in his bedroom, and begged him to desist. The household consisted of Cousin Ellen, her husband, Henry Watts, and the two daughters, Helen and Justine. Justine was about Roberts's own age; Helen three or four years older. Mr. Watts had married rather late in life, and had retired from his office a year or so before. He interested himself chiefly in tuberous-rooted begonias, and in the season went out a few miles to his cricket club and watched the game on Saturday afternoons. Every morning there was breakfast at eight, every evening there was high tea at seven, and in the meantime young Roberts did his best in the City, and liked his job well enough. He was shy with the two girls at first, but Justine was lively, and couldn't help having a voice like a peacock, and Helen was adorable. And so things went on very pleasantly for a year or perhaps eighteen months; on this basis, that Justine was a great joke, and that Helen was adorable. The trouble was that Justine didn't think that she was a great joke.

For, it must be said that Roberts's stay with his cousins ended in disaster. I rather gather that the young man and the quiet Helen were guilty of—shall we say—amiable indiscretions, though without serious consequences. But it appeared that Cousin Justine, a girl with black eyes and black hair, made discoveries which she resented savagely, denouncing the offenders at the top of that piercing voice of hers, in the waste hours of the Brondesbury night, to the immense rage, horror, and consternation of the whole house. In fact, there was the devil to pay, and Mr. Watts then and there turned young Roberts out of the house. And there is no doubt that he should have been thoroughly ashamed of himself. But young men. . . .

Nothing very much happened. Old Watts had cried in his rage that he would let Roberts's chief in the City hear the whole story; but, on reflection, he held his tongue. Roberts roamed about London for the rest of the night, refreshing himself occasionally at coffee-stalls. When the shops opened, he had a wash and brush-up, and was prompt and bright at his office. At midday, in the underground smoking-room of the tea-shop, he conferred with a fellow clerk over their dominoes, and arranged to share rooms with him out Norwood way. From that point onwards, the career of James Roberts had been eminently quiet, uneventful, successful.

Now, everybody, I suppose, is aware that in recent years the silly business of divination by dreams has ceased to be a joke and has become a very serious science. It is called "Psycho-analysis"; and is compounded, I would say, by mingling one grain of sense with a hundred of pure nonsense. From the simplest and most obvious dreams, the psycho-analyst deduces the most incongruous and extravagant results. A black savage tells him that he has dreamed of being chased by lions, or, maybe, by crocodiles; and the psycho man knows at once that the black is suffering from the Oedipus complex. That is, he is madly in love with his own mother, and is, therefore, afraid of the vengeance of his father. Everybody knows, of course, that "lion" and "crocodile" are symbols of "father." And I understand that there are educated people who believe this stuff.

It is all nonsense, to be sure; and so much the greater nonsense inasmuch as the true interpretation

of many dreams—not by any means of all dreams—
moves, it may be said, in the opposite direction to the
method of psycho-analysis. The psycho-analyst infers
the monstrous and abnormal from a trifle; it is often
safe to reverse the process. If a man dreams that he
has committed a sin before which the sun hid his
face, it is often safe to conjecture that, in sheer forgetfulness, he wore a red tie, or brown boots with
evening dress. A slight dispute with the vicar may
deliver him in sleep into the clutches of the Spanish
Inquisition, and the torment of a fiery death. Failure
to catch the post with a rather important letter will
sometimes bring a great realm to ruin in the world of
dreams. And here, I have no doubt, we have the
explanation or part of the explanation of the Roberts
affair. Without question, he had been a bad boy; there
was something more than a trifle at the heart of his
trouble. But his original offence, grave as we may
think it, had in his hidden consciousness, swollen
and exaggerated itself into a monstrous mythology of
evil. Some time ago, a learned and curious investiga-
tor demonstrated how Coleridge had taken a bald
sentence from an old chronicler, and had made it the
nucleus of *The Ancient Mariner.* With a vast gesture of
the spirit, he had unconsciously gathered from all the
four seas of his vast reading all manner of creatures
into his net: till the bare hint of the old book glowed
into one of the great masterpieces of the world's poetry. Roberts had nothing in him of the poetic faculty,
nothing of the shaping power of the imagination, no
trace of the gift of expression, by which the artist
delivers his soul of its burden. In him, as in many
men, there was a great gulf fixed between the hidden
and the open consciousness; so that which could not
come out into the light grew and swelled secretly,
hugely, horribly in the darkness. If Roberts had been
a poet or a painter or a musician; we might have had
a masterpiece. As he was neither: we had a monster.

And I do not at all believe that his years had consciously been vexed by a deep sense of guilt. I gathered in the course of my researches that not long after the flight from Brondesbury, Roberts was made aware of unfortunate incidents in the Watts saga—if we may use this honoured term—which convinced him that there were extenuating circumstances in his offence, and excuses for his wrongdoing. The actual fact had, no doubt, been forgotten or remembered very slightly, rarely, casually, without any sense of grave moment or culpability attached to it; while, all the while, a pageantry of horror was being secretly formed in the hidden places of the man's soul. And at last, after the years of growth and swelling in the darkness; the monster leapt into the light, and with such violence that to the victim it seemed an actual and objective entity.

And, in a sense, it had risen from the black waters of the pool. I was reading a few days ago, in a review of a grave book on psychology, the following very striking sentences:

> The things which we distinguish as qualities or values are inherent in the real environment to make the configuration that they do make with our sensory response to them. There is such a thing as a "sad" landscape, even when we who look at it are feeling jovial; and if we think it is "sad" only because we attribute to it something derived from our own past associations with sadness, Professor Koffka gives us good reason to regard the view as superficial. That is not imputing human attributes to what are described as "demand characters" in the environment, but giving proper recognition to the other end of a nexus, of which only one end is organised in our own mind.

Psychology is, I am sure, a difficult and subtle science, which, perhaps naturally, must be expressed in subtle and difficult language. But so far as I can gather the sense of the passage which I have quoted, it comes to this: that a landscape, a certain configuration of wood, water, height and depth, light and dark, flower and rock, is, in fact, an objective reality, a thing; just as opium and wine are things, not clotted fancies, mere creatures of our make-believe, to which we give a kind of spurious reality and efficacy. The dreams of De Quincey were a synthesis of De Quincey, plus opium; the riotous gaiety of Charles Surface and his friends was the product and result of the wine they had drunk, plus their personalities. So, the profound Professor Koffka—his book is called *Principles of Gestalt Psychology*—insists that the "sadness" which we attribute to a particular landscape is really and efficiently in the landscape and not merely in ourselves; and consequently that the landscape can affect us and produce results in us, in precisely the same manner as drugs and meat and drink affect us in their several ways. Poe, who knew many secrets, knew this, and taught that landscape gardening was as truly a fine art as poetry or painting; since it availed to communicate the mysteries to the human spirit.

And perhaps, Mrs. Morgan of Lanypwll Farm put all this much better in the speech of symbolism, when she murmured about the children of the pool. For if there is a landscape of sadness, there is certainly also a landscape of a horror of darkness and evil; and that black and oily depth, overshadowed with twisted woods, with its growth of foul weeds and its dead trees and leprous boughs, was assuredly potent in terror. To Roberts it was a strong drug, a drug of evocation; the black deep without calling to the black deep within, and summoning the inhabitant thereof to come forth. I made no attempt to extract the legend of that dark place from Mrs. Morgan; and I do not suppose that she would have been communicative if I had questioned her. But it has struck me as possible and even probable that Roberts was by no means the first to experience the power of the pool.

Old stories often turn out to be true. ✛

The Bright Boy

I.

Young Joseph Last, having finally gone down from Oxford, wondered a good deal what he was to do next and for the years following next. He was an orphan from early boyhood, both his parents having died of typhoid within a few days of each other when Joseph was ten years old, and he remembered very little of Dunham, where his father ended a long line of solicitors, practising in the place since 1707. The Lasts had once been very comfortably off. They had intermarried now and again with the gentry of the neighbourhood and did a good deal of the county business, managing estates, collecting rents, officiating as stewards for several manors, living generally in a world of quiet but snug prosperity, rising to their greatest height, perhaps, during the Napoleonic Wars and afterwards. And then they began to decline, not violently at all, but very gently, so that it was many years before they were aware of the process that was going on, slowly, surely. Economists, no doubt, understand very well how the country and the country town gradually became less important soon after the Battle of Waterloo; and the causes of the decay and change which vexed Cobbett so sadly, as he saw, or thought he saw, the life and strength of the land being sucked up to nourish the monstrous excrescence of London. Anyhow, even before the railways came, the assembly rooms of the country towns grew dusty and desolate, the county families ceased to come to their "town houses" for the winter season, and the little theatres, where Mrs. Siddons and Grimaldi had appeared in their divers arts, rarely opened their doors, and the skilled craftsmen, the clock-makers and the furniture-makers and the like began to drift away to the big towns and to the capital city. So it was with Dunham. Naturally the fortunes of the Lasts sank with the fortunes of the town; and there had been speculations which had not turned out well, and people spoke of a heavy loss in foreign bonds. When Joseph's father died, it was found that there was enough to educate the boy and keep him in strictly modest comfort and not much more.

He had his home with an uncle who lived at Blackheath, and after a few years at Mr. Jones's well-known preparatory school, he went to Merchant Taylors and thence to Oxford. He took a decent degree (2nd in Greats) and then began that wondering process as to what he was to do with himself. His income would keep him in chops and steaks, with an occasional roast fowl, and three or four weeks on the Continent once a year. If he liked, he could do nothing, but the prospect seemed tame and boring. He was a very decent classical scholar, with something more than the average schoolmaster's purely technical knowledge of Latin and Greek and professional interest in them: still, schoolmastering seemed his only clear and obvious way of employing himself. But it did not seem likely that he would get a post at any of the big public schools. In the first place, he had rather neglected his opportunities at Oxford. He had gone to one of the obscurer colleges, one of those colleges which you may read about in memoirs dealing with the first years of the nineteenth century as centres and fountains of intellectual life; which for some reason or no reason have fallen into the shadow. There is nothing against them in any way; but nobody speaks of them any more. In one of these places Joseph Last made friends with good fellows, quiet and cheerful men like himself; but they were not, in the technical sense of the term, the "good friends" which a prudent young man makes at the university. One or two had the bar in mind, and two or three the civil service; but most of them were bound for country curacies and country offices. Generally, and for practical purposes, they were "out of it": they were not the men whose whispers could lead to anything profitable in high quarters. And then, again, even in those days, games were getting important in the creditable schools; and there, young Last was very decidedly out of it. He wore spectacles with lenses divided in some queer manner: his athletic disability was final and complete.

He pondered, and thought at first of setting up a small preparatory school in one of the well-to-do London suburbs; a day-school where parents might have their boys well grounded from the very beginning, for comparatively modest fees, and yet have their upbringing in their own hands. It had often struck Last that it was a barbarous business to send a little chap of seven or eight away from the comfortable and affectionate habit of his home to a strange place among cold strangers; to bare boards, an inky smell, and grammar on an empty stomach in the morning. But consulting with Jim Newman of his old college, he was warned by that sage to drop his scheme and leave it on the ground. Newman pointed out in the first place that there was no money in teaching unless it was combined with hotel-keeping. That, he said, was all right, and more than all right; and he surmised that many people who kept hotels in the ordinary way would give a good deal to practise their art and mystery under housemaster's rules. "You needn't pay so very much for your furniture, you know. You don't want to make the boys into young sybarites. Besides, there's nothing a healthy-minded boy hates more than stuffiness: what he likes is clean fresh air and plenty of it. And, you know, old chap, fresh air is cheap enough. And then with the food, there's apt to be trouble in the ordinary hotel if it's uneatable; but in the sort of hotel we're talking of, a little accident with the beef or mutton affords a very valuable opportunity for the exercise of the virtue of self-denial."

Last listened to all this with a mournful grin.

"You seem to know all about it," he said. "Why don't you go in for it yourself?"

"I couldn't keep my tongue in my cheek. Besides, I don't think it's fair sport. I'm going out to India in the autumn. What about pig-sticking?"

"And there's another thing," he went on after a meditative pause. "That notion of yours about a day prep school is rotten. The parents wouldn't say thank you for letting them keep their kids at home when they're all small and young. Some people go so far as to say that the chief purpose of schools is to allow parents a good excuse for getting rid of their children. That's nonsense. Most fathers and mothers are very fond of their children and like to have them about the house; when they're young, at all events. But somehow or other, they've got it into their heads that strange schoolmasters know more about bringing up a small boy than his own people; and there it is. So, on all counts, drop that scheme of yours."

Last thought it over, and looked about him in the scholastic world, and came to the conclusion that Newman was right. For two or three years he took charge of reading parties in the long vacation. In the winter he found occupation in the coaching of backward boys, in preparing boys not so backward for scholarship examinations; and his little text-book, *Beginning Greek*, was found quite useful in lower school. He did pretty well on the whole, though the work began to bore him sadly, and such money as he earned, added to his income, enabled him to live in the way he liked, comfortably enough. He had a couple of rooms in one of the streets going down from the Strand to the river, for which he paid a pound a week, had bread and cheese and odds and ends for lunch, with beer from his own barrel in the cellar, and dined simply but sufficiently now in one, now in another of the snug taverns which then abounded in the quarter. And, now and again, once a month or so, perhaps, instead of the tavern dinners, there was the play at the Vaudeville or the Olympic, the Globe or the Strand, with supper and something hot to follow. The evening might turn into a little party: old Oxford friends would look him up in his rooms between six and seven; Zouch would gather from the Temple and Medwin from Buckingham Street, and possibly Garraway, taking the Yellow Albion bus, would descend from his remote steep in the northern parts of London, would knock at 14, Mowbray Street, and demand pipes, porter, and the pit at a good play. And, on rare occasions, another member of the little society, Noel, would turn up. Noel lived at Turnham Green in a red brick house which was then thought merely old-fashioned, which would now—but it was pulled down long ago—be distinguished as choice Queen Anne or Early Georgian. He lived there with his father, a retired official of the British Museum, and through a man whom he had known at Oxford, he had made some way in literary journalism, contributing regularly to an important weekly paper. Hence the consequence of his occasional descents on Buckingham Street, Mowbray Street, and the Temple. Noel, as in some sort a man of letters, or, at least, a professional journalist, was a member of Blacks' Club, which in those days had exiguous premises in Maiden Lane. Noel would go round the haunts of his friends, and gather them to stout and oysters, and guide them into some neighbouring theatre pit, whence they viewed excellent acting and a cheerful, nonsensical play, enjoyed both, and were ready for supper at the Tavistock. This done, Noel would lead the party to Blacks', where they, very likely, saw some of the actors who had entertained them earlier in the evening, and Noel's friends, the journalists and men of letters, with a painter and a black-and-white man here and there. Here, Last enjoyed himself very much, more especially among the actors, who seemed to him more genial than the literary men. He became especially friendly with one of the players, old Meredith Mandeville, who had talked with the elder Kean, was reliable in the smaller Shakespearean parts, and had engaging tales to tell of early days in county circuits. "You had nine shillings a week to begin with. When you got to fifteen shillings you gave your landlady eight or nine shillings, and had the rest to play with. You felt a prince. And the county families often used to come and see us in the Green Room: most agreeable."

With this friendly old gentleman, whose placid and genial serenity was not marred at all by incalculable quantities of gin, Last loved to converse, getting glimpses of a life strangely remote from his own: vagabondage, insecurity, hard times, and jollity; and against it all as a background, the lighted murmur of the stage, voices uttering tremendous things, and the sense of moving in two worlds. The old man, by his own account, had not been eminently prosperous or successful, and yet he had relished his life, and drew humours from its disadvantages, and made hard times seem an adventure. Last used to express his envy of the player's career, dwelling on the dull insignificance of his own labours, which, he said, were a matter of tinkering small boys' brains, teaching older boys the tricks of the examiners, and generally doing things that didn't matter.

"It's no more education than bricklaying is architecture," he said one night. "And there's no fun in it."

Old Mandeville, on his side, listened with interest to these revelations of a world as strange and unknown to him as the life of the floats was to the tutor. Broadly speaking, he knew nothing of any books but play books. He had heard, no doubt, of things called examinations, as most people have heard of Red Indian initiations; but to him one was as remote as the other. It was interesting and strange to him to be sitting at Blacks' and actually talking to a decent young fellow who was seriously engaged in this queer business. And there were—Last noted with amazement—points at which their two circles touched, or so it seemed. The tutor, wishing to be agreeable, began one night to talk about the origins of *King Lear*. The actor found himself listening to Celtic legends which to him sounded incomprehensible nonsense. And when it came to the Knight who fought the King of Fairyland for the hand of Cordelia till Doomsday, he broke in: "Lear is a pill; there's no doubt of that. You're too young to have seen Barry O'Brien's Lear: magnificent. The part has been attempted since his day. But it has never been played. I have depicted the Fool myself, and, I must say, not without some need of applause. I remember once at Stafford . . ." and Last was content to let him tell his tale, which ended, oddly enough, with a bullock's heart for supper.

But one night when Last was grumbling, as he often did, about the fragmentary, desultory, and altogether unsatisfactory nature of his occupation, the old man interrupted him in a wholly unexpected vein.

"It is possible," he began, "mark you, I say possible, that I may be the means of alleviating the tedium of your lot. I was calling some days ago on a cousin of mine, a Miss Lucy Pilliner, a very agreeable woman. She has a considerable knowledge of the world, and, I hope you will forgive the liberty, but I mentioned in the course of our conversation that I had lately became acquainted with a young gentleman of considerable scholastic distinction, who was somewhat dissatisfied with the too abrupt and frequent entrances and exits of his present tutorial employment. It struck me that my cousin received these remarks with a certain reflective interest, but I was not prepared to receive this letter."

Mandeville handed Last the letter. It began: "My dear Ezekiel," and Last noted out of the corner of his eye a glance from the actor which pleaded for silence and secrecy on this point. The letter went on to say in a manner almost as dignified as Mandeville's, that the writer had been thinking over the circumstances of the young tutor, as related by her cousin in the course of their most agreeable conversation of Friday last, and she was inclined to think that she knew of an educational position shortly available in a private family, which would be of a more permanent and satisfactory nature. "Should your friend feel interested," Miss Pilliner ended, "I should be glad if he would communicate with me, with a view to a meeting being arranged, at which the matter could be discussed with more exact particulars."

"And what do you think of it?" said Mandeville, as Last returned Miss Pilliner's letter.

For a moment Last hesitated. There is an attraction and also a repulsion in the odd and the improbable, and Last doubted whether educational work obtained through an actor at Blacks' and a lady at Islington—he had seen the name at the top of the letter—could be altogether solid or desirable. But brighter thoughts prevailed, and he assured Mandeville that he would be only too glad to go thoroughly into the matter, thanking him very warmly for his interest. The old man nodded benignly, gave him the letter again that he might take down Miss Pilliner's address, and suggested an immediate note asking for an appointment.

"And now," he said, "despite the carping objections of the Moody Prince, I propose to drink your jocund health to-night."

And he wished Last all the good luck in the world with hearty kindliness.

In a couple of days Miss Pilliner presented her compliments to Mr. Joseph Last and begged him to do her the favour of calling on her on a date three days ahead, at noon, "if neither day nor hour were in any way incompatible with his convenience." They might then, she proceeded, take advantage of the occasion to discuss a certain proposal, the nature of which, she believed, had been indicated to Mr. Last by her good cousin, Mr. Meredith Mandeville.

Corunna Square, where Miss Pilliner lived, was a small, almost a tiny, square in the remoter parts of Islington. Its two-storied houses of dim, yellowish brick were fairly covered with vines and clematis and all manner of creepers. In front of the houses were small paled gardens, gaily flowering, and the square enclosure held little else besides a venerable, wide-spreading mulberry, far older than the buildings about it. Miss Pilliner lived in the quietest corner of the square. She welcomed Last with some sort of compromise between a bow and a curtsy, and begged him to be seated in an upright arm-chair, upholstered in horse-hair. Miss Pilliner, he noted, looked about sixty, and was, perhaps, a little older. She was spare, upright, and composed; and yet one might have suspected a lurking whimsicality. Then, while the weather was discussed, Miss Pilliner offered a choice of port or sherry, sweet biscuits or plum cake. And so to the business of the day.

"My cousin, Mr. Mandeville, informed me," she began, "of a young friend of great scholastic ability, who was, nevertheless, dissatisfied with the somewhat casual and occasional nature of his employment. By a singular coincidence, I had received a letter a day or two before from a friend of mine, a Mrs. Marsh. She is, in fact, a distant connection, some sort of cousin, I suppose, but not being a Highlander or a Welshwoman, I really cannot say how many times removed. She was a lovely creature; she is still a handsome woman. Her name was Manning, Arabella Manning, and what possessed her to marry Mr. Marsh I really cannot say. I only saw the man once, and I thought him her inferior in every respect, and considerably older. However, she declares that he is a devoted husband and an excellent person in every respect. They first met, odd as it must seem, in Pekin, where Arabella was governess in one of the legation families. Mr. Marsh, I was given to understand, represented highly important commercial interests at the capital of the Flowery Land, and being introduced to my connection, a mutual attraction seems to have followed. Arabella Manning resigned her position in the attaché's family, and the marriage was solemnized in due course. I received this intelligence nine years ago in a letter from Arabella, dated at Pekin, and my relative ended by saying that she feared it would be impossible to furnish an address for an immediate reply, as Mr. Marsh was about to set out on a mission of an extremely urgent nature on behalf of his firm, involving a great deal of travelling and frequent changes of address. I suffered a good deal of uneasiness on Arabella's account, it seemed such an unsettled way of life, and so unhomelike. However, a friend of mine who is in the City assured me that there was nothing unusual in the circumstances, and that there was no cause for alarm. Still, as the years went on, and I received no further communication from my cousin, I made up my mind that she had probably contracted some tropical disease which had carried her off, and that Mr. Marsh had heartlessly neglected to communicate to me the intelligence of the sad event. But a month ago, almost to the day"—Miss Pilliner referred to an almanac on the table beside her—"I was astonished and delighted to receive a letter from Arabella. She wrote from one of the most luxurious and exclusive hotels in the West End of London, announcing the return of her husband and herself to their native land after many years of wandering. Mr. Marsh's active concern in business had, it appeared, at length terminated in a highly prosperous and successful manner, and he was now in negotiation for the purchase of a small estate in the country, where he hoped to spend the remainder of his days in peaceful retirement."

Miss Pilliner paused and replenished Last's glass.

"I am so sorry," she continued, "to trouble you with this long narrative, which, I am sure, must be a sad trial of your patience. But, as you will see presently, the circumstances are a little out of the common, and as you are, I trust, to have a particular interest in them, I think it is only right that you should be fully informed—fair and square, and all above board, as my poor father used to say in his bluff manner.

"Well, Mr. Last, I received, as I have said, this letter from Arabella with its extremely gratifying intelligence. As you may guess, I was very much relieved to hear that all had turned out so felicitously. At the end of her letter, Arabella begged me to come and see them at Billing's Hotel, saying that her husband was most anxious to have the pleasure of meeting me."

Miss Pilliner went to a drawer in a writing-table by the window and took out a letter.

"Arabella was always considerate. She says: 'I know that you have always lived very quietly, and are not accustomed to the turmoil of fashionable London. But you need not be alarmed. Billing's Hotel is no bustling modern caravanserai. Everything is very quiet, and, besides, we have our own small suite of apartments. Herbert—her husband, Mr. Last—positively insists on your paying us a visit, and you must not disappoint us. If next Thursday, the 22nd, suits you, a carriage shall be sent at four o'clock to bring you to the hotel, and will take you back to Corunna Square, after you have joined us in a little dinner."

"Very kind, most considerate; don't you agree with me, Mr. Last? But look at the postscript."

Last took the letter, and read in a tight, neat script: "PS. We have a wonderful piece of news for you. It is too good to write, so I shall keep it for our meeting."

Last handed back Mrs. Marsh's letter. Miss Pilliner's long and ceremonious approach was lulling him into a mild stupor; he wondered faintly when she would come to the point, and what the point would be like when she came to it, and, chiefly, what on earth this rather dull family history could have to do with him.

Miss Pilliner proceeded.

"Naturally, I accepted so kindly and urgent an invitation. I was anxious to see Arabella once more after her long absence, and I was glad to have the opportunity of forming my own judgment as to her husband, of whom I knew absolutely nothing. And then, Mr. Last, I must confess that I am not deficient in that spirit of curiosity, which gentlemen have scarcely numbered with female virtues. I longed to be made partaker in the wonderful news which Arabella had promised to impart on our meeting, and I wasted many hours in speculating as to its nature.

"The day came. A neat brougham with its attendant footman arrived at the appointed hour, and I was driven in smooth luxury to Billing's Hotel in Manners Street, Mayfair. There a majordomo led the way to the suite of apartments on the first floor occupied by Mr. and Mrs. Marsh. I will not waste your valuable time, Mr. Last, by expiating on the rich but quiet luxury of their apartments; I will merely mention that my relative assured me that the Sevres ornaments in their drawing-room had been valued at nine hundred guineas. I found Arabella still a beautiful woman, but

I could not help seeing that the tropical countries in which she had lived for so many years had taken their toll of her once resplendent beauty; there was a weariness, a lassitude in her appearance and demeanour which I was distressed to observe. As to her husband, Mr. Marsh, I am aware that to form an unfavourable judgment after an acquaintance which has only lasted a few hours is both uncharitable and unwise; and I shall not soon forget the discourse which dear Mr. Venn delivered at Emmanuel Church on the very Sunday after my visit to my relative: it really seemed, and I confess it with shame, that Mr. Venn had my own case in mind, and felt it his bounden duty to warn me while it was yet time. Still, I must say that I did not take at all to Mr. Marsh. I really can't say why. To me he was most polite; he could not have been more so. He remarked more than once on the extreme pleasure it gave him to meet at last one of whom he had heard so much from his dear Bella; he trusted that now his wandering days were over, the pleasure might be frequently repeated; he omitted nothing that the most genial courtesy might suggest. And yet, I cannot say that the impression I received was a favourable one. However; I dare say that I was mistaken."

There was a pause. Last was resigned. The point of the long story seemed to recede into some far distance, into vanishing prospective.

"There was nothing definite?" he suggested.

"No; nothing definite. I may have thought that I detected a lack of candour, a hidden reserve behind all the generosity of Mr. Marsh's expressions. Still; I hope I was mistaken.

"But I am forgetting in these trivial and I trust erroneous observations, the sole matter that is of consequence; to you, at least, Mr. Last. Soon after my arrival, before Mr. Marsh had appeared, Arabella confided to me her great piece of intelligence. Her marriage had been blessed by offspring. Two years after her union with Mr. Marsh, a child had been born, a boy. The birth took place at a town in South America, Santiago de Chile—I have verified the place in my atlas—where Mr. Marsh's visit had been more protracted than usual. Fortunately, an English doctor was available, and the little fellow throve from the first, and as Arabella, his proud mother, boasted, was now a beautiful little boy, both handsome and intelligent to a remarkable degree. Naturally, I asked to see the child, but Arabella said that he was not in the hotel with them. After a few days it was thought that the dense and humid air of London was not suiting little Henry very well; and he had been sent with a nurse to a resort in the Isle of Thanet, where he was reported to be in the best of health and spirits.

"And now, Mr. Last, after this tedious but necessary preamble, we arrive at that point where you, I trust, may be interested. In any case, as you may suppose, the life which the exigencies of business compelled the Marshes to lead, involving as it did almost continual travel, would have been little favourable to a course of systematic education for the child. But this obstacle apart, I gathered that Mr. Marsh holds very strong views as to the folly of premature instruction. He declared to me his conviction that many fine minds had been grievously injured by being forced to undergo the process of early stimulation; and he pointed out that, by the nature of the case, those placed in charge of very young children were not persons of the highest acquirements and the keenest intelligence. 'As you will readily agree, Miss Pilliner,' he remarked to me, 'great scholars are not employed to teach infants their alphabet, and it is not likely that the mysteries of the multiplication table will be imparted by a master of mathematics.' In consequence, he urged, the young and budding intelligence is brought into contact with dull and inferior minds, and the damage may well be irreparable."

There was much more, but gradually light began to dawn on the dazed man. Mr. Marsh had kept the virgin intelligence of his son Henry undisturbed and uncorrupted by inferior and incompetent culture. The boy, it was judged, was now ripe for true education, and Mr. and Mrs. Marsh had begged Miss Pilliner to make enquiries, and to find, if she could, a scholar who would undertake the whole charge of little Henry's mental upbringing. If both parties were satisfied, the engagement would be for seven years at least, and the appointments, as Miss Pilliner called the salary, would begin with five hundred pounds a year, rising by an annual increment of fifty pounds. References, particulars of university distinctions would be required: Mr. Marsh, long absent from England, was ready to proffer the names of his bankers. Miss Pilliner was quite sure, however, that Mr. Last might consider himself engaged, if the position appealed to him.

Last thanked Miss Pilliner profoundly. He told her that he would like a couple of days in which to think the matter over. He would then write to her, and she would put him into communication with Mr. Marsh. And so he went away from Corunna Square in a mood of great bewilderment and doubt. Unquestionably, the position had many advantages. The pay was very good. And he would be well lodged and well fed. The people were wealthy, and Miss Pilliner had assured him: "You will have no cause to complain of your entertainment." And from the educational point of view, it would certainly be an improvement on the work he had been doing since he left the university. He had been an odd-job man, a tinker, a patcher, a cobbler of other people's work; here was a chance to show that he was a master craftsman. Very few people, if any, in the teaching profession had ever enjoyed such an opportunity as this. Even the sixth-form masters in the big public schools must sometimes groan at having to underpin and relay the bad foundations of the fifth and fourth. He was to begin at the beginning, with no false work to hamper him: "from A B C to Plato, Aeschylus, and Aristotle," he murmured to himself. Undoubtedly it was a big chance.

And on the other side? Well, he would have to give up London, and he had grown fond of the homely, cheerful London that he knew; his comfortable rooms in Mowbray Street, quiet enough down by the unfrequented Embankment, and yet but a minute or two from the ringing Strand. Then there were the meetings with the old Oxford friends, the nights at the theatre, the snug taverns with their curtained boxes, and their good chops and steaks and stout, and chimes of midnight and after, heard in cordial company at Blacks': all these would have to go. Miss Pilliner had spoken of Mr. Marsh as looking for some place a considerable distance from town, "in the real country." He had his eye, she said, on a house on the Welsh border, which he thought of taking furnished, with the option of buying, if he eventually found it suited him. You couldn't look up old friends in London and get back the same night, if you lived somewhere on the Welsh border. Still, there would be the holidays, and a great deal might be done in the holidays.

And yet; there was still debate and doubt within his mind, as he sat eating his bread and cheese and potted meat, and drinking his beer in his sitting-room in peaceful Mowbray Street. He was influenced, he thought, by Miss Pilliner's evident dislike of Mr. Marsh, and though Miss Pilliner talked in the manner of Dr. Johnson, he had a feeling that, like a lady of the Doctor's own day, she had a bottom of good sense. Evidently she did not trust Mr. Marsh overmuch. Yet, what can the most cunning swindler do to his resident tutor? Give him cold mutton for dinner or forget to pay his salary? In either case, the remedy was simple: the resident tutor would swiftly cease to reside, and go back to London, and not be much the worse. After all, Last reflected, a man can't compel his son's tutor to invest in Uruguayan silver or Java spices or any other fallacious commercial undertaking, so what mattered the supposed trickiness of Marsh to him?

But again, when all had been summed up and considered, for and against; there was a vague objection remaining. To oppose this, Last could bring no argument, since it was without form of words, shapeless, and mutable as a cloud.

However, when the next morning came, there came with it a couple of letters inviting him to cram two young dunderheads with facts and figures and verbs in *mi*. The prospect was so terribly distasteful that he wrote to Miss Pilliner directly after breakfast, enclosing his college testimonials and certain other commendatory letters he had in his desk. In due course, he had an interview with Mr. Marsh at Billing's Hotel. On the whole, each was well enough pleased with the other. Last found Marsh a lean, keen, dark man in later middle age; there was a grizzle in his black hair above the ears, and wrinkles seamed his face about the eyes. His eyebrows were heavy, and there was a hint of a threat in his jaw, but the smile with which he welcomed Last lit up his grimmish features into a genial warmth. There was an oddity about his accent and his tone in speaking; something foreign, perhaps? Last remembered that he had journeyed about the world for many years, and supposed that the echoes of many languages sounded in his speech. His manner and address were certainly suave, but Last had no prejudice against suavity, rather, he cherished a liking for the decencies of common intercourse. Still, no doubt, Marsh was not the kind of man Miss Pilliner was accustomed to meet in Corunna Square society or among Mr. Venn's congregation. She probably suspected him of having been a pirate.

And Mr. Marsh on his side was delighted with Last. As appeared from a letter addressed by him to Miss Pilliner—"or, may I venture to say, Cousin Lucy?"—Mr. Last was exactly the type of man he and Arabella had hoped to secure through Miss Pilliner's recommendation. They did not want to give their boy into the charge of a flashy man of the world with a substratum of learning. Mr. Last was, it was evident, a quiet and unworldly scholar, more at home among books than among men; the very tutor Arabella and himself had desired for their little son. Mr. Marsh was profoundly grateful to Miss Pilliner for the great service she had rendered to Arabella, to himself, and to Henry.

And, indeed, as Mr. Meredith Mandeville would have said, Last looked the part. No doubt, the spectacles helped to create the remote, retired, Dominie Sampson impression.

In a week's time it was settled, he was to begin his duties. Mr. Marsh wrote a handsome cheque, "to defray any little matters of outfit, travelling expenses, and so forth; nothing to do with your salary." He was to take train to a certain large town in the west, and there he would be met and driven to the house, where Mrs. Marsh and his pupil were already established—"beautiful country, Mr. Last; I am sure you will appreciate it."

There was a famous farewell gathering of the old friends. Zouch and Medwin, Garraway and Noel came from near and far. There was grilled sole before the mighty steak, and a roast fowl after it. They had decided that as it was the last time, perhaps, they would not go to the play, but sit and talk about the mahogany. Zouch, who was understood to be the ruler of the feast, had conferred with the head waiter, and when the cloth was removed, a rare and curious port was solemnly set before them. They talked of the old days when they were up at Wells together, pretended—though they knew better—that the undergraduate who had cut his own father in Piccadilly was a friend of theirs, retold jokes that must have been older than the wine, related tales of Moll and Meg, and the famous history of Melcombe, who screwed up the dean in his own rooms. And then there was the affair of the Poses Plastiques. Certain lewd fellows, as one of the dons of Wells College expressed it, had procured scandalous figures from the wax-work booth at the fair, and had disposed them by night about the fountain in the college garden in such a manner that their scandal was shamefully increased. The perpetrators of this infamy had never been discovered: the five friends looked knowingly at each other, pursed their lips, and passed the port.

The old wine and the old stories blended into a mood of gentle meditation; and then, at the right moment, Noel carried them off to Blacks' and new company. Last sought out old Mandeville and related, with warm gratitude, the happy issue of his intervention.

The chimes sounded, and they all went their several ways.

II.

Though Joseph Last was by no means a miracle of observation and deduction, he was not altogether the simpleton among his books that Mr. Marsh had judged him. It was not so very long before a certain uneasiness beset him in his new employment.

At first everything had seemed very well. Mr. Marsh had been right in thinking that he would be charmed by the scene in which the White House was set. It stood, terraced on a hill-side, high above a grey and silver river winding in esses through a lonely, lovely valley. Above it, to the east, was a vast and shadowy and ancient wood, climbing to the high ridge of the hill, and descending by height and by depth of green to the level meadows and to the sea. And, standing on the highest point of the wood above the White House, Last looked westward between the boughs and saw the lands across the river, and saw the country rise and fall in billow upon billow to the huge dim wall of the mountain, blue in the distance, and white farms shining in the sun on its vast side. Here was a man in a new world. There had been no such country as this about Dunham in the Midlands, or in the surroundings of Blackheath or Oxford; and he had visited nothing like it on his reading parties. He stood amazed, enchanted under the green shade, beholding a great wonder. Close beside him the well bubbled from the grey rocks, rising out of the heart of the hill.

And in the White House, the conditions of life were altogether pleasant. He had been struck by the dark beauty of Mrs. Marsh, who was clearly, as Miss Pilliner had told him, a great many years younger than her husband. And he noted also that effect which her cousin had ascribed to years of living in the tropics, though he would hardly have called it weariness or lassitude. It was something stranger than that; there was the mark of flame upon her, but Last did not know whether it were the flame of the sun, or the stranger fires of places that she had entered, perhaps long ago.

But the pupil, little Henry, was altogether a surprise and a delight. He looked rather older than seven, but Last judged that this impression was not so much due to his height or physical make as to the bright alertness and intelligence of his glance. The tutor had dealt with many little boys, though with none so young as Henry; and he had found them as a whole a stodgy and podgy race, with faces that recorded a fixed abhorrence of learning and a resolution to learn as little as possible. Last was never surprised at this customary expression. It struck him as eminently natural. He knew that all elements are damnably dull and difficult. He wondered why it was inexorably appointed that the unfortunate human creature should pass a great portion of its life from the very beginning in doing things that it detested; but so it was, and now for the syntax of the optative.

But there were no such obstinate entrenchments in the face or the manner of Henry Marsh. He was a handsome boy, who looked brightly and spoke brightly, and evidently did not regard his tutor as a hostile force that had been brought against him. He was what some people would have called, oddly enough, old-fashioned; childlike, but not at all childish, with now and then a whimsical turn of phrase more suggestive of a humorous man than a little boy. This older habit was no doubt to be put down partly to the education of travel, the spectacle of the changing scene and the changing looks of men and things, but very largely to the fact that he had always been with his father and mother, and knew nothing of the company of children of his own age.

"Henry has had no playmates," his father explained. "He's had to be content with his mother and myself. It couldn't be helped. We've been on the move all the time; on shipboard or staying at cosmopolitan hotels for a few weeks, and then on the road again. The little chap had no chance of making any small friends."

And the consequence was, no doubt, that lack of childishness that Last had noted. It was, probably, a pity that it was so. Childishness, after all, was a wonder world, and Henry seemed to know nothing of it:

he had lost what might be, perhaps, as valuable as any other part of human experience, and he might find the lack of it as he grew older. Still, there it was; and Last ceased to think of these possibly fanciful deprivations, when he began to teach the boy, as he had promised himself, from the very beginning. Not quite from the beginning; the small boy confessed with a disarming grin that he had taught himself to read a little: "But please, sir, don't tell my father, as I know he wouldn't like it. You see, my father and mother had to leave me alone sometimes, and it was so dull, and I thought it would be such fun if I learnt to read books all by myself."

Here, thought Last, is a lesson for schoolmasters. Can learning be made a desirable secret, an excellent sport, instead of a horrible penance? He made a mental note, and set about the work before him. He found an extraordinary aptitude, a quickness in grasping his indications and explanations such as he had never known before—"not in boys twice his age, or three times his age, for the matter of that," as he reflected. This child, hardly removed from strict infancy, had something almost akin to genius—so the happy tutor was inclined to believe. Now and again, with his, "Yes, sir, I see. And then, of course . . ." he would veritably take the coming words out of Last's mouth, and anticipate what was, no doubt, logically the next step in the demonstration. But Last had not been accustomed to pupils who anticipated anything—save the hour for putting the books back on the shelf. And above all, the instructor was captured by the eager and intense curiosity of the instructed. He was like a man reading *The Moonstone*, or some such sensational novel, and unable to put the book down till he had read to the very last page and found out the secret. This small boy brought just this spirit of insatiable curiosity to every subject put before him. "I wish I had taught him to read," thought Last to himself. "I have no doubt he would have regarded the alphabet as we regard those entrancing and mysterious cyphers in Edgar Allan Poe's stories. And, after all, isn't that the right and rational way of looking at the alphabet?"

And then he went on to wonder whether curiosity, often regarded as a failing, almost a vice, is not, in fact, one of the greatest virtues of the spirit of man, the key to all knowledge and all the mysteries, the very sense of the secret that must be discovered.

With one thing and another: with this treasure of a pupil, with the enchantment of the strange and beautiful country about him, and with the extreme kindness and consideration shown him by Mr. and Mrs. Marsh, Last was in rich clover. He wrote to his friends in town, telling them of his happy experiences, and Zouch and Noel, meeting by chance at the Sun, the Dog, or the Triple Tun, discussed their friend's felicity.

"Proud of the pup," said Zouch.

"And pleased with the prospect," responded Noel, thinking of Last's lyrics about the woods and the waters, and the scene of the White House. "Still, *timeo Hesperides et dona ferentes.* I mistrust the west. As one of its own people said, it is a land of enchantment and illusion. You never know what may happen next. It is a fortunate thing that Shakespeare was born within the safety line. If Stratford had been twenty or thirty miles farther west . . . I don't like to think of it. I am quite sure that only fairy gold is dug from Welsh gold-mines. And you know what happens to that."

Meanwhile, far from the lamps and rumours of the Strand, Last continued happy in his outland territory, under the great wood. But before long he received a shock. He was strolling in the terraced garden one afternoon between tea and dinner, his work done for the day; and feeling inclined for tobacco with repose, drifted towards the stone summer-house—or, perhaps, gazebo—that stood on the verge of the lawn in a coolness of dark ilex-trees. Here one could sit and look down on the silver winding of the river, crossed by a grey bridge of ancient stone. Last was about to settle down when he noticed a book on the table before him. He took it up, and glanced into it, and drew in his breath, and turning over a few more pages, sank aghast upon the bench. Mr. Marsh had always deplored his ignorance of books. "I knew how to read and write and not much more," he would say, "when I was thrown into business—at the bottom of the stairs. And I've been so busy ever since that I'm afraid it's too late now to make up for lost time." Indeed, Last had noted that though Marsh usually spoke carefully enough, perhaps too carefully, he was apt to lapse in the warmth of conversation: he would talk of "fax," meaning "facts." And yet, it seemed, he had not only found time for reading, but had acquired sufficient scholarship to make out the Latin of a terrible Renaissance treatise, not generally known even to collectors of such things. Last had heard of the book; and the few pages he had glanced at showed him that it thoroughly deserved its very bad character.

It was a disagreeable surprise. He admitted freely to himself that his employer's morals were no business of his. But why should the man trouble to tell lies? Last remembered queer old Miss Pilliner's account of her impressions of him; she had detected "a lack of candour," something reserved behind a polite front of cordiality. Miss Pilliner was, certainly, an acute woman: there was an undoubted lack of candour about Marsh.

Last left the wretched volume on the summer-house table, and walked up and down the garden, feeling a good deal perturbed. He knew he was awkward at dinner, and said he felt a bit seedy, inclined to a headache. Marsh was bland and pleasant as usual, and Mrs. Marsh sympathized with Last. She had hardly slept at all last night, she complained, and felt heavy and tired. She thought there was thunder in the air. Last, admiring her beauty, confessed again that Miss Pilliner had been right. Apart from her fatigue of the moment, there was a certain tropical languor about her, something of still, burning nights and the odour of strange flowers.

Marsh brought out a very special brandy which he administered with the black coffee; he said it would do both the invalids good, and that he would keep them company. Indeed, Last confessed to himself that he felt considerably more at ease after the good dinner, the good wine, and the rare brandy. It was humiliating, perhaps, but it was impossible to deny the power of the stomach. He went to his room early and tried to convince himself that the duplicity of Marsh was no affair of his. He found an innocent, or almost innocent explanation of it before he had finished his last pipe, sitting at the open window, hearing faintly the wash of the river and gazing towards the dim lands beyond it.

"Here," he meditated, "we have a modified form of Bounderby's Disease. Bounderby said that he began life as a wretched, starved, neglected little outcast. Marsh says that he was made into an office boy or something of the sort before he had time to learn anything. Bounderby lied, and no doubt Marsh lies. It is the trick of wealthy men; to magnify their late achievements by magnifying their early disadvantages."

By the time he went to sleep he had almost decided that the young Marsh had been to a good grammar school, and had done well.

The next morning, Last awoke almost at ease again. It was no doubt a pity that Marsh indulged in a subtle and disingenuous form of boasting, and his taste in books was certainly deplorable: but he must look after that himself. And the boy made amends for all. He showed so clean a grasp of the English sentence, that Last thought he might well begin Latin before very long. He mentioned this one night at dinner, looking at Marsh with a certain humorous intention. But Marsh gave no sign that the dart had pricked him.

"That shows I was right," he remarked. "I've always said there's no greater mistake than forcing learning on children before they're fit to take it in. People will do it, and in nine cases out of ten the children's heads are muddled for the rest of their lives. You see how it is with Henry; I've kept him away from books up to now, and you see for yourself that I've lost him no time. He's ripe for learning, and I shouldn't wonder if he got ahead better in six months than the ordinary, early-crammed child would in six years."

It might be so, Last thought, but on the whole he was inclined to put down the boy's swift progress rather to his own exceptional intelligence than to his father's system, or no system. And in any case, it was a great pleasure to teach such a boy. And his application to his books had certainly no injurious effect on his spirits. There was not much society within easy reach of the White House, and, besides, people did not know whether the Marshes were to settle down or whether they were transient visitors: they were chary of paying their calls while there was this uncertainty. However, the rector had called; first of all the rector and his wife, she cheery, good-humoured and chatty; he somewhat dim and vague. It was understood that the rector, a high wrangler in his day, divided his time between his garden and the invention of a flying machine. He had the character of being slightly eccentric. He came not again, but Mrs. Winslow would drive over by the forest road in the governess car with her two children; Nancy, a pretty fair girl of seventeen, and Ted, a boy of eleven or twelve, of that type which Last catalogued as "stodgy and podgy," broad and thick set, with bulgy cheeks and eyes, and something of the determined expression of a young bulldog. After tea Nancy would organize games for the two boys in the garden and join in them herself with apparent relish. Henry, who had known few companions besides his parents, and had probably never played a game of any kind, squealed with delight, ran here and there and everywhere, hid behind the summerhouse and popped out from the screen of the French beans with the greatest gusto, and Ted Winslow joined in with an air of protest. He was on his holidays, and his expression signified that all that sort of thing was only fit for girls and kids. Last was delighted to see Henry so ready and eager to be amused; after all, he had something of the child in him. He seemed a little uncomfortable when Nancy Winslow took him on her knee after the sports were over; he was evidently fearful of Ted Winslow's scornful eye. Indeed, the young bulldog looked as if he feared that his character would be compromised by associating with so manifest and confessed a kid. The next time Mrs. Winslow took tea at the White House, Ted had a diplomatic headache and stayed at home. But Nancy found games that two could play, and she and Henry were heard screaming with joy all over the gardens. Henry wanted to show Nancy a wonderful well that he had discovered in the forest; it came, he said, from under the roots of a great yew-tree. But Mrs. Marsh seemed to think that they might get lost.

Last had got over the uncomfortable incident of that villainous book in the summer-house. Writing to Noel, he had remarked that he feared his employer was a bit of an old rascal in some respects, but all right so far as he was concerned; and there it was. He got on with his job and minded his own business. Yet, now and again, his doubtful uneasiness about the man was renewed. There was a bad business at a hamlet a couple of miles away, where a girl of twelve or thirteen, coming home after dusk from a visit to a neighbour, had been set on in the wood and very vilely misused. The unfortunate child, it would appear, had been left by the scoundrel in the black dark of the forest, at some distance from the path she must have taken on her way home. A man who had been drinking late at the Fox and Hounds heard crying and screaming, "like someone in a fit," as he expressed it, and found the girl in a terrible state, and in a terrible state she had remained ever since. She was quite unable to describe the person who had so shamefully maltreated her; the shock had left her beside herself; she cried out once that something had come behind her in the dark, but she could say no more, and it was hopeless to try to get her to describe a person that, most likely, she had not even seen. Naturally; this very horrible story made something of a feature in the local paper, and one night, as Last and Marsh were sitting smoking after dinner, the tutor spoke of the affair; said something about the contrast between the peace and beauty and quiet of the scene and the villainous crime that had been done hard by. He was surprised to find that Marsh grew at once ill at ease. He rose from his chair and walked up and down the room, muttering "horrible business, shameful business"; and when he sat down again, with the light full on him, Last saw the face of a frightened man. The hand that Marsh laid on the table was twitching uneasily; he beat with his foot on the floor as he tried to bring his lips to order, and there was a dreadful fear in his eyes.

Last was shocked and astonished at the effect he had produced with a few conventional phrases. Nervously, willing to tide over a painful situation, he began to utter something even more conventional to the effect that the loveliness of external nature had never conferred immunity from crime, or some stuff to the same inane purpose. But Marsh, it was clear, was not to be soothed by anything of the kind. He started again from his chair and struck his hand upon the table, with a fierce gesture of denial and refusal.

"Please, Mr. Last, let it be. Say no more about it. It has upset Mrs. Marsh and myself very much indeed. It horrifies us to think that we have brought our boy here, to this peaceful place as we thought, only to expose him to the contagion of this dreadful affair. Of course we have given the servants strict orders not to say a word about it in Henry's presence; but you know what servants are, and what very sharp ears children have. A chance word or two may take root in a child's mind and contaminate his whole nature. It is, really, a very terrible thought. You must have noticed how distressed Mrs. Marsh has been for the last few days. The only thing we can do is to try and forget it all, and hope no harm has been done."

Last murmured a word or two of apology and agreement, and the talk moved off into safer country. But when the tutor was alone, he considered what he had seen and heard very curiously. He thought that Marsh's looks did not match his words. He spoke as the devoted father, afraid that his little boy should overhear nauseous and offensive gossip and conjecture about a horrible and obscene crime. But he looked like a man who had caught sight of a gallows, and that, Last felt, was altogether a very different kind of fear. And, then, there was his reference to his wife. Last had noticed that since the crime in the forest there had been something amiss with her; but, again, he mistrusted Marsh's comment. Here was a woman whose usual habit was a rather lazy good humour; but of late there had been a look and an air of suppressed fury, the burning glance of a jealous woman, the rage of despised beauty. She spoke little, and then as briefly as possible; but one might suspect flames and fires within. Last had seen this and wondered, but not very much, being resolved to mind his own business. He had supposed there had been some difference of opinion between her and her husband; very likely about the rearrangement of the drawing-room furniture and hiring a grand piano. He certainly had not thought of tracing Mrs. Marsh's altered air to the villainous crime that had been committed. And now Marsh was telling him that these glances of concealed rage were the outward signs of tender maternal anxiety; and not one word of all that did he believe. He put Marsh's half-hidden terror beside his wife's half-hidden fury; he thought of the book in the summer-house and things that were being whispered about the horror in the wood: and loathing and dread possessed him. He had no proof, it was true; merely conjecture, but he felt no doubt. There could be no other explanation. And what could he do but leave this terrible place?

Last could get no sleep. He undressed and went to bed, and tossed about in the half dark of the summer night. Then he lit his lamp and dressed again, and wondered whether he had better not steal away without a word, and walk the eight miles to the station, and escape by the first train that went to London. It was not merely loathing for the man and his works; it was deadly fear, also, that urged him to fly from the White House. He felt sure that if Marsh guessed at his suspicions of the truth, his life might well be in danger. There was no mercy or scruple in that evil man. He might even now be at his door, listening, waiting. There was cold terror in his heart, and cold sweat pouring at the thought. He paced softly up and down his room in his bare feet, pausing now and again to listen for that other soft step outside. He locked the door as silently as he could, and felt safer. He would wait till the day came and people were stirring about the house, and then he might venture to come out and make his escape.

And yet when he heard the servants moving over their work, he hesitated. The light of the sun was shining in the valley, and the white mist over the silver river floated upward and vanished; the sweet breath of the wood entered the window of his room. The black horror and fear were raised from his spirit. He began to hesitate, to suspect his judgment, to inquire whether he had not rushed to his black conclusions in a panic of the night. His logical deductions at midnight seemed to smell of nightmare in the brightness of that valley; the song of the aspiring lark confuted him. He remembered Garraway's great argument after a famous supper at the Turk's Head: that it was always unsafe to make improbability the guide of life. He would delay a little, and keep a sharp look out, and be sure before taking sudden and violent action. And perhaps the truth was that Last was influenced very strongly by his aversion from leaving young Henry, whose extraordinary brilliance and intelligence amazed and delighted him more and more.

It was still early when at last he left his room, and went out into the pure morning air. It was an hour or more before breakfast time, and he set out on the path that led past the wall of the kitchen garden up the hill and into the heart of the wood. He paused a moment at the upper corner, and turned round to look across the river at the happy country showing its morning magic and delight. As he dawdled and gazed, he heard soft steps approaching on the other side of the wall, and low voices murmuring. Then, as the steps drew near, one of the voices was raised a little, and Last heard Mrs. Marsh speaking:

"Too old, am I? And thirteen is too young. Is it to be seventeen next when you can get her into the wood? And after all I have done for you, and after what you have done to me."

Mrs. Marsh enumerated all these things without remission, and without any quiver of shame in her voice. She paused for a moment. Perhaps her rage was choking her; and there was a shrill piping cackle of derision, as if Marsh's voice had cracked in its contempt.

Very softly, but very swiftly, Last, the man with the grey face and the staring eyes, bolted for his life, down and away from the White House. Once in the road, free from the fields and brakes, he changed his run into a walk, and he never paused or stopped, till he came with a gulp of relief into the ugly streets of the big industrial town. He made his way to the station at once, and found that he was an hour too soon for the London express. So there was plenty of time for breakfast; which consisted of brandy.

III.

The tutor went back to his old life and his old ways, and did his best to forget the strange and horrible interlude of the White House. He gathered his podgy pups once more about him; crammed and coached, read with undergraduates during the long vacation, and was moderately satisfied with the course of things in general. Now and then, when he was endeavouring to persuade the podges against their deliberate judgment that Latin and Greek were languages once spoken by human beings, not senseless enigmas invented by demons, he would think with a sigh of regret of the boy who understood and longed to understand. And he wondered whether he had not been a coward to leave that enchanting child to the evil mercies of his hideous parents. But what could he have done? But it was dreadful to think of Henry, slowly or swiftly corrupted by his detestable father and mother, growing up with the fat slime of their abominations upon him.

He went into no detail with his old friends. He hinted that there had been grave unpleasantness, which made it impossible for him to remain in the west. They nodded, and perceiving that the subject was a sore one, asked no questions, and talked of old books and the new steak instead. They all agreed, in fact, that the steak was far too new, and William was summoned to explain this horror. Didn't he know that beefsteak, beefsteak meant for the consumption of Christian men, as distinguished from Hottentots, required hanging just as much as game? William, the ponderous and benignant, tasted and tested, and agreed; with sorrowful regret. He apologized, and went on to say that as the gentlemen would not care to wait for a fowl, he would suggest a very special, tender, and juicy fillet of roast veal, then in cut. The suggestion was accepted, and found excellent. The conversation turned to Choric metres and Florence St. John at the Strand. There was port later.

It was many years afterwards, when this old life, after crumbling for a long while, had come down with a final crash, that Last heard the real story of his tutorial engagement at the White House. Three dreadful people were put in the dock at the Old Bailey. There was an old man, with the look of a deadly snake; a fat, sloppy, deplorable woman with pendulous cheeks and a faint hint of perished beauty in her eyes; and to the utter blank amazement of those who did not know the story, a wonderful little boy. The people who saw him in court said he might have been taken for a child of nine or ten; no more. But the evidence that was given showed that he must be between fifty and sixty at the least; perhaps more than that.

The indictment charged these three people with an unspeakable and hideous crime. They were charged under the name of Mailey, the name which they had borne at the time of their arrest; but it turned out at the end of the trial that they had been known by many names in the course of their career: Mailey, Despasse, Lartigan, Delarue, Falcon, Lecossic, Hammond, Marsh, Haringworth. It was established that the apparent boy, whom Last had known as Henry Marsh, was no relation of any kind to the elder prisoners. "Henry's" origins were deeply obscure. It was conjectured that he was the illegitimate son of a very high Englishman, a diplomatist, whose influence had counted for a great deal in the Far East. Nobody knew anything about the mother. The boy showed brilliant promise from very early years, and the father, a bachelor, and disliking what little he knew of his relations, left his very large fortune to his son. The diplomatist died when the boy was twelve years old; and he had been aged, and more than aged when the child was born. People remarked that Arthur Wesley, as he was then called, was very short for his years, and he remained short, and his face remained that of a boy of seven or eight. He could not be sent to a school, so he was privately educated. When he was of age, the trustees had the extraordinary experience of placing a very considerable property in the hands of a young man who looked like a little boy. Very soon afterwards, Arthur Wesley disappeared. Dubious rumours spoke of reappearances, now here, now there, in all quarters of the world. There were tales that he had "gone fantee" in what was then unknown Africa, when the Mountains of the Moon still lingered on the older maps. It was reported, again, that he had gone exploring in the higher waters of the Amazon, and had never come back; but a few years later a personage that must have been Arthur Wesley was displaying unpleasant activities in Macao. It was soon after this period, according to the prosecution, that—in the words of counsel—he realized the necessity of "taking cover." His extraordinary personality, naturally enough, drew attention to him and his doings, and these doings being generally or always of an infamous kind, such attention was both inconvenient and dangerous. Somewhere in the East, and in very bad company, he came upon the two people who were charged with him. Arabella Manning, who was said to have respectable connections in Wiltshire, had gone out to the East as a governess, but had soon found other occupations. Meers had been a clerk in a house of business at Shanghai. His very ingenious system of fraud obtained his discharge, but, for some reason or other, the firm refused to prosecute, and Meers went—where Arthur Wesley found him. Wesley thought of his great plan. Manning and Meers were to pretend to be Mr. and Mrs. Marsh—that seemed to have been their original style—and he was to be their little boy. He paid them well for their various services: Arabella was his mistress-in-chief, the companion of his milder moments, for some years. Occasionally, a tutor was engaged to make the situation more plausible. In this state, the horrible trio peregrinated over the earth.

The court heard all this, and much more, after the jury had found the three prisoners guilty of the particular offence with which they were charged. This last crime—which the press had to enfold in paraphrase and periphrase—had been discovered, strange as it seemed, largely as a result of the woman's jealousy. Wesley's affections, let us call them, were still apt to wander, and Arabella's jealous rage drove her beyond all caution and all control. She was the weak joint in Wesley's armour, the rent in his cover. People in court looked at the two; the debauched, deplorable woman with her flagging, sagging cheeks, and the dim fire still burning in her weary old eyes, and at Wesley, still, to all appearance, a bright and handsome little boy; they gasped with amazement at the grotesque, impossible horror of the scene. The judge raised his head from his notes, and gazed steadily at the convicted persons for some moments; his lips were tightly compressed.

The detective drew to the end of his portentous history. The track of these people, he said, had been marked by many terrible scandals, but till quite lately there had been no suspicion of their guilt. Two of these cases involved the capital charge, but formal evidence was lacking.

He drew to his close.

"In spite of his diminutive stature and juvenile appearance, the prisoner, Charles Mailey, alias Arthur Wesley, made a desperate resistance to his arrest. He is possessed of immense strength for his size, and almost choked one of the officers who arrested him."

The formulas of the court were uttered. The judge, without a word of comment, sentenced Mailey, or Wesley, to imprisonment for life, John Meers to fifteen years' imprisonment, Arabella Manning to ten years' imprisonment.

The old world, it has been noted, had crashed down. Many, many years had passed since Last had been hunted out of Mowbray Street, that went down dingily, peacefully from the Strand. Mowbray Street was now all blazing office buildings. Later, he had been driven from one nook and corner and snug retreat after another as new London rose in majesty and splendour. But for a year or more he had lain hidden in a by-street that had the advantage of leading into a disused graveyard near the Gray's Inn Road. Medwin and Garraway were dead; but Last summoned Zouch and Noel to his abode one night; and then and there made punch, and good punch for them.

"It's so jolly it must be sinful," he said, as he pared his lemons, "but up to the present I believe it is not illegal. And I still have a few bottles of that port I bought in ninety-two."

And then he told them for the first time all the whole story of his engagement at the White House. +

Out of the Picture

I.

In the old days—which means anything from ten to thirty years ago—there was a question which used to be asked now and then at studio parties and Chelsea pubs. The question was:

"But who was the twisted man?"

And it was often followed by another:

"But where did M'Calmont take himself off to?"

Neither interrogation ever got an answer; save that to the second query, a young man in very full dark green corduroy trousers is reported to have said once on a time:

"Somebody told me he had been seen in Quito."

But to this neither credit or attention was given. And it is probable from what follows that the double enigma is to be reckoned with that question as to what song the Sirens sang; if, indeed, it is not past all solution.

Going back, then, to those old days afore-said, and rather to the earlier portion of them, when, as a journalist, I saw many strange things and people; I was once sent to view an exhibition of pictures at the Molyneux Galleries in Danby Place. Perhaps the event may be sufficiently dated by saying that the Exhibition was opened somewhere between the Battle of Sidney Street and the Coronation of King George V; and I have a feeling that it was a misty May morning when I went to see it. It was not a large exhibition: all the pictures were contained in two sizeable rooms, and as soon as I got into them I saw at once that I could make nothing of it—that is, from any serious standpoint. I cared nothing; my point of view in that instance, as in all others like it, was, that if the paper chose to send an outsider and an ignoramus to criticise works of art—especially the works of a new and tentative and experimental school—then, on the head of the paper let the just doom fall. And the school represented on this particular occasion at the Molyneux Galleries evidently represented a fierce revolt against the traditions and conventions of the elders. To begin with; my eye was caught by "The Old Harbour." There were buildings in vertical perspective, their walls appearing to incline together and to aspire to meet in the upper part of the canvas, and with a sense about them as if the whole mass were unstable, impermanent, void of true solidity and settlement on the earth. A mystic once told me that after he had finished his meditation and gone out into the street, he had seen the grey bulk of the houses opposite suddenly melt, evaporate, go up like smoke, leaving void nothingness in their place. And so the painter with his art had made these warehouses and Customs buildings, or whatever they were, in such a fashion that they seemed as if they also were on the very point to turn to mist, to float into the air, and to disappear. And then, for the rest, there was grey water, and segments, and portions, and particles of keels, sails, masts, ropes, decks, and deck furniture, not cohering, or fitting together, but dispersed and apart. Here, I could see, was choice matter on which the expert and art critic could exercise their knowledge and judgement. As I had neither, I made an experiment or two, and was able to inform the readers of the paper that if you walked briskly past the picture, winking both eyes as fast as possible, you really got a sort of impression of movement and activity, of ships and boats coming into harbour and sailing out of it, of sails lowered and hoisted, of an uncertain background, now obscured, now left visible as a ship in full sail passed before it. It struck me that, in my hands, art criticism was in a fair way to become a popular sport.

And then there was another picture that both attracted and distracted me. It was a big canvas, and the subject was a number of geometrical figures of all kinds, most ingeniously fitted into one another, and rainbow painted, no doubt on some occult principle of contrast and complement and correspondence. It was called "King Solomon's Cargoes." I murmured: "Gold and silver and ivory and apes and peacocks," and looked for them. I could not see any of them, and I thought I would go back to Fleet Street, relying on my impressions of "The Old Harbour," which would just fill the "two sticks" that had been allotted to the story. It was, decidedly, a case of least said, soonest mended. In spite of the defence which, as I have mentioned, I had ready; I felt I was on unsafe and treacherous ground. Who was I to sit in judgement on the work of painters? No doubt, I might say that I had looked for apes and peacocks in that picture and had found none; and, likely enough, that remark might merely serve to display my utter ignorance of the subject I was pretending to treat. But it was not written that I should escape "King Solomon's Cargoes" so easily.

It was some years after the exhibition at the Molyneux Galleries that I found myself in a various company one evening. I saw a few people that I knew, and was talking to one of them, when the friend who had brought me along came and said:

"Do you mind if I introduce you to a man? It's M'Calmont, the painter, who says he's been wanting to meet you for years. Some criticism of yours that he read seems to have made a great impression on him."

He took me up to a dark, slight man with a black moustache, and left me. M'Calmont made room on the settee, and began at once:

"I've been wanting to thank you for a long time for that notice you wrote in your paper about the Exhibition in the Molyneux Galleries. You'll remember? It was in Coronation year."

I told him I thought I did remember something about it. But I wondered, internally, what sort of thanks I was going to get from a painter for my vain ribaldry. He went on:

"I said to myself at the time: 'This A.M., whoever he may be, has got an eye to detect the falsities and fallacies, and I'd like to have a talk with him.' Then somebody told me your name, but I left town soon after, and this is the first chance I've had."

And, finally, it came to this: that the falsities and fallacies were the picture of "The Old Harbour," by Frank Guildford, and M'Calmont had enjoyed the way I had stuck my knife into the fellow.

I explained. I said I knew nothing about painting, and had been afraid that I had been guilty of ill-placed and unmannerly humour. He wouldn't hear of this.

"It was just instinct, pure instinct. You may not have the technical knowledge, but you know a silly man when you see him."

I asked what had become of this unhappy man.

"He's what they call a fashionable painter, and makes his eight thousand a year by painting grocers and their wives—damn him!"

And he went on:

"I don't know whether you happened to see a thing I had in that Exhibition? I called it 'King Solomon's Cargoes.'"

I lied. I dwelt again and more forcibly on the utter unscrupulousness of my character when simulating an art critic. I said I had not seen his canvas. I had just dashed into the galleries, invented my silly game with the ships in the harbour, and run out again as soon as I had got material for my two or three paragraphs. But, in fact, I remembered those purple squares, scarlet triangles, sky-blue circles very well.

M'Calmont nodded his head gloomily.

"I'm glad it didn't catch your eye. You might have had something to say to me too. You'd have been right, and you'd have been wrong. I was never a faker like Guildford. I never pretended that if you painted a bit of mast here and a scrap of a sail there and a deck in another part of the canvas you could call it painting a ship. But I did believe in abstract painting—and I do still in a way."

I asked him to tell me all about it.

"I'd like to explain what I was after in those days. You say you know nothing about the technical side of painting. You won't want to know anything about it: it's not a technical question. It's behind all that and beyond it. But you can't talk sense in the middle of all these havers. Come away."

I followed him out, and by devious and obscure ways he led me to an obscure tavern, where we sat down together in a quiet corner of a bulging and old-fashioned bar. They spoke his language there, since his order for "two wee halfyins" was fulfilled without comment. But I looked at the stuff in my glass, and remembered how the poet had said that the half is greater than the whole—"greater," I corrected mentally, "than the double." I added water.

"Don't kill good drink," M'Calmont said reproachfully. "*Scelus est jugulare Falernum*, and this is better. It's the genuine Lagavulin, not the trash they sell in London for whiskey. But you were asking about abstract painting. It will be necessary to go back and away a little if we're to see what we're after. They say distance lends enchantment to the view; I'd put it myself, 'lends vision,' *theoria*. It may turn out, of course, that when you do see, you see enchantment, but that is just secondary; a kind of by-product, you might say, of the proposition. I'll ask you, then, if you know anything about the Kabbala of the Hebrews?"

Whatever I knew of that matter, I dissembled. I am a lover of the rich improbabilities, and I would not check this rare manifestation of them.

"Well, I don't want you to feel like a cow in a fremd loaming; so we won't go too deeply into those dark mysteries. But the Kabbalists tell us that at the Fall of Man, the Serpent did not ascend to Kether in the Tree of Life. It stopped at Daath. And that's their way of saying that the nature of man was not entirely corrupted. The Serpent poisoned and infected the logical understanding, but there was a pure, spiritual region above that which remained untouched.

"Very good. You see that? And there you have the reason why a man that's sunk deep in the blackest mud of materialism may very possibly be overcome with delight at the Fugues of Bach. You'll see how that may be? That's absolute music. It has nothing to do with Daath, the logical understanding. I'm speaking, you understand, of the pattern of sounds that reaches the ears of the hearer; just the ordered noise that he hears, if you like to put it that way. In the making of the music, no doubt, in the technical part of the creation, the understanding had its share, as the slave of the spirit. If you want to build Jerusalem with its Temple you must have your hewers of wood and stone and drawers of water. You're a writer yourself, and you know you can't do much in that way without calling in the aid of the pen-makers and the ink manufacturers and paper merchants; but you don't allow them to teach you how to turn the phrase.

"But the way the thing is fashioned is nothing to do with us. What we're concerned with is the thing we hear; and with that thing the logical understanding has just no concern at all. You'll note there's no tongue or language in which we can speak of it. There's no answer to the question: 'But what does it mean?' when that question is asked of pure music. Bach, you may say, had the gift of tongues; but in his case there's no legitimate gift of the interpretation of tongues. It's impossible to translate the language of Kether into the speech of Daath. I remember well going to hear *Lohengrin*, and there was a manner of commentary attached to the bill of the opera. I just glanced at it and saw that when the overture began I was to picture to myself a blue sky, and then to watch the wee white clouds forming on it. There you have your music critic calling in nature, and I saw in the paper, there was another of them puzzling his head over Berlioz, and decided that he was a 'pictural,' not a 'linear' composer—calling in the terms of another art. And you'll hear often enough of the 'magnificent colour' of this or that passage of music. And I don't say they can do better. But it proves what I am telling you: that the understanding has nothing to do with absolute music, and nothing to say to it.

"Aye, and what about painting? That's the question I asked myself years ago. You know Aristotle says that all art is imitation. It's a very questionable pronouncement. If I'm not mistaken he had the drama chiefly in his mind when he made it. But the drama is just an impure or mixed development of the dance. In its primitive, original form, the dance was not an imitation of anything. It was, like music, an expression of something; but that's different. You may say that the drama of the Greeks was the dance set to words. And then, there's architecture. You can't say that the Parthenon is an imitation of anything, or that Rheims Cathedral is an imitation of anything. And literature. I shan't need to tell you that all the things we value most in the finest literature are just the things that soar above the sense— that is the logical understanding of it. If you turn to the Book and read Second Samuel, one, seventeen, you'll find a statement to the effect that David lamented the decease of Saul and Jonathan; but you'll not tell me that the vital interest and value of that proposition is to be discovered in the logical sense of it. And if you read Coleridge's *Kubla Khan*, I think you'll be puzzled to find out the logical sense in it and to tell me what it is. But there you have literature almost becoming music.

"And now you see what I've been getting at all the while."

I did not; but I forbore to say so.

"It was just this: that I asked myself why should there not be abstract or absolute painting, as well as absolute music and architecture? In the past, painting has been almost entirely Aristotelian, imitative. Why should it continue wholly on those lines? And you'll have gathered that I don't consider you solve the problem by cracking an object up into bits and scraps and pieces, and then painting the bits as they lie abroad. And if you paint a man's hands three times their natural size and draw a jackass with five legs, I'm not thinking you're any nearer to a solution. And that's how I came to paint the picture that I sent, into those Galleries, that I'm glad now you didn't see. I was on the wrong track."

He lapsed at last into silence. I broke it by making a proposition remote from pure aesthetics. He declined to accede to it.

"No, no," said M'Calmont, "I'll not hear of it. In the 'Crown and Thistle,' I'm in Scotland, and you're my guest. Where's the Macfarlane creature?"

When we parted soon after, he wrote his address on a scrap of paper torn from his note-book, and begged me to come and see him one evening.

"I'd like to show you the new track I've found," he said, and vanished into the night, as we came out together.

II.

It may be as well to make it clear at once that I am not the man to be daunted by the unusual. I have seen too much of it for that. I know that there are quarters, and very influential quarters, in which it is considered improper to mention such things. Every age has its conventions of propriety and impropriety: every age and every race. The missionary's wife in Africa shocked her two black servants horribly and unspeakably when she said that she was afraid the fruit was too green for a tart. Her husband's name was Green, and every (black) body knows that for a wife to utter her husband's name is both impious and obscene in the highest degree. We talk quite freely in the drawing-room in a style that would have made Dickens run out of the smoking-room, and when we write books we set down boldly words that were only forced out of the policeman of yesterday by the strict order of the Bench. It is all a matter of convention and taboo, and perhaps it is idle to ask for reasons. Mrs. Green, I daresay, couldn't understand why on earth she shouldn't utter the word "green"; and I suppose I am in much the same case when I say that I have no notion why I shouldn't mention the unusual, the odd, the extraordinary when I come across it. At any rate, I propose to defy this particular convention, here and elsewhere and always. As I was saying, I have seen too much of it to affect disbelief in its existence. I heard from the brass-founders of Clerkenwell about a former member of their craft who had confuted Darwin by the Hebrew alphabet and by the stars, and had buried the pot of gold in a field, where it was found by the navvies who were making the cutting for the Midland Railway. I have discussed with a solicitor, in his London office, the affairs of the J.H.V.S. Syndicate, who were seeking for the Ark of the Covenant from the directions of a cypher contained in that chapter of the Prophet Ezekiel which is called Mercabah. I know all about Campo Tosto, of Burnt Green, near Reigate, who defended his treasures with the bow and arrow. Why, then, should I hush up M'Calmont the painter, who drew his artistic principles from the Hebrew Kabbala?

As a matter of fact, I thought him an interesting man, and determined that I would see more of him. And so, one windy night in October, a few weeks after our meeting, I set out from somewhere in the west and made up the Gray's Inn Road. I am not certain by which street I turned from it. I think, but I am not sure, that it was by Acton Street. I know that I had gone too far north, and that when I came to the bottom of the street, and traversed the King's Cross Road, I found out my mistake, and had to incline somewhat to the right in climbing the hill. It is a district both devious and obscure, and I suppose that its twisting streets and unexpected squares of dusty trees will all come to ruin before they are intelligently explored. I had trod these mazes before, and thought I knew them tolerably well, but it was some years since I had been in that region, and I found myself perplexed and at fault, while the great wind blew the leaves of shadowy trees about my head and at my feet. At last I entered a black passage at a venture, and came down a short flight of steps into an irregular open space, on which there abutted a chapel of the Countess of Huntingdon's Connexion. I went round and about this square or triangle or trapezium, which was sparsely lit, till I found the green door in a wall to which I was directed, and rang the bell under the name M'Calmont. It was M'Calmont who opened the door and, taking hold of my arm, led me down a passage, past a house all lit up, where they were singing, and so to his studio, with trees all about it, bending and tossing and straining in the wind. Inside, there was a hanging lamp, and though it was not cold, the blaze of the fire was cheerful; and lamplight and firelight glittered on the carved and gilded frames of the pictures that hung on the walls. We sat down on a big settee at a comfortable distance from the fire; and he pressed on my attention what he called "Eela"—which is spelt, I found, "Islay."

And then there was more of it. Not of the spirit of the western isle, but of art, as he expounded it. It seemed that he had been forced to modify, one might say, to abandon his earlier views.

"I found out, and I was not so long about it, that you can't have absolute painting any more than you can have absolute literature. There are people, as you know, who are trying their hands at that—by writing gibberish without grammar. And *that* won't do. And I discovered that my endeavours in the direction of pure painting wouldn't do either. The principle of it is all right; but it's not for pigments. If you would carry it out, you must turn Eastern carpet-maker. And I'll maintain that there are Persian carpets as fine as any symphony of Beethoven's. They are the very analogy in colour and form of pure music.

"As it seemed that I couldn't go forward, I went back. And there, as you'll no doubt be well aware, I was in the height of the fashion. The sculptors and painters too have been trying back for the last quarter of a century. There are men who do their best to forget all the bare elements of their art, their drawing and their perspective and all the rest of it, that they may paint as if they were five years old. Another lot are off to Borrioboolah Gha, to learn the principles of sculpture from black savages. And I've no doubt there's a weary band trying to tramp back all the way to the Stone Age to see what they can find there. It's all very interesting. I'd like it fine—if they'd not call their imitations of barbarism Modern Art. And now I shall show you where I've gone back myself, so as to be in the movement."

He barked derisively, and turning up the lamp a little, proceeded to guide me round the studio. And I felt as helpless and as futile as I had been in the old days, when I was an art critic *pour rire*.

For I was not at all sure where he had gone back, to use his own phrase. The pictures were all landscapes, painted, I conjecture, in the manner of the eighteenth century. There seemed to me, the uninstructed, as it were a dark shadow that hung over them all. Now and again there were patches of an intense and glowing blue in M'Calmont's skies; but these were contrasted with purple cloud masses rimmed with fire, with huge white clouds blown up into the sky by gathering thunder, with cloudy walls of black streaked with coppery flame. The green of the trees and of the grass was dark and livid, and the water of the pools and streams reflected something of the threat of the skies. M'Calmont had depicted open spaces in the midst of mysterious woods, narrow valleys edged with grim rocks, paths that wound in and out by lonely lands to shattered walls on a far height, trees of strange growth hanging over a well, glades glooming with twilight and the coming storm. There was an enchantment; but the incantation was of oppression and terror. There were three things that I noticed as curious: the first was that in every picture M'Calmont had introduced fire: logs burning under a broken wall, flames breaking out of yellowish smoke in the forest clearing, a fire by the well, a fire on the far hill-side. Water, also, was represented in each canvas; well, or brook, or pool in the woods; and in every one of them there was the figure of a man, the same man, so far as I could judge. The figure was roughly dressed in the costume of an eighteenth-century countryman, in ragged clothes, with a scarlet cap on his head. He was depicted as tending the invariable fire, perhaps, or leaning on his staff, or half-hidden behind the trunk of a tree, or crouching among thorns on the border of a broken road. As I passed slowly from picture to picture, I noticed that the figure became more prominent. At first, it was barely seen in the background. Then it came forward into the middle distance, and at the end of the tour, the recently painted pictures, as M'Calmont told me, it was prominent in the foreground. In one picture he led a procession of torch-bearers into a wood as the night came on; but mostly he was alone in these desolate places that M'Calmont had made. And there was about this figure an impression of distortion. There was no specific deformity, as of hunched back or misshapen limbs but yet a distinct sense of a form twisted and awry. And the face, where it could be clearly seen, was at once piteous and malignant, as of a stricken snake, wounded and dying.

Whatever my feelings about this odd gallery of paintings may have been, I kept it to myself. I reminded M'Calmont that I was an outsider and (perhaps exaggerating a little) that I could never be an admirer of the famous slaughterhouse, since it told no story.

"You're an awful liar," he said with engaging directness as we sat down again, "but let that flea stick to the wall. I told you I was going back, like the rest, but not to the ignorance of childhood or savagery. I'm returning to a great art, and exploring its possibilities. You know that the Gothic architecture was the result of the builders, first of the dark ages and then of the middle ages, exploring the possibilities of the architecture of the Romans?"

"I have heard that theory advanced," I said, "but I don't know that it holds the field so decisively as you seem to think. I believe that some authorities would tell you that the gothicosity of the Gothic derives, to a great extent at least, from the East."

"I wouldn't believe a word of that tale—not that it signifies one way or the other in the argument. But I've seen churches down on the Rhone where the Gothic seems growing out of the Classic before your very eyes. There's one such at Valence: a regular Classic pediment, and all the detail of it one would call Norman, if one saw it in England. And anyone who will cast an eye over a First Pointed capital will see in a moment that it's a Corinthian capital in disguise; especially if it's got the square abacus."

"Very good, then," I assented, "let us grant your doctrine of Gothic. You're applying it to painting?"

"That is so. As I said; I'm exploring the possibilities of an old school of landscape. I don't know whether it's ever struck you; but there's no doubt that some of the painters of that age anticipated the word that came to Coleridge and Wordsworth. The eighteenth-century literature was Pope. It belonged to Daath, the region of the logical understanding. To the men of that age, the poetry of the sixteenth century and the first half of the seventeenth century was just Egyptian hieroglyphics. They could not interpret a single word of it; they'd forgotten what it meant. And, naturally, they could not dream of what was to come after them. But if you look at some of their painting: you'll see the landscapes of *Kubla Khan*—the awe, and the terror, and the hidden mysteries of earth and air, water and fire. And I just meant to find out what's beyond the turn of those paths they made."

He paused for a moment. "But that's not painter's talk," he went on. "I mean, of course, that I've taken a certain school of landscape painting as my starting-point; and I will see if I can't develop it on its own lines. I hope to draw something new out of the old."

"You have a figure, I notice, in all your pictures."

"You must have the human figure. Without that all your scenery would dissolve and melt away. It would be just nothing at all."

I did not ask if it was necessary that this human figure should be abhorrent of aspect. For that, I was certain, would not be painter's talk. And soon after, I went out into the labyrinth on the hill-side. It was late, and the night had grown misty, and the sound of the streets below came faintly, with strange voices.

III.

I remember being told a good many years ago in the course of a cheerful evening that the one thing fatal to an actor was intelligence.

"Or if you like it better," said the speaker, "I will say intellect. Or, better still, that something or other in a man that can pick a character to pieces, and analyse it, and find out why it does this, that, or the other, and relate it to the plot and the other parts in the cast; and then, continuing the process, build up by careful reasoning, the impersonation out of tones of the voice, facial expression, gesture, habit of body, and so forth."

"But," said a gentleman in the company, "isn't that the way to act? I thought that was how it was done."

"That's how I do it," replied the lecturer. "But I haven't any illusions. The man who depicts by that method will never be a 'feerst actor,' as the German producer called it when I was in *Old Heidelberg* with Alexander. You know the story of Irving and poor Bill Terriss. Bill was ponging away for all he was worth as Henry VIII. Irving stopped him.

"'Very good, Terriss; very good indeed. I suppose you don't understand the meaning of one single word that you have uttered?'

"'No, guv'nor,' said Terriss, not in the least put out. 'But it'll go all right on the night.'

"That's the way to act."

"But, excuse me," said the man who wanted to know, "I'm afraid I don't quite grasp your meaning. *What* is the way to act?"

"You begin by not being able to give a single reason for anything you do or for your particular style of doing it. The rest comes along by itself. And I think I will help myself to another drink ere I go to that bourne . . . I don't want to miss the twelve-forty."

It was probable, I considered, that the old actor—a dignified Priest in *Hamlet*—was right in the main. Creative work, even such secondary creative work as the actor's, is not achieved by theories or by taking thought. A man must know the grammar of his business, whatever it is; the rest, if it is to be of the first order, must be the work of the hidden flame within. And, therefore, I had grave doubts of the validity of M'Calmont's art, when I thought of the elaboration of his theories. I remembered Claude Lantier in L'Oevre. He made up his mind to be a stark realist, to paint bunches of carrots with sincerity. But he listened to theories, and ended by hanging himself before his symbolical picture of Paris as a nude woman, whose flesh glowed with jewels, like a Byzantine icon. It was some time before I went to see him again in that retired and secret studio. I met him in Holborn a few weeks after my visit, and he asked me in a very cheerful manner whether I was recovering from his pictures by degrees—giving his short bark of laughter. I told him that I had been allowed out for the last week.

"But," said I, willing to continue the vein of mild facetiousness, "you know art without a story is no good to me. Do tell me the story of that figure in all your paintings—the figure of the twisted man."

He stared at me blankly as if he hadn't a notion what I was talking about. Then he caught sight of an east-bound 'bus in a slowly moving press of traffic, ran for it, and shook a jocular fist at me from the top of the stair. And that was the last I saw of M'Calmont for a considerable time.

I was occupied as a matter of fact all through that winter with affairs and interests of my own. What is generally and conveniently known as psychical research has always had a strong attraction for me, in spite, or perhaps because, of the obscurities, difficulties and drawbacks of the pursuit. I must say, that the usual demand of the men of physical science does not strike me as in the least rational. This demand is, I believe, that psychical phenomena should be made to conform to the laws of the laboratory experiment. The man of science says: "I can make hydrogen by a simple process of mixing acid and water and zinc. If you don't believe me, come along now to my laboratory, and I will make hydrogen in three or four minutes, and show you how it is done, so that you can make it yourself—and blow yourself up, too, if you don't follow the directions. Or, if you like, I will make hydrogen to-morrow morning at eleven, or to-morrow night at twelve, or on Saturday by written appointment." You confess your belief in the validity and efficacy of the hydrogen process; and your scientific friend goes on: "Very good; but you were telling me of a woman who looked in a crystal one morning, and saw and foretold correctly certain things that happened fifty miles away four hours later. Then, find that woman and bring her along to the laboratory, and let me see and hear her doing it again, and let her explain to me how she does it." And here, I say, physical science strikes me as profoundly irrational. A great poet cannot guarantee a masterpiece to be written on demand, under the eye of an observer, by 6.50 p.m. Shillaker, the famous bat, would never undertake to reproduce his 250 not out and no chances given, against the Patagonians. He knows that when he next meets that famous eleven, he may be out for a duck in the first over. And what painter can explain how he does it? Can Dick, Tom, and Harry go to the Master, listen to a demonstration, and come away, fully prepared to equal his immortal works? Clearly, men are capable of all sorts of performances of body and spirit which are not in the least amenable to the law of the laboratory. Let us remember the historic case of one of whom it is recorded: "at tip-cheese, or odd and even, his hand is out." If Master Tommy Bardell had been required to demonstrate his skill at tip-cheese then and there in Court, under the immediate eye of Mr. Justice Stareleigh, he would, very likely, have made a miserable fiasco.

So I have always ruled out the scientific demand and its implied conclusion as void and vain and foolish. The real difficulties in these enquiries are to be found, partly in the exquisite skill to which the art of the conjurer is sometimes brought, partly to the rarity of the faculty of keen and clear observation, partly to inaccurate and unreliable memory, a little to the commonness of lying: but most of all to the vast and bottomless credulity of the race of men. It is not a case of a plausible tale deceiving a simpleton; it is a case of homely strangers going to an hotel in a busy seaside town, telling the managing director of the concern that they are leaving him a couple of million in their wills, and living at the hotel free of payment for eight or nine months. What is to be expected when the managing director—the type is common—devotes his talents to psychical research?

Still, with all this in my mind, I persevered; perhaps not altogether displeased at the thought that, so far as clear and final and general conclusions were concerned, the quest was a hopeless one. After all, there is something eminently human in the desire of impossible things. To seek for possibilities is rather the business of the lower animals than of man. To be more specific: it had often struck me that from the singular phenomena grouped together under the heading of *poltergeist* there might, possibly or even probably, emerge a good deal of light on the doings and showings of modern spiritualism. In both cases, naturally, a huge discount has to be made. No doubt, the *poltergeist* was often a bad child, delighting in annoying, alarming, and humbugging its elders, delighting also in playing the leading part in the comedy. Sometimes, hysteria was to be expected; and hysteria is capable of anything. But it seems to me that there was a very considerable remnant of *poltergeist* cases in which mischief and trickery and ordinary hysteria were necessarily excluded from consideration. As to the other end of the enquiry, spiritualism; its history might, in a sense, be called a sad one. The last time I looked into the leading spiritualist journal I saw on one page a description of the unpleasing methods by which the medium had hidden the flowers that were to drop later from the spirit world on to the seance table; on another page was a brief announcement that an eminent spiritualist had declared the equally eminent Mr. X, the spirit photographer, to be a highly fraudulent person. For the time, at all events, I decided on occupying myself with the manifestations of the simple *poltergeist*.

And, as it happened, a favourable opportunity came in my way. Soon after my encounter with M'Calmont in Holborn, I ran across an old acquaintance of Manning, who was something in the British Museum. A few years before, when he had been a lodger in a Bloomsbury street, I had been accustomed to see a good deal of him; but he had married and gone to live with his wife on some remote heights up at Hornsey, and we had not encountered one another for some time. We found a nook in which we could exchange such news as we had, and I heard a good deal about the fine old garden, "above the

London smoke," and of great success with roses. Then came something interesting.

"Six months ago," Manning began, "we took a boarder. He's a boy of fifteen, and his father, Richards, an old friend of mine, has got a job in the East, which will keep him there for some years. He asked me if my wife and I would take charge of the lad for the next year or two, anyhow. The mother is dead, and, as Richards put it, he didn't want to leave his son with strangers. The young fellow is a day boy at Westminster, so we don't see too much of him, in term-time at all events.

"Well, he came along and seemed a decent young chap enough, and didn't give any trouble—till the last week or so. And now we don't know what to do about him."

"What's wrong?" I asked. "Stays out late at night and comes home drunk? That sort of thing?"

"Not a bit of it. He sticks to his work all of the evening and goes to bed soon after ten. But, wherever he is, things go smash. It began with a stone coming through the dining-room window. I thought, naturally, some hooligan had thrown it from the street, and rushed out. The only people near enough to have done it were a couple of quiet old ladies walking along and chatting to each other about the vicar. Another night the clock jumped from the shelf on to the table. Then he went into the kitchen to get me a box of matches, and the plates on the dresser began falling about. It worries my wife—and it bothers me too. Young Richards says he doesn't do it. No doubt he does, all the same; but I haven't succeeded in catching him at it, so far. I suppose I shall have to write to his father, and that won't be pleasant."

I saw my chance. I told Manning that young Richards must be regarded, not as an infernal nuisance, but as an interesting case. On my earnest petition, Mrs. Manning being, I believe, rather glad to have another man on the premises, I became the second paying guest at the Hornsey house, promising myself important and first-hand evidence. And I had better say at once that I was disappointed. As young Richards pored over his home-work at a side table, I saw a small piece of Samian ware rise up from the table at the other end of the room, hover, or seem to hover, for an instant, and then fall to the floor, breaking into fragments. I could not see how Richards could possibly be the conscious agent in this event. There was, certainly, no apparatus of threads or wires concerned in the destruction of the Samian bowl. The boy looked frightened and furious; and I found out that he had been thrashed at his preparatory school for "wilful destruction." But, from the enquirer's point of view, "what next?" It seemed that one was reduced to posit an unknown force, devoid of conscious or intelligent direction, and wholly outside and beyond the sphere of physical science. And yet; this was something.

Richards in himself was an entirely ordinary and normal boy; a very decent fellow, I should say, neither too stupid nor too intelligent. It was only in his appearance that there was something not quite ordinary. I do not know that he was short for his age, but his breadth of chest made him appear short, and gave a certain vague impression of deformity, and also of considerable strength.

I had been staying with the Mannings for six or seven weeks, and it was drawing towards the darkest and shortest days in the year. There was a succession of heavy fogs, and it was after one of these that the "Horrible Dwarf" scare began its course in the papers. A small child, living with its parents in a back street of Westminster, had been sent on some errand to a shop round the corner. The fog was thick down there by the river, but the distance was short, the little girl went to the shop for her mother every other day, and there were no roads to be crossed. She came back crying, and evidently badly frightened, having dropped the sixpenn'orth of tea, or whatever it was. When she had been soothed into coherence, she told a tale of a "dreadful little man," who came out of a passage, and bent down with all his teeth showing, and put out his hands as if he would take her by the throat and kill her—and then disappeared into the fog, without saying a word. Of course the neighbours came swarming to hear all about it, and deafened each other with conjectures of an impossible kind, and proposed moves and measures which led nowhere. On the whole, it was to be gathered that the horrible little man must be a stranger, since no dwarfs were known to inhabit the neighbourhood. The police were called in, and made very little of the business, ranking the offender with those tiresome but not dangerous semi-lunatics who cut off girls' hair on the bus, or slash their clothes in the street. The paragraphs in the press were brief; and some people were inclined to think that the small messenger had let the tea or sugar spill into the gutter and had invented the dwarf in order to escape punishment. But, then, in a couple of days, there was something more serious. Late on a dismal afternoon, a man who was taking a short cut through an unfrequented by-street off the Tottenham Court Road, felt, as he said, a violent punch in the back, and found himself at the bottom of a flight of area stairs. He was bruised and shaken, but conscious, and as he looked up, he saw an ugly little man grinning at him through the railings. He struggled to his feet, and ran up the steps, shouting: "Stop thief!" There were two or three people about, who came running; but they had seen nothing. Then, on another evening, five or six days later, a girl looking into a shop window in Camden Town, became aware that there was a short man, "with a nasty look on his face," standing beside her, and the next moment she felt a piercing pain in her arm, screamed out in agony and fear, and fainted. There was hurry and bustle, shouting and confusion, running here and there from all quarters, but by the time the girl had come to herself and was able to say what had happened to her, the assailant had disappeared. A doctor came up and found a long needle almost buried in her arm. The newspaper paragraphs had become half-columns, and people began to be afraid. And the next outrage of the "Horrible Dwarf" was again at Westminster; and close to the place where the small messenger had been frightened. Again there was a dense fog; rather a thick white mist, deadening to sound, so that in those narrow streets where there is little wheeled traffic on the brightest days, such noises as these were could hardly be heard, and seemed dull and muffled as if they came from a place far off. But through this thick, stilled silence there broke a lamentable complaint. A man, making his way homeward, cautiously, warily, and slowly, passed through one of these by-streets where, for some years, there had been a patch of wretched and wasted land. Four or five cottages had been pulled down, and for some reason or another the plans for re-building had fallen through, and the plot where the houses stood lay as the house-breakers had left it. There were cavernous remains of underground rooms or cellars, brickbat mountains, plaster valleys, all scattered over with fragments of mouldering beams and jagged with slates; a very dismal and ruined place, separated from the pavement by a line of broken-down palings. As the homeward-bound man felt his way along the street, he thought he heard a noise of crying, a very faint, sad sound. He stopped and listened by a window, where the light from within was barely apparent through the thick, white folds of mist, and wondered whether the sound came from a child, shut up alone and frightened. He could not satisfy himself that this was so, and walked on a few paces, still listening, and thinking that he was drawing nearer to the noise of crying. He was now by the palings that hedged off the waste land, and he became sure that here was the scene of the trouble. He broke through the rotten fence, and went prowling and stumbling about, well aware, as he had often passed that way, that he might very well come to grief himself in the broken-down ruin and confusion of the place. But, with good fortune, he came without disaster to a wretched child lying on his back amidst the rubbish, sobbing and wailing most piteously. The man gave him a cheerful "What's the matter, Tommy? Come along, and we'll make it all right," and tried to lift the child to his feet. But the poor misery cried out in sharper anguish, and the man raised him as gently as he could and bore him away, dreadfully afraid all the while that he might stumble and fall and, as he said afterwards, do the poor little beggar in.

However, he brought his burden safely out of the horrible pits, and rang the bell at the first house he came to. The rescuer and the people of the house saw a terrible sight. It was a poor place, with a bed in the sitting-room, and on this they laid the wreckage. It was a boy of nine or ten. One leg seemed bent under him, and when they tried to straighten it the child screamed with pain. But it was the boy's face that frightened them. It was all swollen and bloody, and black with bruises, and the blood was still gushing from the nostrils, which were as if they had been stamped on by the hoof of a horse. One went out and shouted through the fog for the police; and in time the poor boy was taken in an ambulance to the hospital. In a day or two, a little mended and recovered, he told his tale of a twisted man that came out of the mist, and took him up as if he would have broken him, and carried him over the fence and threw him down, and then stamped with his feet on his face.

The newspapers altered their headline to "Devilish Dwarf," and cursed the police—and so forth.

And it was after this most detestable outrage that Manning horrified me one night, as we sat by the fire with the rest of the house abed. He told me that he was seriously afraid that young Richards was guilty of these abominations. He urged that they had all taken place at a time when the boy was on his way from Westminster to Hornsey, that he had certainly been late home on the occasions of the first and last of the outrages. He dwelt on his dwarfish appearance, on his great strength, but above all on those abnormal activities which had interested me in the first place.

"You know yourself there's something queer about the fellow. Upon my word, I'm afraid he's the man. And if we don't do something, it will come to murder."

I was, indeed, horrified for a moment when he began, but at the end I laughed, I am glad to remember. I told him that the fog would amply account for Richards's late return on the two occasions he had mentioned; that to the best of my recollection he had been back in good time on the other two evenings of outrage; and finally, and most conclusively, that he was talking nonsense. "Excepting only that singular faculty or fatality of his, he's a very ordinary boy, and a good sort."

In short, I laughed him out of it. Happily, there were no more horrors of the "Devilish Dwarf" order for the rest of the winter. They stopped as suddenly as they had begun; and in the succeeding calm somebody found sense enough to write an article pointing out the helplessness of the police when confronted with the motiveless outrages of a maniac. The new generation heard all about the doings of Jack the Ripper, and the analogy seemed fair enough. And at the same time—it was, of course, pure coincidence—the *poltergeist* activity, or possession, or whatever it was, of young Richards dwindled and ceased. The house on the Hornsey heights was in all respects at peace with itself when I left it for the valley of London in the early spring.

IV.

Extract from a letter received about eighteen months after "the early spring" mentioned above.

. . . Now, as to this M'Calmont business. In your place, I should certainly go no farther—or "further"—I never know which is right and which is wrong. There's no question of bringing the story to its logical conclusion, because there isn't one. Your theories, and conjectures and the rest of it may be all right—and they may be all wrong. And just remember that for all we know M'Calmont may turn up any day, and that might be a nasty business for you. I remember Sandy M'Calmont very well, and he always struck me as a man who would be extremely (shall we say) tenacious, if he got in a temper.

I note what you say about your visit to his studio in the spring of last year. In the first place; as to the man himself. You say he struck you as very much changed: "silent, morose, and apparently not in the least glad to see me." And I gather that the Lagavulin touch was conspicuous by its absence. I don't think there's much significance in that. There are genial Scotchmen and frozen Scotchmen, and sometimes and naturally enough you have samples of both temperaments in one man. And, as I've just said, he always struck me as having a reserve of grimness. One of his race gave me a most cordial invitation to dine with him at his club, and when the evening came, I was going to say, he didn't speak half a dozen words. That's a figure of speech; but, to be strictly accurate, if he had been "measured up," I don't think his remarks all through the evening would have exceeded a hundred words. He was all right the next time we met. Some of them are like that.

You say that all the pictures you had seen when you went to the studio the autumn before had been cleared away, and that there was a new lot on the walls. The change you noticed is certainly interesting: the seduction of the elaborate landscapes into mere backgrounds, the trees barely indicated, the detail shadowy, and so forth: the Twisted Man promoted from a sort of super to be the real subject of the picture—"a devilish figure," as you say, with, I gather, minor demons grouped about him, being instructed in strange traps and chases, in obscure employments, in pastimes that did not strike you as too agreeable. I was rather reminded of an old lacquer bureau I grew up with. I remember one of the drawers was decorated with a design of a golden garden of unearthly trees, in which Chinamen in golden robes tormented a porcupine with long wands of gold. All this was certainly very odd. You didn't like M'Calmont's manner when he said: "You asked me for the story of the Twisted Man and here it is"? I don't see much in that. But that particular gesture in one of the pictures: the man pointing to an indistinct figure on the ground, and lifting up his foot above it: well . . . Still, as you can see for yourself, there's nothing you can fasten on in that. You can't charge a painter with the crimes he chooses to paint. And that's the fatal flaw in the whole of your case; if you think you have a case.

Of course I remember that awful business of the poor girl in the July following. It was one of the most hideous and revolting things that have happened in my time; and I think that we should both agree that Fleet Street, with all its faults, rendered a public service by its suppression of most of the facts. I knew Selwyn of the *Gazette*, who was put on the country end of the story. He managed to see a sort of diary the girl had kept—about her visits to London and all that. I don't care to recall what he told me. But there again, when you try to put two and two together, you'll find it can't be done. There was nothing in those papers that Selwyn looked at to connect the unfortunate wretch with the studio. As you say, that square in Bloomsbury where the body was found is not a great distance off; but that's nothing to go on.

And, after all, it seems to me that either way, you would be well advised to let it alone. The man has gone away, and it seems likely that he will stay away, so there's no fear of any recurrence of these abominations. But, on the other hand, he may come back, and if he did, you might find yourself in the dock on a charge of criminal libel. And I don't think that such evidence as you have is anything like strong enough for you to put up a good defence. I say again: drop it.

I took this advice, so far as making any representations to the police authorities was concerned. After some years—nine, getting on for ten—nothing has been heard of M'Calmont. A cousin of his eventually received authority to deal with the pictures in the studio. Some of the earlier canvases appeared in due course in the dealers' shops round St. James's and Bond Street, and others went to the auction rooms, and realised very fair prices. There is a movement, I have gathered, in certain circles of art criticism, to appreciate M'Calmont's work very highly. One critic wrote lately: "It is all old school, if you like, but there is something there that the old school never had; and I don't think that any of us quite know what it is. And I am convinced that collectors, public and private, will do well to keep a very keen eye on M'Calmont. At the present prices they are undoubted bargains."

And the studios are still asking where M'Calmont got his model for the wonderful Twisted Man.

There was one circumstance which I failed to mention, when I consulted the friend who wrote me the letter of advice. I am not sure why I left it out of my story; possibly from a whimsical dislike of making the case too complete, possibly from a feeling, equally whimsical, that it was as well to keep one card at least safe and secret in my own hand.

But, two nights after the discovery of the package in Irving Square, when horror was still black and raging, I felt that I must visit that secret studio on the hill-side. It was a clear night with a red moon, just past the full, rising out of a low band of clouds, and this time I found my way without any difficulty. And just as I came down the flight of steps that led into the open square, I saw the green door of M'Calmont's studio open; very cautiously at first, inch by inch, and then wider, and a figure, vague against the darkness behind it, seemed to peer about for a moment. Then, the door was opened wide, and as quickly shut, and I saw a man, all twisted and bent so as to be dwarf-like, go capering with fantastic and extravagant gestures across the scene of light, and vanish into a narrow passage which led down the hill between garden walls and the shadowy boughs of trees. I stood still, beaten back into the shelter of my steps, drawing a long breath. I had recognised very well that dancing and terrible figure, and I was quite overcome by the utter impossibility of that which I had certainly seen. I had been living for some time with gathering suspicions of some dreadful and mysterious connection between the work of the studio and the horror of the waste place in Westminster; but they had been vague surmises and unshapen fears. But this was delirium; nightmare walking visibly abroad. I shook myself out of my terror and went briskly up to the studio door and rang the bell.

The door was opened by M'Calmont's handy man whom I had seen pottering about on my last visit. I asked him if Mr. M'Calmont were at home.

"Not at the moment, sir," he replied. "But please to step in. Mr. M'Calmont told me he'd be back in a minute; he's only gone to post a letter—and I'm sure he'd be very sorry to miss you."

I followed the man to the studio, which was all lit up. I stood there in a great bewilderment.

"But, William," I said, "I saw somebody come out by that door just as I was coming down the steps. But it was a twisted sort of man, like that man in all Mr. M'Calmont's pictures. I thought it must be the model." The notion had flashed into my mind that moment, as with a deep sigh of relief.

William looked puzzled.

"It must have been Mr. M'Calmont, sir. There's nobody else been here to-night. He went out a couple of minutes ago."

"But the man I saw was twisted; crooked. And he was dancing about like a lunatic."

"Then, sir, I think that was Mr. M'Calmont all right. I expect he was doing what he calls his Physical Jerks, thinking there would be nobody about to see him. He says it's strongly recommended by the doctors. But do be seated, sir, if you please."

I was staring at a great sheet of paper on an easel. It was covered with black charcoal outlines, to me significant and most awful. I had heard something of the contents of the package that had been found under the bushes of Irving Square.

I told the man I really could not wait. I hurried out of the place, and struck away up to the north, and made as quickly as I could for the broad and jangling streets, and so got home at last, avoiding dark narrows and short cuts all the way.

I do not know how long William waited for his master to return. But he waited vainly. ✣

Change

"Here," said old Mr. Vincent Rimmer, fumbling in the pigeon-holes of his great and ancient bureau, "is an oddity which may interest you."

He drew a sheet of paper out of the dark place where it had been hidden, and handed it to Reynolds, his curious guest. The oddity was an ordinary sheet of notepaper, of a sort which has long been popular; a bluish grey with slight flecks and streaks of a darker blue embedded in its substance. It had yellowed a little with age at the edges. The outer page was blank; Reynolds laid it open, and spread it out on the table beside his chair. He read something like this:

>   a aa e ee i e ee
>   aa i i o e ee o
>   ee ee i aa o oo o
>   a o a a e i ee
>   e o i ee a e i

Reynolds scanned it with stupefied perplexity.

"What on earth is it?" he said. "Does it mean anything? Is it a cypher, or a silly game, or what?"

Mr. Rimmer chuckled. "I thought it might puzzle you," he remarked. "Do you happen to notice anything about the writing; anything out of the way at all?"

Reynolds scanned the document more closely.

"Well, I don't know that there is anything out of the way in the script itself. The letters are rather big, perhaps, and they are rather clumsily formed. But it's difficult to judge handwriting by a few letters, repeated again and again. But, apart from the writing, what is it?"

"That's a question that must wait a bit. There are many strange things related to that bit of paper. But one of the strangest things about it is this; that it is intimately connected with the Darren Mystery."

"What Mystery did you say? The Darren Mystery? I don't think I ever heard of it."

"Well, it was a little before your time. And, in any case, I don't see how you could have heard of it. There were, certainly, some very curious and unusual circumstances in the case, but I don't think that they were generally known, and if they were known, they were not understood. You won't wonder at that, perhaps, when you considered that the bit of paper before you was one of those circumstances."

"But what exactly happened?"

"That is largely a matter of conjecture. But, anyhow, here's the outside of the case, for a beginning. Now, to start with, I don't suppose you've ever been to Meirion? Well, you should go. It's a beautiful county, in West Wales, with a fine sea-coast, and some very pleasant places to stay at, and none of them too large or too popular. One of the smallest of these places, Trenant, is just a village. There is a wooded height above it called the Allt; and down below, the church, with a Celtic cross in the churchyard, a dozen or so of cottages, a row of lodging-houses on the slope round the corner, a few more cottages dotted along the road to Meiros, and that's all. Below the village are marshy meadows where the brook that comes from the hills spreads abroad, and then the dunes, and the sea, stretching away to the Dragon's Head in the far east and enclosed to the west by the beginnings of the limestone cliffs. There are fine, broad sands all the way between Trenant and Porth, the market-town, about a mile and a half away, and it's just the place for children.

"Well, just forty-five years ago, Trenant was having a very successful season. In August there must have been eighteen or nineteen visitors in the village. I was staying in Porth at the time, and, when I walked over, it struck me that the Trenant beach was quite crowded—eight or nine children castle-building and learning to swim, and looking for shells, and all the usual diversions. The grown-up people sat in groups on the edge of the dunes and read and gossiped, or took a turn towards Porth, or perhaps tried to catch prawns in the rock-pools at the other end of the sands. Altogether a very pleasant, happy scene in its simple way, and, as it was a beautiful summer, I have no doubt they all enjoyed themselves very much. I walked to Trenant and back three or four times, and I noticed that most of the children were more or less in charge of a very pretty dark girl, quite young, who seemed to advise in laying out the ground-plan of the castle, and to take off her stockings and tuck up her skirts—we thought a lot of Legs in those days—when the bathers required supervision. She also indicated the kinds of shells which deserved the attention of collectors: an extremely serviceable girl.

It seemed that this girl, Alice Hayes, was really in charge of the children—or of the greater part of them. She was a sort of nursery-governess or lady of all work to Mrs. Brown, who had come down from London in the early part of July with Miss Hayes and little Michael, a child of eight, who refused to recover nicely from his attack of measles. Mr. Brown had joined them at the end of the month with the two elder children, Jack and Rosamund. Then, there were the Smiths, with their little family, and the Robinsons with their three; and the fathers and mothers, sitting on the beach every morning, got to know each other very easily. Mrs. Smith and Mrs. Robinson soon appreciated Miss Hayes's merits as a child-herd; they noticed that Mrs. Brown sat placid and went on knitting in the sun, quite safe and unperturbed, while they suffered from recurrent alarms. Jack Smith, though barely fourteen, would be seen dashing through the waves to swim to the Dragon's Head, about twenty miles away, or Jane Robinson, in bright pink, would reappear suddenly right way among the rocks of the points, ready to vanish into the perilous unknown round the corner. Hence, alarums and excursions, tiresome expeditions of rescue and remonstrance, through soft sand or over slippery rocks under a hot sun. And then these ladies would discover that certain of their offspring had entirely disappeared or were altogether missing from the landscape; and dreadful and true tales of children who had driven tunnels into the sand and had been overwhelmed therein rushed to the mind. And all the while Mrs. Brown sat serene, confident in the overseership of her Miss Hayes. So, as was to be gathered, the other two took counsel together. Mrs. Brown was approached, and something called an arrangement was made, by which Miss Hayes undertook the joint mastership of all three packs, greatly to the ease of Mrs. Smith and Mrs. Robinson.

It was about this time, I suppose, that I got to know this group of holiday-makers. I had met Smith, whom I knew slightly in town, in the streets of Porth, just as I was setting out for one of my morning walks. We strolled together to Trenant on the firm sand down by the water's edge, and introductions went round, and so I joined the party, and sat with them, watching the various diversions of the children and the capable superintendence of Miss Hayes.

"Now there's a queer thing about his little place," said Brown, a genial man, connected, I believe, with Lloyd's. "Wouldn't you say this was as healthy a spot as any you could find? Well sheltered from the north, southern aspect, never too cold in winter, fresh sea-breeze in summer: what could you have more?"

"Well," I replied, "it always agrees with me very well: a little relaxing, perhaps, but I like being relaxed. Isn't it a healthy place, then? What makes you think so?"

"I'll tell you. We have rooms on Govan Terrace, up there on the hill-side. The other night I woke up with a coughing fit. I got out of bed to get a drink of water, and then had a look out of the window to see what sort of night it was. I didn't like the look of those clouds in the south-west after sunset the night before. As you can see, the upper windows of Govan Terrace command a good many of the village houses. And, do you know, there was a light in almost every house? At two o'clock in the morning. Apparently the village is full of sick people. But who would have thought it?"

We were sitting a little apart from the rest. Smith had brought a London paper from Porth and he and Robinson had their heads together over the City article. The three women were knitting and talking hard, and down by the blue, creaming water Miss Hayes and her crew were playing happily in the sunshine.

"Do you mind," I said to Brown, "if I swear you to secrecy? A limited secrecy: I don't want you to speak of this to any of the village people. They wouldn't like it. And have you told your wife or any of the party about what you saw?"

"As a matter of fact, I haven't said a word to anybody. Illness isn't a very cheerful topic for a holiday, is it? But what's up? You don't mean to say there's some sort of epidemic in the place that they're keeping dark? I say! That would be awful. We should have to leave at once. Think of the children."

"Nothing of the kind. I don't think that there's a single case of illness in the place—unless you count old Thomas Evans, who has been in what he calls a decline for thirty years. You won't say anything? Then I'm going to give you a shock. The people have a light burning in their houses all night to keep out the fairies."

I must say it was a success. Brown looked frightened. Not of the fairies; most certainly not; rather at the reversion of his established order of things. He occupied his business in the city; he lived in an extremely comfortable house at Addiscombe; he was a keen though sane adherent of the Liberal Party; and in the world between these points there was no room at all either for fairies or for people who believed in fairies. The latter were almost as fabulous to him as the former, and still more objectionable.

"Look here!" he said at last. "You're pulling my leg. Nobody believes in fairies. They haven't for hundreds of years. Shakespeare didn't believe in fairies. He says so."

I let him run on. He implored me to tell him whether it was typhoid, or only measles, or even chicken-pox. I said at last:

"You seem very positive on the subject of fairies. Are you sure there are no such things?"

"Of course I am," said Brown, very crossly.

"How do you know?"

It is a shocking thing to be asked a question like that, to which, be it observed, there is no answer. I left him seething dangerously.

"Remember," I said, "not a word of lit windows to anybody; but if you are uneasy as to epidemics, ask the doctor about it."

He nodded his head glumly. I knew he was drawing all sorts of false conclusions; and for the rest of our stay I would say that he did not seek me out—until the last day of his visit. I had no doubt that he put me down as a believer in fairies and a maniac; but it is, I consider, good for men who live between the City and Liberal Politics and Addiscombe to be made to realize that there is a world elsewhere. And, as it happens, it was quite true that most of the Trenant people believed in the fairies and were horribly afraid of them.

But this was only an interlude. I often strolled over and joined the party. And I took up my freedom with the young members by contributing posts and a tennis net to the beach sports. They had brought down rackets and balls, in the vague idea that they might be able to get a game somehow and somewhere, and my contribution was warmly welcomed. I helped Miss Hayes to fix the net, and she marked out the court, with the help of many suggestions from the elder children, to which she did not pay the slightest attention. I think the constant disputes as to whether the ball was 'in' or 'out' brightened the game, though Wimbledon would not have approved. And sometimes the elder children accompanied their parents to Porth in the evening and watched the famous Japanese Jugglers or Pepper's Ghost at the Assembly Rooms, or listened to the Mysterious Musicians at the De Barry Gardens—and altogether everybody had, you would say, a very jolly time.

It all came to a dreadful end. One morning when I had come out on my usual morning stroll from Porth, and had got to the camping ground of the party at the end of the dunes, I found somewhat to my surprise that there was nobody there. I was afraid that Brown had been in part justified in his dread of concealed epidemics, and that some of the children had 'caught something' in the village. So I walked up in the direction of Govan Terrace, and found Brown standing at the bottom of his flight of steps, and looking very much upset.

I hailed him.

"I say," I began, "I hope you weren't right, after all. None of the children down with measles, or anything of that sort?"

"It's something worse than measles. We none of us know what has happened. The doctor can make nothing of it. Come in, and we can talk it over."

Just then a procession came down the steps leading from a house a few doors further on. First of all there was the porter from the station, with a pile of luggage on his truck. Then there came the two elder Smith children, Jack and Millicent, and finally, Mr. and Mrs. Smith. Mr. Smith was carrying something wrapped in a bundle in his arms.

"Where's Bob?" He was the youngest; a brave, rosy little man of five or six.

"Smith's carrying him," murmured Brown.

"What's happened? Has he hurt himself on the rocks? I hope it's nothing serious."

I was going forward to make my enquiries, but Brown put a hand on my arm and checked me. Then I looked at the Smith party more closely, and I saw at once that there was something very much amiss. The two elder children had been crying, though the boy was doing his best to put up a brave face against disaster—whatever it was. Mrs. Smith had drawn her veil over her face, and stumbled as she walked, and on Smith's face there was a horror as of ill dreams.

"Look," said Brown in his low voice.

Smith had half-turned, as he set out with his burden to walk down the hill to the station. I don't think he knew we were there; I don't think any of the party had noticed us as we stood on the bottom step, half-hidden by a blossoming shrub. But as he turned uncertainly, like a man in the dark, the wrappings fell away a little from what he carried, and I saw a little wizened, yellow face peering out; malignant, deplorable.

I turned helplessly to Brown, as that most wretched procession went on its way and vanished out of sight.

"What on earth has happened? That's not Bobby. Who is it?"

"Come into the house," said Brown, and he went before me up the long flight of steps that led to the terrace.

There was a shriek and a noise of thin, shrill, high-pitched laughter as we came into the lodging-house.

"That's Miss Hayes in blaspheming hysterics," said Brown grimly. "My wife's looking after her. The children are in the room at the back. I daren't let them go out by themselves in this awful place." He beat with his foot on the floor and glared at me, awestruck, a solid man shaken.

"Well," he said at last, "I'll tell you what we know; and as far as I can make out, that's very little. However. . . . You know Miss Hayes, who helps Mrs. Brown with the children, had more or less taken over the charge of the lot; the young Robinsons and the Smiths, too. You've seen how well she looks after them all on the sands in the morning. In the afternoon she's been taking them inland for a change. You know there's beautiful country if you go a little way inland; rather wild and woody; but still very nice; pleasant and shady. Miss Hayes thought that the all-day glare of the sun on the sands might not be very good for the small ones, and my wife agreed with her. So they took their teas with them and picnicked in the woods and enjoyed themselves very much, I believe. They didn't go more than a couple of miles or three at the outside; and the little ones used to take turns in a go-cart. They never seemed too tired.

"Yesterday at lunch they were talking about some caves at a place called the Darren, about two miles away. My children seemed very anxious to see them, and Mrs. Probert, our landlady, said they were quite safe, so the Smiths and Robinsons were called in, and they were enthusiastic, too; and the whole party set off with their tea-baskets, and candles and matches, in Miss Hayes's charge. Somehow they made a later start than usual, and from what I could make out they enjoyed themselves so much in the cool dark cave, first of all exploring, and then looking for treasure, and winding up with tea by candlelight, that they didn't notice how the time was going—nobody had a watch—and by the time they'd packed up their traps and come out from underground, it was quite dark. They had a little trouble making out the way at first, but not very much, and came along in high spirits, tumbling over molehills and each other, and finding it all quite an adventure.

"They had got down in the road there, and were sorting themselves out into the three parties, when somebody called out: 'Where's Bobby Smith?' Well, he wasn't there. The usual story; everybody thought he was with somebody else. They were all mixed up in the dark, talking and laughing and shrieking at the top of their voices, and taking everything for granted—I suppose it was like that. But poor little Bob was missing. You can guess what a scene there was. Everybody was much too frightened to scold Miss Hayes, who had no doubt been extremely careless, to say the least of it—not like her. Robinson pulled us together. He told Mrs. Smith that the little chap would be perfectly all right: there were no precipices to fall over and no water to fall into, the way they'd been, that it was a warm night, and the child had had a good stuffing tea, and he would be as right as rain when they found him. So we got a man from the farm, with a lantern, and Miss Hayes to show us exactly where they'd been, and Smith and Robinson and I went off to find poor Bobby, feeling a good deal better than at first. I noticed that the farm man seemed a good deal put out when we told him what had happened and where we were going. 'Got lost in the Darren,' he said, 'indeed that is a pity.' That set Smith off at once; and he asked Williams what he meant; what was the matter with the place? Williams said there was nothing the matter with it at all whatever but it was 'a tiresome place to be in after dark.' That reminded me of what you were saying a couple of weeks ago about the people here. 'Some damned superstitious nonsense,' I said to myself, and thanked God it was nothing worse. I thought the fellow might be going to tell us of a masked bog or something like that. I gave Smith a hint in a whisper as to where the land lay; and we went on, hoping to come on little Bob any minutes. Nearly all the way we were going through open fields without any cover or bracken or anything of that sort, and Williams kept twirling his lantern, and Miss Hayes and the rest of us called out the child's name; there didn't seem much chance of missing him.

"However, we saw nothing of him—till we got to the Darren. It's an odd sort of place, I should think. You're in an ordinary field, with a gentle upward slope, and you come to a gate, and down you go into a deep, narrow valley; a regular nest of valleys as far as I could make out in the dark, one leading into another, and the sides covered with trees. The famous caves were on one of these steep slopes, and, of course, we all went in. They didn't stretch far; nobody could have got lost in them, even if the candles gave out. We searched the place thoroughly, and saw where the children had had their tea; no signs of Bobby. So we went on down the valley between the woods, till we came to where it opens out into a wide space, with one tree growing all alone in the middle. And then we heard a miserable whining noise, like some little creature that's got hurt. And there under the tree was—what you saw poor Smith carrying in his arms this morning.

"It fought like a wild cat when Smith tried to pick it up, and jabbered some unearthly sort of gibberish. Then Miss Hayes came along and seemed to sooth it; and it's been quiet ever since. The man with the lantern was shaking with terror; the sweat was pouring down his face."

I stared hard at Brown. "And," I thought to myself, "you are very much in the same condition as Williams." Brown was obviously overcome with dread.

We sat there in silence.

"Why do you say 'it'?" I asked. "Why don't you say 'him'?"

"You saw."

"Do you mean to tell me seriously that you don't believe that child you helped to bring home was Bobby? What does Mrs. Smith say?"

"She says the clothes are the same. I suppose it must be Bobby. The doctor from Porth says the child must have had a severe shock. I don't think he knows anything about it."

He stuttered over his words, and said at last:

"I was thinking of what you said about the lighted windows. I hoped you might be able to help. Can you do anything? We are leaving this afternoon; all of us. Is there nothing to be done?"

"I'm afraid not."

I had nothing else to say. We shook hands and parted without more words.

The next day I walked over to the Darren. There was something fearful about the place, even in the haze of a golden afternoon. As Brown had said, the entrance and the disclosure of it were sudden and abrupt. The fields of the approach held no hint of what was to come. Then, past the gate, the ground fell violently away on every side, grey rocks of an ill shape pierced through it, and the ash trees on the steep slopes overshadowed all. The descent was into silence, without the singing of a bird, into a wizard shade. At the farther end, where the wooded heights retreated somewhat, there was the open space, or circus, of turf; and in the middle of it a very ancient, twisted thorn tree, beneath which the party in the dark had found the little creature that whines and cried out in unknown speech. I turned about, and on my way back I entered the caves, and lit the carriage candle I had brought with me. There was nothing much to see—I never think there is much to see in caves. There was the place where the children and others before them had taken their tea, with a ring of blackened stones within which many fires of twigs had been kindled. In caves or out of caves, townsfolk in the country are always alike in leaving untidy and unseemly litter behind; and here with the usual scraps of greasy paper, daubed with smears of jam and butter, the half-eaten sandwich, and the gnawed crust. Amidst all this nastiness I saw a piece of folded notepaper, and in sheer idleness picked it up and opened it. You have just seen it. When I asked you if you saw anything peculiar about the writing, you said that the letters were rather big and clumsy. The reason of that is that they were written by a child. I don't think you examined the back of the second leaf. Look: 'Rosamund'—Rosamund Brown, that is. And beneath; there, in the corner."

Reynolds looked, and read, and gaped aghast.

"That was—her other name; her name in the dark."

"Name in the dark?"

"In the dark night of the Sabbath. That pretty girl had caught them all. They were in her hands, those wretched children, like the clay images she made. I found one of those things, hidden in a cleft of the rocks, near the place where they had made their fire. I ground it into dust beneath my feet."

"And I wonder what her name was?"

"They called her, I think, the Bridegroom and the Bride."

"Did you ever find out who she was, or where she came from?"

"Very little. Only that she had been a mistress at the Home for Christian Orphans in North Tottenham, where there was a hideous scandal some years before."

"Then she must have been older than she looked, according to your description."

"Possibly."

They sat in silence for a few minutes. Then Reynolds said:

"But I haven't asked you about this formula, or whatever you may call it—all these vowels, here. Is it a cypher?"

"No. But it is really a great curiosity, and it raises some extraordinary questions, which are outside this particular case. To begin with—and I am sure I could go much farther back than my beginning, if I had the necessary scholarship—I once read an English rendering of a Greek manuscript of the second or third century—I won't be certain which. It's a long time since I've seen the thing. The translator and editor of it was of the opinion that it was a Mithriac Ritual; but I have gathered that weightier authorities are strongly inclined to discredit this view. At any rate, it was no doubt an initiation rite into some mystery; possibly it had Gnostic connections; I don't know. But our interest lies in this, that one of the stages or portals, or whatever you call them, consisted, almost exactly, of that formula you have in your hand. I don't say that the vowels and double vowels are in the same order; I don't think the Greek manuscript has any *aes* or *aas*. But it is perfectly clear that the two documents are of the same kind and have the same purpose. And, advancing a little in time from the Greek manuscript, I don't think it is very surprising that the final operation of an incantation in mediaeval and later magic consisted of this wailing on vowels arranged in a certain order.

"But here is something that is surprising. A good many years ago I strolled one Sunday morning into a church in Bloomsbury, the headquarters of a highly respectable sect. And in the middle of a very dignified ritual, there rose quite suddenly, without preface or warning, this very sound, a wild wail on vowels. The effect was astounding, anyhow; whether it was terrifying or merely funny, is a matter of taste. You'll have guessed what I heard: they call it 'speaking with tongues,' and they believe it to be a heavenly language. And I need scarcely say that they mean very well. But the problem is: how did a congregation of solid Scotch Presbyterians hit upon that queer, ancient and not over-sanctified method of expressing spiritual emotion? It is a singular puzzle.

"And that woman? That is not by any means so difficult. The good Scotchmen—I can't think how they did it—got hold of something didn't belong to them: she was in her own tradition. And, as they say down there: *asakai dasa*: the darkness is undying."

✢

The Dover Road

The disappearance of Sir Halliday Stuart, the well-known antiquary, was really a very puzzling affair. And even the solution of it is in itself something of a puzzle.

Some of the circumstances that surrounded and involved this singular business were recalled by the painstaking though futile attempt undertaken by the B.B.C. to pin down a ghost that was supposed to haunt an old manor house in an out-of-the-way part of Kent. The B.B.C. people, it will be remembered, put themselves in the hands of a recognized expert. This gentleman took the precautions which considerable experience of sprites, some of them exceedingly tricky, suggested as necessary. He sealed the doors with a special seal, he established microphones at critical points. In that quarter which was supposed to be afflicted now and again by icy draughts of air he set up an automatic temperature registering instrument. A watch went on guard outside the house, and patrolled the ground from eight o'clock to a quarter to twelve. Then the expert and four or five others sat down to watch and listen.

Everything, in short, that could be done was done. And nothing, or next to nothing, happened. The instrument that registered the temperature showed some odd alternations, moving up and down within four or five degrees Fahrenheit, but there was no indication of the blasts of ice-cold air of which the legends spoke. Beyond this, there was nothing, and the expert and his assessors broke off the inquiry, observing very sensibly that the local ghost in particular and ghosts in general had neither been proved nor disproved by the proceedings of the night.

Very much the same kind of thing happened at an earlier investigation of a supposed case of haunting, which was conducted without the aid or countenance of Broadcasting House. In this case, the building supposed to be haunted was an old manor house called Morton Grange, situated in Essex, fourteen or fifteen miles from London, to the north-east. In those days, it might fairly be said to be in the country, but now it stands, if it does stand at all, in the very middle of the Morton Grange Estate, a sad grey rock in a red suburban sea. At the time of the experiment in ghost-detection, the Grange was not only in the country, but lonely—for a house within reasonable distance from Liverpool Street. Following the main road, dotted here and there with pleasant old cottages, and not unpleasant oldish villas—the sort of villa that has a trellised porch, a verandah, and a curving penthouse over a window here and there—one came to the hamlet of Morton; a whole row of cottages, a Queen Anne house for a doctor, a public-house with dim green seats and tables before it, the rectory, with a drive, behind shrubs and elms, and a small, unrestored church. At the end of all this, a yellow washed farmhouse, with famous barns, red brick, half-timber, and dipping roof-trees; and a bare quarter of a mile farther, on the other side of the road, and some way from it, where the land rose up in a slope, Morton Grange, a confused appearance of buildings, part stucco and part stone, and altogether of a neglected aspect.

It was approached, in spite of what must have been its former dignity, by a lane that could hardly have been a formal drive in its best days, since it had rough high banks with old timber growing on them. Then, a stone wall with good iron-work gates, beginning to rust away, and a grove of dark ilexes. Before the front of the house, a lawn sloped down to a sunken fence or ha-ha: there were remnants of flower beds, their edges vague and overgrown with grass and weeds, remnants of a rosary, in which the suckers of the wild stock had overpowered the cultivated flowers, and grown into matted and thorny thickets. A leaden statue, with one arm missing, stood in the midst of a stagnant pool; some grey stone urns on pillars showed vague and mouldering indications of stone garlands.

Where the stucco had begun to peel away on the right, as you faced the house, the architecture looked early Georgian; the left, the grey stone portion, was a good deal older, though the mullions had been knocked out of most of the windows. At the back; kitchens, pantries, butteries, brew-house and the rest smacked of the sixteenth century; low, solid, cavernous places. The living-rooms were dank and damp; the gorgeous Chinese paper of the drawing-room was smeared with grey shapes of rising wet, the heavy crimson flock paper of the dining-room was beginning to peel and rip from the sweating wall. In three or four of the rooms there was a skeleton furnishing: cheap modern stuff, shabby after forty, fifty years of little use and long neglect. And the usual story was told about the house. It was empty because no one could live in it. It was haunted.

Of course, there was a legend; and here again it was the usual legend; more or less. I believe there was a monk who was looking for treasure, and might have had some difficulty in explaining his *locus standi*, if he could have been brought to book, since the Grange had never been a religious house. There was a Priest, who had been stifled in his hiding-hole, contrived in the hall chimney. And there was a Cavalier, who perished in some very unhappy manner. These three stock phantoms hovered about the legend of the Grange; now one troubled the peace of its inhabitants, now another. There was every reason to suppose that all three of them were invented some time in the 'thirties or 'forties of the last century, together with the Mysterious Terror of Glamis Castle, and the *chère reine* of Charing.

Yet, though the Monk and the Priest and the Cavalier were, doubtless, idle and late inventions; there was a certain remnant of strangeness about Morton Grange, which, it seemed, could not be explained as the result of natural and normal causes. Andrew Lang, if I remember, was taken into counsel over the place, and on hearing of some of the alleged abnormal phenomena, was inclined to suggest rats and defective waterpipes. There was also a singular moaning sound, distinct and different from the whine of the wind in the chimneys; and Lang advised a close structural examination of the other parts of the house; it was possible, he thought, that there might be a tunnel or vent in the thickness of the walls, which might catch the wind blowing from a particular quarter.

This surmise, I believe, was justified on examination, such a tunnel was found in the old brew-house at the back of the Grange. But, beyond the moans and whines and sighs, there were other manifestations of a more difficult order. There was a cellar door which persisted in staying open, whatever you did with it. A new lock was affixed, the bolt turned, and the other two keys taken away in the occupant's pocket; but when he came back from London in the evening, the door was wide open. The man, not to be beaten, had another and a very special mechanism, with an alphabetical combination, affixed but again the door was opened—somehow. Lang confessed that he could not account for this circumstance; and there the matter rested until Professor Warburton took the Grange in hand ten or a dozen years ago.

Warburton was a distinguished man of science, and a strong exponent of the purely materialistic theory of the universe; he was even reckoned by some of his own school as a little old-fashioned in this respect. I am not sure that the particular instance applied in his case; but he was certainly with the older men who held that the stigmata—for example—were lies and impostures and didn't happen, rather than on the side of the younger scientists, who would discuss cases of the stigmata that they had observed in the hospital wards, and show that they had no more spiritual significance than carbuncles.

Somehow, this very valiant and determined man heard of the Morton Grange puzzle, and felt certain that either trickery or a purely mechanical cause was the only agent. He made up his mind to investigate, not without hesitation, since he held that the man of science should hardly partake so far of the evil thing—which he sometimes called Mysticism and sometimes Spiritualism—as to admit that it required investigation. However, in this case, the end seemed to justify the means; and the Professor began to make his arrangements. The then occupant of the Grange, who seldom occupied it, made no difficulties; and Professor Warburton chose as assistants three or four friends and acquaintances: Rodney, the biologist, W. K. Forster, a Chancery barrister, Sir Charles Lemon, the throat specialist, and Ian Tallent, who was supposed to have inherited a good share of the Andrew Lang mantle, and had a very ingenious hypothesis as to the fire-walking problem.

The night of the inquest was fixed, the caretaker and his wife were warned to get in sufficient fuel and have a fire burning all day in the room nearest to the cellar stairs, and to await the party at eight o'clock, thereafter to betake themselves to the village inn, where a room had been ordered for them. On the morning of the appointed day, Professor Warburton was sitting in his study at his house in Philpot Crescent, Kensington, contemplating the campaign of Morton Grange, when his servant announced a caller.

The Professor knew the name, Sir Halliday Stuart, the famous antiquary, very well, though he had never met the man. Sir Halliday was asked to come up, and the two eminent personages met with grave courtesy. After a phrase of apology, the caller came directly to his point.

"I understand," he said, "that you are going down this evening to investigate certain phenomena which are alleged to take place at Morton Grange, in Essex. Well, if I may venture, I would put it that you would do me a very great favour, if you would allow me to be of your party. Do you think you could stretch a point?"

Warburton was agreeably impressed by the antiquary. He was of a dark, agreeable presence, and his face lit up with a very engaging smile, as he made his apology and petition.

"We shall all be most pleased, I am sure," he said, "and honoured too by your company. But I didn't know that Spiritualism was much in your line."

"It's not, not a bit of it," said Sir Halliday. "And if you'll forgive me, I've always understood that it was still less in yours."

The Professor explained.

"You're perfectly right. Thirty years ago I shouldn't have dreamed of having anything to do with such unmitigated nonsense. There were exceptions, of course—there was Crookes—but men of science wouldn't hear of such stuff or of any approach to it. They didn't refute it. They didn't know it was there. And any scientist who was suspected of having any kind of interest in all this mystical humbug would have forfeited the respect of his colleagues.

"But the War had changed everything. It was, no doubt, a very severe national shock. It has had all sorts of bad effects and repercussions; and one of the worst, in my opinion, is this hysterical credulity that one sees everywhere. There's no tale too monstrous to be believed. We're threatened with the return of the most childish superstitions of the Middle Ages. Here's an instance; this tale of a door that can't be kept shut whatever locks you put on it. And there are people of supposed intelligence who are ready to discuss this nonsense seriously! I feel it's my duty to expose the trick, whatever it is. It will be 'doing my bit,' as the men used to say in the War."

"I quite understand," said Sir Halliday, "and I may as well explain my interest in the matter. I made a study of Morton Grange some years ago and included it in my 'Essex Manor Houses and Halls.' There are some extremely interesting features in the building. The vaulting in the cellar is, in my opinion, unquestionably Roman, though Markham won't admit it. I think there is a very strong evidence that the Grange cellar was, originally, a Mithrian temple. I should like to have the opportunity of making a re-examination. And it also occurred to me that my knowledge of the structure of the place might possibly be of some service to you in your investigation."

Sir Halliday Stuart was cordially included in the party of ghost-hunters. He refused with thanks the offer of a seat in Warburton's car: he was going down earlier, he explained, as he wished to have another look at the very singular squint in the Grange brew house: an undoubted thirteenth-century building, he explained, the original lancets having been replaced by square headed windows of 1530–40.

"And for this I shall want daylight. So you will find me at the Grange when you arrive. It is extremely kind of you to let me join your party."

Warburton was pleased with this addition to his committee of investigation. There was a genial gravity about the antiquary that won favour; and he was evidently a man of an accurate habit of mind, accustomed to careful observation, a minute weighing of evidence, the very man for the occasion. The

Professor told the others about the inclusion of Stuart, when they all met at his house in the late afternoon, and they agreed he would be valuable. They all knew him by reputation, and Tallent had read his revised edition of "Isca Silurum" with very great interest. When the cars drew up before the door of Morton Grange that evening, Stuart was waiting on the steps. He was mildly excited.

"I've examined that squint very minutely," he said to Warburton. "I have Markham at my mercy."

The introductions were made, and the party entered the house. Warburton had brought down flasks of strong coffee, and the caretaker having set cups and saucers on the table, departed with his wife. Warburton locked the front door, the back door, and the door communicating with the brew-house, and put the keys in his pocket. A systematic tour and search of the mouldering and desolate house was made. The cellar came last in the inspection, and Professor Warburton pointed out the bolts he had added to the alphabet lock.

"One top, one bottom," he said. "The best steel, fitted under my supervision."

The door stood open; a powerful lamp was fixed above it, and another on the other side, within the cellar. Sir Halliday Stuart went in eagerly, and peered about him.

"Look at the entablatures," he said. "There's no room for doubt."

Warburton called him out, adjusted the lock, and shot the bolts. The party went up the steps of the winding stair, and sat down to their hot coffee, while Warburton explained his plan.

"One of us," he said, "is to be on guard at the bottom of the cellar stair, by the door, the whole evening from eight to twelve-fifteen. The watch will be for an hour; I will take the first watch, and Rodney will relieve me at nine. The door at the top of the stairs will be open, and the door of this room will be open. The instruction to the man on guard is: to call out at the top of his voice if he sees or hears anything in the least out of the way. That is understood? Very good. It is now half-past seven; perhaps Sir Halliday will tell us something about the history of Morton Grange while we are drinking our coffee?"

Sir Halliday cordially assented, and proceeded to deliver a bristling lecture. He merely touched on the evidences for stone and bronze age occupation, was diffused and elaborate on the Roman period; thinning again with the Saxon-invasion; but becoming merciless from Doomsday Book to the end of the seventeenth century. Strange terms and allusions were heard; *inquisitis post mortem,* Fine and Recovery, *diem elausit extremum, mortuus sine prole,* Pipe Rolls, vert, a chevron or. Some of these terms awoke memories in Forster, the barrister; to the rest they were as the hooting of owls. The Monk, the Priest, and the Cavalier were mentioned only to be puffed away like thistledown.

"So you see," said the antiquary, "the place has a very ordinary history; the typical history, in fact, of the East Anglian manor house. So far as I know, apart from certain remarkable features in construction, which I have explained to you as well as I can, the only point of interest I can recall in the history of the Grange is the discovery, a few years ago, of a hiding-place in the chimney of the great hall, used from 1690 onwards as a brew-house. A workman employed in putting right some loose bricks, found a small oak chest in a place contrived in the thickness of the chimney. The contents were legal documents, of the late sixteenth and early seventeenth centuries, relating to the passing of the manor and estate from the Mullins Moleyno family to the Roches."

At eight o'clock, punctually, the watch was set, Warburton went down, impressing on the others that they were to join him at top speed if he called out. The two doors: the sitting-room door, and the door at the top of the stairs, were left open as arranged. The party in the room broached another flask of coffee, smoked a little, and talked a little in low tones. Some of them thought they were making fools of themselves, and were sorry they had come.

The hours went by without event. The antiquary, having delivered his lecture, seemed to sink into a gentle abstraction, from which he roused himself now and again to make remarks which seemed to be dictated by a sense of conversational duty, rather than by interest in the (possible) ghost. He pulled out his watch, looked at it and observed with bland satisfaction, "We are keeping good time, I think." Warburton, who had just come up from his turn at the door, assured him that the time-table was being strictly adhered to. Sir Halliday nodded, and again became quiescent.

Nothing happened. Rodney had crept like a snail down the stairs on hearing Warburton's summons. The barrister, Forster, succeeded the biologist. Sir Halliday, brightening once more, said it was a calm night, at all events, "and that's in our favour." People were puzzled for a moment, and then concluded that he meant that their observations were not to be confused by the noises of high wind and restless trees. Sir Charles Lemon took up his position at the bottom of the stairs at eleven. The low-voiced conversation flagged. Most of the men looked tired and bored to the extreme. Sir Halliday's head shook and nodded, not with sleep, but rather as if he were following a train of reasoning, an argument with an imaginary opponent, dissenting, and agreeing by turns. Finally, as Lemon's watch drew on, and midnight was at hand, the antiquary, feeling, perhaps, that he had cultivated silence at the expense of courtesy, remarked in a very amiable manner:

"Well, I suppose Dover *is* rather a hole. But I must say I've always liked it; Strond Street and the old harbour; all that part, you know."

The company in general, who were longing to make and end of a tiresome and futile sitting, as they considered it, looked up crossly, and wondered what on earth Stuart thought he was talking about. Tallent chuckled quietly; the key word of Sir Halliday's sentence, and its lack of precise relevance to the business in hand had reminded him of a certain immortal axiom relating to milestones on the Dover Road, but he speculated also as to whether Sir Halliday's intellect was quite the keen instrument of their belief.

It was on the first stroke of twelve that at last something happened. Lemon, who had by this time quite made up his mind that he had wasted the evening, was just calling on Ian Tallent to take his place, when the summons changed to a dismal sound, something inarticulate, between a croak and a cry. The whole company in the sitting-room jumped up and pelted out of the door, and jammed in the narrow stair. Sir Charles, gasping, with a grey-white face, was hauled up, on the verge of a fainting fit, to the higher region. Brandy was administered, and he was soon able to say, rather tartly, that beyond damned foul air, he had nothing to report. They were all yawning and looking at their watches and agreeing that there was nothing to be done but to go home, when Warburton, glancing from one to another, said with a jerk:

"Where's Stuart?"

And, in a second or two, it was evident that he had asked a question that nobody could answer. Sir Halliday Stuart was not there, nowhere in the room at all. They bustled into the passage, went again, not quite so madly, down the stair to the cellar; presently, explored every room in the house with the aid of electric torches, returned, looking helpless, to the room where they had held their session. They had not found a trace of the antiquary. And Warburton, who had the keys of every exit in his pocket, knew perfectly well that he must be in the house—somewhere. Then a notion struck him.

"Will you all stay in this room?" he said. "I should think it would be as well if you sat down. It has just struck me as possible that Sir Halliday is in the cellar, examining those accursed entablatures of his. I can't think how he can have got there, if he is there, without knowing the lock combination—but perhaps there is some trickery about that door which circumstances have prevented us from detecting so far. At any rate, I am going to make sure that Sir Halliday has not been caught in some sort of trap. May I ask you again to keep your positions exactly as you are at present?"

Warburton was absent for seven or eight minutes. His face was blank when he returned.

"I've been over every inch of the cellar," he said. "There's no one there. I've put out the lights and refastened the door. We mustn't leave a bolt-hole. Not that I would suggest for a moment that Stuart could or would desire to bolt; of course that's absurd. Still . . . what on earth can have become of the man? I was standing just behind him when the doctor gave the alarm, and we all ran down. Did anybody else notice him, then or afterwards?"

Nobody had. They were all staring at Sir Charles Lemon. They saw nothing else during the critical moments.

"There is nothing to be done," concluded Professor Warburton after some minutes of perplexed meditation, "but to make a thorough and systematic search of the whole house. Perhaps we were a little haphazard before. I will take Forster with me, and we will go over every room in the house."

The two went off with their torches. They were away for half an hour. They had failed to discover Sir Halliday, or any trace or hint of his presence. It was evident that there was nothing more to be done. Tallent put the position of affairs to himself that Sir Halliday was both in the Grange and not in the Grange at the same time; he remembered having seen something of the kind in Eastern Philosophy. But he kept the contradiction to himself, not thinking it suitable for the company. He substituted the sagacious and commonsensical remark:

"A difficult thing to be sure you've gone into every nook and cupboard of an old place like this. A little chap of Stuart's build could pack himself away in a very small space."

"Little chap?" said Forster. "I should have said that Sir Halliday was above the average height."

Finally, they all returned to town in a condition of stupified bewilderment.

The first thing, the next morning, Professor Warburton found out Sir Halliday Stuart's address. He had a place in Oxfordshire, it appeared, but when in town he occupied a suite of rooms in service chambers near St. James's. Warburton went there at once and saw the management. Sir Halliday had been in residence for five or six weeks, the manager told him.

"Yesterday morning, soon after twelve he came round to the offices and handed in his key. He said he might be away for some little time. I was not at all surprised; there was nothing unusual in the proceeding. Sir Halliday often went away without giving us notice in advance. He would be out of town for a week, a month, even three months. Sometimes he would send a postcard announcing his return; but as a rule he merely walked in and asked for his key."

"And there is no address to which I could write?"
"You might try Sir Halliday Stuart's Oxfordshire

address. I can give you that: 'Campden House, High Street—the name of the village, I understand—Oxfordshire.' It is possible that Sir Halliday is there."

The Professor went home and wrote two letters. One to Sir Halliday, politely begging to be reassured as to his safety, asking no questions, going into no detail. This letter he put into a small envelope, which was enclosed in a large envelope, addressed "Occupant," with a letter begging for Sir Halliday's present address. The large envelope, marked "Urgent Immediate," was despatched by registered post. There was an answer by return. M. Timpson begged to say that Sir Halliday Stuart was at present residing in his London chambers, the address of which was enclosed.

Meanwhile, Professor Warburton had taken counsel with the friends who had been with him in the strange adventure of Morton Grange. They had all agreed together that it would be well to keep the whole affair in strict secrecy. It was clear, they decided, that in some way or another, Sir Halliday Stuart had contrived to get out of the house in the midst of the confusion over Lemon's collapse. Nobody could suggest how he made his exit or why he made it; but it was evident that he *had* made it. One of them, given on the quiet to the reading of very old-fashioned fiction, babbled of sliding panels and secret passages. But Warburton, who had reluctantly thought of this, had paid another visit to the Grange, going there in broad daylight, and taking with him an expert with a foot-rule, who tapped and measured and surveyed within and without, and gave it as his technical and considered opinion that in this case, at all events, the notion of sliding panels, hidden doors, and secret passages was bunkum. There was nothing to be said; they all felt that they had come to a blank and intolerable wall. And if, by some unconjectured way and dark passage, Sir Halliday had got out of Morton Grange, where was he?

No doubt they all tried their best to keep the secret, but Sir Halliday, it seemed, had an aunt, very old and energetic, and this lady, hearing that her nephew was not to be found, went to the police, and the constables of Essex called in Scotland Yard, which was interested by the peculiar circumstances of the disappearance.

Now, there is nothing illegal about disappearing. Hundreds, or dozens at any rate, of people disappear every year, and nobody bothers about them. Night by night, "Time, Weather, and News," on the Wireless is prefaced by one, two or three S O S's: "S O S Lawkins. Will Thomas Lawkins, last heard of about five years ago in Dulverton, go to Hampstead Heath Hospital, Hampstead, London, where his father Albert Lawkins, is dangerously ill." Clearly, Thomas Lawkins disappeared five years ago or more, and did so in perfect peace. A few years since, a man was found murdered in a car on the highway; and even the violent notoriety of his death did not suffice to identify him, he also must have disappeared, leaving neither trace nor inquiry behind him. But, presumably, Lawkins and the murdered man and men like them have been undistinguished and obscure people, who for one reason or another have shed relations and connections, and have left no great curiosity as to their whereabouts behind them. But Sir Halliday Stuart was none such: he was highly distinguished, a figure in his own world, a man of many friends and colleagues. Moreover, there were the peculiar circumstances, and other people, also well-known, were, one must not say involved, but at any rate present on the occasion when Sir Halliday, as it appeared, was last seen by his fellow-men. Ten days after this event, Professor Warburton received a call from a high official of Scotland Yard, purely in search of exact information.

The Professor gave it, told the whole story, gave the name of the men who were associated with him in the affair, and at the end said very frankly:

"And I should be very much obliged to you, sir, if you would tell me what has happened to Sir Halliday Stuart."

The Scotland Yard man said that that was a question which could not be answered off hand. Inquiries of the most searching nature would be made: there must be a flaw somewhere, a weak spot, in the statement he had just heard, and, no doubt, a trained man would be able to put his finger on it—in time. They would send their own experts to make a special examination of Morton Grange; they might find something.

"Here's a possibility, now, that has just occurred to me. It's not uncommon to come across old, disused wells in such houses as Morton Grange. They are sometimes in the most unexpected places; at the end of dark passages, in a corner at the bottom of a staircase: you never know where to look for them. And the covering, the trap at the top, has sometimes gone rotten. The solution may lie in that direction; though I sincerely hope it doesn't. And in the meantime, would you give me the addresses of your friends who were engaged with you in this business? They may give us some help; you never know. And would you let me have the best description you can manage of Sir Halliday Stuart's personal appearance? Height, fair or dark, colour of hair and eyes, fat or thin, any peculiarities, facial or otherwise; scars; you know the sort of thing?"

The four men were run down at once; they were all Londoners. Each had been asked to give the best description he could of the missing man, together with his account of what had happened, as each had observed the events of that singular night. By the evening, the shorthand notes had been transcribed, and were laid before the personage at the Yard.

"Now, look here," he said to his lieutenant. "This is going to be a very complicated business. For the moment we won't bother about the accounts of the proceedings at this dam' silly business of theirs. I've run through them and compared them with what I got from Professor Warburton this morning, and as far as I can make out they all agree as to the main facts. There are no important discrepancies, anyhow. It's these descriptions of Sir Halliday's personal appearance that are bothering me. Here, you see, is the stuff we got from two of his most intimate friends: Dr. Manning, of Brasenose, and Lord John Ashley of Queen's Row. You see they agree practically in every particular: height, about 5 ft. 7 ins; hair, dark brown, thinning; eyes, grey; Lord John Ashley says, blue—nose aquiline; short upper lip—Manning doesn't mention that—thin; white scar on forefinger of right hand; chestnut eyebrows; and so forth and so forth. As I say, the two descriptions agree."

"By the way," said the lieutenant, "no photographs?"

"He hasn't been photographed for twenty years. There's a sketch in black and white; but I don't think its going to be of much use. But here's the important point. Look at these descriptions of Sir Halliday by Professor Warburton and his four friends you see, they don't agree. One man says short, another tall; the Professor says, hair black; Forster, light brown. They're all at odds. Yet by their own account they were sitting with Sir Halliday and talking to him for four hours on end. What do you make of it?"

The other man studied the documents carefully.

"It's a pity," he said, "that detective fiction is so seldom of much use to detectives. You remember, 'The Murders in the Rue Morgue' the witnesses differing about the language which they had heard the unseen murderer speaking? The Frenchman thought it was English—he didn't know any English. The overwrought Dutchman held it to be Russian; the Englishman, who was ignorant of French, was sure it was French. The deduction to be drawn was that the murderer wasn't speaking any language at all; that he was an ape, and merely gibbering. But I don't see how we can apply Poe's invention to our difficulty."

"No, I don't think we can," said the chief with some dryness and a touch of impatience.

"Unless," said the lieutenant, "we argue that there was nobody there—no Sir Charles Halliday, I mean. That seems the legitimate conclusion; and, obviously, it won't do."

Then the chief said that it was a serious business and they must go about it seriously. He had put a man who knew his job into the Grange, and had told him to go over every inch of it. And if he wanted to do any digging outside, he was to telephone for help.

"You don't think so?"

"No; I don't; but it may perhaps be as well to make sure."

The problem remained the secret of Scotland Yard, and of a circle that was moderately small, considering all things. It was kept out of the Press; and the inquiries went on without result for a month, less three or four days, when a solution was given in a very singular manner. The scene returns to Professor Warburton's study. The Professor is discovered at his bureau, trying hard to occupy himself with his proper business, but wondering at intervals when he would be arrested for the murder of Sir Halliday Stuart. That was what he told his friends later, as a matter of fact he was not beset at all by any such nonsensical fears; but he was still intensely puzzled by the antiquary's disappearance, and intensely curious to know what had really happened. And while he was in this state of mind, his man brought in a card.

Warburton took it impatiently; he didn't want to be bothered by anybody. He read: *Sir Halliday Stuart.*

He stared at the servant with an expression that the man found dreadful in its sheer amazement. He gave the necessary order with difficulty, and got up from his chair and stood waiting, in such surprise and confusion of mind as made him realize for the first time that he had never thought to see Sir Halliday again amongst living men.

The door opened, and the servant announced the visitor. A middle-aged, baldish man with a beaky nose entered the room, and, smiling, confronted the bewildered Professor.

"I gather that you wish to see me, Professor Warburton," he began. "When I got back to High Street yesterday, my housekeeper handed me this envelope, with the enclosure addressed to me. You ask"—he took out his glasses—"to be reassured as to my safety. I hope you will excuse me: but I assure you that I haven't the remotest notion of what you mean."

Warburton feebly motioned the visitor to a chair, and sat down himself, so far incapable of coherent speech.

"You see," Sir Halliday went on, "I don't think I've had the pleasure of meeting you till the present moment, and I, naturally, feel a little puzzled. Is it possible that there has been some mistake, some confusion possibly on the part of your secretary? Were you by any chance mixing me up with Mackinlay Stuart, the Science Don? You know him, no doubt?"

Warburton felt that he was sinking into yet deeper and dimmer depths of confusion. "Not had the pleasure of meeting you till the present moment," he quoted helplessly to himself, and though not deeply versed in Holy Writ, he thought of somebody who could have roared for the very disquietness of his heart. He gaped at the man sitting before him;

amazed at his barefaced denial of their former encounter, and of the hours they had spent together at the Grange. "Is it possible," he asked himself, "that he doesn't recognize me as I recognize him?"

He scrutinized Sir Halliday's features more intently, and then realized, astonished, that the Sir Halliday of a month ago compared with the Sir Halliday now in presence, was rather like an old, yellowed, and blurred photograph in an ancient album, put beside a clean, recent likeness; or, one might say, a first sketch contrasted with the finished drawing. One saw the resemblance, of course, but the Sir Halliday of the Grange had been, as it were, faint.

But how did that help? Not in the least. It rather added confusion to a business that was already utterly confounded. But after a long silence, Warburton struggled from his morass of dazed perplexity and climbed his way into speech. On the whole, he did not do badly; he told Sir Halliday the story of his morning call and evening's occupation, finishing with his mysterious disappearance from Morton Grange.

"And at the present moment," he ended, "Scotland Yard are looking for you. Unless, of course, they have heard of your return."

And it was hard to say which of the two were the more astounded. Warburton, by telling it, had revived all his first amazement, when Sir Halliday could not be found. Sir Halliday could not control himself as he heard an account of his movements on a particular day in October which he knew to be at total variance with the facts. He looked hard at Warburton. There is always a certain way of escape open, when a man is confronted with an incredible and intolerable statement. That is, to hold the person who makes the statement to be a liar. And, undoubtedly, this is often the right solution of such problems. But the antiquary, scanning the visage of the man of exact science, measuring the manner of his utterance, felt that, in this case, mere lying was not the required answer to the riddle. And, besides . . .

"There were four men with you, you said. Who were they?"

Professor Warburton gave the names.

"They're responsible men," he said. "All of them of a certain distinction."

"And they all share your impressions of what happened that night?"

"Absolutely. We are all agreed; I think I may say in every detail."

He suppressed the fact that there had been some discussion and divergence in the party as to Sir Halliday's build and appearance; firstly, because it seemed personal, and then, because he thought very few men were capable of exact observation and subsequent description, and lastly, because he was still puzzled by the difference he had just observed between the look and show of Sir Halliday on his former and his latter visits, and didn't know what to say or think about it.

Sir Halliday pondered. He knew the names of the people who had been associated with Warburton, and, as the professor had observed, they were responsible men. None of them was at all likely to conspire in the concoction of an aimless and preposterous fiction. To believe that would be simply to substitute one incredible story for another. He would take it, then, that the whole five of them supposed that they were telling the truth. He broke his silence.

"I really don't know what to say. The absolute antinomy between your statement and what I know to be the facts as to my doings on the day in question is quite overwhelming. But I'll tell you what really happened, so far as I am concerned, and I hope you'll forgive the small quantity of shop I may have to introduce.

"Well, then. You may be aware that a few years ago there was a good deal of discussion in the Press as to certain discoveries in Central France of objects in baked clay which were said to belong to a very remote period. There were considerable names in favour of their antiquity. However, in the long run, evidence of a destructive character was produced, and in spite of a very spirited defence, the verdict was that the supposed prehistoric pottery was nothing more or less than a modern forgery. Naturally, therefore, we were inclined to treat reports of similar finds with a good deal of distrust, and it was some time before I paid any attention to accounts of discoveries of very early pottery at a place near Loches, in the department of Indre-et-Loire. However, on the morning of October 13th last—your date, I think, Professor—there was an article in *The Times*, which seemed to leave no room for suspicion. I felt I must see for myself: the occurrence of the maze of labyrinth pattern on Neolithic objects struck me as of very great significance and importance.

"I left my chambers late in the morning, took a long walk out into the country, dined in some strange place in Soho, and left London by the night service. I got to Paris the next morning, caught the *Rapide* to Tours, and stayed the night at Loches. Next day, I walked through the forest to the village of Genille, and through the courtesy of M. Pic-Paris, the distinguished French antiquary, whom I had met before, I was able to make a thorough examination of the objects discovered in the rock caves, a short distance from the village. In this case, I may say, I am convinced of the entire genuineness of the find—but that doesn't concern our present purpose. After a week of very close study and of conferences with M. Pic-Paris and other French colleagues, I went on to

Tours; a most agreeable city. I left Tours for England a couple of days ago. I should be glad to show you my hotel bills."

There was a pause. Very evidently and certainly Professor Warburton considered within himself, the man was telling the truth. Then Sir Halliday began talking again, with a sudden plunge.

"But here's a very odd thing, which has just struck me. It is the case that some years ago Morton Grange engaged a good deal of my attention. I made a special study of it for a book of mine, called, 'Essex Manor Houses and Halls.'"

Warburton interrupted, "You told me that before—the last time you were here."

Sir Halliday choked down an inarticulate noise in his throat. "And you were a good deal interested in something you called a squint in the brew-house at the Grange. Also in the vaulting of the cellar. You said, I think, that you were convinced that the cellar had been originally a temple of Mithras."

The effect of this utterance on the two men was tremendous. It was the great name of Mithras that produced this effect. Sir Halliday had been shaken by Warburton's, "You told me that before." He took his host for a truthful man; his familiarity with "Essex Manor Houses" title was, therefore, not a feigned one. And it might be taken as certain that this physiologist, or physicist, or whatever he was, had never so much as seen the publication in question—a subscription book issued to the members of a learned society—and yet he talked of the cellar vaulting and the brew-house squint. But the matter of Mithras! That was a secret, held in reserve, not breathed to his nearest associates. The evidence for the Mithraic origin and use of that Morton Grange cellar, drawn from many sources and accumulating for years, was almost ready to be welded into a demonstration. Other affairs had pressed on Stuart, and he had not been able to bring this matter to an absolute conclusion; he had been waiting for time and opportunity to make one more visit to the Grange, to satisfy himself by a final and meticulous examination of certain details that his theory was well-founded and assured. And here was this man speaking as easily of the great secret of Mithras as of cucumbers in June. He was astounded and confounded: and he looked it.

And Warburton on his side, marked the effect he had produced. He did not altogether understand the full force of his own words, but he noted the shock, and interpreted it in his own manner. He thought that the antiquary must be one of those unfortunate people who suffer from lapses of memory; that he had honestly forgotten his call of a month ago, and his subsequent visit to the Grange; and that the mention of his researches and theories had suddenly recalled the lost memories. The next thing would be that he would explain how he got away, unobserved, from the Grange; very likely it would turn out to be quite simple. Very possibly, he had really been to France on the business he had specified; he had merely antedated his journey by a day. Warburton was going to hint, very gently, something of all this to Sir Halliday, but his guest forestalled him.

"You will excuse me, I am sure," he said, "but I think I had better leave you. I do not think that we can do any good by discussing this subject further. I do not know how you feel, but to me it is intolerable. Something very awful must have happened. I do not dare to think what it can have been. I am afraid—I am afraid that I must be on the other side of death."

He stumbled out of the room. Warburton, going to the window, saw the unfortunate man swaying and staggering like a drunkard, as he picked his blind way along the pavement.

The Professor went down thoughtfully to his lunch. He felt sure that he had been right in his theory. Loss of memory; or perhaps it might be a case of double personality. He had heard, somewhat doubtfully, of such cases. It had struck him as rather fanciful, but men of good scientific repute were said to have been convinced, and to have undoubted evidence in favour of the doctrine. Well, one or the other, at all events he was afraid that Sir Halliday had been very much upset.

Warburton, on the other hand, was immensely relieved by the solution he had propounded to himself. He was an extremely worthy man, but a materialist and a rationalist to the core; the determined and unrelenting foe of all mysteries. If you had told him that a man of sense passes his whole life in wondering awe and amazement before the mysteries which perpetually confront him, he would have thought you either a madman, or else an intolerable and pretentious humbug. He dismissed the whole affair from his mind, and lived in extreme comfort for the remainder of his days.

It was Ian Tallent who provided an hypothesis, extravagant and improbable in the highest degree, no doubt, and yet the only tolerable solution of a most difficult problem. He conferred with Professor Warburton, and had the story of his conferences with Sir Halliday out of him, noting his point of view, the loss of memory or if you like—double personality—theory, and leaving him to enjoy it. He had more trouble with Sir Halliday Stuart, who had gone down to his retreat in Oxfordshire in sorry condition, and was making a slow recovery there, restoring himself to a normal state by degrees as he found that the common processes of life still continued in their usual order. At first, Sir Halliday refused Tallent's petitions for an audience with the driest negative; he said that he wished to dismiss "the wretched business" entirely from his thoughts. But Tallent persisted. He had got from Warburton an account of the shattered condition in which Sir Halliday had left him; but, naturally, Warburton had given his own reasons, as he had conceived them, for the shock which the antiquary had very evidently received.

"You see," Warburton had explained, "my reference to the conversation we had had together on his former visit brought the whole thing back to him. It made him aware that for a whole month there had been—a lapse in his personality; the transactions of a day and a night had been blotted out as if they had never existed. He was prepared to deny, as he did deny, that he had ever seen me before, that he had visited Morton Grange in our company, and had somehow or other succeeded in avoiding our observation and getting away from the place. And it was then, in my opinion, that the break in consciousness occurred. He got home to his chambers, I don't pretend to say how, in a dazed, confused state, went to bed, and woke up next morning—with the whole of the previous day missing from his memory. And it was no doubt a very startling and a very painful shock when he realized from my remarks the true state of the case."

Tallent heard all this and seemed to accept Warburton's theory. Indeed, it might be true; but he did not think so. He had a dim glimmering in his mind of possibilities far stranger than this; but he felt that he must talk to the antiquary, with whom the secret must rest. He saw that Warburton, pleased with his solution of the problem, was willing to treat the manner in which Sir Halliday had withdrawn himself inexplicably from their midst as an affair of secondary importance. But to Tallent, this appeared of vital moment: he could not let it go by as a trifle. And if it had happened as he began to dream it might have happened: then, by all means he must see Sir Halliday. But he let him rest a little, and gather his broken forces together, and refit. Then, in a couple of weeks, he wrote again, urging a meeting which might do a great deal, he said, to clear up a very obscure business.

After a few days, he got a letter of reluctant consent, and Tallent went down to High Street, and found Sir Halliday obviously in much better condition than that described by Warburton. And Warburton, it should be said, had not mentioned the odd impression he had received on the antiquary's last visit; the feeling that his visitor's aspect was more fully defined, more sharply "bitten in" than before. This circumstance had become negligible; indeed it was dismissed as a passing fancy—since it did not minister to the master theory of the loss of memory and the consequent annihilation of a day. But Tallent in his turn was impressed in much the same fashion. Sir Halliday looked worn and anxious; but he was distinct and present, as he had not been at the Grange. As Tallent put it to himself: a faint mist seemed to have cleared away from before him.

There was something of a nervous air in Sir Halliday's welcome; a suggestion of disquiet and almost of fear, as if he dreaded a renewal of the very painful and terrifying sensations that had sent him trembling from Warburton's presence a few weeks before. Tallent moved tactfully; he had come prepared to avoid any rough-and-ready handling of this very delicate and difficult case. He made no secret of his interest in the affair, he admitted that there were extraordinary complications and obstacles in the way of a clear issue.

"But before we go down into the deep waters," he added, "there are one or two trifling matters that I believe you would be able to clear up without any trouble. I don't know that they're of much consequence: still, it's as well to start fair. Now, Warburton tells me that on the night of October 13th you went to Paris?"

"I most certainly did," said Sir Halliday, with the strongest emphasis.

"By what route? Dover-Calais?"

"By Dover-Calais. I'm an extremely bad sailor, and I always shorten my discomfort as much as possible. Luckily, it was a calm night. I remember remarking on that fact with considerable satisfaction to a fellow-traveller."

Tallent all but smacked his lips. He remembered the sentence: "It's a calm night, at all events; and that's in our favour."

"Well," he said, "you're meeting me halfway. All these little impressions and recollections of the journey down to Dover: that's exactly what I want you to tell me, if you will. They're trifles, no doubt, but we may possibly find a use for them. Go ahead, sir."

"Really, there's very little to tell: London-Dover isn't generally very eventful. There were two other people in the carriage with me; a middle-aged man and a youngish man. For a good part of the way, I was reading some papers that I had brought with me. And that does remind me of something: I found myself distracted to a certain extent in my reading—somewhat technical matter, I may say—by what struck me as a hum of low-voiced conversation. An odd effect; as if one were listening at one end of a large room to three or four men talking quietly together at the other end. I could just distinguish, as I thought, one man speaking and then another; but I couldn't make out a word they were saying. It quite worried me at last. So far as I've observed, I don't think one hears one's neighbours in the next compartment talking; but I supposed that that was where the sound came from. So, at last I got up from my lace and strolled up and down the corridor for a few minutes; and the queer thing was that one of the compartments next to us was empty, and in the other there were two men fast asleep. So I went back to my place and shut the door after me. I took up my papers again, but the hum of talk went on, and it bothered me so much that I gave up the attempt, and began to talk myself to the young man opposite me—the youngish fellow."

Tallent heard Sir Halliday intently.

"And where were these people talking, do you think?" he asked.

"I haven't a notion. I know nothing whatever about acoustics, and I may be talking great nonsense; but I wondered whether by any possibility the sound may have been somehow transmitted from a remote carriage to my own. Sound does play very odd tricks sometimes."

"Whispering galleries? Echoes? That kind of thing, you mean? Well, I don't know. But . . . did you distinguish one voice from another? Do you think you could recognize them if you heard them again?"

"I don't know about that," said Sir Halliday, doubtfully. "But, as you ask me, I must say that your own voice reminds me a good deal of one of these unseen conversationalists. One of them spoke on a slightly higher pitch than the others; and really, the tone was very like yours."

"That's odd, indeed. So you gave up trying to read, and began talking to one of the men in the carriage. Just about the weather and the news, I suppose; things in general?"

"That sort of thing. Then, if I remember, he propounded his solution for the unemployment problem; he would provide work for the workless by pulling down all the old buildings in the country and running up new ones, constructed on purely functional lines, and adapted to the needs of the age. As you may imagine, I don't often hear that sort of talk at the Antiquaries, and I was a good deal amused. I tried to argue with him. I asked him if he didn't take a certain pleasure in looking at an old church or an old house.

"'No more pleasure than you would take,' he replied, 'if you were speeding and saw a heap of old stones and rubbish in the middle of the road, right in front of your car. Old churches, old houses, old castles; they're obstructive rubbish, nothing more or less.'

"Well, he went on at a great rate in this style, and I put in an objection now and again, without any effect, I must confess. We were getting near Dover by this time, and the young iconoclast began to abuse that harmless old place; he said it was a hole. I stuck up for it; and told him that I liked Dover; especially Strond Street and the old harbour."

Tallent remembered this utterance very well.

"And that's all, I suppose. You got out of the train and got on board the boat—and I hope you had a good crossing?"

"Perfectly calm, I am glad to say. But, since you mention it, getting on board was not quite so quiet a business as usual. There seemed a good deal of pushing and excitement; I am sure I don't know what about. There was plenty of time, of course; but people positively plunged down the gangway; it was almost an ugly rush. But I am afraid I have bored you terribly with all these trivial details. Still, I warned you that you can hardly expect very exciting adventures on the Dover boat-train."

Then the wild hypothesis stood fully confirmed; so Tallent murmured in his mind. "And now," he said to himself, "for the deep waters." He had not only obtained matter of extraordinary value and significance from Sir Halliday's recital of his traveller's trivialities—as he thought them—but the simple story of the Dover boat-train had been soothing to the teller of it. Tallent put his question:

"Professor Warburton," he began, "gave me to understand that you seemed a good deal put out when you left him, after your talk together a few weeks ago. Now, we want to clear things up; and I feel quite sure that it would help very much if you would tell me the exact reason of the distress which I am afraid you experienced."

Sir Halliday Stuart rose from his chair and began to pace slowly up and down the room; evidently in deep and perplexed consideration. At the end of a few minutes, he stopped and faced Tallent.

"I think you are right. Apart from any question of clearing or elucidating a most perplexing business, which I am sure is most desirable, I feel that I shall be the better for plain talk. At the moment, I certainly received a hideous shock."

Tallent perceived that the hour of the forceps had come.

"Tell me exactly what it was."

"It was this. I knew and I know exactly how I had spent that particular day. I knew and I know how every hour of it had been occupied. I knew and I know that I had never set eyes on Professor Warburton before the visit I paid him a few weeks ago. But . . . from certain things that he said, I also knew and know that I had seen him before and told him my most reserved secrets."

He sat down, and covered his face with his hands, bowing his head.

Then Tallent said:

"Do you know that your casual remark about your liking for Dover was heard that night in a room in Morton Grange, where Warburton and the rest of us were sitting? And do you know that you, to all appearance, were sitting also in that room, and that we saw you as you spoke? So it was."

He was met by a blank stare; uncomprehending, utterly incredulous.

"That is quite impossible," said Sir Halliday, quietly and finally.

"There are very few things that are impossible," Tallent replied. "In pure mathematics, perhaps, there may be; though I believe that of late even these eternal canons—as we used to think them—have begun to admit of doubts and uncertainties. Still, I hope we shall not be required to admit the possibility of three-sided squares and two-sided triangles. But, once outside these regions, can we dare to talk of impossibility at all? We can use the word, of course, and I have no doubt that we shall continue to use it; but I think we shall all have to recognize the fact that when we say any event is impossible, we merely mean that we've never heard of such a thing before, and that we don't begin to understand how it can happen so. That is very well, and very applicable to your own case, for I don't think I have ever heard of anything quite on all fours with the extraordinary manifestation in which you were concerned. And I certainly don't begin to understand how it could happen so.

"But, look here; I've just remembered something. I mentioned mathematics just now: I take it you believe there are such things as lines, don't you? Well, have you ever seen one? If so, I should be interested to hear how *that* happened; how length without breadth became visible to the human eye. If you think it over, I believe you will recognize that there are more evident impossibilities lurking in this elementary axiom of geometry than in your own—adventure, shall we call it?"

Sir Halliday was dazed and amazed, and yet attentive. Tallent thought he could hold him, and went on:

"As I said, I think that there are circumstances in your case that are unique; but in the main outlines it falls under a well-ascertained category. There have been many instances of what used to be called Doubles, but are now generally known as Apparitions of Phantasms of the Living. In its early years, the Society for Psychical Research published a thick volume of such cases, all carefully examined and well attested. If I remember, a number of these appearances were of people at the point of death, and the large majority of them were, so far as can be seen, purposeless.

"I remember one case, which might be called typical. A Berkshire farmer, coming down to breakfast one morning, sees on the stairs a Buckinghamshire miller, a market acquaintance, no more, coming up to meet him. The farmer is astonished to see him; and as he stares, the miller is not there. The miller, it was found, was dying at the time, but nobody could guess why he had projected this image of himself into the consciousness of a man with whom he had been barely on nodding terms."

"But, you see," broke in Sir Halliday, "I wasn't dying, or anything like it. I was perfectly well at the time, and that must be seven weeks ago."

"Quite so, but these appearances are by no means invariably the images of the moribund. Indeed, I think that the most remarkable case I know of is a man who was perfectly well and at ease when he became apparent—can we say?—where he was not. This is not one of the Psychical Researchers' cases, it is recorded by Charles Dickens. I have it in my notebook and here it is—

> "'I once saw the apparition of my father at this hour (the early morning). He was alive and well, and nothing ever came of it, but I saw him in the daylight, sitting with his back towards me, on a seat that stood beside my bed. His head was resting on his hand, and whether he was slumbering or grieving, I could not discern. Amazed to see him there, I sat up, moved my position, leaned out of bed, and watched him. As he did not move, I spoke to him more than once. As he did not move then, I became alarmed and laid my hand upon his shoulder—as I thought—and there was no such thing.'

"You see? There you have the apparently purposeless projection of the image of a man in good health. And I think I may say that in the Psychical Research records, there is hardly a single case—if there is such a case—where the apparition was any thing but purposeless. To quote a passage from one of the publications of the S.P.R.: "One has to admit a total absence of any apparent aim or of any intelligent action on the part of phantoms." We may venture, then, to say that this is the rule: that the apparition or projection of the image is not (in our modern jargon) a 'wish-fulfilment' on the part of the projector. The miller did not want to see the farmer; old Mr. Dickens did not want to see his son.

"Here is where your case parts company from all the others on record. We know that you had made a special study of Morton Grange, and I gathered from Warburton that for some time you had wished to revisit the place, to make a further examination of certain details of importance. That is so, isn't it?"

"Yes, that is quite true. There were points on which I wished to satisfy myself by a second inspection, before finishing some work I had in hand."

"Exactly; and there, I believe, we have the distinction between your particular case and all the others that we have been considering. You say you had a fixed purpose to revisit Morton Grange, in order that you might satisfy yourself finally on certain matters which to you were of the first importance? Good. Then, I think, having established that distinction—the purpose behind the projection, we come, not unnaturally, to the other distinction or difference—the superior intensity of the image projected. The normal phantasy of the living manifests and vanishes. It does not speak, it does not abide our question, its visibility is its only energy, and that is rapidly exhausted and dispersed. In your case, on the other hand, the phantasm was in all respects like an ordinary human being; it was both persistent and energetic; to all apparent intents and purposes it was yourself as you sit there before me.

"Beyond the extraordinary character of the whole manifestation, there are one or two very curious points. For instance. While the phantasm was with us, we saw nothing, as I have just intimated, at all peculiar or out of the way about it. But when it had disappeared, and we were wondering what on earth had happened, it came out accidentally that the figure—I was going to say, 'you'—had not impressed us all in the same way. One man thought Sir Halliday was short and small, another described him as above the average height. And another thing: when I came into this room about an hour ago, I noticed at once the difference between Sir Halliday of Campden House and the Sir Halliday of Morton Grange; the former figure was by far more definite and vivid than the latter. You know in the old Christmas Ghost stories, the apparition is often described as 'a shadowy figure.' A traditional phrase, no doubt, and an instance, as I think, of the fact that tradition often tells the truth under the form of a picturesque symbolism. We couldn't see the furniture through the phantasm of Sir Halliday; but, in a sense, the image was certainly shadowy, indeterminate.

"And again: here is a puzzle. As you sat in the train on the way to Dover, you heard the murmur of the conversation in the room at Morton Grange. You recognized my voice just now. And, on the other hand, we heard some—not all—of your remarks to your fellow-travellers in the carriage. Of course we thought you were speaking to us. These are difficulties which I do not attempt to explain. But I hope that on the whole you are relieved."

Sir Halliday Stuart had listened in a deep, meditative silence; assenting, now and again, with a nod of the head, when Tallent appealed to him.

"'Journeying very far, I found what I had not sought,'" he murmured to himself, sighing, in great wonder.

"Well, yes," he said aloud. "In a way, I suppose you have relieved me—of the sense of an intolerable contradiction."

"Well, I am glad," said Tallent, rising. "Though I believe it may be held at last that true wisdom consists in accepting contradictions and rejoicing them greatly." +

Ritual

Once upon a time, as we say in English, or *olim*, as the Latins said in their more austere and briefer way, I was sent forth on a May Monday to watch London being happy on their Whitsun holiday. This is the sort of appointment that used to be known in newspaper offices as an annual; and the difficulty for the men engaged in this business is to avoid seeing the same sights as those witnessed a year before and saying much the same things about them as were said on Whit-Monday twelvemonth. Queuing up for Madame Tussaud's waxworks, giving buns to diverse creatures in the Zoo, gazing at those Easter Island gods in the portico of the British Museum, waiting for all sorts of early doors to open; all these are spectacles of the day. And the patient man who boards the buses from suburbs may chance to hear a lady from Hornsey expounding to her neighbour on the seat, an inhabitant of Enfield Wash, the terrible gaieties that Piccadilly Circus witnesses when the electric signs are fairly lit.

On the Whit-Monday in question, I saw and recorded some of these matters; and then strolled westward along Piccadilly, by the palings of the Green Park. The conventional business of the day had been more or less attended to: now for the systematic prowl: one never knows where one may find one's goods. And then and there, I came across some boys, half-a-dozen or so of them, playing what struck me as a very queer game on the fresh turf of the Park, under the tender and piercing green of the young leaves. I have forgotten the preliminary elaborations of the sport; but there seemed to be some sort of dramatic action, perhaps with dialogue, but this I could not hear. Then one boy stood alone, with the five or six others about him. They pretended to hit the solitary body, and he fell to the ground and lay motionless, as if dead. Then the others covered him up with their coats, and ran away. And then, if I remember, the boy who had been ritually smitten, slaughtered, and buried, rose to his feet, and the very odd game began all over again.

Here, I thought, was something a little out of the way of the accustomed doings and pleasures of the holiday crowds, and I returned to my office and embodied an account of this Green Park sport in my tale of Whit-Monday in London; with some allusion to the curious analogy between the boys' game and certain matters of a more serious nature. But it would not do. A spectacled Reader came down out of his glass cage, and held up a strip of proof.

"Hiram Abiff?" he queried in a low voice, as he placed the galley-slip on my desk, and pointed to the words with his pen. "It's not usual to mention these things in print."

I assured the Reader that I was not one of the Widow's offspring, but he still shook his head gravely, and I let him have his way, willing to avoid all *admiratio*. It was, I thought, a curious little incident, and to this day I have never heard an explanation of the coincidence—mere chance, very likely—between the pastime in the Park and those matters which it is not usual to mention in print.

But a good many years later, this business of the Green Park was recalled to me by a stranger experience in a very different part of London. A friend of mine, an American, who had travelled in many outland territories of the earth, asked me to show him some of the less known quarters of London.

"Do not misunderstand me, sir," he said, in his measured, almost Johnsonian manner, "I do not wish to see your great city in its alleged sensational aspects. I am not yearning to probe the London underworld, nor do I wish to view any opium joints or blind-pigs for cocaine addicts. In such matters, I have already accumulated more than sufficient experience in other quarters of the world. But if you would just shew me those aspects which are so ordinary that nobody ever sees them, I shall be greatly indebted to you."

I remembered how I had once awed two fellow-citizens of his by taking them to a street not very far from King's Cross Station, and shewing them how each house was guarded by twin plaster sphinxes of a deadly chocolate-red, which crouched on either side of the flights of steps leading to the doorways. I remembered how the late Arnold Bennett had come exploring in this region, and seen the sphinxes and had noted them in his diary with a kind of dumb surmise, venturing no comment. So I said that I thought I understood. We set out, and soon we were deep in that unknown London which is at our very doors.

"Dickens had been here," I said in my part as Guide and Interpreter. "You know 'Little Dorrit'? Then this might be Mr. Casby's very street, which set out meaning to run down into the valley and up again to the top of the hill, but got out of breath and stopped still after twenty yards."

The American gentleman relished the reference and his surroundings. He pointed out to me curious work in some of the iron balconies before the first floor windows in the grey houses, making a rough sketch of the design of one of them in his note-book. We wandered here and there, and up and down at haphazard, by strange wastes and devious ways, till I, in spite of my fancied knowledge, found myself in a part that I did not remember to have seen before. There were timber yards with high walls about them. There were cottages that seemed to have strayed from the outskirts of some quiet provincial town, off the main road. One of these lay deep in the shadow of an old mulberry, and ripening grapes hung from a vine on a neighboring wall. The hollyhocks in the neat little front gardens were almost over; there were still brave displays of snapdragons and marigolds. But round the corner, barrows piled with pale bananas and flaming oranges filled the roadway, and the street market resounded with raucous voices, praise of fruit and fish, and loud bargainings, and gossip at its highest pitch. We pushed our way through the crowd, and left the street of the market, and presently came into the ghostly quiet of a square: high, severe houses, built of whitish bricks, complete in 1840 Gothic, all neat and well-kept, and for all sign of life or movement, uninhabited.

And then, when we had barely rested our ears from the market jangle, there came what I suppose was an overflow from that region. A gang of small boys surged into the square and broke its peace. There were about a dozen of them, more or less, and I took it that they were playing soldiers. They marched, two and two, in their dirty and shabby order, apparently under the command of a young ruffian somewhat bigger and taller than the rest. Two of them banged incessantly with bits of broken wood on an old meat tin and a battered iron tea tray, and all of them howled as barbarously as any crooner, but much louder. They went about and about, and then diverged into an empty road that looked as if it led nowhere in particular, and there drew up, and formed themselves into a sort of hollow square, their captain in the middle. The tin pan music went on steadily, but less noisily; it had become a succession of slow beats, and the howls had turned into a sort of whining chant.

But it remained a very horrible row, and I was moving on to get away from the noise, when my American interposed.

"If you wouldn't mind our tarrying here for a few moments," he said apologetically. "This pastime of your London boys interests me very much. You may think it strange, but I find it more essentially exciting than the Eton and Harrow Cricket Match of which I witnessed some part a few weeks ago."

So we looked on from an unobtrusive corner. The boys, evidently, agreed with my friend, and found their game absorbing. I don't think that they had noticed us or knew that we were there.

They went through their queer performance. The bangs or beats on the tin and the tray grew softer and slower, and the yells had died into a monotonous drone. The leader went inside the square, from boy to boy, and seemed to whisper into the ear of each one. Then he passed round a second time, standing before each, and making a sort of summoning or beckoning gesture with his hand. Nothing happened. I did not find the sport essentially exciting; but looking at the American, I observed that he was watching it with an expression of the most acute interest and amazement. Again the big boy went about the square. He stopped dead before a little fellow in a torn jacket. He threw out his arms wide, with a gesture of embrace, and then drew them in. He did this three times, and at the third repetition of the ceremony, the little chap in the torn jacket cried out with a piercing scream and fell forward as if dead.

The banging of the tins and the howl of the voices went up to heaven with a hideous dissonance.

My American friend was gasping with astonishment as we passed on our way.

"This is an amazing city," he said. "Do you know, sir, that those boys were acting all as if they'd been Asiki doing their Njoru ritual. I've seen it in East Africa. But there the black man that falls down stays down. He's dead."

A week or two later, I was telling the tale to some friends. One of them pulled an evening paper out of his pocket.

"Look at that," said he, point with his finger. I read the headlines:

MYSTERY DEATH IN NORTH LONDON SQUARE

HOME OFFICE DOCTOR PUZZLED

HEART VESSELS RUPTURED

"PLAYING SOLDIERS"

BOY FALLS DEAD

CORONER DIRECTS OPEN VERDICT ✢

Appendix: The Literature of Occultism

There is a sense, of course, in which all fine literature, both in prose and in verse, belongs to the region of things mysterious and occult. Formerly it might have been maintained that music was the purest of all the arts, that the shuddering and reverberant summons of the organ, the far, faint echo of a distant choir singing, spoke clearly to the soul without the material impediment of a story, without that "body" which must clothe the spirit of pictures and sculptured forms, being as they are presentations of the visible things around us. But since Wagner came and conquered, music has become more and more an intellectual exercise, and to the modern musical critic every bar must be capable of interpretation, of an intelligible translation, if it is to be absolved in the judgment.

Since then music has frankly become a "mixed" art, a "criticism of life" in the medium of sound, we who try to understand literature may well insist that our fine prose and our fine poetry have a part in them, and that part the most precious, which is whole super-intellectual, non-intelligible, occult. The lines of Keats, the "magic casements, opening on the foam of perilous seas, in faëry lands forlorn," will occur to every one as an instance of this mysterious element in poetry, Poe's ode to Helen is another example, and there are passages in the old prose writers, sentences in Browne and Jeremy Taylor, and sometimes a sudden triumphant word in Ken, which thrill the heart with an inexplicable, ineffable charm. This, perhaps, is the true literature of occultism.

These are the runes which call up the unknown spirits from the mind.

But there is a literature which is occult in a more special sense, which either undertakes to explain and comment on the secrets of man's life, or is explicitly founded on mysterious beliefs of one kind or another. Books of this sort have, it is well known, existed from the earliest times; perhaps, indeed, when the last explorer leaves Babylon, bringing with him positively the most antique inscription in the world, he will find an incantation written on the brick or on the rock. It will be said, no doubt, that there would be nothing strange in such a discovery, that early man living in a world which he understood either dimly or not at all, would naturally devise occult causes for occult effects, would imagine that he too by esoteric means could pass behind the veil, and attain to the knowledge of the secret workings of the universe. But we know that such beliefs were by no means peculiar to the Egyptian and the Accadian of prehistoric times, we are able to trace all through the ages the one conviction of an occult world lying a little beyond the world of sense, and probably at the present day, in our sober London streets, there are as many students of and believers in magic, white and black, as there were in the awful hanging gardens of Babylon. But though belief is as fervent as ever, the expression of it has lamentably deteriorated as may be seen in Mr. W. T. Stead's "Letters from Julia," written by the hand of Mr. W. T. Stead, which we reviewed some time ago. The modern disciples of Isis speak in a tongue that differs from that of the ancient initiates. They who wish to learn the message of the new hierophant may read the review, or even the book in question, but here, where we discourse of literature and of literature only, we cannot enter into the squalid chapter of back-parlor magic, into the follies of modern theosophy and modern spiritualism. And here we must not even speak of "imposture," for we know nothing of most of these persons, save that they cannot write books.

But this literature of occultism was not always vulgar. Futile, perhaps, it was always, or perhaps, like the ritual of Freemasonry, it did once point the way to veritable enigmas; if it could never tell the secret, it may have whispered that there was a secret, that we are the sons of God and it doth not yet appear which we shall be. But no one could look into the alchemical writings of the middle ages and deny them the name of literature. Alchemy, in spite of all confident pronouncements on the subject, remains still a mystery, the very nature and object of the quest are unknown. The baser alchemists—there were quacks and impostors and dupes then as now—no doubt sought or pretended to seek some method of making gold artificially, but the sages, those who practised the true spagyric art, were engaged in some infinitely more mysterious adventure. The Life of Nicholas Flamel is decisive on this point, and Thomas Vaughan, the brother of the Silurist, was certainly not hinting at any chemical or material transmutation when he wrote his "Lumen de Lumine" and the "Magia Adamica." The theory has been advanced that the true alchemists were, in face, the successors of the hierophants of Eleusis, that their transmutation was a transmutation of man, not of metal, that their "first matter" was "that hermaphrodite, the son of Adam, who though in the form of a man, ever bears about him in his body the body of Eve, his wife," that their fine gold, glistening and glorious as the sun, symbolized the soul, freed from the bonds of matter, in communion with the source of all things, initiated in the perfect mysteries. However that may be, there can be no question as to the beauty of the best alchemical treatises, of that strange symbolism which spoke of the Bird of Hermes, of the Red Dragon, of the Son Blessed of the Fire. The curious in such matters may consult Ashmole's "Fasciculus Chemicus," and the extraordinary "Opusculum" of Denys Zachaire, at once an autobiography and an alchemical treatise.

In the space of an article it is, of course, impossible to sketch out even a brief scheme of old occult literature. We must pass over the Greeks, in spite of the songs of the Initiated that Aristophanes has given us, in spite of that Thessalian magic which Apuleius moulded to such exquisite literary ends. We must decline the question of the origin of alchemy, which a distinguished French chemist has characteristically referred to some misunderstood trade receipts, relating to methods of gilding and bronzing the baser metals. Then there is the great question of the Sabbath. History tells us that in the Dark Ages people were mad about witchcraft, and that they tortured old women till they confessed to anything rather than suffer another turn of the rack. It was a familiar superstition, that of the poor old woman with her black cat, but it may be noted that Payne Knight's monograph on the "Worship of Priapus" throws a very different light on it, and that Hawthorne understood something of the real Sabbath. The terror and the flame of it glow behind all the chapters of the "Scarlet Letter," and those who can read between the lines see the same red glare in "Young Goodman Brown." We must leave, too, the problem of Rosicrucianism, concerning which Mr. A. E. Waite has said the last words in his "Real History of the Rosicrucians," a kind of historical counterblast to the fantastic and entertaining, but wholly unreliable work by the late Hargrave Jennings. The "Black Mass," which M. Huysmans exploited to such purpose in "La Bas" is a degenerate, *decadent* descendant of the medieval Sabbath, and is really only a revival of the blasphemous fooleries that went on in France about the time of the Revolution, when great persons assembled to adore a toad, which had received "all the Sacraments of the Church." Indeed, there seems to be a constant Satanic tradition in France; in the middle ages one finds Gilles de Raiz, and about ten years ago a clever writer described an appearance of Satan in Paris with extraordinary effectiveness, and this, be it remarked, was long before Leo Taxil had invented Diana Vaughan, and the diabolic rites of an inner Masonry. Those who know anything of occultism will be aware that we have scarcely touched the fringes of the subject; we have said nothing of the Kabbala, nothing of the Evil Eye, perhaps the most widespread, ancient, and persistent of all beliefs, nothing of the malefic images, such as "Sister Helen" made in Rossetti's ballad, which are being made in our Somersetshire at the present time by village women who love and hate. And all these beliefs and many others have left deep marks on our literature, and perhaps on our hearts also.

So far our subject has been chiefly the "expository" literature of the secret sciences. We have noted some few of the forms which occultism has assumed, and have mentioned one or two of the leading books and leading cases. The imaginative literature inspired by or dealing with the mysteries is a far smaller field for criticism. Passing by the "Golden Ass" and all the mass of legends and songs that the middle ages have given us, doing reverence to King Arthur as we read that "here in this world he changed his life," leaving the strange Hermetic Poems of Sir George Ripley, and that mystical romance the "Chymical Marriage of Christian Rosycross," we may glance at the fiction of the present century and see how it has been influenced by the occult idea. Sir Walter Scott dabbled slightly in the subject, as he dabbled in most antique and curious things, but occultism to him was merely a "property" with which he decked some of his pages, as he chose to deck his hall at Abbotsford with helmets, and broadswords. "Mervyn Clitheroe," by

Appendix: The Literature of Occultism

Harrison Ainsworth, and the "Lancashire Witches," by the same writer, are books to make boys quake of dark nights when they pass the black end of the lane, but Bulwer Lytton's "Strange Story" strikes a genuine and original note of terror, and few will forget the appearance of the *Scin Loeca*, the Luminous Shadow of Icelandic belief. And perhaps the "Haunters and the Haunted" comes still nearer to perfection, with its theory of the malignant dead, of the instruments by which they work. Hawthorne and Poe, so utterly unlike in most things, were at one in their love of haunting, but while Hawthorne suggested the presence of the infernal army camped all about us and around us, Poe found his terror and awe in the mortal human body, in his theory of a living death. He wrote the story of the corporeal frame that rots in death, and thinks while it decays. Those who have read Mrs. Oliphant's "Wizard's Son" have seen a splendid theme spoilt by weak and diffuse execution, but her "Beleaguered City" may stand with Mr. Kipling's very different "Mark of the Beast," that is amongst the little masterpieces of occult fiction. In the one case spiritual awe, in the other panic terror, and the hint of awful possibility are developed with the extremest skill, and after such successes as these it would be painful to contemplate the sorry imitation, the lath and plaster mysteries of "Mr. Isaacs," a book which recalls Madame Blavatsky and her sliding panels. At the outset of our article we barred all discussion of "Theosophy," so it will only be necessary to say that Mr. A. P. Sinnett once wrote two novels, which may be Theosophic but are certainly not literature. "Jekyll and Hyde" remains to some of us Stevenson's most perfect work, and it may be that a too obvious undercurrent of allegory is its only flaw. But those who revel in the creations of a bizarre and powerful imagination may perhaps find something to satisfy them in Mr. M. P. Shiel's "Prince Zaleski," and

"Shapes in the Fire," stories which tell of a wilder wonderland than Poe dreamed of in his most fantastic moments. And "Pierrot," by Mr. De Vere Stacpoole, stands alone, perfect in its pure and singular invention. We must say at the end as at the beginning that perhaps the true occultism is to be found in the books of those that never consciously designed to write of hidden things, that the "melodies unheard" are the mightiest incantations, that the "magic casements" open on the very vision of the world unseen. +

ABOUT S. T. JOSHI

A well known editor and literary scholar, S. T. Joshi's 1996 biography, *H. P. Lovecraft: A Life,* was widely praised and reviewed. Mr. Joshi edited the standard edition of Lovecraft's fiction, published by Arkham House, and also compiled the standard bibliography for Dunsany, published in 1993. In 1995 his critical study, *Lord Dunsany: Master of the Anglo-Irish Imagination,* appeared. His current interests include George Sterling and Ambrose Bierce. He lives in Seattle, Washington.

Ordering Chaosium Fiction

All Chaosium titles are available from bookstores and game stores. You can also order directly from Chaosium. To order by credit card via the net, visit our web site at www.chaosium.com, 24 hours a day.

CALL OF CTHULHU® FICTION TITLES

THE WHITE PEOPLE and other stories
The Best Weird Tales of Arthur Machen, Vol. 2

Born in Wales in 1863, Machen was a London journalist for much of his life. Among his fiction, he may be best known for the allusive, haunting title story of this book, "The White People," which H. P. Lovecraft thought to be the second greatest horror story ever written (after Blackwood's "The Willows"). This wide ranging collection also includes the crystalline novelette "A Fragment of Life," "The Angel of Mons," (a story so widely reported that it was imagined true by millions in the grim initial days of the Great War), and "The Great Return," telling of the stately visions which graced the Welsh village of Llantristant for a time. Four more tales and the poetical "Ornaments in Jade" are all finely told. This is the second Machen volume edited by S. T. Joshi and published by Chaosium. The first volume was *The Three Impostors*.

5 3/8" x 8 3/8", 312 pages, $14.95. Stock #6035; ISBN 1-56882-172-7.

THE TSATHOGGUA CYCLE (forthcoming)

Can a god be a pet? Even a devil-god who relishes human sacrifice? It is hard to deny that for his creator and godfather, Clark Ashton Smith and H. P. Lovecraft, Tsathoggua was exactly that. They found the Saturnian-Hyperborean-N'klaian (huh?) toad-bat-sloth-deity as cute and adorable as horrific, and this strange ambivalence echoes throughout their tales over which Great Tsathoggua casts his batrachian shadow! Some are droll fables of human foibles; others are terrifying adventures of human delvers who perish in the fire of a religious fanaticism fully as awful as its super-sub-human object of worship.

In this arcane volume you will read Tsathogguan tales old and new by various writers, chronicling the horrors of the amorphous amphibian's descent into new decades and deeper waters. The mere fact that such a thing is possible attests mightily the power of the modern myth of Tsathoggua, and the men who created him!

5 3/8" x 8 3/8", $14.95. Stock #6029; ISBN 1-56882-131-X

CALL OF CTHULHU® FICTION TITLES

DISCIPLES OF CTHULHU 2
Blasphemous Tales of the Followers: New Tales of the Cthulhu Mythos

Bad things tend to happen to people who go where they are not wanted, or who over-stay their welcome once they reach their destination. This book contains thirteen new personal explorations of the Cthulhu Mythos. As its title suggests, this is a companion volume to Edward P. Berglund's earlier classic Mythos collection, *The Disciples of Cthulhu*. Both books are published by Chaosium, but their contents are entirely different. Twelve of the stories in *Disciples 2* are original and have never been published before. All the stories record the dire fates of people whose destinies intertwine with the Mythos. Edited by Edward P. Berglund.

5 3/8" x 8 3/8", 224 pages, $13.95. Stock #6033; ISBN 1-56882-143-3.

NAMELESS CULTS

Robert E. Howard is the world-renowned author of the *Conan* series and the stories that were the basis of the recent *Kull* movie. He frequently corresponded with H. P. Lovecraft, and authored many pivotal Mythos tales. This book collects together all of Howard's Mythos tales, including those which originated Gol-Goroth, the *Black Book* (*Unaussprechlichen Kulten*), and Friedrich Von Junzt—all the stories that are usually considered his Cthulhu Mythos yarns, plus another batch that make use of Arthur Machen's lore of the Little People and help fill out the picture implicit in a couple of the overt Mythos tales. A third group are tales which Howard did not intend in a Lovecraftian vein but which feature creations later assimilated into the Mythos, whether by Howard, Lovecraft, or later writers. Four Howard fragments are presented here with additional text by Robert M. Price, C. J. Henderson, Joe Pulver, and August Derleth.

5 3/8" x 8 3/8", 358 pages, $15.95. Stock #6028; ISBN 1-56882-130-1.

CALL OF CTHULHU® FICTION TITLES

NIGHTMARE'S DISCIPLE
Even in the modern day, horrors arise in Innsmouth. In this brand-new novel the curse of the Marshes falls upon an entirely new generation when a serial killer terrorizes Schenectady, New York. Detective Christopher James Stewart must follow a trail of mutilated bodies and piece together enigmatic clues before the murderer strikes again. Here is a wealth of terror and exuberant scenes, a detailed Cthulhu Mythos novel of the present day. Warning: contains explicit scenes.

5 3/8" x 8 3/8", 408 pages, $14.95. Stock #6018; ISBN 1-56882-118-2.

SINGERS OF STRANGE SONGS
Most readers acknowledge Brian Lumley as the superstar of British horror writers. With the great popularity of his *Necroscope* series, he is one of the best known horror authors in the world. Devoted fans know that his roots are deep in the Cthulhu Mythos, with which most of his early work deals. This volume contains eleven new tales in that vein, as well as three reprints of excellent but little-known work by Lumley. This book was published in conjunction with Lumley's 1997 trip to the United States.

5 3/8" x 8 3/8", 244 pages, $12.95. Stock #6014; ISBN 1-56882-104-2.

CALL OF CTHULHU® FICTION TITLES

SONG OF CTHULHU

Tales of the Spheres beyond Sound

Lovecraft's most famous portraitist was Richard Upton Pickman, whose ironic canvases of ghouls and humanity's relation to ghouls have become famous, even though they existed only in Lovecraft's keen imagination. Among HPL's writers, Randolph Carter and the tragically destined Edward Pickman Derby stand out. And of course there is Erich Zann, the inhumanly-great violist, whose powers are detailed in "The Music of Erich Zann," included in this volume.

In HPL, the artist is the detached observer of society, a cultural reporter of the sort whose function has since become familiar. But Lovecraft also saw a deeper role, one such as played by Henry Wilcox the sculptor in "The Call of Cthulhu": "Wilcox's imagination had been keenly affected. [He had] an unprecedented dream of great cyclopean cities of titan blocks and sky-flung monoliths, all dripping with green ooze and sinister with latent horror. . . . [and] a voice that was not a voice; a chaotic sensation which only fancy could transmute into sound, but which he attempted to render by the almost unpronounceable jumble of letters, *Cthulhu fhtagn."*

Here are nineteen Mythos tales, melodies of prophecy and deceit. *Cthulhu fhtagn!*

    5 3/8" x 8 3/8", 222 pages, $13.95. Stock #6032; ISBN 1-56882-117-4.

CALL OF CTHULHU® FICTION TITLES

THE BOOK OF DZYAN

Mme. Blavatsky's famous transcribed messages from beyond, the mysterious *Book of Dzyan,* the heart of the sacred books of Kie-te, are said to have been known only to Tibetan mystics. Quotations from *Dzyan* form the core of her closely-argued *The Secret Doctrine,* the most influential single book of occult knowledge to emerge from the nineteenth century. The text of this book reproduces nearly all of *Book of Dzyan* that Blavatsky transcribed. It also includes long excerpts from her *Secret Doctrine* as well as from the Society of Psychical Research's 1885 report concerning phenomena witnessed by members of the Theosophical Society. There are notes and additional shorter materials. Editor Tim Maroney's biographical essay starts off the book, a fascinating portrait of an amazing woman.

5 3/8" x 8 3/8", 272 pages, $13.95. Stock #6027; ISBN 1-56882-114-X.

THE YELLOW SIGN and other stories

This book contains all the immortal tales of Robert W. Chambers, including "The Repairer of Reputations," "The Yellow Sign," and "The Mask." These titles are often found in survey anthologies. In addition to the six stories reprinted from *The Yellow Sign* (1895), this book also offers more than two dozen other stories and episodes. These narratives rarely appear in print. Some have not been published in nearly a century.

This is a complete collection of Robert W. Chambers' short weird fiction—his published horror, science fiction, and fantasy/supernatural, as well as some self-conscious whimsy. The writing can be facile and out of fashion, of interest to collectors and those desiring to comprehend the writer. But other stories are as delicate and durable as those wrought by Lord Dunsany, and worthy of every reader's time. Selected by S. T. Joshi.

5 3/8" x 8 3/8", 652 pages, $19.95. Stock #6023; ISBN 1-56882-170-0.